RANDOM ACTS
of HEROIC LOVE

DANNY SCHEINMANN

BLACK SWAN

TRANSWORLD PUBLISHERS
61–63 Uxbridge Road, London W5 5SA
A Random House Group Company
www.rbooks.co.uk

RANDOM ACTS OF HEROIC LOVE
A BLACK SWAN BOOK: 9780552774222

First published in Great Britain
in 2007 by Doubleday
a division of Transworld Publishers
Black Swan edition published 2008

Addresses for Random House Group Ltd companies outside the UK
can be found at: www.randomhouse.co.uk
The Random House Group Ltd Reg. No. 954009

The Random House Group Limited supports The Forest Stewardship Council
(FSC), the leading international forest certification organisation. All our titles
that are printed on Greenpeace approved FSC certified paper carry the
FSC logo. Our paper procurement policy can be found at
www.rbooks.co.uk/environment

Design by Julia Lloyd
Typeset in 11/14pt Giovanni Book by
Falcon Oast Graphic Art Ltd.

Printed in the UK by CPI Cox & Wyman, Reading, RG1 8EX.

2 4 6 8 10 9 7 5 3 1

Mixed Sources
Product group from well-managed
forests and other controlled sources
www.fsc.org Cert no. TT-COC-2139
FSC © 1996 Forest Stewardship Council

Danny Scheinmann is a writer, actor and storyteller. He has performed at the National Theatre and in over thirty countries. His tours include storytelling in Siberia and a year and a half working for an avant-garde theatre group creating shows with street children in Colombia, the Philippines, Cambodia and Vietnam. He also co-wrote and acted in the acclaimed independent film *The West Wittering Affair*. He was born and brought up in Manchester and now lives in London with his wife and three children. *Random Acts of Heroic Love* is his first book.

Entry no. 17

Tell her, brief is life but love is long.
Tennyson

Eleni Eleni
Eleni
Eleni Eleni

Eleni

1

THE MIND AFTER A SHARP BLOW TO THE HEAD IS LIKE A house after a hurricane: unrecognizable shards, shreds and splinters.

Fragments of memory lie scattered in the wreckage. All the pieces are there, somewhere – but the landscape is so distorted that, stumbling across them, the brain has no idea what they are or where they are from.

'Where is Eleni?'

'*Muerta*,' says the doctor.

Leo's eyes close, he is oddly calm watching the bomb hurtle towards him. One last look before he is swept away. He searches his mind and does not recognize the view. A thick fog smothers everything; he can just make out a few faintly familiar shapes. *Muerta*. He already knows she is dead. At the point of asking he had no idea but when he hears the answer it sounds like the confirmation of a memory he can't seem to bring to his mind. Something lurches out of the blur into sharp focus. Eleni. Droplet brown eyes, rich mane of ebony curls, bundle of electric energy, singing. Always singing, like others breathe. For a fleeting moment he feels her brightness and warmth. They were like a single atom, indivisible.

The bomb is almost upon him. The atom is about to be split. The energy to be unleashed, ferocious and uncontrollable.

'Can I see her?'

'No es buena idea'.

'Where is she?'

'Here, in another room.'

A game is being played. The doctor doesn't want the patient to see his dead lover – at least not yet. He is saying, 'Let's pretend she is not really dead. *Muerta* – it's just a word.' This is a game of damage limitation. Leo plays along. He doesn't know where he is or how he got there. He has no memory of recent events. He knows only that he loves a girl called Eleni and that he must see her at all costs. He senses the panic in the doctor. If he shows any sign of cracking, the doctor will keep them apart. So he plays calm.

'Please let me see her.'

The doctor clocks the steely determination in Leo's eyes and seems reassured; maybe the boy can cope after all. He doesn't know the story of these two young foreigners. He doesn't know the strength of their relationship.

'Venga,' he says softly and indicates the door.

It is only then that Leo realizes he is lying on a bed and that he must have been unconscious. His waking words were for Eleni. Something of that delirious soup lingers with him. Why does the doctor speak Spanish? The question hangs in his thoughts like a piece of string whose other end is lost in the haze. He pulls it and a thread emerges from the fog. A memory clings to it. I'm in Latin America. I came here with Eleni. But where? Guatemala? No, we flew to Colombia from there. Colombia then? No. He tugs at the string harder. No, not Colombia. After Colombia came Ecuador. Ecuador, what comes after Ecuador? Where were we going next? He pulls harder, the twine is fraying. Peru. From Ecuador to Peru. How? How did we get to Peru? The string snaps. No memory of getting to Peru. I must be in Ecuador or Peru. Probably Ecuador. I can't remember Peru. He contemplates the broken thread; he has no idea where to find the other end. He is at the edge of a hole whose size is as yet unfathomable. He stares into the void like a senile man who in a moment of lucidity knows that his mind is lost.

He pulls himself to his feet. His head swirls and he puts his hand on the bed to steady himself. He blinks hard and tries to focus on the enamel basin on the wall opposite. One of the taps dribbles annoyingly; it must have been leaking for years because the water has left an ugly brown stain in the sink. Wherever he is, it is in a state of neglect. The paint peels from the walls and thick spiders' webs hang undisturbed in the corners. A solitary gecko surveys the scene from the ceiling. The doctor takes Leo by the arm and leads him down a corridor.

They stop in front of a closed door. Leo knows she is on the other side. The doctor pushes it open. Eleni lies on a trolley bed. There is blood on her blue shirt; her shoulder is out of joint. There is a graze on her cheek. Now the

11

bomb hits. Something inside him yields and the full implication of events explodes inside him. His blood thunders out of control, coursing through him like a river that has burst its banks; legs shudder and give way at the knees; breath shortens and rasps in his throat. His heart rejects the returning blood and empties itself; stomach locks, sending undigested waste crashing into the colon; anus pulls tight to prevent evacuation. His nose charges with fluid mucus, eyes blink obsessively, vision blurs with tears. He collapses to the floor and screams a high guttural scrape. Nurses three rooms away stop in their tracks like mothers responding to a baby's cry. People come running from all directions. The doctor closes the door. A murmuring crowd gathers outside. Some of the people know what has happened. They are witnesses who are being treated in the clinic themselves. They have been wondering what would happen when the gringo came round and was told his girlfriend had died. 'My God,' they have been saying, 'when that boy wakes up . . . it is too terrible to contemplate.' And they cross themselves and thank Jesus that they will see their loved ones again.

Leo is sobbing in a crumpled heap. He has never been so alone. Lost in some nameless South American town with his mind half gone. He stands up and goes to Eleni. He caresses her face tenderly. Her skin is still warm. Perhaps she is not dead, maybe she can be brought back to life. He looks at the doctor with a wild stray optimism in his eye. The kiss of life, maybe he can bring her back with the kiss of life. He pinches her nose and opens her mouth and breathes his desperate hope into her. Again and again he pours his life into her. Then he beats on her heart to make it beat. Harder he pummels. He knows that he is hurting her, that she will be bruised, but it is the only way. The doctor puts his hand on Leo's shoulder. But a pathetic tenacious hope has gripped Leo.

'Electric shock. Have you got shock treatment? Er . . . *choc electrico. Tienes?*'

'*No hay, señor. Esta muerta.*'

She can't be dead, he will not believe it. He continues to breathe into her. He begs for a miracle and a miracle happens. A low raspy breath comes up from deep within her. It is a sound he will remember for the rest of his life.

'She's alive. She's breathing. Did you hear it?'

The doctor is motionless. Leo is suddenly animated, he doesn't need this stupid, lazy doctor, he can resuscitate Eleni on his own. He fills her up feverishly and each time she responds with a breath.

'Señor, señor!' The doctor places his hand again on Leo's shoulder. He ignores it, his heart is flying, he almost wants to laugh.

'Señor, she is not breathing. It is your breath coming back from her lungs.'

Leo feels for Eleni's pulse. There is nothing. Once more he plummets into despair. He kisses her forehead and whispers words learned from her native Greek: '*Matyamou, karthiamou, psychemou.*' My eyes, my heart, my soul.

He strokes her hair as he used to sometimes when she was sleeping. Slowly the heat leaves her body. A minute later he is howling like a dog. How long this lasts he has no idea.

The old doctor looks on from a corner. He battles back his own tears, he does not want to let his feelings conquer his professional dispassion. Later he will return home and weep in his wife's arms and hug her hard for many minutes, savouring her breath, her perfume and her love.

The story has spread through the hospital and the crowd outside the door have been overcome by that unsavoury curiosity that grips people in the face of tragedy. Someone pushes open the door. They see a man ravaged in grief, his face raw and twisted, and next to him a small woman lying gnarled and lifeless on a bed. As one they draw in a sharp breath, and for a moment their faces mirror Leo's.

'Go away, clear off. This is not a freak show. Leave me alone . . .' And even as he speaks Leo's voice cracks and fades away. They have seen enough, they are ashamed and someone closes the door.

The episode triggers a thought in his clouded mind. Why do I recognize those people? He turns to the doctor.

'What is the date?'

'It is the second of April, señor.'

'The second of April?' He searches desperately inside for a connection.

'Where am I?'

'Latacunga, señor.'

Latacunga – he knows the name. Yes, now he

remembers that he has been through Latacunga before. There is a busy market in the town square. He changed buses there with Eleni to go into the mountains. He is in Ecuador.

'What date is it?' He forgets that he has just asked this question.

'It is the second of April.'

'The second of April? What happened?'

'You were in a bus crash, señor.'

Nowhere in his memory can he place this information. It does not even create the slightest ripple across his psyche. He sits with the idea for a moment. No, he does not remember a bus or a crash. The thought hangs outside him like an alien trying to gain entry. His brain refuses to connect this information to any synapse or nerve ending. And yet somewhere lost in the internal wreckage sits the little black box, the flight recorder which carries the truth of what happened. A strange protective mechanism has kicked in which prevents him getting too close to the epicentre of his trauma. Like a witness in a court case who is not obliged to give evidence which could implicate him, so the body refuses the mind access to the information which could damage it.

'What date is it?' He wonders if he has asked this question before.

'The second of April, señor,' the doctor repeats patiently.

'What year?'

'1992.'

Leo grapples with the year. He set off in 1991. When in 1991? The end, near the end. December 1991. So what happened over the last four months? A small light switches on and he sees himself lying on a beach with Eleni. It is New Year's Eve; they have taken a day trip from Cartagena in Colombia to a tropical island. Eleni is wearing her pink swimsuit. They lie there in sunbleached bliss with the surf at their feet. He turns to her and kisses her warm cheek.

'You know, I can't think of anything in the whole universe that I want. I've got you at my side and I love you and that's it. There's nothing more to life than this.'

Eleni smiles, leans over and kisses him. 'Let's photograph it,' she says. She takes out their small instant camera and holds it at arm's length above their heads and points it towards them. They check their positions in the reflection on the lens and take the picture. Click.

He looks down at her corpse. The memory acts like a pair of hands that plough through his breastbone, rip open his ribcage and expose his heart to the elements. His spine melts away and he stands before his dead lover like a piece of limp flesh. He cannot breathe. His only thought now is that he wants to die and go with her.

From nowhere he feels a shooting cramp through his leg. He looks down and notices his jeans are ripped and covered in blood. Next he feels a throb in his hands. They are cut and bleeding. Shards of glass stick out from the skin. For a moment he becomes quite self-absorbed picking out the splinters.

His right shoulder is badly bruised and his hip joint fires sharp warning shots up his back. He realizes that he has suffered injuries all down his right side. But worst of all is his right knee. He cannot bend it or even feel it. How could he not notice the pain until now?

What is the date? he wonders. He is too embarrassed to ask again. The door opens. The crowd has disappeared. A policeman enters and asks Leo to accompany him to the bus station to identify his bags. Leo is reluctant to leave Eleni's side but he is strangely open to suggestion. There is no fight left in him and he obediently follows the policeman out of the room. The doctor follows and Eleni is left in peace.

'What is your name?' asks the policeman.

'Leo Deakin.'

'It is very close, Leo, it won't take a minute,' the policeman says in Spanish.

They step out of the clinic into the blinding evening sun and a wall of heat. The huge central plaza sprawls before them. A bustling South American market in full flow. On one side live cattle are being auctioned, llamas and cows foul the floor and chickens, foot-tied in hanging clusters, fill the air with fevered clucking. The fruit sellers sit on blankets in rows with their produce fanned out before them, and the wealthy Ottovalo Indians, hair in long plaits, hawk their multicoloured hand-woven hammocks and ponchos. Leo breaks out into a sweat. How unbearable the world is, so callous and indifferent. He shudders and recoils like a snake prodded with a stick. Lives beset with trivia and humdrum chores. Tedious mundane pathetic existences spent serving material gain.

He is looking at the world through binoculars held the wrong way round. All is small and distant, unreachable and detached. He belongs to another world now, a bubble where he can hear his heartbeat and feel his skin wrinkle. The marketplace is a muffle a million miles away. Sounds are cushioned and unreal. He is underwater and no one notices that he is drowning.

On his previous visit to that square, he and Eleni could barely walk a yard before being swamped by hawkers and draped in clothes or jewellery they did not want. They resisted all offers until Leo caught sight of two tiny carved Inca heads, one male and one female. He bought them without haggling, and gave the male head to Eleni as a keepsake.

But now as he walks through the square the traders instinctively turn away. For once he is avoided and ignored. There is something in the eyes of this man who is locked in a state of tragic bewilderment that disturbs the stallholders and dries the throat. This man is definitely not on a shopping spree.

The policeman leads them to a small hut at the bus terminal. Normally it is full of bus drivers and ticket collectors but today they are huddled outside animatedly discussing the accident. They fall silent when they see Leo approaching. The hut is packed high with bags and there, right in the middle, are two large rucksacks. He clambers towards them, unsure if they are his. He tries to lift the bags but a wave of dizziness overcomes him and he totters and winces. The doctor steps forward and picks the two bags up. Leo notices an ice pick and a pair of crampons sticking out from one of the bags. He stares at them curiously. He double-checks the nametag and sees Leo Deakin written on it.

As they walk back across the square Leo's eyes flick side to side as he desperately tries to remember. Neurons and synapses spark inside him and suddenly something bolts out of the gloom. They are in a mountain hire shop in Quito. Leo loved climbing mountains; it was one of the most perfect pleasures in life. Perfect, because once you had gained the summit you knew you could go no further. You had a complete sense of achievement. This was a rare sensation for him in a life where so many activities were ongoing, never-ending, where you had to look into the future for any sign of contentment. Cotopaxi, which towered over the plateau like an alluring cone-shaped exotic dessert, was going to be a huge challenge. The assistant in the shop told them to spend the night at the mountain lodge at five thousand metres, maybe even two nights, to acclimatize. He advised them to set off at 2 a.m. on the day of the climb so as to reach the summit for dawn, and return before the afternoon thaw, which would be treacherous. Crampons and picks would be a necessity, but if the weather held the walk would not be too difficult.

'Are you both going to the top?' he asked.

'Not me,' said Eleni. 'I'm climbing to the lodge and that's as far as I go.'

'Don't take any risks,' he warned. 'A couple of novices died up there last year.'

Leo recalls eating breakfast. They had gone to their favourite café near their hotel. He had eaten a fruit salad with granola and honey. 'Breakfast of the gods,' he had called it; pineapple, maracuya, mango and passion fruit. As he recalls it he tastes it again. Eleni had scoffed down a banana pancake with melted chocolate, and could not prevent the hot sauce dribbling down her chin. They had lingered over coffee. Afterwards they had returned to their hotel and picked up their heavy backpacks and set off for the bus station. There it was at last, the bus station. They were later than they had planned by over an hour. Would Eleni be alive now if they hadn't taken so long over breakfast? His memory stops at the bus station; he still cannot see any aspect of the journey in his mind. Perhaps it is better not to know, but he cannot seem to stop his thoughts racing. The holes are slowly filling up, and despite itself the brain will work until the job is completed.

2

THE CLINIC IS A SMALL DILAPIDATED BUILDING TYPICAL OF Spanish colonial architecture. To the local people it is a hospital but to a European it is definitely a clinic. Starved of equipment and qualified personnel, it cannot deal with anything other than routine illnesses.

In the foyer the doctor puts his arm round Leo's shoulder. 'We have to take her to the morgue.'

'No, please, can't I stay with her tonight?' Leo begs.

'I'm sorry, of course you can spend the night here, but I'm afraid the lady cannot. Tomorrow I will do an autopsy to establish the cause of death and then you must decide what to do next. Where are you from?'

'I am English, Eleni is Greek.'

'Well, I suggest you call the Greek embassy and ask for their help,' the doctor says. He turns to the policeman. 'Call Pedro, we need to get the ambulance to take Eleni to the morgue.'

The policeman shakes his head. 'Pedro has finished today. He's not back until Monday.'

'Well, get Carlos to come with the pickup van.' The doctor sighs and throws Leo a look of placid resignation. 'I'm sorry, señor. This is a small town. We only have one ambulance and the driver is a volunteer. He doesn't work weekends.'

What a godforsaken place for this to happen, Leo curses to himself. 'Before you take her away can I have some time alone with her?' he asks.

'You loved her very much, señor. I can tell. I am so sorry for you. My name is Doctor Jorge Sanchez, you can ask for me any time. I will do everything I can to help you. Now go. I will call you later when Carlos arrives with the van.' The doctor gives him the bags, squeezes his arm and pushes him towards the room where Eleni lies unattended.

Something has changed in her face, she has become more inert as if her soul has fully left her body. He kisses her and feels a terrible coldness on her lips. He takes her hands and rubs them to keep them warm. But it makes no difference, she is like a frozen rock, and a blue tinge has appeared in the veins beneath the skin where her blood has deserted her. Her dislocated shoulder arcs upwards out of joint. Leo winces at the imagined pain of the injury. She looks uncomfortable, and he can't leave her like that. He tenderly places his hand beneath her shoulder and tries to straighten it out, but it is locked rigid and he can feel the gap between the ball and joint.

'My poor baby, I hope you weren't in too much pain,' he whispers. He takes her right hand again and places it on her stomach so that she appears less twisted. Her long dark curly hair is still soft and he strokes it. Tears stream down his cheeks and drip on to her face. The door opens and a nurse walks in.

'Get out, please get out. Leave me alone.'

The nurse drops her head, turns sharply and leaves, muttering an apology.

Leo always knew when Eleni was happy, which was most of the time, because she made a sound. It might be humming or singing or silly lip noises. No matter what she was doing, whether she was on her bike, in the bath, working, cooking, she would make a sound. Everywhere, all the time, noise. Perhaps it would have driven some people crazy but Leo had grown to love it. She was only quiet when she was sad. Once she had been silent for a week and Leo had found it intolerable. It was a year into their relationship, and she had received a call from an ex-boyfriend who had told her that he had just discovered he was HIV positive and she should have an AIDS test. She had hurried to the university clinic and had hardly been able to speak as she waited seven interminable days for the results. Leo had had no idea what was wrong with her until the day she got the all-clear and came home singing.

Now the singing had stopped for good. A numbing silence hangs over the hospital room. Leo will have to live with this silence for ever. He slumps into a chair and listens intently to the void. The grief inside him settles for a moment. He sees himself from above sitting quietly on a chair with Eleni lifeless and still on the bed. Nothing moves. The air feels heavy and thick like sludge. He absorbs the silence, his heartbeat slows and his breath halts. The broad landscape of his future collapses into a pinhead. He stops crying and his eyes dull. He sits like this for some time, willing himself to fade away, when from nowhere a voice sounds in his soul. It is Eleni. 'Live,' she says simply.

What is this?

'Live,' there it is again.

He had never before been sensitive to the call of angels.

Indeed he positively railed against such nonsense. He was a PhD biology student, a rationalist and the outspoken ex-chairman of the University College Darwin Society. He despised quackery, metaphysics, and most of all religion.

'Live,' Eleni repeats softly.

Was he now developing an antenna for messages from beyond the grave? He battles against it. There has to be a logical explanation for this voice that seems as clear as his own. But he can't deny that he wants to believe she is there.

It is all he has left.

'All right,' he says to no one, 'I'll live if that's what you want.'

Leo notices that an orderly has entered the room. He did not see him come in and does not know how long he has been there. There is an unearthly lightness about the

24

man's presence, like a snowflake, and he moves with the delicacy of a butterfly landing on a leaf. The man does not make eye contact but busies himself with their rucksacks. A jar of honey, which they had been carrying, has smashed in the crash and the bags are sticky. He is cleaning them with a wet cloth. The man says nothing, but for some reason Leo feels comforted by him, so he lets him stay. He works quietly and with such humility that Leo is drawn to join him. He kneels awkwardly by the orderly and unzips his rucksack to remove the broken glass.

'What is your name?' Leo asks.

The man looks Leo in the eye and smiles serenely. He is a small man with dark Indian features.

'José.'

'Thank you, José.'

Inside the bag Leo finds the honey-dripped journal that Eleni wrote in every night. It is a familiar object to him with its blue faded cover and dog-eared pages, yet he has never ventured inside. He tries to flick through the sticky pages but the notebook falls open stubbornly in the middle. He dwells on the page that the journal wants him to read. Making no sense of the words he travels up and down the foothills of her rolling calligraphy, plunging headlong into her deep u's and v's, sliding down her curly y's, then looping round her o's, before reaching the glorious heights of her soaring l's and t's, and swinging off the pimples on her i's to land on the brow of an n or the breast of an m. All Eleni's beauty captured in the sensuality of her consonants and the voluptuousness of her vowels; the contours of her body traceable in the gentle coils of her writing. He slowly retreats from the detail of the lettering to seek its meaning.

31 DEC 1991

Got up early to catch a boat from Cartagena to the islands. Some of them were so small they just had one house on them with a boat launch or a helipad. Guide said they were mostly owned by drug barons. Leo offered to buy me one when he was rich, which means he'll never buy me one. We'll never be rich but I'm beginning to think we'll always be happy. Maybe happiness is the new rich.

It was weirdly cold on the boat, a combination of wind and spray from the sea. We were completely underdressed, so we huddled together at the back of the boat being silly trying to pinch each other's nipples when no one was looking, and then all of a sudden I had this uncontrollable urge to have Leo's babies. I wanted to be like a sea horse and shoot them out by the hundreds. To fill the world with little Leos and Elenis. I've never felt like that before. Lovely Leo, lovely dreamy-eyed Leo.

We stopped on one of the bigger islands for lunch in this straw beach-hut restaurant. We ate swordfish and then the owner put on some salsa and we all had a good bop. God I adore these people, they know how to have fun. You wouldn't see that in Peckham of an afternoon. Leo must have known what I was feeling because later we lay on the beach and he said so many sweet things to me that I felt like crying. I took a photograph of us as evidence so that I would never forget that moment. We have reached another level and I know in my heart that I have found everything I'm looking for. Still

*can't quite believe Leo loves me though. I know he does but
I can't quite believe it. He looks at me like I'm this fabulous
human being or something and I wonder when is he going
to realize what I'm really like? The funny thing is that the
more he looks at me like I'm fabulous the more I feel
fabulous. Today on the beach for the first time in my life I
actually thought maybe I am fabulous, and that maybe I've
always been fabulous but never realized it.*

*We came back at dusk and ate some frijoles at the youth
hostel. Shattered after another day of unadulterated
pleasure.*

Leo closes the diary and holds it tightly to his chest. José
has finished cleaning up the broken jar and offers Leo the
bag to put the journal back in, then he takes Leo's hand
gently and inspects the cuts. He carefully pulls out the last
few splinters and dresses the wounds. He washes Leo's
knee, dabs on disinfectant and wraps it neatly with a
bandage. Next he goes over to Eleni and starts to wash the
blood from her face.

Suddenly the door bursts open and Doctor Sanchez and
another man enter. In comparison to José the two men
seem oddly heavy and clumpy. The doctor again puts his
hand on Leo's shoulder, 'Carlos is here with the pickup
van. I'm afraid we must take your girlfriend to the morgue
now.'

'No, please give me a little more time.'

'I'm sorry, señor. You must understand it is not hygienic
to leave her here.'

27

'Yes, yes, I understand but you can't take her away. I don't want her to go to a morgue. Let me look after her. Please.'

He seeks out José from the shadows and looks pleadingly at him. José sighs and shakes his head and Leo knows that there is no point arguing.

'All right but I want to go with her to make sure everything is OK. And I want to go back in the morning.'

Doctor Sanchez thinks for a moment and says, 'It would be better if you stayed here, señor. Maybe you should make a few phone calls and rest.'

'No,' says Leo emphatically, 'I'll do that later.'

'As you wish, my friend,' says the doctor, and he signals to Carlos to open the double doors as he pushes the trolley out. Leo turns to thank José for his help but he has vanished. Leo never sees the gentle Indian again.

They make their way through the foyer to the main entrance of the hospital. Leo is surprised to see that the sun has set and it is pitch black outside. He has no idea of the time and he wonders what day it is. He still cannot remember anything of the bus crash or even the journey, but events preceding it are beginning to slip into place. Previous perilous journeys through the mountains come back to him. The buses had terrified Eleni right from the start. There seemed to be no rules or regulations when it came to buses. A family might have clubbed together to buy an old second-hand bus built in the fifties and this bus would provide their living. If the bus broke down they went hungry so they became very adept at botch-job mechanical repairs. The roads were cluttered with these unroadworthy dinosaurs with dodgy brakes and broken exhausts. The owners could choose their own destinations and timetables and buses would wait at the depot until they were full before they left. It benefited the owners to have people standing between the seats and sitting on the roof hanging on to a couple of poles that made up a makeshift roof rack. Then they drove as fast as they humanly could in order to fit in as many journeys as possible. It might have been tolerable for a short trip round town, but often the journey was several hours long through the Andes and the roads were dreadful. Pockmarked and bumpy with death-defying drops on either side and no barriers to stop the inevitable. A couple of times Leo and Eleni had seen a rusty bus deep in the valley below and all the other passengers had crossed themselves and said a little prayer. On several occasions Eleni had asked a driver to slow down and he had snorted at her and said, 'Don't you trust me? Do you think I can't drive? Get off the bus if you don't like it.' And sometimes Leo and Eleni had done just that.

Carlos's red pickup is waiting at the entrance to the hospital. There is a cab for the driver and one passenger and the rest of the van is open to the elements. The back hangs open awaiting its cargo. There are no seats or blankets, just the bare metal smeared with soil.

'We can't put her in there, it's disgusting,' Leo pleads.

But the men have already picked Eleni up by her feet and shoulders and are struggling to get her on to the back of the van.

'Please be careful.' Leo takes hold of her head to protect it. Carlos backs on to the van but as Leo tries to step up his knee gives way and he slips and falls backwards. Carlos loses his grip and Eleni falls on top of Leo. She is much heavier dead than alive. She is rigid and cold and Leo struggles to pull himself out.

She lies there like a slaughtered sheep ready for market, with no semblance of dignity. There is nothing to tie her down or keep her from bouncing on the bumpy roads. It is all so piecemeal and makeshift. While Eleni was alive he had been charmed by the chaos of South America; now he craves an ambulance, cleanliness, efficiency. He wants an authority he can trust, guilt to be apportioned and a system of redress. With so much chaos already in his head, he desperately seeks external order.

As he watches Eleni sliding around in the back, Leo becomes sensitive to every pothole in the road and begs Carlos to drive carefully. For once it is not taken as an insult and Carlos slows to a crawl. They drive right through town and no one seems in the slightest bit perturbed by a van with a corpse in the back. Eventually they arrive at a graveyard.

'I thought we were going to a morgue,' Leo says.

'It is here, señor, at the back,' Carlos reassures him.

It is menacingly dark; Leo can just make out the gravestones and the outline of a small chapel. The front gates are closed and Carlos hoots. After a while an old thin man appears in the headlights and limps up the gravel path holding a torch. He opens the gates and invites Carlos to drive through and park behind the chapel.

They pull up outside a heavy stone structure, which, with its sharply pointed roof, reminds Leo of an Egyptian pyramid. The attendant, hobbling back from the gate, smiles a toothless tobacco-stained grin. Do I have to leave her with him? Leo wonders, remembering that human organs are traded in South America. The guidebooks were full of stories of unsuspecting travellers being drugged in bars and waking up the next day in some godforsaken alley with a large scar and a kidney missing. Leo battles against haunting imagery from horror films and night-mares. Carlos leaves the headlights on so they can see the door of the pyramid, which is half-open. Candles are flickering inside, there seems to be no electricity.

They carry Eleni in. It is damp and surprisingly cold for a chamber that is not refrigerated. The room is bare except for five concrete slabs; one holds the corpse of an old man. There are no windows, and a stench of bleach and stale flesh hangs in the air. Leo's stomach lurches and quivers. Up on the high grey stone ceiling ghosts dance in the candlelight. The men put Eleni on the central slab.

Leo is crying, 'I can't leave her here. It's like a dungeon.' As he speaks the ghosts answer back and his voice echoes around the room.

'Señor, it is best to leave now,' says Carlos.

Leo grabs her icy hand and his sobs are amplified by the mocking devils in the ceiling until the morgue howls with him. His resolve to live for Eleni vanishes, now he wants death, he wants communion with her.

'She is already in heaven, señor. Her spirit has left her body. Come on, let's go back to the hospital.'

'I won't leave her. I won't ever leave her.' A draught blows in from outside and extinguishes two candles. 'You see, she is still here.'

Carlos and the attendant exchange a glance.

'Eleni, Eleni,' Leo shouts at full voice. 'Don't go.'

'Eleni,' the walls bounce back. 'Go, go.'

The corpse of the old man watches silently. He had slipped away unnoticed and content. No one had fought for him. But Eleni was only twenty-one years old, just two weeks away from her twenty-second birthday. She wanted a family. She loved life. Growing up, Eleni was always the first to get dirty, jump in puddles and roll in mud. As a young teenager she would climb olive trees and skinny-dip in mountain streams. Leo was envious of her affinity with nature; he admired her for the way she would bush-whack through mountain forests in search of waterfalls or dive head first into a cold English sea in May. Her connection to the world was as a baby to its mother.

'Eleni, Eleni, come back,' he thrashes the air and pulls at his shirt.

'We have to get him out of here, he's losing his mind,' Carlos says to the attendant.

They try to take Leo by the arm but he pushes them off, 'Eleni, don't go without me.'

'Eleni . . . without me,' the ghosts reply. Carlos grabs Leo round the waist and pulls him towards the door.

'Señor, you must go. You need to rest.'

'I'll never leave you, Eleni,' Leo thunders into the void. Another candle blows out and their shadows loom on the wall behind the old corpse. And as the light glimmers over its face the corpse seems to leap into life and stare angrily at the disturbance.

The attendant panics, 'Oh mother of Jesus, help us. The morgue is alive.' He bolts for the door. Leo is kicking and crying and begging for Eleni to come back. Carlos tugs him with all his strength. '*Hijo de puta*, get out of here before the devil has you.'

Carlos pulls Leo backwards, and as they crash through the door a breeze blows out the last candles. The attendant dives in with his key, slams the door closed and locks it. Leo buckles on to the grass holding his head on his knees, rocking and sobbing, rocking and sobbing.

Carlos leans on the van, breathless. Oh God, oh God, he says to himself. Oh God, deliver me from this awful place.

Eventually Leo pulls himself to his feet. 'I'm sorry,' he says weakly.

Carlos puts his arms around him and hugs him hard. The two strangers stand like that for a couple of minutes until their two hearts slow to a calmer beat.

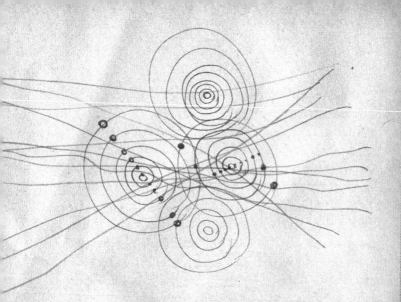

Entry no. 53

The butterfly that lives a day
Has lived eternity.

T. S. Eliot

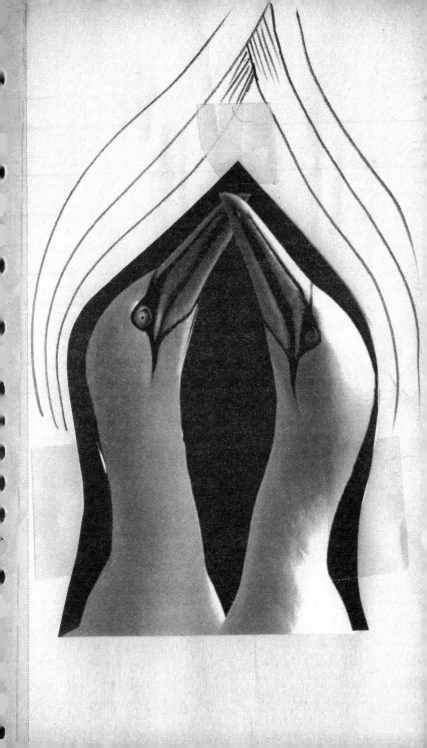

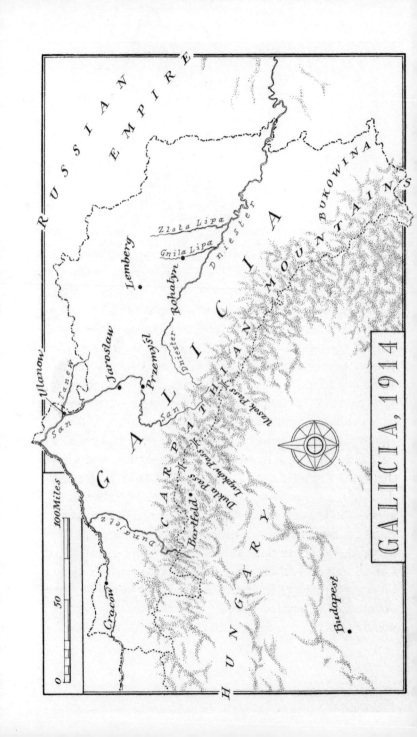

3

AH THERE YOU ARE. I'M GLAD. I'VE GOT A STORY TO TELL you. Come closer, that's it, right up to my bed. Don't be shy. Bring the chair right up. It's all right, I'm not contagious. You can rest your feet on it if you like. There. I've been worried about you, Fischel; you haven't said a word for days. Your mother said it started when you saw them take me away. Well I'm back now, a little worse for wear maybe, but I'm back and they won't come for me again. Maybe you're worried about me, too. You children have finer senses than we give you credit for. You know that I'm going to die, don't you? It's all right, my boy . . . don't speak if you don't want to . . . you don't have to say a word. To tell you the truth, for a long time I didn't even think I'd live this long. Death has been chasing after me for years. I've come close to being caught so often that I've lost all natural fear of it. Now I see life and death as two lovers embracing. Inseparable. Each obsessed by the other . . . Oh excuse me . . . this wretched cough . . . please pass me . . . the spittoon . . . yes and my hanky

. . . thank you. I'm sorry, you can't bear the sight of it, can you? Here, put it back on the table. Oh dear, does it smell that bad? I've got so used to it, I don't even notice any more. Now listen, they've taken everything . . . the workshop . . . everything. But there is one thing that even they cannot steal and that is my story.

That's it; get comfortable. I want you to imagine a fast clean river flowing through a dense forest. A pathway, beaten through the trees, leads to the river's edge. Here the rocks have reached round to create a pool of calm still water. Sitting on the rocks, with their feet dangling in the pool, are a boy and a girl. No one knows they are there. It is their secret place, a place to talk and hold hands. The boy turns to the girl, the girl turns to the boy. Their hearts are racing. There is no reason. He gently takes the girl's head in his hands and for the first time he kisses her. Her lips are as soft as ripe peach. A lock of her curly dark hair falls about his face and an eyelash flutters against his cheek. They close their eyes and feel the forest melt around them. They float upwards and glide with swallows on the summer breeze. Then drift down like falling leaves. 'I love you,' he whispers.

'I love you too,' she sighs. No sooner spoken than their words are lost in the sound of rushing water and carried downstream to a bigger river, which whisks them off to the sea. The moment is cast in memory for ever. The kiss holds a promise from which there is no return.

A year later that same boy finds himself once more in a forest with a river running through it. It is a different forest. On his side of the river is the Austro-Hungarian

Army, on the other is the might of the Russian Army. It is August 1914, the war is a month old and the boy is me. In my hand is a letter from the girl. It carries her perfume and reminds me of that moment. It begins:

Moritz, my love,

You have won my heart and now I can't stop thinking about you . . .

I am sitting with my back to a sandbag, waiting to be killed. For the moment it is quiet, there is a lull. Next to me is my best friend Jerzy Ingwer. Next to him is Frantz Király, a burly and unpopular Hungarian peasant boy. On the other side is Piotr Baryslaw, a well-meaning Pole from Cracow who blinks too often. There are others, thousands of others but you don't need to know them, I hardly remember any of them myself. Oh there is one more, I almost forgot. Lieutenant Neidlein. He is pacing in front of us, all two metres of him. We call him the Great Viennese Sausage. Long, thin and Austrian. He is waiting for the next order.

Never have I loved life more than in this moment, for the beauty of life is etched in the face of death. How sweet life is. I want to open my every pore and soak it up until I'm rolling full and then inhale it, drink it in and drown in it some more. I am thinking of all the tiny things I took for granted. How golden they now seem; the taste of fresh bread on the Sabbath, the feel of underclothes warmed by the fire in winter, the scrunch of shoes on autumn leaves, the yawning magnificence of a day spent doing nothing. What would I give to live the carefree days once more? But on this day, Fischel, I am sure that I am going to die. I have only been at the front one day and I have seen enough in that day to convince me of it.

I put the letter down and begin to shake with fear. I long to be back home in Ulanow. I think about my mother and father. I want to see my favourite sister Eidel and the rest of my noisy siblings. But most of all I think of Lotte and our sun-dappled pool by the River San. I see a carpet of kisses unravelling majestically ahead of me. I picture a wedding and try to imagine the children that we might have had. For on that day in Galicia with the Russians bearing down on us, it does not seem possible. They will rip me to shreds with their artillery and trample me into the mud. I will die a virgin in the blood-soaked earth of my homeland. Terror holds me in its icy grip. My mind is dark. I look over to Jerzy Ingwer for reassurance. We grew up together, went to school together, did everything together. I know his feelings as I know my own. I can read him by the glimmers on his face. He is shivering even though it is warm. Jerzy smiles weakly and I know that he too is in Ulanow with his memories. It is the best place to be.

Fischel, go and bring me that map on the shelf. It will help you understand. Yes, that big one. Find Poland for me . . . There, good, that's it. Look down here in the south-east, can you see it, there where the River San meets the Tanew. Ulanow. Have you found it? That's where all your family is from. You have to remember, Fischel, that back then there was no Poland. This bit up here, the north, was Russia and this bit in the south called Galicia was in the Austro-Hungarian Empire. Look, you see how close Ulanow was to Russia – barely fifteen kilometres. So close in fact that we would regularly cross over and trade with them. I learnt to speak Russian from an early age and my uncle Josef used to take me over to help him sell crucifixes. Don't look so shocked, Fischel, Josef made all the crucifixes in Ulanow, no one could match him for detail. He took great pleasure nailing Jesus to the cross twice a day. It was a revenge of sorts for the persecution he suffered as a boy at the hands of the Cossacks when he lived over the border.

Now, find Lvov on the map. It was called Lemberg back then. Go forty kilometres south-east, you see a little blue line there. That's the Gnila Lipa River and halfway down there is a village called Rohatyn. Got it? And there are some woods to the north. Well that's where Jerzy and I are sitting dreaming of Ulanow. We're not so very far from home but it feels like a million miles.

I try and recall the precise moment I fell in love with Lotte. It was some time in 1912; I was young, a few years older than you, about sixteen, and it all began with a pair of shoes. Do you remember your grandfather, Fischel? Perhaps not, he died when you were four years old. He was a poor cobbler and when I had time I would help him out in his shop. I didn't like it much but one day the door opened and there before me was Lotte Steinberg and her father. I knew who she was, everyone knew the Steinbergs, they were the wealthy furriers with the big house on the edge of town. They had come to collect a pair of dress shoes that my father had made for Lotte.

'Can I try them on now, Daddy?' she asked.

'Of course you can, angel. Go on, young man,' Steinberg thundered. He had a huge voice.

Lotte sat down on a chair and I knelt down in front of her. She kicked off her shoes and the insignificant denuding of her feet had the same effect on me as if she had disrobed entirely. I gasped and blushed and couldn't move. I caught myself staring at her ankles and then her toes, and then I didn't know where to look. After a moment's hesitation I picked her left foot up in my hand and felt its loveliness. It was pale and delicate and I guided it as tenderly as I could into the new shoe. And then the same with her right, but this time I hovered and fussed over it because my hands had urgently acquired a need to touch her.

Lotte stood up and walked purposefully around the room turning her feet this way and that.

'So how are they?' her father boomed.

'Yes, they're perfect,' she replied happily, 'very comfortable. I shall wear them to the waltz.'

First love is an extraordinary thing, I felt jubilant and melancholic all at once; one minute I was skipping through the cornfields, the next I was sulking in dark corners. My mind was in constant conversation with her, she was the subject of countless florid daydreams. At home I meandered aimlessly, oblivious to my loud-mouthed family. Sometimes I would find myself staring out of the window when the last thing I could remember was reading on a chair. I was on the cusp of manhood and love was my chaperone. I was like a bud opening in

42

spring, elated and confused by my new awakening. I was changing physically, hair was sprouting on my face and body, my sweat took on a musky odour, my muscles gained definition, I was a butterfly emerging from a pupa and I was embarrassed by my own beauty.

I went out of my way to pass Lotte's house, running useless errands up and down town like a demented donkey, but whenever I saw her, love robbed me of my tongue. What could I say without betraying myself? When I told Jerzy that I was in love with Lotte Steinberg he shook his head and held up his hands. 'Don't waste your time. Why would Lotte care for the son of a cobbler when she can have who she wants?' He was right. Her parents were grooming her for a big society wedding in Vienna. They knew all the wealthy Jews there and were already taking her to the great waltzes to meet prospective husbands. Her father was looking for men who had experience of the world, men who earned money and could provide for her. I was the last person on earth he would have taken into his family.

In the end it was my sister Eidel who told her that I was pining like a moonstruck dog. I was furious with Eidel but the next time I saw Lotte she walked right up to me and said hello. I was taking a sack of firewood to old Mr Kaminsky's place when she approached. I was so shocked to see her coming towards me that I dropped it on my foot and yelped in pain. She pretended not to notice, but much later when we had got to know each other she told me that she had found the incident most endearing. I remember the summer of 1913 as the sweetest time of my life. We still had no idea of the terrible things that would happen to us.

Fischel, please could you pass me the water? My throat is dry . . . thank you. Don't look so worried. I'm all right . . . well, perhaps I should be resting but these doctors say the strangest things. One minute they tell you that you're going to die and the next they tell you to rest. So I ask you what is the point of resting if you are going to die anyway? Won't I be resting enough soon? Oh, I'm sorry, you don't want me to talk about it. Come here, Fisch, give me a hug.

I'm sure you know what happened next. Anyone old enough to remember knows exactly where they were when they heard that Archduke Franz Ferdinand and his wife had been assassinated in Sarajevo. It was one of those moments when a whole nation quivers in shock. The world turned on its head and nothing was quite the same ever again. It was a bit like what happened here in 1933 when Hitler won.

It was a balmy hot evening towards the end of June 1914. We were at the Steinbergs' annual summer party. Children were running riot through the garden, pockets stuffed with fine biscuits. Labourers and craftsmen lounged in deckchairs like ruddy-faced dukes as waiters in white gloves served nibbles and schnapps. No one paid any attention to the overdressed string quartet that was toiling in the heat. By this time Jerzy and I had been conscripted and were proudly wearing our uniforms. Lotte was busy being the perfect hostess, chatting politely to the guests. She dared not pay me any special attention. Jerzy and I stood by the house together talking of how I might win her hand. 'Maybe if you were to move up the ranks and become an officer her father would let you marry,' Jerzy offered.

'What chance is there of that?' I said, dejected.

'You never know, there are some prominent Jewish officers. You just have to work hard at it. Make a career of it.'

From the corner of my eye I saw Mrojek, Ulanow's police captain, burst into the garden. He was in a sweat. He must have run the entire length of town. He quickly downed a vodka to steady his nerves and then stood on a chair and begged for quiet. The quartet broke off abruptly and the revellers gathered round. He announced in a solemn tone that he had just received a telegraph from Vienna. The Archduke was dead. As he read it out he burst into tears. The party erupted in protest and lament. 'The Serbs will pay for this!' they shouted. Lotte shot me a worried glance from across the crowd. Jerzy and I knew what it meant for us.

There was so much activity surrounding our departure from Ulanow that it was virtually impossible to find a moment alone with Lotte. We snatched conversations here and there. She told me that she couldn't care less if I became an officer. 'Just come home alive. And I will marry you anyway,' she said. Those words were a rare gift, better than any weapon, for during the dark times ahead when death held more promise than life it was those words that kept me alive.

There were thirteen of us who left for war, and the way we were cheered on the day we left you would have thought we had won already. No one expected it to last long. We were going to teach the Serbs a lesson and be home within a month. As we rode out on horseback towards the station at Rudnik the road was lined with people clapping and shouting. At the top of town we passed the Steinberg mansion. Lotte and her family were all standing outside waving us on. Lord knows why, but I felt so proud to be an Austrian soldier going to war. I sat tall in my saddle and doffed my cap as I passed them. Lotte was fighting back her tears. Suddenly she called out, 'I'll wait here for you, Moritz, don't forget to write,' then she put her hand to her mouth as if to stop the words, for her father was glowering disapprovingly at her side. And as I rode off I could see that he was talking angrily to her.

Jerzy and I were on a train with the Austro-Hungarian Second Army, quite close to Serbia, when we heard that the Russians had declared war against us. Half our troop was ordered back to Galicia but the rail network had come to a standstill under the strain of mobilization and it took us four weeks to get back. By the time we were marching to the front the Germans had declared war on the Russians, the British and French had come out against us and we had missed some ferocious battles already. What had started as a scrap on our southern border had blown up into a full-scale war and Ulanow was right in the middle of it.

So you have the picture now, Fischel: Piotr Baryslaw,

me, Jerzy Ingwer and Frantz Király all sitting in a row waiting for Neidlein to tell us what to do. It is almost light and we haven't been there long. We are exhausted and demoralized, more so than all the others, because we have just returned from a gruelling night of 'voluntary' work kindly organized for us by Lieutenant Neidlein and we are haunted by the spectres we have seen through the night. The others at least have slept. Not us. Király blames me for getting us into trouble but the truth is that he is as guilty as I am. The only innocents are Ingwer and Baryslaw, they were punished for laughing.

You see, when at last we got off the train that had brought us back up from the Serb border we still had to walk for three days in the scorching heat to get to the front. It didn't have to be that way, there were stations closer to the front, but for some reason we were deposited near Przemyśl and told to walk. Have you ever heard people say *'L'Autriche est toujours en retard d'une armée, d'une année et d'une idée'*: Austria is always an army short, a year behind and clueless? Well, it was true, especially then. You can imagine that, after the month we had just spent going up and down the country like idiots, the men were losing faith in those who were leading them. Király was the first to complain.

'Come on, Lieutenant, can't we stop for a rest?' he called out in his heavily accented German.

Lieutenant Neidlein looked back over his shoulder and grimaced.

'Stop moaning, it's just a stroll in the country. Enjoy it while you can.'

'A stroll in the country! We've been walking non-stop for days,' Király groaned.

'Oh shut up,' Lieutenant Neidlein hissed, 'we have to get to the front by sundown. The Third Army need re-inforcing. If it's action you want I'll make sure you get some soon.'

'That's right, and we all know what happened the last time the Great Viennese Sausage said that, don't we, lads? We twiddled our thumbs for ten days in a field full of cow-pats waiting for a train,' I shouted out in Polish. There was a roar of laughter from Jerzy and Piotr.

'What was that?' Neidlein enquired angrily.

'Nothing, Lieutenant,' I replied.

You see, Neidlein couldn't speak Polish, nor could Király for that matter. Some bright spark had had the idea that every regiment should contain a smattering of all the nationalities for social cohesion and to prevent rebellion from hostile minorities like the Czechs and Romanians. A recipe for disaster. The officers who were mostly Austrian couldn't understand half their men and we couldn't understand each other. I think Neidlein wanted to assert his authority over us after that but he got the actual idea for our punishment a little later. As we got nearer to the front we heard the rumbling sound of lorries in the distance. We watched as an ambulance truck rolled by in the opposite direction on its way back from the front. It was overflowing with wounded men. We could just make out their vacant faces squashed up against the mud-spattered windows.

The first ambulance was followed by another and

48

another and then all manner of military vehicles carrying men prostrate in the back with their limbs mangled or missing, their faces burnt and peeling. Soon there was a constant flow of traffic coming the other way. I felt sick, what had happened? No one said a word. Up ahead was a forest and I could see now a trickle of foot soldiers emerging from the trees.

'Oh my God,' Jerzy gasped as they drew closer, 'look at them.'

These were the walking wounded, their uniforms covered in filth and blood, their weary heads lolling forwards, their eyes wide open, intent on the horizon, determined to escape whatever was behind them. I wondered where they were going. Why weren't they being tended to in the field hospitals?

'Perhaps they are full. Maybe they're going to the nearest base station. Where would that be?' Jerzy asked.

I thought it would probably be in Lemberg but some of the men wouldn't make it that far, they were in a state of near collapse, sprawled along the roadside. They bled copiously from open wounds to their arms, stomachs and heads. Their retreat was over.

The nearer we got to the forest the thicker the stream of injured men that gushed out of it. It worried me that none of these men had been bandaged. If their wounds were dressed properly nearly all of them would live. I could not understand why we weren't stopping to help. Eventually I became so irritated that I broke ranks to help a man who was lying face down in the mud. But Neidlein screamed at me to get back in line. And that's when he got the idea about what to do to us.

Later that afternoon, after we had pitched camp in the woods and cleaned out our rifles, Neidlein summoned us to his tent. He was sitting behind a small fold-out table covered in maps.

'Ah, come in boys,' he smiled, then he looked me in the eye. 'I must say, Daniecki, I was deeply touched by the concern you showed for your fellows today, so I have decided to give you all an opportunity to volunteer your services to the field hospital at Rohatyn for the night. They are desperately short-staffed and can't cope with the numbers. They've made a specific request for assistance and I immediately thought of you. I want you to know that this is not a punishment but a worthy and important task. My only concern is that it will exhaust you ahead of tomorrow's battle, but you are all spirited lads, you'll be all right.'

The forest was swarming with retreating soldiers as we made our way to Rohatyn. No one seemed to know where to go or what to do; they were just running. This was my first taste of war and I had never seen such pandemonium. Then from behind us a cavalry captain surged forward on his horse and shouted at the men to stop running and to regroup by the river. There were some who ignored the order and the captain took out his rifle and shot one of them in the back. It was enough to halt the rest. The words 'Hold your ground' echoed through the trees as soldier called to soldier. The tide was stopped and the men sank to the ground exhausted, awaiting their next order. We came across a soldier sitting forlornly at the foot of a hornbeam tree and asked him what was happening.

'There's been a massacre at the Zlota Lipa twenty kilometres east of here,' he explained. Apparently they'd been advancing in close order over the hills and rivers, making good progress, when quite unexpectedly they met the Russians coming the other way; it was, he said, like running into a steamroller. Our men had held their ground for two days but the Russians were better armed and at least double in number. The soldier had a stray look in his eye; I'd seen it in some of the wounded men we had passed earlier in the day. It was as if his eyes had seen something that his mind could not comprehend. We wanted to know what the battlefield was like.

'The shells fell like rain on our heads,' he said, 'I saw whole regiments wiped out in a matter of minutes. No matter how many Russians we killed there were always more of them advancing. In the end we were crushed like flies. We fled for our lives. It was horrific. The battlefield was stained red and covered with bits of body and brains. But worse were the desperate pleas from the dying who we left howling in the wind as we retreated. That was dreadful.'

If this were not enough to rob us of our youthful bravado then what we were about to see would finish us off completely. There can be nothing more demoralizing for those about to face the enemy for the first time than to see at close quarters what a shell can do to a man. Of course I would grow accustomed to such sights but I cannot overemphasize the impact it had on me at first.

A makeshift field hospital had been set up inside the Roman Catholic Church of St Peter and Paul in the village of Rohatyn and our assignment was to bring in the wounded and throw out the dead. They came in their hundreds from every direction, like a swarm of locusts converging on the little church, traipsing down from the uplands or tramping through forests. It was as if the graves had opened and spilled their contents into the street. Men with half their faces missing, men with limbs mashed to a pulp, some dragging their legless rumps along the road trailing blood behind them, others, more hopeless still, being carried in the arms of their friends. A few of these last were so severely burnt that they were barely recognizable as human at all. Gristle in uniform, and yet miraculously they were still alive.

At first we tried to help them all but the nurses quickly reprimanded us. If they could walk we were to send them on. Only those who needed urgent attention and could be saved were treated. Those who were beyond hope were ignored. It was dreadful, but choices had to be made because there was neither the time nor the resources to tend to them all. Once they had succumbed we carried them out on stretchers to the graveyard where they were dropped into a mass grave that the villagers had dug. The priest stood in constant prayer over the grave. Occasionally a hospital transport would arrive to take some of the wounded back to Lemberg, and we were able to carry some new arrivals into the church.

Inside, the pews had been moved to one side. There were only a dozen beds so most of the wounded lay shoulder to shoulder on the floor and there was barely any room to walk. It was dark but for a sharp ray of sunlight that pierced the western window and created a glowing halo of light over a particular soldier, such that whenever I walked in my eye would immediately fall upon that soldier, as if he were somehow special. And as the sun set, the solitary ray shifted from soldier to soldier and lifted each one in turn out of the obscurity, as if God himself were scrutinizing them and choosing who should live or die.

After a few hours I became accustomed to the grim stench of pulverized flesh and the groans of the wounded. They were to be my unwanted companions throughout the war. At dusk we lit candles, and the nurses carried on tirelessly cleaning and bandaging long into the night. We did not notice that the guns had gone quiet until there was a sudden barrage much closer than before. The approach of the Russians only served to hasten our activities. My arms and back ached from the carrying and I was parched. My canteen was empty; I had given every last drop to the dying, upon whose lips it was wasted. Frantz Király was the only one who had kept his water for himself. If anyone asked him for a drop he told them to go to hell. He was out for himself. Like all peasant labourers he knew the pace that he could sustain, and would not surpass it even when all others around him were in a frenzy.

We were in a rush now to load up the wounded as

quickly as possible and send them west. Baryslaw and I were helping a soldier, who had lost a leg, on to a transport wagon, when there was a terrific explosion that shook the ground and caused a few tiles to drop from the roof of the church. I instinctively ducked behind the wagon, as did Baryslaw, but the soldier panicked and began to shout 'retreat'; he pushed us aside and with newfound strength hopped away down the street. When we returned to the church, we found that half the stretchers were empty: fear had driven the men scraping and crawling into the night. Men who we thought were incapable of moving had vanished. What had these men experienced in only two weeks of war that drove them to blind panic every time they heard a bomb drop?

Within twenty-four hours I would understand, for at that very moment somewhere safe and warm 150 kilometres away Field-Marshal Conrad von Hötzendorf was issuing an order for the Austro-Hungarian Third Army led by General Brudermann, supported by reinforcements from the Second Army recently arrived from the Serbian Front, to attack the Russians at the Gnila Lipa River. General Brudermann, who was keen to avenge the humiliation suffered at the Zlota Lipa where he had lost half his men, was only too happy to oblige.

We received new orders to return to our posts and be ready for a morning offensive. Meanwhile the divisional surgeon had already decided to pack up and pull back to the next village. A dozen hospital transport wagons had drawn up outside the church and we managed to get most of the wounded hoisted on to them but there wasn't room for them all. One of my last chores was to lift a dying man from a camp bed on to the floor because the bed had to be packed away. He had a shrapnel wound the size of a tennis ball in his chest, which gurgled strangely at every breath. As I put him down he grasped my hand with uncanny strength. He tried to speak but his lips were unable to form the words. Then he pulled my hand towards his chest. I recoiled but he would not let go. He clasped it firmly over his uniform, the side that had not disappeared into his wound. 'Pocket,' he whispered, summoning the last of his will. I reached inside his breast pocket and felt a piece of card. I picked it out carefully and saw that it was a bloodstained photograph. It was a picture of him with his wife and baby girl. Taken against a simple white wall, he was standing with his hands resting on the shoulders of his wife, who was sitting on a chair with the baby on her knee. They were wearing their Sunday best and to my tired eye in that dark church they looked like the most beautiful people in the world. I turned the photograph towards him so that he could take a last look. He stared at it for a moment then closed his eyes. I kept that photograph throughout the war, in fact I still have it now, Fischel. Would you like to see it? It's over in the drawer in my desk . . . yes that one . . . under the envelopes. That's it. Have a good look. Beautiful, aren't they? Here, let me see. Ah yes . . . yes. I love these people.

Have I really drunk all that water? Fischel, please go and fill the jug, and if you don't mind, clean out the spittoon. There's a good boy. Hurry back and I'll tell you the rest.

Entry No. 33

And when Love speaks, the voice of
  all the gods
Make heaven drowsy with the harmony.

Shakespeare

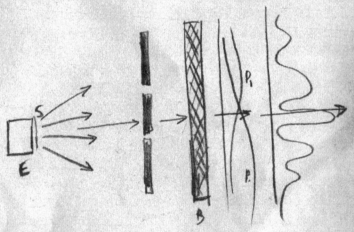

$$i\hbar \frac{\partial \psi}{\partial t} = -\frac{\hbar^2}{2m}\frac{\partial^2 \psi}{\partial x^2} + V(x,t) \equiv H\Psi(x,t),$$

$$\psi(x,t) = \varphi(x)e^{iEt/\hbar}$$

$$= \sum_n c_n \psi_n(x)e^{-iE_n t/\hbar}$$

4

LEO IS LYING IN THE SAME ROOM, ON THE SAME MOBILE BED his girlfriend had lain on a few hours previously. It is late, he is supposed to be asleep. The doctor has told him to rest, but it is the first night in two years that Eleni has not been at his side. He aches for her, rolls over, falls down the crevice where she once lay, tumbles head-long through space and chases her through the ether.

He grapples to fill the empty holes that still plague his memory. He has now been told that the bus crashed into a lorry, that the lorry driver was drunk and swerved across the pan-American highway into their path. The lorry driver had sustained a concussion but nothing serious. Still now this information means nothing to him. If it wasn't for the devastation the accident had wrought, he wouldn't know it had anything to do with him.

Eventually he begins to slip in and out of conscious-ness, his thoughts and his nightmares merging into one. This is not sleep but a relentless wringing of the spirit as if it were a wet rag that needed to shed its filth. Eleni appears to him, she is dancing with him and he is relieved. 'I thought you were dead,' he says, and he holds her tightly. This is the cruellest nightmare of all, a nightmare he is to have night after night for many years. Eleni is alive, she returns to play with him and the nightmare is so real that he actually believes it to be true. His body relaxes and he breathes easily. They talk and kiss and he can feel the warmth of her skin, he softens and opens like a passion flower. But then she begins to dissolve in his arms, her smile fades and she disappears. Now he is screaming for her to come back, he searches for her in the recesses of his dream, trying desperately not to wake up. In his half-waking state he locks his eyes shut and thrusts himself backwards towards his dream, but he has lost the route map. When finally he awakes it feels like he has lost her all over again.

Muerta.

The only evidence of his dream is two lines of salt down his face where he has been crying in his sleep. Morning is moon miles away.

Now irreversibly awake, he replays his first meeting with Eleni, back when they were both students. He was in the final year of his biology degree at University College, London. He had been out clubbing in Camden with some friends. It was three in the morning and he had decided to walk back to his hall of residence in town. As he passed a bus stop a voice called out to him.

'Excuse me, are you going towards Tottenham Court Road?'

Leo stopped and turned. The first thing he saw was hair. Long, black and curly. Then he saw the girl beneath, short with tight jeans, and no more than eighteen years old.

'Yes, I am.'

'Do you mind if I walk with you?' She seemed worried.

'No, not at all,' he said.

'It's just that my friends went off without telling me and I've been waiting for a night bus for ages.'

It turned out she was a fresher at the same university and she had seen him around in the college bar. She wouldn't have asked a complete stranger to walk her home. She was chatty and they talked all the way back, although Leo could no longer remember anything they talked about, the only thing that stuck with him from that first encounter was her mass of hair and her distinctive gait. She seemed to bounce on the front of her foot, her weight slightly forward, her head bobbing up and down. There was something about that walk that was so joyful and carefree that Leo had to try it for himself. He dropped her off at her hall of residence and walked the Eleni walk home to see what it felt like. The shift forward in weight gave him a sense of purpose, the bob of the head after each step made him feel naively optimistic, and the extra energy through the foot had an enthusiasm about it. It was a revelation to him that the way he walked could affect his feelings. Perhaps every emotion had its corresponding walk. He tried walking slowly, he stooped and he staggered. If anyone had seen him that night they would have mistaken him for a lunatic. This is better than therapy, he thought; depressed people should just walk differently. They should look to the sky, they should breathe deeply and they should bounce like Eleni.

The next time he saw her she was sitting at an Amnesty stall in the student union trying to get people to write letters to Colonel Gaddafi to complain about victims of torture in Libya. Leo sat down at the desk and they chatted about the work of Amnesty. Eleni spoke like she walked. Listening to her he rediscovered the purpose, the optimism and the enthusiasm that he had felt in her walk. He wondered what came first: the bouncy walk or the bouncy talk? Which had influenced the other? She was persuasive and passionate and Leo felt good about writing to Colonel Gaddafi. Unfortunately Gaddafi was not a very good pen pal, he never wrote back, he never thanked Leo for his interest or let him know how his letters had moved him. But nevertheless Eleni encouraged him to come back again and again. During the next couple of months Leo wrote to a whole cartload of obscure African kings, Arab dictators and the odd American senator to plead for the life of political activists, poets and death-row interns. He became Amnesty's most avid letter writer. He wrote so frequently that every fascist, Stalinist, military crackpot, nutcase despot in the world must have known him by name. If there had been an award for the dogged pursuit of justice by one man and his pen Leo would have won it. Until eventually he could bear it no longer; he sat down at the Amnesty desk and wrote:

Dear Saddam Hussein,
How many of these bloody letters do I have to write before
Eleni will go out with me?
Lots of love, your old friend,
Leo Deakin

He gave it to Eleni who perused it carefully. She nodded to herself and then looked up disapprovingly at Leo. His cheeks flooded with embarrassment. Eleni put the letter on the table.

'And I thought you really cared about human rights,' she said.

'I do, I really do, I care about everything you care about. If you ran a dog home I'd come round every day with dog biscuits. Don't you see I just want to be near you?'

'You don't have to write letters if you want to go out with me.' She appeared totally unimpressed by his charm.

'Well, what do I have to do?' he asked. This was desperate, he felt like he was sinking into a bog and she was watching him drown.

'You just have to ask me.'

'Oh, right . . . will you go out with me?' he asked meekly.

At last she smiled and Leo felt a rush of hope, suddenly he was above the clouds. She was teasing him. Of course she liked him.

'I'll think about it,' she said.

'You'll think about it?'

'I'll give you an answer in a week.'

What kind of response was that? Think about it? What

was there to think about? It was a torturous week. At first Leo was confused. His pride was hurt. What would she know in a week's time that she did not know already? She obviously didn't care for him and he didn't want to be with a girl who had to persuade herself that she did. He mulled it over at night, imagined a thousand scenarios, planned his responses and prepared little speeches. Like a small boy with two armies of toy soldiers he played out Eleni's possible motives and then calculated his best defensive strategy. As the week progressed he became exhausted by his obsession and began to feel manipulated. She had isolated him from the decision-making process. It was now her choice alone whether they were to embark on a relationship. She had manoeuvred him into a position of weakness and he resented it. He began to despise her. Didn't she know she was torturing him? He decided that whatever she said to him at the end of the week he was no longer interested. She had blown her chance and that was that. With the issue resolved in his own mind he adopted an air of false joviality whenever he saw her. She was in for a surprise.

Eleni was not confident in love. She was deeply suspicious of anyone who expressed an interest. She had had too many experiences of surrendering herself to boys who only wanted to practise on her until someone better came along. That night, after Leo had surprised her by asking her out, she sat in front of the mirror and examined herself. It just wasn't plausible that Leo, a sweet-looking third year who always seemed to be surrounded by what she considered to be infinitely more attractive girls, could want to be with her. Everywhere she looked there were better propositions than her, taller, funnier, fairer, smarter. What did she have? A podgy face, a wide nose, heavy black eyebrows on broody eyes, tiny short legs which dissolved into doughy thighs, and a general lack of definition. If she were to sum herself up in three words, it would be 'out of focus'. In school photos she was the kid whose features you couldn't quite make out when everyone else was smiling and clear. Her only redeeming feature was her long curly dark hair; an expensive wrapping on a poor gift.

And she was even convinced that if someone looked closely they would notice the black cloud that hung over her head like a curse. For Eleni had been born with a specific purpose: to build a bridge between her parents, the philandering Georgios and the depressive Alexandria. But she failed spectacularly in her duties and was only able to prove unequivocally that they should never have been together in the first place. Her home on the small Greek island of Kithos was a war zone in which she was the battleground. When she was four years old the marriage finally imploded in an orgy of recrimination and Georgios ran off to the mainland with another woman. For a few years he struggled to sustain even a lazy contact with Eleni, and the biannual visit, monthly phone call, holiday postcard and late birthday present slowly dwindled to nothing so that by the time she was eight he had disappeared altogether.

When Eleni was fourteen Alexandria hit another depression and decided to pack her off to England to live with her aunt. She wanted her daughter to be free; free of the claustrophobia of Kithos and free of her mother's mood swings, but it left Eleni feeling intrinsically unlovable. It was easy for her to suspect Leo of being a philanderer, why else would he be interested? Was she really going to succumb to a charmer only to be dumped yet again? But she adored him; he was attentive, humorous and without a trace of vanity. He never combed his hair, he wore ill-fitting clothes from the charity shop and yet, with his tall, slender body and bright green eyes, he always managed to look lovely in a haphazard kind of way. She wrestled with herself and finally resolved to chance her weary young heart one more time, fully expecting that it would all be over by the next new moon.

She could not foresee that two years later, sitting in the Camden flat she shared with Leo, she would look in her mirror again and realize that the black cloud had gone and that she was beautiful. Nor could she know that her relationship with Leo would be her last and most loving and that she would be dead before the end of her twenty-second year.

Exactly one week later, she found Leo in the bar and said somewhat formally: 'Regarding that business last week, the answer is yes.'

Leo's resolve unravelled on the spot; he instinctively put his arm round her and kissed her. 'I hate you with all my heart,' he said, and threw the rest of his prepared speeches into the dustbin of his thoughts. He was ecstatic. All he wanted to do was run his hands through her magnificent mane of hair and bounce.

5

LEO SHUFFLED OUT OF THE ROOM, DOWN THE CORRIDOR OF the sleeping clinic to the telephone in the foyer. He hovered over the receiver wondering who to call first. Start with the easiest, he thought, so he dialled the hotel in Quito where they had been staying. They had kept their room on for the Cotopaxi excursion and left half their luggage there. Leo and Eleni had grown very fond of the owner, Celeste, in the few weeks they had stayed there. She was more matriarch than manager; a zestful attractive lady in her forties who advised and mothered the young back-packers who frequented her hotel. When she discovered that Eleni could sing she taught her a host of Ecuadorean love songs. Leo couldn't think of anyone else in the country who he could rely on for help, and true to her caring image Celeste promised to be in Latacunga by morning.

Then he called his parents, but it was 5 a.m. in England and the answering machine was on, so he tried his friend Charlie, who answered in a dozy mumble. He listened to Leo's strained voice and wondered whether he was not in one of those twilight nightmares that appear so real you are convinced you are awake. 'Is this a joke?' he kept repeating and: 'Do you know what time it is here?' He pulled himself up to sit on the side of his bed and turned on the lamp. It was only the dual shock of gravity and light that eventually brought him tumbling out of his torpor. There was a long silence.

'Leo, what happened?'

'It was a bus crash, but I can't remember anything about it.'

'My God, are you all right?'

'Bruised and cut, nothing broken. I'm fine.'

Charlie could not disguise his relief and he felt guilty for enquiring after the living.

'Charlie, I can't get hold of my mum and dad, and I've got to tell Eleni's mum. I can't call direct from here. Will you ring her and tell her to call me?'

'Oh, er . . . I don't think I can do that, I don't really know her.' Breaking the news to Eleni's mother, Alexandria, would be like opening a window in a flood. There would be a deluge of grief that would flatten all in its path. 'Look, I'll keep trying your parents, maybe they should contact her.'

Ten minutes later Leo's father called; Charlie had managed to rouse him from his bed. He was clearly shaken and he spoke in an unfamiliar high pitch that cracked and wavered yet never quite broke. Leo's father, Frank, was as soft as a runny Brie, a gentle man who had survived a difficult childhood. Both his parents were dead before he was thirteen and he had been adopted into a poor family from Leeds who made him sleep in an attic, but he was not one for discussing his past or his emotions. Occasionally in a cinema or theatre some ancient trigger would be released and he would be catapulted back to his youth, right into the heart of the grief that he had been too young to name, bypassing in an instant the intervening years of middle-class stability, and he would find himself silently crying.

Now, once more, he saw himself as a child without his mother and his heart opened up like an oyster, his intestines knotted and his breath faltered. He'd harboured a soft spot for Eleni ever since their first meeting, when she had thrown her arms around him and hugged him like a long-lost relative.

Frank knew what Leo was going through but he offered no words of comfort. He never knew what to say, so he generally said nothing. From a very young age Leo had known that it was pointless trying to discuss anything emotional with his father. Whenever Leo was going through a rocky patch Frank would go inside himself and behave like a helpless bystander while Leo's mother, Eve, would try to sort things out. Leo attributed his father's silent impenetrability to his childhood as an orphan, not that Leo knew much about it. He had given up hope that they would ever have a proper adult relationship.

'Dad, I want to come back with Eleni as soon as possible. I may need you to check out flights and help organize the funeral, but I've got to speak to Alexandria first,' Leo said curtly.

'You mean she doesn't know yet?'

'No, you can't call Greece from here – don't know why. Eleni used to go to the central telephone exchange. Anyway, I wondered if you could speak to Alexandria and ask her to phone me?'

There was a long pause. Leo could hear his father blowing his nose. 'I don't know,' Frank said, his voice rising as he tried to suffocate his tears. 'Don't you think it would be better coming from you?'

Again this refusal. Breaking the news to Alexandria was a morbid responsibility and no one wanted to put their hand in the fire, least of all Frank. 'Please, Dad.'

Frank sighed. 'All right, wait by the phone . . . I'll . . . I'll wake up Eve and get her to call.'

Within minutes the phone rang again. Leo looked at the receiver and began to shake involuntarily. He took a deep breath and picked it up. He could hear Alexandria's voice before he even got the phone to his ear. She was in full flow as though she was in the middle of an argument.

'You promise me you look after her. You promise.'

'There was nothing I could . . .'

'Leo, you give me your word. I knew it was stupid idea to go there. You should have stop her. Why didn't you stop her?'

'I couldn't stop her, the best I could do was follow her.'

'Now she's gone. My baby, my baby. It's my fault I should never have relax.'

'What?'

'All this time I worry about her. I was so thinking about

70

her all the time but this last two weeks I relax. I stop even to praying for her.'

'Alexandria, it's not your fault, it's not my fault. It was a bus crash.'

'But I should have been more strict from the start. I had bad feeling about this trip. I should have force her not to go. She would have hate me but at least she would be alive.'

She was not the only one who had had a bad feeling about their trip. Leo's own mum, Eve, had sought many reassurances that it would be safe. They had discussed every worst-case scenario imaginable and he had calmed her with a confidence which masked his own fears. For Eleni, Latin America was a lifelong dream, she was going whether he came or not. But Leo had never been drawn to the place, and so he found himself in the strange position of rebutting advice which he secretly agreed with. There was only one reason he was going and that was because he loved Eleni so much that he could not contemplate a year without her. If he'd been given the choice he would have gone east to Thailand or Indonesia.

'Why did God do this?' Alexandria said. 'Why take someone so young? She was such a good girl. Why? I don't understand!'

'I don't know. I don't think God cares who dies,' Leo said. 'If God did this then I don't know why you believe in Him. Why bow down to a murderer?'

Alexandria was stunned by this remark and for a moment she fell in thrall to its cynical logic. After a long pause she said quietly, 'Bring her back to me, Leo. I want to bury her here on Kithos. Here I look after her,' and she hung up.

                    *   *   *

Leo was exhausted as he trudged back to his room. A bolt
shot up from his knee and he gasped in pain. He
manoeuvred himself gingerly into bed and slumped down
once more to keep vigil over the eternal night, desperately
chasing sleep, wondering how long he could stare at the
crack in the ceiling before his eyes would bore through it
and the entire weight of the universe would come crashing
down on top of him. He threw the word 'bus' to the dogs
in his mind that were scavenging for memories of the
crash, but all he got back were the chewed remains of a
different journey.

They were in Esmeraldas on the northern coast of Ecuador.
The town's reputed remoteness was its biggest draw, there
was no access by road so they had come by boat through
lush mosquito-infested marshlands. The only other way
was by an old plantation train which dropped steeply
down from Ibarra high on the Andean plateau. It was
supposed to come every three days or so but there was no
timetable. Every morning at dawn a crowd would gather at
Esmeraldas station for an hour or so in case it came. On
the days the train did come the whole town knew about
it in minutes and people would come flooding to meet it.
But only those who had waited could be sure of a seat out
of town, the rest would scramble for standing room.
    Leo and Eleni had spent a couple of days in this charm-
ing humid town where the electricity went off at eight in
the evening and, with no cars, it was so quiet that they
could hear people chatting several streets away. They were

lucky that on the very day they wanted to leave, a train magically showed up and they managed to get seats.

They had been travelling an hour or so and climbed maybe a thousand metres when suddenly all the passengers began to gather their bags and clamber out of the windows. The train was slowing down but had not stopped and people were hanging out of the windows and doors.

'What's going on?' Leo asked Eleni.

'I don't know but perhaps you should do what they're doing,' she said.

Leo climbed out of the window and shouted to the next man along to ask what was happening.

'There's only one bus. No more buses for two days,' the man called. Leo did not have a clue what he was talking about. They were miles away from Ibarra, and he could not understand why everyone was getting off and in such a hurry. Before he could ask any more questions two more men had climbed out of his window and they were all hanging on shoulder to shoulder like swimmers at the beginning of an Olympic backstroke competition. By now all the men were on the outside of the train and the women, children and elderly were pushed up against the doors. There was such pandemonium on the train that Leo knew that, for whatever reason, it was best to be ready to jump out.

Eleni shouted out of the window to him, 'There's been a landslide further along the track and we have to get out here. Apparently there is a road from here up to Ibarra. A woman told me that we have to get the bus because there's

73

nowhere to stay here and there are a lot more people on this train than can get on that bus. She said there was only one bus driver prepared to make the journey. The track's been blocked for a fortnight. Someone could have told us!'

As she spoke the train crossed over a bridge, Leo looked down and saw a shallow gorge beneath his feet. 'Jesus, what the fuck am I doing here?' he gasped, but he felt a thrill of excitement race through him. The train was pulling up into another plantation stop. There was nothing but a few small huts and a field of bananas climbing up a gentle slope. Beyond the field was a vertical wall of rock. They were still at least another fifteen hundred metres below the plateau. Past the huts a dirt track began, and there was the bus waiting with its engine running.

'I'll save you a seat,' Leo shouted.

'I'm coming out of the window, I'll be right behind you,' Eleni replied.

As soon as the bridge had been crossed, men started jumping from the train. Some of them fell in the mud. Others, more nimble, were already pelting towards the bus carrying their woven bags and chickens. Leo jumped, skidded but avoided the fall and hurtled after them. By the time he reached the bus every seat was either taken or reserved for a woman. People were squashed against the door. Now there were people standing the whole length of the bus and Leo was right at the door when the driver shouted out that he could take only two more. He gestured Leo to get on.

'My girlfriend, what about my girlfriend?'

'Of course, your girlfriend too.' The driver smiled. 'Do I

look like a man who would separate a man from his woman?'

The crowd, which was mostly men, pulled back from the door to let the women and children get to the seats their husbands and fathers had reserved. When Eleni got on she laughed, 'That was fun.'

Leo marvelled at the way the men had let the women on, back home it would have been strictly first come first served.

'Thank God we made it,' Eleni said. 'I mean look at this place, we would have been buggered if we had to stay here.' It was true, there was absolutely nothing to the place, no hotel, no restaurants, nothing. 'We would have had to sleep rough and eat bananas.'

They both started giggling, they were breathless and excited, the absurdity of the moment had got to them.

'Hey, *chica*,' the driver called to Eleni, 'you can sit on my gearbox.'

She looked at him and burst out laughing. The driver was mystified for a moment, then he too started laughing. 'Oh she is naughty, that one. That's not what I meant.'

'I know, I know, I'm sorry.' She struggled to contain herself and turned to Leo and said in English, 'I think I'm going to wet myself,' and she cracked up again.

'Not a good time, Eleni, we've got all day on this bus.'

'Oh dear,' she gasped, 'I don't even know why I'm laughing.' And she sat down on the boulder-sized plastic moulding of the gearbox next to the driver.

As they set off and Leo watched the crowd disperse he asked the driver why he hadn't let anyone on the roof.

'The road is very bad. It is too dangerous.'

'That never stopped anyone before,' Leo remarked.

'This road is not normally used by buses and there has been a lot of rain. You will see, señor.'

They were not even around the first corner when the bus came to a standstill and the wheels were spinning in the mud. The driver got out of his seat to make an announcement. 'The bus is too heavy. All the men must get off the bus. I will try to get out of this hole and if I cannot manage it I will ask you to push.'

All the men trooped off the bus. They were no more than fifty metres from the plantation, and some of the unlucky men who had not made it ran up the hill to help. Leo could see that the rear wheels were caught in a huge soggy ditch. This is no place for a bus, he thought. A man from the plantation came up with a couple of planks and put them under the wheels. The bus lurched forward, the planks broke and the bus slipped back.

'Everyone push,' the driver shouted. The men bounced the bus out and it drove ahead a little way and waited for the men to get back on board. A hundred metres further on and the men were off again. And so it continued for hours. One stretch of the road was so bad that the men did not bother getting back on, they just walked behind the bus until the next ditch. Eleni jumped off to find a bush, as did everyone at some point or another on that hellish journey. A great spirit of camaraderie built on the bus and the driver put a salsa tape on full volume. Everyone knew the words and was singing together at the top of their voices. Whatever Leo and Eleni felt about the buses in South

America there was always a party atmosphere. People made friends, offered their food and sang. No matter how wretched the journey, Leo and Eleni could only marvel at the irrepressible joy of these people.

Rain began to thud on the metal roof of the bus. For ten hours they had soldiered on before reaching anything that resembled a road. It was dusk and everyone was exhausted. They were beginning to relax in the knowledge that the worst was over when the bus turned a corner and the driver let out a shriek. Around this bend nature had turned on its head. For a dizzying moment their eyes were confused; the landscape seemed to be moving in the shadows. The mountains were collapsing and changing shape. The road had disappeared under a huge slide of mud and rocks, which cascaded down into the valley like some primeval soup. There was a screech of brakes as the driver tried desperately to bring the bus to a halt. To their right was a sheer drop, to their left a jagged rock face. The driver fought to keep control, but the road surface was wet and they careered into the rocks. Metal scraped stone and sparks were thrown up against the windows. Passengers began to jump out of the rear door of the bus, tumbling on to the tarmac. Leo and Eleni hung on to each other in dismay, the bus bounced back off the rock and came to a halt just short of the landslide.

The men gathered to inspect the damage; the side of the bus was badly dented, but, worse, the engine wouldn't start. Leo felt sorry for the driver who had taken so many risks to get them this far. If he couldn't get the bus moving he would lose a lot of money. That night they slept on the bus, and in the morning they picked their way across the landswept road before finding a taxi to take them the last ten miles into Ibarra.

How strange, Leo thought, that they should have been involved in two bus crashes. Could that really be a co-incidence or had fate been chasing Eleni? What if fate did exist? Eleni was frightened of only one thing in Latin America: buses. Not illness or crime or any other horror, only buses. And in the end the buses had got her. Perhaps somewhere deep in her soul she had known her fate.

On the other hand, Leo reasoned, maybe it had nothing to do with fate at all. It could work the other way round. We might be so frightened of something that we bring it upon ourselves. You're standing on a ledge and you have a fear of falling, the fear makes you lose your balance. You're frightened of dogs, the dog smells the fear and bites you. That makes some sense, but how does this apply to a bus crash? Could Eleni's fear make a bus crash? That would imply the existence of the paranormal. Leo couldn't stop himself from entertaining the idea.

Was Alexandria right? Could God have been harvesting for heaven? Or was Eleni just unlucky: in the wrong place at the wrong time?

His mind was racing, searching for an explanation of the inexplicable. Fate, telekinesis, luck, religion – now there was no territory that he would not explore. He was like a leaf buffeted in the breeze, unable to find his way back to the tree that had given him stability.

remained. And yet she was still beautiful, indeed more so than ever. All the tensions and dramas of her short life had dissolved from her features and she seemed relaxed and serene. How simple and fragile life is, nothing more than the ebb and flow of air. Still the air and there is nothing.

Doctor Sanchez hated doing post-mortems. In a larger town it would be left to experts, but in Latacunga he had to do everything. He had cut open the children of poor Indians to give a medical name to poverty, he had found the hidden cancers and clots in the elderly, he had looked into the fatal stab wounds of young men, but he couldn't remember the last time he had dealt with a woman in the prime of her life. He began to unbutton her shirt and then stopped, flushed with embarrassment. Perhaps he should see what he could ascertain without removing her clothes. He could feel four broken ribs but none of these was the cause of death. He would have to look further. It was absurd that the law required him to fill out a form establishing the exact cause of death for someone who had died in a crash. There were no suspicious circumstances, what could be gained by this desperately unpleasant rigmarole? He pulled open her shirt and saw signs of severe bruising across the chest. It looked like she had been smashed by a metal bar. He was 90 per cent certain she had died from internal bleeding. Her lungs must have filled with blood and she would have died within minutes. He would fill in the forms and no more questions would be asked. 'She died instantly,' he told Leo. 'She would have felt no pain.' This was not strictly true, but why make him suffer more? Would it help him to know that, had a fully equipped ambulance arrived quickly, Eleni might even have been saved? Or that she might have died in agony?

By three o'clock, the death certificate had been stamped and Eleni was in the back of a Quito-bound ambulance. Sanchez had achieved in hours what would normally have taken days. Leo's knee had deteriorated through the night and he could no longer walk without a stick. The pain was increasing at the same rate that the shock was subsiding. He hugged the doctor in gratitude. 'I won't forget what you have done for me. And please send my wishes to José.'

'José?'

'The orderly . . . who helped me at the clinic?'

'There is no José here.'

'Oh . . . who was he then?' Leo asked.

The doctor shrugged.

Celeste was waiting in the ambulance when Leo got in the back. He took his seat next to the bed where Eleni lay under a sheet and they set off. There was only one road to Quito; they would have to pass the place of the accident. He wondered whether he would see the wreckage and Eleni's blood on the road. Nothing on the way seemed familiar until they rounded a bend and the imposing Cotopaxi came into view.

It triggered a memory of the bus reaching the brow of a small hill; the other side was lost in a cloud that had descended into the valley. They had driven into the mist and for a few minutes had seen nothing beyond a few metres. Suddenly the fog had cleared and there before them had been the magnificent snow-capped peak. A man close to them had asked, 'Are you sure you still want to climb that beast, you crazy gringos?'

'Oh yes,' Leo had replied, but in the face of the mountain his confidence had drained away. It would be the most dangerous thing he had ever done in his life. Death entered his thoughts. What if I fall? Or get stranded in a blizzard? Or freeze to death? What madness to risk a life for what ultimately would be no more than bar-room brag.

In the ambulance Leo dropped his head into his hands. Perhaps death had been given a choice that day: either take the man on the mountain or the woman on the road. Maybe Eleni had sacrificed herself for him. He kicked himself, why couldn't he stop himself from having such ridiculous ideas? Better stick to the facts. Leo now knew that the accident must have happened only minutes before they were due to get off the bus. He also had a picture of where they had been sitting. They had been on the front row. He was directly behind the driver, his bag was on the floor next to him and Eleni was over the aisle behind the vertical metal bar which passengers used to climb on to the bus. He was saved by the driver's seat, and the ice pick must have slammed into his knee on impact. Eleni had been thrown with terrific force into that bar. Had they not been on the front seats Eleni would still be alive, she was the only fatality.

He wanders deep into the fog again in search of the black box and is rewarded only by the memory of a conversation with an engineer from Ohio whom they met in their hotel in Ibarra. They were telling him about the landslide and the crash on the mountain road. 'It's always best to sit in the middle of the bus,' he said, 'because in 90 per cent of accidents it is the front or rear of the bus that is hit.'

From that day on they had always sat in the middle of the bus, but for some reason on 2 April they had been sitting at the front and Leo did not know why.

Leo couldn't see any signs of a smashed bus on the side of the road as they passed Cotopaxi. The owner must have scraped up the wreckage and botched it back together. It was probably back in service already. Leo was twitchy for the whole journey, driving about in slabs of metal now seemed like a perilous activity, and he shuddered every time they passed a lorry going the other way.

It was dusk when they pulled up outside the morgue in Quito. It was a new whitewashed building with no windows and everything that Latacunga was not; modern, clean and completely devoid of spirits. But so dead that it was none the less terrifying. Eleni was brought in while Leo and Celeste were shown around as if they were on a tour of a stately home. They entered a white tiled room containing huge metal drawers from floor to ceiling. 'This is where we normally keep the bodies before we do autopsies and embalmings, although in your case I believe the Greek consul has paid for the deluxe service so we will be going straight to theatre. This room is always kept at 5 degrees centigrade. We have our own generator, so we can keep it cold even in a power cut,' said a man in a white coat, proud of his shiny spanking new death emporium. Their feet echoed on the floor, the neon lights buzzed; it was so over-lit that they cast no shadows as they walked. The waft of disinfectant bruised their nostrils. The place was so sterile that even the ubiquitous ants had quit it. The man showed them into another room, the mirror image of the first, except that a drawer had slid open and a battered purple naked man was staring at the ceiling.

'They do that sometimes,' their guide said and casually pushed the man back into the cabinet. They were just leaving when Leo heard a squeaking sound, he turned and watched the same man slowly slide out into the room again. Even morgues have their rebels.

They were led through to a small amphitheatre with raked seating and a huge stainless steel table in the middle. 'This is where we do the autopsies. Notice the drains in the side of the operating table. This is to allow the blood to drain away during embalming. We got the table from America. We used to be knee-deep in blood but this is so much cleaner.'

'What are the seats for?' asked Celeste.

'Well, we often have students from the medical school here. It's really the best possible way to see inside the body and learn where everything is. So you see in our own way we are helping the living as well,' said their guide.

Some compensation, thought Leo.

'I am sure you will agree that your friend will be well looked-after here.' Their guide smiled.

Leo wanted to punch him.

'Now if you would like to wait outside, the process won't take more than a couple of hours.'

'I'm staying here,' Leo said.

'I wouldn't recommend it, señor.'

'I'm staying here,' Leo shouted, and sat down angrily.

'Well as you wish . . . but really I . . .' Leo stared at him disdainfully, the man shook his head and left the theatre.

Celeste sat down next to him. 'Are you all right?'

'This place is an abattoir, I can't leave her alone in here . . . with these butchers . . . it's a fucking meat-processing plant . . . who knows what they'll . . .' His rant was cut short by a pair of swing doors rocking open and the sight of Eleni being wheeled out on a trolley by two morticians. She was naked.

Leo jumped to his feet. 'Who the fuck said you could undress her . . . without my permission . . . you imbeciles!' he screamed in English.

The morticians looked up in shock, only their frightened eyes were visible; the rest of their faces were hidden under surgical masks and elasticated hats. Loose-fitting white disposable tops and trousers, rubber shoes and gloves covered their bodies and it was impossible to tell if they were men or women.

Celeste pulled Leo back. 'They'll make you leave. Now control yourself. They're just doing their job.'

Leo took a deep breath and sat down sullenly. 'Well, they should have asked me,' he hissed.

Eleni was transferred on to the metal drain table. Her bones were rigid like a shop mannequin's and she seemed to be frozen. Her flesh had sagged like a deflated balloon and she looked brittle and translucent. Only her hair was unchanged, still pliant, lustrous black and beautiful. One of the figures withdrew into the shadows and returned with a tray of steel implements. The other attached a pipe to a huge bottle of chemicals that stood by the table.

Celeste stood up. 'I can't watch this. I'll wait outside. I think you should come with me.'

'No.'

'Oh Leo, don't do this to yourself.'

'I don't trust them.'

Celeste sighed in resignation and walked out.

The morticians set about washing and disinfecting Eleni's body. Leo watched aghast as they inserted plugs in her mouth, ears, nose, anus and vagina to prevent excretion of the embalming chemicals. Their every touch felt like an infringement of the intimacy Leo had once shared with Eleni. He bit his tongue and turned away, his eyes bruised by the horror of it. When next he looked they had made an incision in her stomach and were removing her viscera. These soft organs they soaked in a formaldehyde bath before replacing them in her body and sewing up the cut. Then they pulled out a large syringe and Leo gripped his seat as they injected chemicals into an artery in her left arm. At the same time they cut open a corresponding vein and, as the chemicals were pumped in, Eleni's blood and body fluids leaked away down the drains on the table. When formaldehyde began to flow out of the vein, the job was done. The agents of decomposition no longer had anything to feed upon. Leo had watched this act of clinical rape in determined silence and when he saw that it was finally over he got up, staggered to the door and threw up on the pavement outside.

A blue Rolls-Royce pulled up in front of him. It was the Greek Consul.

7

ON ARRIVING IN EACH COUNTRY LEO AND ELENI WOULD register with their respective embassies for security reasons. But when they had arrived in Ecuador, Eleni had not been able to locate the Greek embassy, it was not listed in any directory and none of the hotels they stayed in knew of its existence. Indeed none of the hotels they stayed in could remember a Greek ever having checked-in within living memory. Clearly the Greeks and the Ecuadoreans did not do much business. Greece was the lost nation, and it became Eleni's mission to educate Ecuador in all things Greek. With a resurgent national pride she would tell all and sundry about the gods, the Parthenon and democracy. People had heard of Socrates, Plato and Aristotle. But what had happened in the intervening two thousand years between Aristotle and Eleni was anyone's guess.

Eventually Eleni had tracked down a woman called Maria Clemencia de Leon who handled Greek affairs. She was a wealthy, upper-class Ecuadorean in her fifties whose only contact with Greece seemed to be that she had been there on holiday. She had no Greek blood and could not speak a single word of the language, though her English was excellent. She worked full-time as a lawyer in downtown Quito, and looked after Greece from her luxurious home, where her retinue of servants and secretaries would answer the phone in her absence. For Maria Clemencia de Leon being Greek consul was not a job but a society fashion accessory; she wore her diplomatic status like a Gucci handbag, and it allowed her to attend important dinners and shake well-perfumed hands. But her shiny, easy-to-wear, low-maintenance, diplomatic handbag was about to lose its appeal, for that very morning Maria Clemencia de Leon was halfway through a facial when one of her minions disturbed her with the tragic news that the only Greek in Ecuador had died. This would entail, to her horror, some work.

Leo was still heaving on the pavement as the chauffeur, decked in uniform and hat, emerged from behind the wheel of the blue Rolls-Royce and in one well-rehearsed flowing movement spiralled back and flipped open the rear door. He held out a gloved hand and four gold- and diamond-soaked manicured fingers appeared on top. A left shoe in white patent leather landed on the pavement. Leo looked up momentarily; under the opened door he caught sight of tan-coloured satin tights and the edge of a grey linen skirt cut just below the knee. A right foot joined the left, the calf muscles locked together and stiffened, the chauffeur gave a delicate pull on the fingers and Maria

Clemencia de Leon appeared from the car; suit creaseless, rumple-free, fitted to the slightest contour of her body, matching handbag hung over padded shoulder. Hair bunned up in twists and curls, pulled back from the forehead so tightly that a less well-fed woman would have bled. Face veneered like a newly varnished oak table, knotty and lined but shiny smooth. Eyes lashed, browed and shadowed like a Van Gogh flower. The Greek consul was as incongruous as caviar on a peasant's plate.

Leo was clutching his stomach forlornly, he had not changed his underpants for three days, nor washed for two. He was sweaty and stubbled and his jeans were stained with dry blood. He stank like a camel trader. Maria Clemencia de Leon did not so much as turn a pore towards him, but carefully side-stepped the pool of vomit, glided past him with all the disdain of a lifetime's indifference to poverty, and held out her hand to Celeste, who was rushing to Leo's aid. 'We spoke on the phone, I am the Greek consul, Maria Clemencia de Leon.'

'Yes, that's right, this is Leo,' Celeste said, pointing to the urchin who was now wiping his mouth on his sleeve in front of her.

The consul turned to him, glued a fake sympathetic smile to her lips and said in a near faultless American English, 'Pleased to meet you, I am the Greek consul, Maria Clemencia de Leon.' She seemed to enjoy saying that, but this time she did not offer her hand. 'I was so sorry to hear about Eleni, my secretary says she was very sweet. May I offer you my condolences?'

'Thank you,' gasped Leo.

'Are you all right?'

'Fine now, thanks – it was a bit sordid in there.'

'Oh I see. I am here to help you arrange whatever you need. I will put my driver at your service for a couple of days. We have many things to sort out. But it's late and I was going to invite you back to my apartment for something to eat . . . though perhaps you're not so hungry,' she said, eyeing the splattered contents of Leo's stomach on the pavement.

'No, I am, I haven't eaten all day. What about Eleni?'

The consul's smile evaporated and she paused, not quite knowing what to say, then added rather uncomfortably, 'I think it would be better if she stayed here.'

Leo laughed, 'I wasn't asking you to invite her round for tea. I meant that she is still in the amphitheatre.'

Celeste tried to hide a smile. Maria Clemencia grimaced. 'Well, you're just going to have to let them sort it out. It's perfectly nice here.' She began to talk about funeral arrangements but Celeste started to snigger uncontrollably, which in turn set Leo off, and for the next couple of minutes they both hovered on the edge of hysteria, not knowing why they were laughing, only that they needed to for the sake of their sanity. Maria Clemencia de Leon was appalled by their vulgarity. She shuddered at the thought of Leo dirtying her car seats and soiling her sofa. The boy would leave a trail of fluid behind him like a slimy gastropod. She would have to disinfect everything he touched. Worse than this she would have to pollute herself with his company unless somehow she could wriggle out of her consular duties. Indeed why should she help Leo at all? He was a British citizen and not her responsibility. All she would have to do was pay for Eleni to be embalmed and flown back to Greece and then claim it back on Eleni's travel insurance. She should have let Leo sort himself out. But it was too late now.

There was no choice but to leave Eleni at the morgue. Leo had to persuade himself that there was nothing of Eleni left in her body.

'I'll see you at the hotel later,' Celeste said hugging him tightly and she disappeared into the night, leaving Leo in the reluctant hands of Maria Clemencia de Leon.

No sooner had they set off, than she instructed the chauffeur to open the rear windows in the Rolls-Royce.

'Are you sure, señora?' he asked. 'Perhaps you would like me to put up the air conditioning?'

'No, open the windows.'

The chauffeur obliged but was ill at ease. They never travelled with the windows open for fear of theft, especially after dark. The car attracted enough attention as it was, but now he was frightened to stop at traffic lights in case someone should stick a knife in and snatch a ring and maybe even a finger with it. But Maria Clemencia seemed happier to risk her life than to suffer the stench of this stale Englishman.

They were driving at terrifying speed through the town. Swerving on to the other side of the road to pass standing traffic and flying through red lights. At one point a police-man gave chase on a motorbike but when he saw the diplomatic number plates he pulled up sharply. Leo asked the driver to slow down, but he paid no attention. He only took orders from the lady. She told Leo not to worry, but he began to swear at her, begging her to stop the car. 'We're almost there,' she said. Then, before she knew it, he had burst into tears. She was dealing with an emotionally disturbed child, a delinquent. Leo began to scream, he had his head in his hands, 'Oh my God, it was my fault, it was my fault.'

Maria Clemencia did not understand what he was talking about, but she could see his attention had shifted away from the road and that he was lost inside himself.

A cavern in Leo's memory had begun to fill and was sending shock waves through his psyche. He remembered them waiting at the bus station sitting on their bags. They had just missed a bus and were waiting for the next one, the ill-fated one. They were nervous, travellers in South America are always twitchy at bus stations. Leo and Eleni had heard stories of people being robbed while they were carrying their packs on their backs, by thieves who slashed open rucksacks and let the contents tumble into a bag. Within seconds the bag would have switched hands and disappeared in the crowd. They had met a man who had accepted a sweet from an old lady at a bus station and woken up two days later in the main square of Cali in Colombia wearing only his underpants and socks. Fortunately he had hidden a hundred-dollar bill in one of his socks. Some travellers lined their rucksacks with chicken wire and put mouse-traps in their pockets. Leo had sewn secret pockets into all his trousers. He carried his credit cards by his ankles and wore a hidden money belt inside his pants.

Quito bus station was humming with traders. Eleni was thirsty, but she refused to buy the home-made drinks which the traders sold in plastic bags with a straw, because there was no guarantee that the water was clean. She marched off to find a shop and returned a couple of minutes later with two bottles of water. When eventually the bus arrived they were first in the queue. Eleni got on first and headed towards the middle of the bus as usual.

The image of Eleni walking to the centre of the bus, walking to safety, is on constant replay in Leo's mind. What happens next is too painful to bear. 'Let's sit at the front,' he says. 'We're not going far and this bag is so big and heavy that if the bus fills up I'll never be able to get it off.' It was only foreigners who carried their packs with them on buses. Everyone else put them on the roof. He dumps his rucksack on the nearest seat. Eleni turns round obediently and bounces back down the bus. There isn't enough room for her to sit right next to Leo because of his pack so she parks herself on the front seat over the aisle, the seat reserved for death.

'Let's sit at the front.'

He had killed her with those five words. Leo had guided her to the most dangerous place on the bus. And why? For the sake of a heavy bag. And now it seemed everything had led inexorably to that moment. The choice to climb Cotopaxi on that day, the breakfast of the gods followed by the languorous coffee, the missed bus and Eleni walking towards her survival at the centre of the bus.

'Let's sit at the front.'

She hadn't argued with him, she trusted his judgement, she would have put her life in his hands willingly, because whose hands could be safer, more loving than his? Her only thought was for him, she felt sorry for him, he always carried the heavier bag. Leo freeze-framed the moment when she turned back. There was pity and love in her dark eyes. She was so alive at that moment that she sparkled, it was impossible to relate her sprung step and zest to the crumpled corpse she had become. It had not occurred to her, as it now did to Leo, that he was planning to carry that bag up a mountain and yet here he was moaning about walking down the bus with it. Had she pointed out that irony and laughed at him he would surely have followed her. He would even have abandoned the climb if she had insisted. Perhaps, deep down, that's what he had really wanted but he had been too proud to admit his fear. He had a reputation for stubbornness but she knew how to get round him.

On one occasion they were climbing a lesser mountain near Ottovalo in the north. They had planned to eat lunch at the summit. On at least three occasions they had gained the top only to find that it was a false summit and there were still rolls of hills ahead of them. They had continued way past lunch, Leo obstinately refusing to stop until they had made it. Eventually she had got so irritated and hungry that she had just sat down on the hill and said, 'I'm eating here.'

'But we're only a few metres from the top,' he had protested.

'How do you know? We could be miles away.'

Leo had not complained, he had been glad of the excuse to stop. They had spent an hour there dozing and canoodling. When they set off again they had climbed for only another minute before finding themselves at the peak with a stunning 360-degree view.

'You were right,' Eleni had laughed.

But this time he had been wrong and he would have to live with it for the rest of his life.

8

THE GREEK CONSUL LIVED ON A PRIVATE ROAD IN THE diplomatic quarter of Quito. Her 'apartment', as she called it, was situated in an old colonial building with a courtyard at its centre. Throughout Ecuador these buildings had a crumbling beauty to them, but in the diplomatic quarter they had been magnificently restored to their former grandeur. They were framed by orange trees and palms, and topped with the flags of various countries.

Leo was slumped in an antique, green velvet, Castilian sofa in the reception room. He had slipped into a listless torpor since the flashback. He had nothing to say to Maria Clemencia de Leon, he desperately wanted to talk to someone but couldn't unburden himself to a stranger. She had sat in silence with him for a few minutes, and when she could tolerate his morose presence no longer she had got up sharply and left the room saying: 'I have some business to tend to, I'll let you know when dinner is served.'

After twenty minutes she returned and asked him to join her in the dining room.

'Can I call my mum and dad?' he asked.

'Of course, after dinner.'

'No, now,' he said.

'But it will be three in the morning in England.'

'I don't think they'll mind.'

She was clearly irritated with him. He had sat there for half an hour saying nothing, and now just as dinner was ready he wanted to make a phone call. She should have sent him down the road to the British embassy and washed her hands of him there and then, but now she felt obliged to see the wretched business through. She pointed to the telephone and walked out.

When finally he came into the dining room his dinner was cold. Maria Clemencia had finished and she was clicking her heels impatiently on the parquet floor. As he hacked at his cold steak and greedily shovelled in the congealed pepper sauce, Maria Clemencia took him through the travel arrangements.

'On Wednesday Eleni flies to Frankfurt on a Lufthansa cargo plane, there she will be transferred on to another plane to Athens and from there to Kithos. She arrives at two o'clock local time on Thursday the eighth of April. You will leave on Tuesday . . .'

'No, wait, I want to be on the same plane,' Leo interrupted.

'That's not possible. They won't carry this kind of freight on an international passenger plane.'

'She is not fucking freight,' Leo shouted.

'Well, she's not exactly luggage either! It's not about Eleni, Leo, it's something to do with hermetically sealed containers, drugs, bombs, South America . . . the usual thing. But the rules are different for internal flights in Greece, so you can fly with her from Athens to Kithos.'

'Well, in that case I'll take a flight after her. I'm not leaving her here alone, then at least I can make sure she is on the plane and that . . .'

'Leo, I've already looked into all of this,' Maria Clemencia snapped impatiently. 'Please trust me! If you leave on Thursday you will miss the funeral on Friday. Don't worry, Celeste and I will take care of everything here.'

Leo fell silent. Once again he had to resign himself to leaving his sweetheart in the hands of people he barely knew. He cursed himself for failing to look after her properly.

It was midnight when Maria Clemencia's chauffeur dropped him off at Celeste's hotel. All the guests were gathered around Celeste in the bar. She was explaining what had happened. Leo could feel the sombre atmosphere as soon as he entered. Where was the loud music and chatter? He shuffled past the bar; they fell silent, stared at him and felt their appetite for adventure waning. Leo's ravaged face seemed to carry all their nightmares. He stopped. He felt like he was expected to speak but he didn't know what to say. He was now the leading player in an unfolding Greek tragedy and the chorus looked on. None of them knew what to say, either. There was an uncomfortable standoff; after an awful silence Celeste said, 'Would you like a drink?'

'No thanks, if I start now I'll never stop.'

That was enough to uncork the others and they muttered their condolences, one echoing the next. He nodded his appreciation and disappeared up the stairs, a sad and lonely shadow of himself.

Eleni's clothes were hanging in the open wardrobe and her sandals were waiting for her small feet next to the bed. A few black-and-white postcards, mainly portraits of sun-beaten Indians, lay scattered on the table. On the windowsill was a collection of oddly coloured stones that she had picked up on their walks and the tiny carved male Inca head that he had given her in the market at Latacunga. He picked it up, felt its marble coolness in his hands and slipped it into his pocket to join the female head he still carried. Then he went to the wardrobe and pulled out her favourite top; a short-sleeved pale blue cotton shirt with flowers embroidered around the neck-line. He brought it to his nostrils and breathed in deeply, and for a moment there she was, with her arms wrapped around his neck, kissing him. She was pressed against him, the rich scent of her hair filling his lungs, he was running his fingers over the small of her back, stroking the invisible patch of fine baby hair that only grew at the very base of her spine. The world was Eleni. The world was sweet. When the vision began to fade he went over to her rucksack, found her perfume and sprayed it on the shirt, just so he could prolong her presence a few seconds longer. He pulled open a drawer and threw her underwear and socks on the bed and sprayed them all. He took the fleece from her rucksack and sprayed that too. The room was dense with musk and flowers, but she was gone. Leo collapsed on the bed and began to laugh through his tears, 'You didn't much like that perfume, did you?' Someone had bought her some Anaïs Anaïs once as a present. She only wore it because she couldn't afford to buy anything else. Everyone assumed she loved it and it became an easy gift to buy for her. She didn't have the heart to tell anyone that it wasn't her favourite. Besides, Leo liked it and that was all that mattered.

The commotion had woken up a few flies and moths and they were gathering under the light wondering what was going on. A marvellous garden aroma had entered their dreams but there were no flowers in sight. Still it was a good excuse to dance with each other. Leo watched the insect antics with fascination. They were just like him, little creatures trying to make sense of it all. He watched two flies come together and dive-bomb down towards the floor before separating and meeting again to repeat the game. Weren't all animals on a similar journey to him? Looking for a mate, seeking companionship? Perhaps Eleni was now a fly or an ant.

Leo thought about the doctorate that was waiting to be finished back home. After his biology degree he'd applied for a job that he saw advertised in the department to work as a lab technician at the Institute of Zoology under the eminent Professor Lionel Hodge, who was a world authority on ant behaviour. It was just a job, but it soon

101

became an obsession, the ant world was so organized and intricate that he decided to do a PhD on it. Now he wondered if he could ever return to his studies, or indeed any kind of normality. The scientist in him was waning, and grief was opening him to a new way of relating to the world.

He drifted into sleep and woke up in the morning in his clothes with the light still on. Eleni had visited him again in the night and he had slept easy, convinced that she was still alive. He dreamt he had made an extraordinary mistake and that she had only died in a nightmare. But dreams are deceivers, and by morning she had left him.

He showered and changed clothes more out of habit than desire. He had nothing to do, nowhere to go so he spent the day reading Eleni's journal. It helped him remember everything up to a few minutes before the crash. But he still did not know if he had been conscious just after the crash. He thought that maybe he had seen Eleni die and then passed out. Why else would he have known that she was dead when he came to in the hospital? He was terrified that, at some unsuspecting moment, his mind would throw up this last horror and that it would devastate him. He did not know what would be worse: the memory itself or the lingering dread of its anticipated arrival.

Monday came and Leo and Celeste duly made their way back to the morgue. Eleni was pulled out of the corpse-filled filing cabinet. The same purple man lay on his broken drawer in the middle of the room. He had won the battle of wills because the attendant didn't bother to push him back.

She was wheeled to a side room where Leo began to dress her. He opened his bag and took out her long grey summer skirt and the blue cotton shirt he had sprayed with perfume. He felt her freezing skin against his for the last time. Her pallid flesh seemed to have gained a softness and elasticity from the embalming. For a long moment he just held her then, slowly, and with all the love left in his fractured heart, he manoeuvred her like a docile puppet into her clothes. When it was done he asked Celeste to put some make-up on her face. He would have done it himself but he had never applied make-up before and he thought he would do it badly. She powdered over the cut on Eleni's cheek until it was hardly noticeable, then plastered on the blusher in order to give Eleni a flush of life. She applied a line of red lipstick to her lips and delicately took a black eyeliner to her closed eyes. There is vanity even in death: the need to hide the twisted body, the cuts and the contorted face frozen in pain under a mask of serenity. Eleni never wore make-up in life but in death it was mandatory. Leo wanted her to look as good as possible.

Eleni was transported to a nearby undertakers where she was placed in a special metal coffin which Leo had ensured would meet with airline regulations. There was nowhere in the shop that they could solder on the lid without causing mess and disturbance so Eleni suffered the further indignity of being carried out of the back door into a car park. Leo took the two tiny Inca heads from his pocket and placed the male one in her cold hand and wrapped her fingers around it. The other one he put in his breast pocket opposite his heart. He kissed her forehead, 'Eleni, *karthiamou*, thank you for loving me.'

Their adventure had separated them, but she was still ploughing on, travelling through the hidden world, deeper than he could go, a forester into the unknown. Now they were like the sea and the moon, far apart but still in harmony. When his life was done their time would come again and when it did there would be no more hurdles between them, they would dance as one for ever. What is life but a holiday sandwiched by eternity?

He softened her face with his tears and then withdrew. The undertakers picked up the heavy lid of the coffin and clumsily slid it on top of her. They took a soldering iron to the rim and Eleni was unceremoniously sealed inside her casing like a sardine in a tin.

9

THERE WERE THREE OF THEM WAITING HUNCHED AND miserable at Athens airport on the Thursday morning. Leo had arrived the previous day and now he stood with his father and Alexandria at the cargo collection point. He wished his mother had been there but, to her fury, she hadn't been given leave from the bank where she worked.

The three did not converse, each silenced by their own thundering heartbeat. The flight from Frankfurt had just flashed on to the arrivals display, 'on time' it said. Until that moment Alexandria had been grilling Leo on the details of the accident. It is impossible to grieve properly if mystery clouds the death of a loved one. A whole business of inquiries, investigations, post-mortems and court cases has been built around that one truth. The fact of death is not enough, there has to be certainty as to the cause. Leo patiently took Alexandria through what he had been told and what he remembered, omitting only the five words that had killed her: 'Let's sit at the front.' That was his secret and the guilt was still as fresh as a gaping wound.

The plane landed and they waited quietly for the coffin to be brought out, their black mournful presence incongruous in the immense hangar. They watched as dusty lorries thundered in and out of huge portals, mailbags were loaded on to vans and various large boxes and crates were shunted around on forklift trolleys. The roar of engines, the crashing of metal doors, the dumping thuds of unloved cartons clogged the building. At last the coffin emerged on the back of an electric luggage cart driven by a man in a blue overall.

'There she is,' Frank shouted.

Alexandria let out a cry of dismay. It was unthinkable that her little brown-eyed girl could be inside the shiny metal casket that was trundling towards them. Her heart filled with all the Elenis that she had loved; the baby who had suckled at her breast and slept in her arms, the tottering infant who had delighted her with her first word, the skipping child whose hand she had held to school, the passionate and temperamental teenager who had been sent to England and the politically active woman with a taste for adventure. Not even in her nightmares had Alexandria imagined that her only daughter would be cut down so young and returned to her mother in a box, like a cruel gift from Hades. She began to shudder uncontrollably. Leo instinctively put his arm around her but she shrugged him off and walked away to be alone. She was utterly inconsolable.

Within the hour they were seated on the small propeller plane to Kithos, painfully aware that Eleni was directly beneath their feet in the freezing hold of the plane, no better off than their luggage.

The wind had risen steadily throughout the day and the normally bright but smoggy sky above Athens was heavy with storm cloud. The pilot had been advised not to fly, but as he was an islander and Alexandria had taught his children, he would not countenance any delay.

As soon as they took off, the plane was at the whim of the storm. It tipped from side to side giving them unnatural views of the sea beneath them. They were buffeted from all directions, great thunderclaps blasted the cabin and the lightning was so close that they recoiled in terror. Suddenly the plane hit an air pocket and plunged momentarily into freefall, lifting them weightless from their seats before catching them again with a painful thud. Frank feared for his life, Alexandria retched into her lap but Leo was content to flirt with death. The storm was Eleni's doing, she was calling him, and the heavens exploded at her command. He could feel her anger at being separated from him. Now all of nature was a message with her signature on it. She was everywhere; more present in Leo's heart than ever. Two weeks ago he would have dismissed such thoughts as ludicrous, he would have said that after death there is nothing but rotting flesh. His reversal was absolute.

Kithos fizzed with gossip and rumour. Many suspected there was more to Eleni's death than met the eye; some were convinced that she must have been involved in drugs, for why else would anyone visit Colombia? One man even claimed she had been murdered by the cartels. The sense of anticipation on the island had reached such a climax that when Leo, Frank and Alexandria walked off the plane all they could see was a wall of black pressed up against the airport windows. They had barely set foot in the arrivals hall before they were mobbed by a rush of weeping well-wishers, hugging and patting them and offering their condolences. When the coffin eventually appeared there was a collective howl of grief. Then a fevered whispering spread through them, they parted and a diminutive grey-haired man in a tailored black suit was ushered forward. Leo wondered if this was some local dignitary. The crowd fell silent. Alexandria stared at him uncomprehendingly.

'Georgios!'

'I'm so sorry, I came as soon as I heard.'

'Now you make an effort! It's too late, Georgios, it's too damn late.'

Georgios bit his lip and dropped his head. 'Take me to her,' he said quietly.

Alexandria didn't move.

'Please, Alexi.'

She led him through the crowd to the coffin where Frank was standing. Georgios brushed past him without a word and threw himself at the coffin.

'I have to see her, I have to see my girl,' he cried, trying to open the lid.

'It's been sealed, you can't open it,' Alexandria said. She put her hand gently on his shoulder and tried to pull him away, but Georgios didn't seem to hear her and he tugged ferociously at the lid, to no avail.

'Are you in there, *karthiamou*, are you really in there?' His voice was barely audible. 'My little girl, is that you?' He ran his hand over the box as if he was trying somehow to contact her. When at length he got to his feet his eyes were bloodshot. 'Oh, Alexandria. What have I done?'

When the cortège arrived in town people poured from their homes to walk behind the hearse, holding down their coats and hats in the squall. They processed slowly down the tiny streets of the old quarter and then up the hill until they arrived at the gates of the tiny chapel of Agia Sofia where Papa Nikos with his great white beard and flowing black robes was waiting for them. Eleni was placed on a long table in the central apse where, following tradition, she would spend the night whilst the family sat vigil over her.

The storm brought rain, a month's worth in one night pummelling the rooftops and clattering the windows. The grave, which had lain open for two days, filled with water and collapsed. In the morning they found it silted and boggy. The gravedigger had to drain it and re-dig it while the service for Eleni took place in the chapel. It was overflowing with people and Leo did not understand a word of the Orthodox ceremony. He slipped out of the back and went to watch the gravedigger sweating over the grave.

The sky held no memory of the previous night's storm, the air was crisp and light. Alexandria had picked a peaceful spot. Leo and Eleni had often walked up to the chapel on their visits to Kithos, then wound their way down along goat paths through olive groves to the empty beaches on the other side. They would pause at the top to sit on the wall of the small graveyard, enjoy the cooler air and admire the plunging view into the emerald sea. Once at the beach, if no one was there, they would strip naked and lie like lizards in the sand. Then when the sun was unbearable they would run into the sea and play like children, ducking, splashing and hugging.

Now Eleni could enjoy the cooler air and admire the view for ever. She could sing along with the goats' bells.

The gravedigger had just put down his spade and wiped the sweat from his brow when Papa Nikos emerged from the chapel with the coffin and entourage in tow. Leo joined the back of the group. The coffin was lowered into the grave and a prayer was said. There was then a hesitation in the proceedings, there seemed to be some confusion, a man had made a comment and those around him had nodded their assent. Soon there was a full-scale discussion. There seemed to be something wrong. Then he heard a loud bang, and he pushed his way through the crowd to see that the gravedigger had jumped back into the grave and was trying to break the lid off the coffin with the handle of his spade.

'What are you doing?' Leo shouted. 'Don't open it. It's been a week since she died.' He tried to grab hold of the spade but his father caught hold of his arm.

'Leo, they want to let nature do its work. It's a metal coffin, they have to let the air in.'

He looked over at Alexandria, who nodded. This was

what she wanted. The spade crashed down again on the lid and echoed off the walls.

'Dad, don't let them do it . . .' Leo begged.

'They need to see her, Leo, how can they grieve until they've seen her? She'll haunt them on every street corner unless they do. They have to know for sure that she is in there,' Frank said, as the gravedigger bashed the coffin with all his strength.

'Of course she's in there. I saw to it myself, for God's sake,' Leo protested.

'It's not enough, Leo, I should know,' Frank insisted.

'What do you mean?'

'I'll explain another time, just believe me,' Frank said, closing the conversation. Leo relented but he could not watch.

The hammering was increasingly desperate. The lid would not budge. Someone went to fetch a crowbar and the poor gravedigger used it to lever into the coffin. Leo turned his back and walked away. He did not want to see Eleni's rotting flesh crawling with maggots. He did not want that memory burned into his retina with all the other awful images he had seen in the last week. The brutal hacking at the coffin destroyed all sense of what a funeral should be. Hearts quickened, prayer was abandoned and solemnity replaced by fear and fore-boding. The lid began to give way. There was a terrible scraping of metal and a gasp from the mourners. The crowbar was driven in again and the lid came free. For a second there was total silence as the grieving crowd stared open-mouthed into the coffin. Leo froze; what unrecognizable horror had stilled them? Then there was a screeching howl which tore right through his spine. Never in his life had Leo heard such a dreadful sound. Despite himself, he turned round and saw Georgios on all fours with his head bent to the grave, his spine arched like a cat. He opened his mouth wide and wailed again and again. This was a keening alien to Leo's culture. A keening that expressed all the guilt and regret that a man's soul could bear. Alexandria seemed to lose balance, her legs could not hold the weight and her sisters rushed in to prevent her falling. Leo took a step forward and looked into the open grave. There Eleni lay exactly as he'd left her, with her little fingers curled around the Inca head, her face flushed with make-up. She was sleeping sweetly. It was her youth and beauty that had silenced them. He felt himself being pulled into the grave. He was under her spell. He wanted to be buried with her. But something stopped him, some ancient instinct. Leo thought it was cowardice.

Then he heard her voice. 'Live,' she said, 'and live beautifully.'

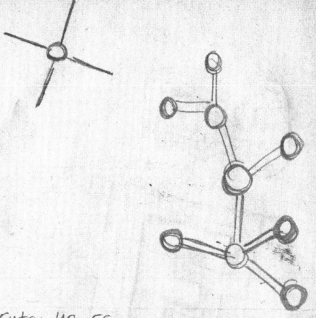

Entry No. 58

This division between past, present
and future doesn't mean anything,
and has only the value of an
illusion, tenacious as it may be.

Einstein

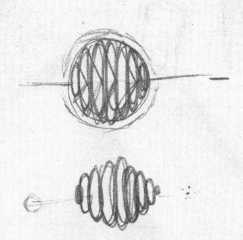

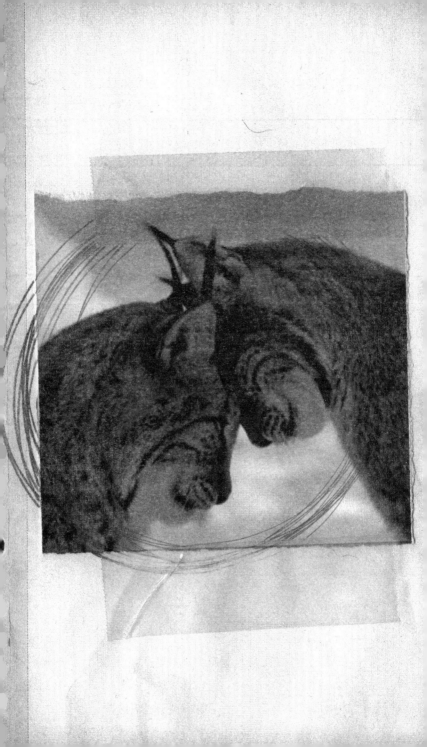

10

GOOD, GOOD, PUT THE WATER THERE . . . A LITTLE CLOSER where I can reach it . . . thank you. You know, maybe the doctor was right after all . . . maybe I should rest. I do feel like sleeping. No? You want me to go on? All right, Fischel. Enjoying it then, are you? Oh I see . . . still not talking. Just listening, are we? Well, that's fine young man. You listen away but remember how much Mother worries about you. It's been three weeks since Kristallnacht. And you know, son, I was already ill before they took me away – all right so I came back with a shaved head and a few bruises – maybe that's why you're not talking – but you mustn't worry, they can't kill us. Remember, above the clouds the sun is still shining . . . you're not so sure, eh? I understand. There's a lot to think about. Talk when you're ready. Shall I go on?

When we were eight, Jerzy Ingwer and I decided that it would be a good idea to pull up all the flowers in front of the school. Of course we were caught and sent to the headmaster. We were so terrified of what he might do to us that we sat outside his office crying like it was the end of the world. Now here we were again sitting side by side, waiting, terrified. When at last Neidlein gave the order for us to relieve the night shift and make our way to the front line a chill crawled down my spine and I felt like that little boy again. All I wanted was for my mummy to cradle me in her arms and tell me everything would be all right. I brought Lotte's letter to my nose and breathed in her perfume one more time before putting it in my breast pocket next to the photograph that you have in your hands there.

'Come, Daniecki,' Király mocked in his clumsy German, 'it's rude to keep death waiting.' I picked up my rifle and marched off with the others the short distance through the supply lines to the front.

I have revisited the battle of Gnila Lipa many times, Fischel, not just in my nightmares but also through the history books. As infantrymen we merely followed orders and fought for the patch of grass we were standing on. We had no notion of the bigger picture, but now I know that there were nearly half a million Russians stretched along a fifty-kilometre front east of the river. We had a hundred and seventy-five thousand men. We were doomed from the start.

There had been no time to entrench properly. All we had was a small knee-high furrow which only offered protection if you lay on the ground. We were set back fifty metres from the river in a clump of trees. To our right was open ground and to our left was thickening forest. The lay of the land was similar on the other side of the river: woods, meadows and rolling hills.

I remember the air was still and silent, and that I was so tired from the night's work that my eyes hung heavy on their lids. I reached over to Jerzy and squeezed his arm, 'Good luck, my friend,' I whispered.

'We've got to win, Moritz,' he said, 'not for the Austrians but for Ulanow.'

The order to attack came at daybreak. The artillery let loose an ear-splitting barrage, but what seemed thunderous at our end translated into a mild peppering of dust clouds over the Russian lines a thousand metres away. It was a random scattering of shells, but hardly a body blow to prepare the ground for an effective infantry assault. The bombardment lasted twenty minutes and the gunners sweated over their cannon but we simply did not have enough big guns to inflict serious damage. So it came as a shock when Lieutenant Neidlein told us to advance. 'Advance'; the word sent my heart into my mouth. Király turned to the gangling Austrian and shouted, 'Advance, what do you mean, advance? We've hardly laid a glove on them. More artillery, man, we need more artillery.'

'It's an order, Király, not a debate,' Neidlein retorted angrily. 'Now get out and fight, and may God be with you.'

We picked ourselves up and clambered out of our furrows with bayonet rifles forward. Behind us the drummers beat out a driving rhythm to spur us on. I was expecting an instant volley of gunfire to rain down on our heads, but there was only an eerie silence. We left the cover of the trees and headed down to the river. To my right I could see a long line of men running shoulder to shoulder, three or four deep. Still the Russians were quiet. What were they doing? Perhaps I had been mistaken about the power of our artillery. Were they retreating? As we reached the river our shells let loose again to provide us with cover for the crossing. At its shallowest points the river was spanned with duckboards which had been laid in the night, but many men chose to wade across holding their rifles high above their heads.

The sloped bank on the other side offered us some cover but we were told not to stop there. Ahead of us now was open meadow with a smattering of bushes and trees. The grass was long and wild, rising to the waist in places. Onwards we pounded, a wall of glinting bayonets bearing down on the enemy. The thick grass wound itself around our boots, slowing us down, willing us to stop. We were two hundred metres away and within rifle range, yet still the Russian guns were quiet. But they had not retreated, for now I could clearly make out the silhouettes of men against the fiery red morning sky, waiting solemnly like the keepers of hell. My blood froze and my legs began to shake. We were charging into a trap. I kept running forwards only because the Austrian stampede carried me, but my instinct was to crawl deep into the earth and commune with the worms. At a hundred and fifty metres I could see the Russians looking down the sights of their rifles, aiming at us and awaiting the order to fire. We, too, had brought our rifles up to our shoulders when suddenly there was a whistling sound above our heads. I dropped to the ground and at the same instant there was a terrific explosion somewhere close by. The earth shook beneath me and a second later another shell landed, then another. The air vibrated strangely around me as shell after shell dropped down upon us. Smoke clogged my lungs and burnt my eyes. Something thudded against my back. A bullet must have struck me. I remained rooted to the spot, paralysed by fear, with only the long grass as cover. I was going to die in that meadow, I was sure of it. I reached round and felt for the wound on my back. When I looked at my hand it was covered in blood but I could feel no pain. Then I saw a boot at my side leaking scarlet into the grass. A severed foot shredded at the ankle was still attached. I had not been shot, just kicked in the ribs. I looked around for Jerzy but he was no longer at my side. Our men were still advancing suicidally towards the Russians. I said goodbye to my family and told Lotte that I loved her. Then I got to my feet again and stumbled on. A brown haze hung over the battlefield. Bullets were flying in both directions now and men were falling all around me. A shell exploded ahead of me and three of my countrymen were blown to smithereens. I tripped over a body hidden in the grass and fell on to my face. I checked back to see if the soldier was all right and saw Piotr Baryslaw. Or what was left of him. He had been sliced in half; the left side of his face and chest were missing. His heart was hanging by a vein near his leg and one of his arms lay in the grass a few metres away. I turned away. Now the shells were cracking off every few seconds, sending shrapnel in all directions, and the noise was deafening. Lieutenant Neidlein dropped down beside me. He was trembling. 'Come with me, we're going to take out the gunners,' he barked, 'there's an artillery post over there.' He pointed to a clump of trees a hundred metres away. I could see a pile of sandbags and a gun poking over the top.

'We're going to have to get closer – keep crawling until we get a proper view of them. I've got men coming at it from the other side.'

We inched along on our bellies through the grass until we reached a welcome ditch. Volleys of rifle fire were flying in both directions above us. The Russians still hadn't broken cover to advance, and some of our men had reached their trench and were engaged in hand-to-hand combat; others held their ground and were firing from the meadow. We were fragmented; all our training ground strategies were for nothing here. Orders were lost in the clamour of the battlefield and it was every man for himself. Except for me, my fate was not my own, I had an officer breathing in my ear, and he told me to raise my head above the grass to see how close we were to our target. This seemed like madness to me, it was a miracle that we had not been shot already. If I raised my head even ten centimetres above that ditch it would be blown off. I hesitated.

'Come on, Daniecki, don't be such a cowardly Jew, you bastards are going to lose us this war,' Lieutenant Neidlein hissed.

It was a provocation that I could not accept.

'No, no, it's you stupid, pig-headed Austrians who are going to lose this war,' I shouted. 'You're nothing more than a nation of waltzing pastry-makers. What the hell makes you think you can beat the Russians? You have a look if you're so damn brave.'

We were lying on our stomachs side by side with our cheeks pressed against the earth, eyeballing each other like a married couple on the verge of divorce. Lieutenant Neidlein was indignant. 'You will be punished for this, Daniecki,' he roared.

'If I'm still alive by the end of the day, I shall look forward to it.' I thought the odds on us both surviving to play out the charade of retribution were negligible.

'Daniecki, I am ordering you to look.'

'Oh, come on, Lieutenant, please,' I begged.

Neidlein pulled out his pistol and put it against my head.

The will to live is so strong that given the choice of two deaths one will always choose the one that buys more time even if it is a matter of seconds. People will jump to their death from a burning building rather than burn with it. For in those few seconds of accelerating flight the god that refused to save them from the fire might still reach down from heaven and bring them to earth alive. Battered, broken maybe – but alive. Hope defies reason.

I held my breath and raised my head slowly above the long grass. A stream of bullets tore up the grass around me and I ducked back down sharply. God had delayed my death a little longer. Neidlein laughed. 'Still alive, little Jew? What did you see?'

'We're less than thirty metres from the enemy, Lieutenant, but we're right at the edge of the long grass. There's no more cover. What do we do?'

Neidlein rubbed his moustache nervously; he was going through the options in his head. They were bleak. 'Wait here,' he barked and slithered back through the grass. It seemed like an age before he returned, though it probably wasn't more than a few minutes.

'All right,' he said breathlessly, 'we've got Hausmann and Kovak following up thirty metres to our left and Wodecki and Rolka beyond them. When the Russians finish a round, we run at them while they're reloading, the others will follow; let's see if we can shoot them in their lair. Then we'll turn the gun round on them, try and get a foothold.'

We waited for our moment and then Neidlein gave me the nod. We scrambled to our feet and hurtled towards the artillery outpost through a barrage of bullets and shells. I was vaguely aware of other men running alongside us but by the time Neidlein and I had made it only Kovak was still standing. We pointed our rifles over the top at the unsuspecting Russians. There were three of them and as they looked up startled we shot them in the head, then as we were clambering over the sandbags Kovak was hit and collapsed lifeless on the other side. There was no way we could hold the position on our own, and Neidlein knew it. He fired a couple of shots into the mechanism of the gun to render it useless, and we turned on our heels and fled back towards a cluster of bushes. Lieutenant Neidlein stumbled over a root, but before he could recover he was shot in the leg. I should have stopped to help him but I just kept running. Neidlein got back to his feet and hobbled away as fast as he could. I reached the bushes and dived into the ground. Neidlein was limping some way behind me now. He was hit again in the back and he lurched forward but somehow stayed on his feet and staggered on. Another bullet passed through him and I saw blood spurt out of his belly. He fell to his knees but he would not die, the memory of life coursed through his leaking veins and with bulging eyes he crawled painfully towards me. He was only ten metres away when a shot appeared to puncture his head and he sprawled into the meadow. His legs continued to jerk mechanically for a minute and then he was still.

For two hours we were butchered mercilessly in the fields and woods along the length of the river. Whole regiments were emasculated and hundreds of foolhardy officers sacrificed their lives cheaply as they led their men into undefendable positions. The meadow was covered in shell holes and scraps of blue-grey cloth. Severed fingers gripped rifle butts tenaciously. Bloody fragments of flesh stained the grass. The groans of mutilated men were ever increasing. It was about ten in the morning when the Russian infantry finally attacked, smashing through XII Corps who were holding the line on our left. At last someone gave the order to retreat, and it was shouted from man to man. Those of us who could, turned and fled helter-skelter through the fields, across the river and into the forest, chased all the way by

Russian artillery. I passed six of our drummers all lying dead in a straight line with their drums still about their necks, their eyes and mouths wide open. They looked like toy soldiers knocked down by a petulant child. I don't know what killed them, but their pallid faces had aged suddenly beyond their years.

We continued running like demented chickens for several kilometres until we were brought under control and ordered to re-form. In the ensuing chaos I bumped into Király, the Hungarian. He stood out from the ranks because his uniform was clean. I asked him where he'd been hiding. He just laughed and winked.

We found our way back to our company and it was only then that we learnt the full extent of the devastation. A register was taken and of the 260 in our company only half were present. Twenty thousand men died that morning at the Gnila Lipa.

And where was Jerzy Ingwer? I couldn't find him anywhere. I rushed from man to man asking if anyone had seen him, but to no avail. I was bereft. After only a day fighting I'd lost my two good friends Ingwer and Baryslaw and witnessed the death of my lieutenant. But my grief was premature, because two hours later a dejected figure emerged from the trees. He was carrying a body over his shoulder and plodding slowly towards us. As he approached I saw that it was Jerzy with Lieutenant Neidlein on his back. I ran up to him and helped him bring Neidlein to the ground. Then I threw my arms around him and hugged him tightly. I cannot tell you how happy I was to see them.

Amazingly Neidlein was still alive. A double miracle. He was carried off for treatment but I did not expect to see him again. Jerzy was decorated for his bravery. As for me, I never received anything throughout the war. Your father is a survivor but not a hero.

There was no time to rest. Word reached us that the Russian cavalry were coming. The thought of Cossacks filled us with dread. We hadn't had time to get into a fighting formation, so a further retreat was ordered. As we headed west, the roads became busier and busier, as troops mingled with peasants and villagers who had been evacuated from their homes. And as if this miserable human traffic was not enough, we shared the road with vehicles of every possible description: gun wagons, hospital trucks, mobile kitchens and carts over-laden with the furniture and treasured possessions of the fleeing peasants. And with nearly every family there came a cow and a couple of chickens. Progress was slow, and occasionally the cry '*Kosaken kommen*' came forward from the rearguard, and sent whole battalions scurrying across the fields in panic. By nightfall we had retreated some thirty kilometres, we were dead tired and starving. When the halt was given I was so exhausted I collapsed on the side of the road and fell asleep.

We marched day and night for a fortnight, and to compound our misery it began to rain. And once it started, it did not stop. Day in, day out, the skies emptied on our heads. The roads clogged up with mud and soon we were up to our knees in it. The artillery wagons were sunk to their axles and the horses pulled them at a crawl until they were dropping dead from exhaustion. In places the wagons were stuck four abreast across the way. The cavalcade came to a standstill. Road and field were indistinguishable from one another. We were in a bog that stretched to all horizons. There was no choice but to unyoke the rest of the horses and abandon the wagons and their booty to the enemy.

We crossed the River Dneister and surrendered Lemberg. At each village we passed we saw a similar sight, the Jews were fleeing but the Ruthenians were staying. They welcomed us, gave us food and lodged our officers, but they could not be trusted, for they were waiting to welcome their fellow Russians. Rumours were rife that they were betraying our positions to the enemy. Sometimes we were lucky enough to sleep in a barn but more usually we were left in our wet clothes in the rain to sleep under trees. Our only comfort were the fires we burned from the fences and gates that we ripped up on our way. If any peasant objected to this practice they were beaten on the spot. The Jews, most of whom were desperately poor, wandered through the fields in their sodden rags, sometimes gathering under a tree to pray alongside one of their famous rabbis. It was the Chassids with their unshaven forelocks who attracted the most attention from the soldiers as they passed. They called them vermin and in the case of Király even spat at them.

'Why do you shave your women, Daniecki? It's disgusting,' he asked me.

'We don't all do that, only the Chassidim.'

'All right, so why do they do it?'

'Because for hundreds of years the Cossacks have been raiding Jewish villages and raping the women, so they started shaving their heads to make themselves un-attractive. Now it's a custom. A constant reminder that there are still bastards around like you who want to hurt them,' I explained. But it didn't stop Király from insulting them. I despised Király. He was pure vitriol, and my God could he moan. He moaned every step of the way. He would invariably begin in Hungarian and then translate into broken German, because to complain was not enough for him; his complaints had to be understood by those unfortunate enough to be near him.

'I curse the cow that produced the calf that bore the hide that formed the leather that makes up this wretched backpack that weighs a tonne and rubs me raw,' he would say. Or 'I curse the river that flows into the sea that makes the clouds that piss on my head.' His complaints were nothing if not elaborate. He poured scorn on all humanity for its greed and stupidity. It was a stance that was easy to understand in the context of war, but Király would have been just as abrasive anywhere. He lived to hate as I lived for Lotte.

I hadn't washed or changed for twenty days. My feet were never dry and my skin felt rotten to the bone. At the time I had never known such hardship, but God was preparing me for far greater trials than a twenty-day walk in the mud.

On 16 September 1914 we crossed the San. Jerzy and I stopped on the bridge and wept. Ulanow was lost. We looked down on the brown soily water that a few hours earlier had passed through our town and wondered when we would see our loved ones again. I dropped two stones in the river and vowed that wherever Lotte was, even if she was in the hands of the Russians, I would find her. We had dangled our feet in those waters and made our plans, the San was our river, it flowed through our dreams. And even though the Russians had taken the river and the forest they could never take the dream. Not even death can steal our dreams, Fischel. When I pass away, the river and the forest will come to meet me. Lotte will be there, a girl again, catching the sun in her hair and washing her toes in the San. And I will see you there, too, Fischel, with Dovid and little Isaac running between the trees chasing butterflies.

11

I N THE EARLY PART OF THE WAR WE SUFFERED DEFEAT AFTER defeat. After only six weeks of war we had withdrawn all the way to the River Dunajetz. That's a long way . . . maybe three hundred kilometres. Not only was Ulanow in enemy hands but so was most of Galicia. It's almost impossible to imagine the scale of the loss but by the time we reached the Dunajetz some half a million men were dead on that front alone. Most of them ours. Can you understand the madness that had befallen mankind? And remember, Fisch, that's half a million dead in only six weeks. Galicia was a graveyard. The earth was blood and bone.

By now I was suffering from the most dreadful dysentery. If there's anything going round, your dad will catch it first. I was never first in anything at school, that was Jerzy, he won everything. As for me? Well, I was good at languages but otherwise I was neither too clever nor too fast, but if there was a cold in the air I would catch it first. Oh it was dreadful – this dysentery – I must have fertilized a thousand trees. I can laugh now but . . . ah . . . ow . . . actually remind me not to laugh . . . it hurts too much. Thank God we had time to regroup at the Dunajetz. We were there for a while. Long enough for our supply lines to be re-established and for the kitchens to stock up with proper food. My stomach knitted back together and little by little the exhausted rabble began to resemble an army again. The Germans had lost confidence in us – hardly surprising really – they promised to send reinforcements. We were glad of it, we needed all the help we could get, but the best news of all was that the mail service had resumed and letters began to arrive. Every day I would wait for the postman like a loyal dog. When nothing came I would leave with my tail between my legs. There was never anything for me. Where were my parents, my brothers and sisters, and where was Lotte? Had the Russians swallowed them up? Were they on the road west? Were they even alive? As time went by I feared the worst. Eventually I stopped waiting for the postman because I couldn't bear to see the excitement on the faces of my friends when their names were called. Király, with whom I had the misfortune of sharing a tent, mocked me. He too had received no mail but it didn't seem to trouble him. He said he loved nobody and was loved by nobody. Life was simpler that way. It didn't lead to disappointment.

For the next couple of months we advanced and retreated like yo-yos, but for all our efforts we never managed to cross the San. I could tell you many a story, Fischel, about what I got up to in the war but in the end they'll all sound the same, so I'll spare you the details. Let it suffice to say that by the end of November we were back at the Dunajetz, the German reinforcements were nowhere to be seen, the Russians were within twelve kilometres of Cracow and for the first time they had crossed the Carpathians into Hungary and taken the town of Bartfeld. So winter was upon us and the empire was quaking, the Russian hordes were about to stampede down the mountains towards Budapest.

Now did I tell you about Przemyśl . . . no? . . . I must have forgotten. Przemyśl was a strategic fortress town on the San; it was of great psychological importance to our commander in chief, Baron Conrad von Hötzendorf, because it had been his headquarters at the start of the war. Conrad vowed never to surrender it, so even as the rest of us were retreating he left a hundred and twenty thousand troops inside to defend it. Now it was completely surrounded and the men were trapped. But Przemyśl was well fortified and had provisions to last until spring. Everything we did from then on was aimed at pushing the Russians back from the Carpathians and recapturing the fortress before our men starved to death. To lose Przemyśl with so many men would have been the ultimate humiliation, so what did Conrad do in his desperation? He conceived the most ludicrous plan of the whole war. At the turn of 1915, he sent his army up a mountain in winter.

On the day of our departure Király came into the bivouac carrying a large brown-paper package.

'Someone loves you after all,' I laughed.

'No, someone loves you,' he said bitterly, and threw the package at my head.

I examined it carefully before opening it. It had been posted in Vienna and my name was written on the front in bold black ink. On the back in smaller letters was the name Lotte Steinberg and an address that I did not recognize. I brought it up to my nose and inhaled deeply. There was a faint scent of perfume mixed with a much stronger leathery smell. Király was staring at me jealously. There was no way I was going to share this moment with a Hungarian peasant, so I left the tent and opened my parcel outside. Inside was a fur waistcoat and gloves, both made from the thick golden brown skin of a bear. Tucked inside the pocket of the waistcoat was a letter. It was the last letter I received from Lotte during the war, and over the coming years I read it so many times that I virtually know it by heart. Fischel, open the top drawer in the writing desk behind you . . . under the round paperweight you'll see a couple of envelopes . . . yes those are the ones . . . could you pass them to me? Thank you. This is the one.

My dear Moritz,
Please forgive me for not writing earlier. The last few months have been extremely difficult. We fled Ulanow in September taking what we could, which was not much. My father hid the rest of his pelts and coats under the floorboards of the factory. We went to Rudnik to catch a train to Cracow, but all the trains were crammed with wounded men

and equipment. My father tried to bribe one of the officers. Unfortunately for us he picked an honest man who told us he could not let civilians board the trains under any circumstance. So we went back to the road with our horses and carts and joined the exodus to the west. I have never known such misery and degradation. We slept on the carts in the rain, and even though we were lucky to be under furs we were never dry. At every village we tried to find accommodation in a tavern or hotel, we even offered good money to stay in people's homes, but wherever we went the army had already commandeered everything. The best rooms were taken by the officers and there were so many soldiers that even the barns were full. We Jews were like a plague of rats roaming the countryside. Everything was mud, my father's beard was matted and all of my poor mother's dresses were stained and shredded. We collected rainwater in pans and used up half in a vain attempt to keep clean, but within minutes of washing we were filthy again. I saw men and women stop and defecate at the side of the road in front of hundreds of onlookers. They had lost all sense of propriety. What state of mind must a person be in to do such a thing? Surely we must maintain our sense of dignity even in times of hardship? For without it we are no better than animals.

Perhaps the worst part of the journey was the insults and abuse we received at the hands of the Poles. The Poles have never been good to us at the best of times but they have really turned on us now. Do you know that in some villages no sooner had the Jews packed their bags than the Poles were waiting at the door to move into their homes? Surely they wouldn't do that in Ulanow? We threw so many summer parties and treated our staff well; they wouldn't turn on us there, would they, Moritz?

We didn't have enough fodder for the horses and they could barely pull our carts, which were heavy with fur coats. The coats were stopping our progress. My father, ever the businessman, saw an opportunity to make some money. 'Money will be more useful to us than fur,' he said. He stood on the cart and shouted, 'Furs going cheap, rabbit, fox, mink. You name it we've got it.' Can you believe it, Moritz? It really made us laugh. And you know what? A little crowd of people gathered round the cart and started to finger the furs with their muddy hands as if they were in the market. We had become an island of normality in the midst of chaos. A good trader can tell what a customer can afford by the cut of his jacket, the quality of his fingernails, the ruddiness of his face, but here even the rich looked poor. My father was canny, he was not going to give his goods away for nothing, he knew there was not a man, woman or child on that sodden road who did not dream of wrapping themselves in a soft warm fur; so he held an auction. 'What do I hear for this lovely pure white coat, made from the finest rabbit in Galicia?' he cried, holding up a coat which was now as white as a soup-stained tablecloth. At that moment fur was clearly more useful than money to the people gathered round, because the bidding was fierce. People reached deep into their ragged pockets and bags and pulled out fistfuls of grimy notes to wave at us. We sold thirty coats and twenty-three hats in three hours, and none for less than half price. My father was delighted, he said he had never sold so many coats so quickly in all his life.

I kept a bear pelt to sleep under because it has the warmest and most lovely soft fur of all the skins that we sell. They're very rare you know, we don't have many. When at last we got to Cracow I set about cutting and sewing it for you. We're in Vienna now staying with a friend of my father who owns a department store. We can't stay here for ever and my father wants to go back to Ulanow as soon as we win it back. Do you think we'll ever win it back, Moritz? The news from the front is so grim. We seem to be losing horribly, although the Germans are doing much better in Prussia. Anyway I think about you all the time and worry about you. I've been several times to check the lists of fatalities from the front and am horrified by the numbers we have lost, but always relieved that your name is absent. Quite a few boys from Ulanow died in the first month, we could hear mothers wailing in the street when the news arrived. Please be careful, be a coward if you must, I'd rather marry a coward than weep over a dead hero.

Have you heard from your family? Your mother and father decided to stay behind in Ulanow, they said they were too old to leave. But your brothers and sisters left with the rest of us. Eidel said they were going to Berlin. Perhaps your elder brothers won't have to serve as reservists. Or maybe they'd rather fight for the Germans, they seem to be so much better organized than us.

I fear this war will last much longer than we were told. They said it would be over by winter and it's January already, so who says it won't last until next winter or the one after? I made you these gloves and I thought a waistcoat would be better than a coat because you can wear it under *your uniform if you get cold. Can you imagine if you went into battle wearing a fur coat? You would be a laughing stock. Anyway this skin will keep a bear warm in winter so it should do for you. Remember, I slept under it for a month so think of me when you wear it.*

Now listen, my angel, you must write to me whenever you can. Your letters give me hope. Send them to Vienna for now but if the army recapture Ulanow my father will take us back there. He is lost without his factory. At first he had nothing better to do with his time than invite eligible young men (and some not-so-young men) round to meet me. It was a dreadful business; I could not even look at them. They seemed so stuffy and shallow compared to my boy from the San. Eventually I plucked up the courage to tell my father that so long as you are alive my heart is yours. And you know, I think the war has softened him a little because he stopped his matchmaking there and then and said he would agree to whatever made me happy. So there, Moritz, isn't that good news? We can wed as soon as you get home. So hurry up and beat the Russians. I love you more each day.
Your Lotte

There . . . you can put it back in the drawer, Fischel . . . thank you.

I hurried over to the latrines, slipped off my greatcoat and jacket and tried on the waistcoat. It was a good fit. I ran my fingers through the fur and imagined Lotte's sleeping body lying under it. It was pleasing to touch and I could feel its warmth immediately. It was a squeeze to get my jacket on over it but I managed. The gloves were magnificent, but so bulky they looked like oven gloves. The fingers were too fat to fire a rifle. I stuffed them into my haversack next to my silver-grey water bottle and ran off to find Jerzy and tell him my news. As I was making my way to the canteen I was stopped in my tracks by a piercing voice behind me.

'Daniecki, come here.'

A jolt went down my spine; I knew that voice immediately. Could he still be alive? And if he was alive what was he doing here? I turned slowly and saw the tall figure of Lieutenant Neidlein. The Great Viennese Sausage was back. He'd been patched up and reconditioned and, my goodness, did he look terrifying. His face was horribly distorted. His right ear was nothing more than a scarred stump, his cheek on the same side had caved in under his eye socket and his misshapen mouth slanted up to meet it in a sordid grin. The red raw scar tissue that covered his wounds was painful to look at.

'Welcome back, Lieutenant,' I offered.

Neidlein stared at me intently. I was unable to read his expression. 'It's good to be here, I was bored to death in hospital,' he slurred. 'We have a war to fight and we're going to win it. But first I have a few scores to settle.'

From then on I was made to suffer.

There are few roads in the Western Carpathians and only three passes, and as far back as I can remember they were always impassable in winter. It was our unenviable task to defend the Lupków Pass, the middle one of the three. It's not so much that the mountains are high, but they are rugged and steep and the snow lies heavy in the passes. We toiled like slaves to carry our guns and supplies up the southern slopes. On the northern side the Russians were also planning a winter offensive.

I lost count of the number of times Neidlein made me go up and down the mountain those first few days. We all worked hard but the worst jobs always fell to me. There was no shortage of back-breaking chores, and while I was endlessly lugging up great trunks laden with ammunition or heavy kitchen equipment, Jerzy had become the lieutenant's tea boy; he was promised promotion and spared any hard labour.

During our first night up the mountain a snow blizzard battered the tent. No one could sleep for the thumping wind that thwacked against the canvas. The guy ropes groaned under the strain. We had a new recruit, a Pole by the name of Zubrisky who fancied himself as a comedian. Still not tainted by the cynicism of the battle-weary, he found the whole thing rather exciting. He had an in-exhaustible repertoire of filthy jokes which had Jerzy and me in stitches. All night long he entertained us with his repartee. I tried to translate them into German for Király but somehow I didn't have the delivery, or his German wasn't good enough, because he didn't laugh once and he kept saying, 'Yes, and why so funny?'

By morning, half a metre of snow had fallen and we had to dig ourselves out. From that day on we slept with our spades inside the bivouac. We grew to love the snow because when the snow fell it was warm, but sometimes it was too cold for snow and then we froze. On those days the triggers on the rifles jammed and we could only get them working by holding them over fires; even the water in our bottles froze. Our supply lines, which were already stretched, virtually closed as the paths turned into sheet ice. I saw men plummet to their deaths when they lost their footing struggling up the mountain under their loads. As for the fighting, Fischel, well I'm afraid it was more of the same. We attacked on many occasions but failed each time to capture any more than a few hundred metres of snow, and of course we lost thousands of men in the process.

Somewhere in a warm command centre hundreds of kilometres from danger, a handful of generals were quaffing port, puffing cigars and sinking into their leather armchairs as they pushed us around a map spread out on their mahogany coffee table. Millions of lives callously disposed of in a game of chess where all the pawns would be sacrificed to save the king. Meanwhile the soldiers in Przemyśl were beginning to starve as they waited for the Carpathian deadlock to be broken.

On still nights the silence of the padded snow-capped mountains carried our voices around the peaks and we could hear the Russians talking in their tents. I was tired of hating them.

There was no escaping the cold: it crept into our boots and gnawed at our toes, it burnt our ears, numbed our limbs. Our fingers grew stiff and brittle, our minds dull. We became listless and inert. We stumbled around our posts, rubbing our hands and slapping our thighs to get the blood moving. We were ageing quicker than nature intended, we shambled about the camp with shoulders hunched and heads bowed, speaking in croaks and aching all over. The lucky ones lost toes and fingers from frostbite or caught pneumonia and were ferried down the mountain. If I hadn't worn Lotte's waistcoat I would have been the first to succumb.

I can't remember how long we'd been in the Carpathians when an icy Siberian wind howled through the pass and chilled us to the marrow. A ferocious blizzard sent us scurrying to our tents. That night the temperature plummeted so low the thermometers cracked. We shivered uncontrollably and no one, not even Zubrisky the Polish chatterbox, spoke as we fought our personal battles against the cold. I began to lose feeling in my toes, and the numbness was climbing up my legs. I brought my knees up to my chest and tried to wriggle my feet inside my boots. My head was splitting, the liquid in my brain seemed to be clotting and my thoughts ambled aimlessly before losing sense and dissolving to nothing. A terrible lethargy overcame me. All I wanted to do was sleep, and silence the insistent little voice that told me to stay awake. I put my head in my hands and warmed my breath in the fur. I let my heavy eyelids fall shut, just for a moment, just to let them rest . . . and then I couldn't remember why I had to keep them open. The fight had left me.

I woke up with a start; something was tugging at my head. I opened half an eye and saw that Király was sitting on top of me trying to pull off my gloves. I was frozen to the bone and didn't have the strength to push him off. 'What the hell are you doing?' I croaked.

He jumped back in shock. 'Oh my God, you're still alive!'

He was wearing three greatcoats and had a blanket wrapped around his head. I looked about me and saw that all of the men were sleeping without blankets and coats. Király had taken them all.

'Of course I'm alive, what are you doing?' I was still shaking off sleep.

'You're the only one – they've all frozen to death,' he gasped.

I pulled myself up on to my elbows and looked more closely. I hadn't noticed that their faces were tinged with blue and their lips were purple. I crawled over to each man in turn and felt for his pulse. Kellman dead, Zubrisky dead, Polisensky dead, Schonnbrun dead, Landau dead. Finally I got to Jerzy Ingwer and placed my finger on his wrist. 'He's still alive, Király, I can feel a pulse.' I grabbed a couple of the stolen blankets from Király's bed and laid them over Jerzy. 'So they weren't even dead when you took their blankets.'

'I forgot to ask,' Király snorted sarcastically. 'They didn't stop me, so they must have been dead . . . or nearly dead.'

There was no point talking to Király, he was beyond contempt. Jerzy's face was as cold as stone; I shook him to see if I could wake him up, but he didn't stir, so I rubbed him vigorously first across his chest and then down his arms and legs. Király, who had slumped back on to his bed, looked on impassively. After a couple of minutes he said, 'I think you've killed him.'

'What do you mean?' I hissed.

'Never rub a man with hypothermia – you'll give him a heart attack. When the blood from the extremities flows back into the heart it's so cold that it causes a shock to the system,' he said glibly.

I felt for Jerzy's pulse again. This time there was nothing. Király was right, I had killed him.

'You bastard, why didn't you tell me that earlier?'

'Because now we've both killed someone and we're even. I couldn't bear the thought of you getting on your high horse. If I hadn't taken those blankets we would all have died except you with your bloody waistcoat. What a terrible waste of life that would have been, when one of us could have lived to keep you company. The question was, who was that one going to be? Well, I stayed awake the longest, and as I waited for the others to sleep I realized that although I hate this miserable life with all my heart I hate the thought of dying even more. You need that hatred to stay alive. So there it is, Daniecki. Long live Frantz Király. And don't blame yourself for Ingwer, perhaps he wouldn't have made it anyway. We'll never know.' Király casually reached over for Ingwer's haversack and rooted around for the cigarettes that he knew were kept there. When he found them he put one in his mouth and fumbled with the matches in his gloved hand. Once lit he offered it to me. 'Cigarette?' he grinned provocatively.

That was when I punched him. He just laughed, picked up the cigarette that had fallen from his lips, took a deep drag and said, 'Thought as much.'

When I emerged into the pale dawn light I was greeted by a scene of utter desolation. The dead were being dragged from every tent and lined up in neat rows while Lieutenant Neidlein checked them off a register. We dug temporary graves in the snow and piled up the frozen blue corpses of our friends. This was a ritual we were to repeat time and time again.

That night I wrote to Jerzy's parents, who were now in Cracow. I told them that their boy was the bravest and most popular man in the company and would be sorely missed, I related how he had saved Lieutenant Neidlein's life when I had given him up for dead, and that he was about to be made an NCO, but I couldn't face explaining the circumstances of his death. Instead I wrote that he had died a hero in action. He was my dearest friend.

I have always thought that if I'd not been so stupid I could have saved Jerzy Ingwer. I should at least have called the divisional doctor. I felt so guilty that until today I have never told anyone what really happened. We make many mistakes in life, Fischel, and most of them we can put right. But some mistakes can never be righted and the guilt eats away at the soul. Of all the emotions we have, I have learnt that guilt is the most corrosive. Anger passes quickly, and hatred mellows with age and learning, but guilt endures.

You know what was crazy about the Carpathian campaign? Our biggest enemy was the cold; it was more ruthless than the Russians. Replacements arrived from every corner of the empire. Many of them didn't speak German and had hardly had enough time to learn the eighty words of command that we were all supposed to know. There were many misunderstandings, morale was non-existent and men surrendered under the slightest threat. The fabric of the army began to unravel. The Czechs, who were never particularly loyal to the Habsburgs, openly discussed how they might achieve independence, some even proposed switching sides. The Romanians of Transylvania wanted to be part of a greater Romania. The Ruthenians sympathized with Russia, and an ever-increasing number of Poles also wanted an independent state. So who could you trust in the heat of battle?

To compound this the Russians launched a ferocious attack on the Dukla and Lupków Passes, and again we were butchered. And then towards the end of March disaster struck: the garrison at Przemyśl surrendered and every last desperate starving man passed into Russian hands. What stupidity! Those poor men should never have been left there in the first place. But what really makes me angry is that in a vain attempt to save them, we had lost the service of another eight hundred thousand men. Not all killed by the Russians, Fischel. No, most of them were actually incapacitated by cold weather; frost-bite, pneumonia, that kind of thing. But despite these losses Conrad von Hötzendorf did not order a retreat, he didn't even change tactics. For us on the front line it was clear that this cretin would fight to the last man. He would first empty the empire of its youth, then turn to their fathers. When finally the war was lost the royal families of Europe, the tsars, the kaisers, the emperors and the kings – who were all related anyway – would sit down over lunch, congratulate the winner and give him a bit of land.

The day after the fall of Przemyśl the clouds dropped down over the mountains and we were enveloped in a thick fog. I was in a small work party returning from trench-digging duty along the new line, which now crossed the southern approach road to the Lupków Pass. The atmosphere in the group was sombre; we were dispirited and exhausted. Király was simmering with fury like a volcano before eruption. The new boys had quickly lost their hunger for war; they felt duped by the propaganda machine which had sucked them into this icy hell promising them honour and glory on the battlefield. They had come to save Przemyśl but they had never got close, all they did was freeze in their tents and dig holes in the snow. When they did fight, their shells bounced off the ice and failed to explode, and their rifles jammed. We were humiliated and impotent. The Russians were formidable, unbeatable, their progress relentless. We didn't know that they were running out of weapons, or that revolutionaries were infiltrating the army and undermining its morale. We didn't know that their men were treated worse than ours and that their officers operated the brutal Prussian rule, a military orthodoxy left over from the Napoleonic War which posited that the most effective soldier was one who feared his own officers more than the enemy. We didn't know that within four months the Russians would have withdrawn from Galicia. It was inconceivable. If you had asked any Austro-Hungarian where we would be in July 1915 he would have said 'defending Budapest'. So it was with utter dejection that we traipsed back in a long line through the snow and mist towards our encampment. The going was slow, the visibility poor. I kept my eye on the footholes of the man in front and followed in his steps. After a while Király, who was two ahead of me, came to a halt.

'I've lost them,' he said.

There were six of us lost in a disorientating whiteness which stretched out in all directions. A debate ensued as to which way we should go. I and three others instinctively felt that we should head one way but Király insisted that the last man he saw had been walking another way. So we followed Király. After half an hour of walking we saw shadows looming in the snow. As we got closer I could make out the distinctive brown greatcoats of the Russians. But before we could turn and flee Király had surrendered on our behalf; he held his white handkerchief aloft and threw his rifle and spade into the snow. The Russian guns were pointing at us. We followed Király's lead, and I would be lying if I didn't say that it was a relief to see our rifles hit the ground. Our war was over. Two days later the Lupków Pass was in enemy hands. The Russians were staring down on Hungary from the Carpathian heights with spring ahead of them. They had us by the throat.

<u>Entry no. 59</u>

The universe hangs on a kiss.
Zalman Shneor

12

FOR THREE WEEKS LEO STAYED IN HIS PARENTS' HOUSE IN Leeds and waited for time to heal him. Each day he asked himself why he felt worse. His memories replayed obsessively and his mind was in paralysis. At least in that first week after Eleni's death there had been things to organize, there had been a purpose to each day, but now she was buried there was nothing to do other than sit by the garden window and dwell on his misfortune. He was in a cryogenic state, frozen on 2 April 1992. If they had thawed him out and brought him back to life they would have found him babbling about that day. He could not look forward to the future, he could not even exist in the present. The only thing that distinguished one day from the next was the slow dwindling of the light in his eyes. At night he battled against sleep but when he inevitably lost he was haunted by nightmares so painful that his parents were often woken by his cries.

First it was the fox. Late one night in the back garden, caught in the burglar light, the fox stopped in its tracks, turned slowly towards the window and stared at him. Leo shuddered. The following morning came the squirrel. It scampered down a tree and ran into the garden in search of food. After a moment's foraging it ran straight towards the big patio door, checked left, checked right, then stood up on its hind legs and stared at Leo just as the fox had done. Finally it was the pigeon that landed on the windowsill in front of Leo. She jerked back her neck in surprise and gazed at him intently.

'Eleni,' he heard himself say.

'Hello,' the pigeon said, with a jerk of the neck. She threw a glance back towards the garden. 'I always loved your parents' garden,' she said. The pigeon turned back and eyed him quizzically, 'Look at you, Leo, you're so lifeless a fly could lay eggs on you. Don't be alone.'

'But I am alone, Eleni.'

The pigeon ruffled up her feathers and walked along the window ledge nodding to herself in contemplation. She stopped, looked into the distance and shook her head. She fluttered her wings as if to leave, then seemed to change her mind. She looked him in the eye one more time, 'I'm lonely too, Leo, but I feel worse when I see you like this.' She buried her head in her wing momentarily, then abruptly took to the sky and disappeared over the fence.

Eleni was everywhere. She had transformed into beetles, cats, hedgehogs and sparrows. When a solitary sunbeam pierced through the cloud cover and alighted on the old beech tree he saw her brilliance. She was running in the random gusts of wind that picked up rubbish and sent it swirling down the street. She danced in the little pools of rainwater that gathered where the flagstones dipped. At dusk she withered with the petals of the morning glory. She invaded every thought and coloured every vision. He would not shake her off. She would not let go. They clung on to each other across the frontier of death, magically transcending all that is intangible, invisible, unknown.

Grief drifted like a pollutant through the house, sucking the spontaneity out of his parents, making their stomachs curdle after meals, and straining their conversations. Eve hovered over Leo but couldn't get through to him. As her frustration grew she turned increasingly against Frank, who shuffled around like a worn-out slipper pretending everything was normal. 'There are no shortcuts for grief,' he would say ineffectually.

One night Eve snapped. 'Why don't *you* ever try and talk to him? He's *your* son too, for God's sake. Stop avoiding him. You can be so selfish. You of all people, Frank, should know what he's feeling. Tell him the truth. Can't you see he needs you?'

'What happened to me was different. I was much younger,' he said stonily.

'What exactly are you frightened of?'

Frank threw his arms up in anger, 'What do you want me to do, Eve, tell him I spent every day of my childhood weeping for my parents? Tell him about that wretched letter from the Red Cross? And how is that going to help him? How is it going to help him to know that his dad was also a miserable sod? I loved Eleni and it breaks my heart to see Leo lose her. But nothing is going to make him feel better right now.'

Eve had scraped a raw nerve, he rarely raised his voice and she knew that he did not want the conversation to go further. There was a whole lot more to Frank's past than he was prepared to discuss. It had taken her several years after they first met to get the truth out of him, but he still hadn't told Leo anything. Leo had always been told that his paternal grandparents had died when his father was a baby. He knew too that his father had been adopted, although he never met the family who had adopted him. It wasn't until he was ten that he had asked how and when his grandparents had died. Frank had opened his mouth and the first words that fell out were 'in the war' which was half true, followed by 'in the Blitz' which wasn't. And the lie was completed with 'a wall collapsed on top of them'.

Frank persuaded himself that Leo was too young to know the truth. Eve strongly disagreed and had made him swear that he would come clean when Leo was older. But with time the lie put down roots and Frank found himself repeating it. Soon it had assumed the mantle of truth and Frank was afraid to unpick it, and, for all her irritation, Eve had never dared to push him. His peace of mind seemed to rest on his choice not to discuss his past.

'I'm sorry, Frank,' she said, changing tack. 'I didn't mean to stir things up. You may well have been miserable once but you've come through. Perhaps there's something in that for him. Surely he's old enough now.'

Frank sighed; he couldn't escape this any longer. He'd

been meaning to tell Leo for some time but the opportunity had never arisen, and besides the thought of it made him feel sick.

'All right, I'll have a chat with him.'

The following day father and son sat side by side staring into the garden, both silent. Frank couldn't think of anything to say. Or rather he did not know how to start saying what he ought to say. Like a teenager on a first date he played out a series of opening lines in his mind and rejected them all for some reason or other. It was better not to speak than say the wrong thing. After a while Frank wanted to get up and leave, but by then he felt the silence was demanding to be broken. It would be worse to leave without saying anything at all. Eventually he put his hand on Leo's shoulder and squeezed hard. Leo turned and looked at his father mournfully and Frank remembered his golden-haired son of four running naked on the sands of Rhossilli Bay, screaming when the icy sea caught his toes. How could that carefree boy have become this weary young man? Speak, Frank, speak, he said to himself. Say something, something fatherly, something wise and soothing. Tell him the truth, just open your mouth and let the words drop out. Tell him how much you love him, tell him you will pick him up and carry him on your shoulder just as you did when he was little, tell him you will hug him until the hurt has gone and he can walk for himself again. No words came to his lips.

Leo stared at his father expectantly, 'Is everything all right, Dad?'

There was another long silence. Then at last, 'Listen, Leo, I want to talk to you about something very important. It might make you feel better.'

'Yes, Dad?'

'Well . . . how can I put this . . . you see, it's about your inheritance.'

'My inheritance?'

'Yes . . . well that's the word your grandfather used before he died,' Frank said.

'Dad, I don't care about my inheritance right now. Why are you even talking about it? It's not important to me.'

'No, of course not, Leo. I'm sorry, we'll talk about it another time. I'm sorry . . .'

Frank picked up his chair, placed it back in the kitchen, and disappeared upstairs in a cloud of regret.

Elephants are a bit like us. They live to seventy, reach adulthood at twenty and socialize in groups. Today I went into the Institute to find out what evidence there was of elephants grieving. This is what I found out. When an elephant dies in the wild, the other members of the herd will stand over the corpse for days mourning. In one case over a hundred elephants stood vigil over a dead elephant. One of them tried to pick it up and stand it on its feet nearly sixty times before eventually giving up. Sometimes they will cover the body with leaves and branches. Eventually with visible signs of distress they will leave the corpse but they often return over the following days to pay their respects. One female elephant was observed leaving the herd and walking thirty miles to visit the bones of a recently departed mate. Whenever elephants pass the place where another elephant died they will stop and stand in silence for long periods. They might pick up the bones affectionately and hug them as if mourning the loss.

In a zoo in India a female elephant watched her cage mate die while giving birth to a stillborn calf. She stood stock still for a long time until her legs eventually gave way. For three weeks she lay in one spot with her trunk curled up, her ears drooping and her eyes moist. No matter how hard they tried, her keepers could not persuade her to eat. They watched her slowly starve herself to death.

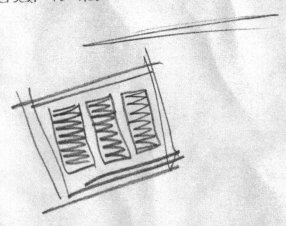

13

'I'M GOING OUT,' SAID LEO ONE AFTERNOON. A SOUND FROM nowhere. His mother looked up from the newspaper she wasn't reading. She had taken to sitting near him and pretending to read. She did not want him to feel alone, nor did she want him to feel watched. So she would sit quietly, hoping that soon he would need to talk and she would be there to help him.

'Do you want some company?' Eve asked.

'No.'

'We could go for a nice walk,' she offered.

'No.'

'No, well that's fine, have a good time . . . Where are you thinking of going? Would you like to borrow the car?'

'No thanks, I've just got to get out of here for a while.' He stood up, yawned, went to the cupboard under the stairs, found his trainers, forced his feet into them without undoing the already tied laces and walked out of the front door.

He walked without aim past the suburban houses of his

parents' neighbours, past shops and parks, to a part of town he hardly knew. He paid little attention to the derelict houses and run-down warehouses that now surrounded him, but instead tried to use each step to suppress the rising sense of panic that had gripped him since the morning. He had awoken with the aching fear that the numbness that was slowly eating his soul would never leave him, and that time would heal nothing. The longer he waited for time the more he festered. He was rotting, as all living matter does, any semblance of order was crumbling into chaos. Time, the heralded healer, had become his enemy.

It was dark. He had been mugged by dusk without noticing. And now he was lost. He felt a pang in his knee, the swelling had gone, only a scar remained. He was glad of it, it was the last physical reminder of his travels with Eleni and he wore it like a badge of honour. He walked on looking for a familiar landmark. At the end of the street he happened across a dingy looking pub and realized how thirsty he was. He expected it to be one of those quiet little pubs with a couple of drunk warehousemen tottering at the bar. The sort of place that never earns the publican a penny, the sort of place he would normally avoid but now suited his mood. He could not see inside for the thick purple curtains that covered the windows. He pushed open the door and was hit by a wall of cigarette smoke and the roaring vulgar sound of men who have left their women at home. The place was so full he could hardly get beyond the door. The men stood with their backs to him, drinks in hand, pushing up their ruddy necks, straining to get a view of something.

'You're just in time, mate, show's about to start,' a man by the door shouted in his ear. 'If you make it to the bar mine's a Guinness.' Leo pushed his way through the bodies. The men started stomping and cheering. Leo followed their focus and saw a young woman wearing a fake fur coat walk on to a small stage. So this is life, Leo thought.

The woman stopped in the middle of the stage, turned her back to the audience and held a pose with hands on hips and legs a metre apart. For a good twenty seconds she stood absolutely still while the crowd clapped and whistled. Then she raised both hands, clicked her fingers, and the voice of Marilyn Monroe singing 'I Want To Be Loved By You' filled the smoky bar. The coat fell to the floor, a flick of the head and a pout over the shoulder. An old formula but it had its effect, for in a moment the room went quiet as the men ravaged the girl with their eyes. Now, in black lace camisole, suspenders and high heels, she turned to face them. She couldn't have been more than twenty years old.

At last Leo was at the bar, he was sweating and his eyes were smarting from the smoke. 'Here's twenty quid,' he said to the portly barman, 'get me drunk.'

'Well, there's a challenge. What would you like, sir, beer, wine, spirits?'

'I don't know . . . beer and spirits.'

'How about I give you five pints and five chasers?'

'Fine, whatever. You choose.'

As he watched the stripper, Leo felt Eleni hovering

silently above him. 'Go away, stop judging me. This is where I belong now. I feel good here.' He gulleted a couple of drinks to chase her from his mind but nevertheless he, too, began to wonder what he was doing there. Maybe this is me, the new me. If I am going to lead a life without love then why not indulge in baser pleasures?

The girl was down to bra, knickers and stilettos. She was at the front of the stage now, inviting a group of six or seven beer-bellied boys to put their money into her bra. They whooped, whistled and egged each other on, excited and embarrassed all at once. It must have been their first time. They looked from one to the other to see who was bravest, each looking for permission, unsure of what to do. Hands in pockets to see if they had any notes. The shortest of the lads, a spotty red-faced kid with lank hair, seizing the opportunity to raise his status, pulled out a fiver and was pushed to the fore by his mates. He held out the note tentatively towards her. The girl grabbed his hand and pushed it down her bra. The others cheered and within seconds they all had their money out and jostled to get closer to the stage. When she had taken all their money they turned on one of their number, lifted him up and rolled him on to the stage at her feet. 'It's his eighteenth birthday,' they clamoured, 'go on, give him something special.' Pumped up with drink and teenage hormones the hapless boy scrambled to his feet and held his fists aloft in victory. The audience responded by singing 'Happy Birthday'. The overexcited youth turned to the stripper and began to wiggle his hips in some hopeless erotic dance. She grabbed him by the shirt, pulled him up close and fixed him in the eyes. The boy froze; his knees were shaking. She wrapped her right leg around his lower back, thrust her hips into his and flung her hair back in simulated pleasure. The boy tried to kiss her neck but she was having none of it. She withdrew and circled him very slowly looking him over and shaking her head as if to say he was not up to it. She then turned him to the audience and made him raise his hands above his head. She put her finger on his lips and slowly traced it down his chest to the top of his trousers. The crowd cheered. Leo whistled and shouted in delight. Eleni had disappeared in the smoke.

She lifted the lad's shirt, revealing his hairless, bulbous belly, and walked her fingers down inside the top of his trousers. Instinctively the boy's arms shot down to protect his manhood. She removed her hand and again pushed his arms up towards the ceiling. The audience laughed. This time she went for his belt, unfastening it provocatively, and slowly pulling it through the trouser loops until she had it in her hand. She took hold of his arms and brought them down behind his back and tied them together with the belt. The lad did not know what to do; half-eager and lusty, half-terrified, he laughed nervously. He was both hero and victim. His tormentor unzipped his trousers and let them fall to his ankles. The audience erupted. Leo looked at the ruddy faces around him, baying like wolves at the kill. He liked what he saw. These men were earthy, honest, in touch with their angry, self-loathing cores. Man as fucker and murderer, beholden to no one, with all the sticky layers of culture and civilization peeled off. He beat his fists on the bar. Go all the way, fuck him. Go on do it, do it. Yes, now he was beginning to find himself, the truth was grovelling on its knees to the surface. He was not worthy of love, not worthy of anything more than whores and sluts.

He was guilty of murder and this was the punishment. 'Let's sit at the front.' With these words he had led Eleni to her death. He wanted to be ripped open and feel salt in the wounds because he deserved it. His humanity had died with Eleni, now he was brute. From this day on I shall live the rest of my life as an animal, he thought, and to encourage himself on his new journey he finished off the remainder of his drinks without pausing between them.

The stripper was in control, she slipped one red varnished fingernail inside the rim of the birthday boy's black underpants. There was not a man in the crowd who did not feel that finger against his own skin. Little by little her whole hand sank down inside the boy's pants until she had hold of his penis. They could all feel her hand on them. A hundred penises bulged and sweated. But not the boy's, he was too nervous. He was limp and the ruthless stripper pulled his pants down to join his trousers and exposed his flaccid humiliation to the crowd. She pushed him hopping and stumbling back towards his friends; he fell to his knees and rolled off the stage to be rescued by his jeering mates.

Leo headed for the toilet. He felt wretched. He pushed his way past the stage, where the stripper had now removed her bra, and through a door on the far side of the room. He was in a corridor and he leant heavily against a wall for a moment while he wiped the sweat from his forehead. A rush of nausea rose up from his stomach, he doubled up and made for what he thought was the toilet door. He found himself in an unlit dressing room. He closed the door behind him and pushed his back against it. He steadied himself, took a deep breath and fought off the urge to vomit. When at last he had mastered himself again he groped along the wall until he found a switch and flicked it on. There was a large mirror edged with vanity lights at one end. In front of the mirror was a table strewn with lipstick and make-up and a chair with a pair of jeans flung over the back. Leo sat down and stared into the mirror. His eyes were torpid and his face seemed to sag. Flesh hung from his jowls in pale shapeless wads. Skin too big for bones. His brow looked corrugated, freshly furrowed. He could see no redeeming features, he had lost his youth. It was too bright and the mirror too cruel. Out in the bar there was a loud cheer and a round of applause.

Leo staggered on to the street, and as he gulped down the cool air, his head swirled and his stomach emptied itself on the pavement. He fell back against a wall and cursed. He was bitterly angry and suddenly it was obvious who to hate, for he had noticed a white lorry approaching on the other side of the street. Lorry drivers were responsible. As a breed they were collectively guilty. He tottered to his feet and lunged into the road.

'The lorry's going to hit us,' Eleni yelled. The lorry had strayed on to the wrong side of the road. Leo saw the *frightened face of the Ecuadorean driver as he tried to bring his vehicle under control. He could hear Eleni screaming and another disembodied voice, which must have been his own.*

'You murderer,' he slurred as the white lorry bore down on him. 'I hope all of you die . . .' The lorry swerved to avoid him, mounted the kerb and skidded to a halt. The driver jumped out of the cab, ran over to Leo, pulled him by the shirt on to the pavement and began to throttle him. 'You fuckin' idiot . . . what the hell do you think you were doing?' he shouted in Leo's face.

'You killed Eleni . . . you killed Eleni,' Leo retorted.

'What? Drunk are we? I should have run you over. One less moron to worry about,' the man said, shaking Leo vigorously.

'No, you were drunk,' Leo contested, '. . . the doctor told me you were drunk . . . that's why it happened . . . now see . . . what you've done to me . . . you've ruined my life.' A surge of hatred rose inside him and he found the strength to push the driver backwards and lunge at him with fists flailing. The driver fought back, kicking and punching him until he fell to the ground. A group of people watched from afar but no one dared intervene.

Leo came round in a police cell, bewildered and bruised. Once he had found his senses he was escorted from his cell up a flight of stairs into a whitewashed room where he was examined by a police doctor, breathalysed and then questioned. At six in the morning he was informed that he had been reported missing by a Mr

Frank Deakin and was allowed to phone home. By eight he was told that no charges were being pressed and that he was free to leave. His parents were waiting for him at reception.

'We thought you'd killed yourself,' Eve said as they led Leo to the car.

Later, slouched at the kitchen table, Leo was vaguely aware that his father was loitering behind him.

'Shall I make you some tea?' Frank offered after a while.

'No, I just need some water.'

'Would you like some ice?'

'For Christ's sake, just give me some bloody water,' Leo snapped.

'Sorry,' Frank said meekly and handed over the glass.

Leo drank it in one go and held out the glass for more. Obediently, Frank filled it up and passed it back.

'How about some toast?'

'I can look after myself, thank you,' Leo hissed.

There was a silence while Leo finished his second glass of water.

'Your mother wants me to have a chat with you,' Frank began and immediately regretted bringing Eve into it. He should have said, '*I* want to have a chat with you.' 'She wants me to tell you about my own experiences. She thinks it may help you. You see I . . . I know how you're feeling because . . . I lost my parents when I was young and I . . .'

But Leo wasn't listening, he still felt drunk and he hadn't slept all night. His thoughts were elsewhere. He was shocked about what he had done the night before. He'd never got drunk like that in his life, he could have been killed. It would have been darkly ironic if he had been killed by a lorry, too. He knew Eleni would have been furious with him for his stupidity. He was ashamed of himself and he knew he had to take some kind of action to halt this slide into self-indulgence. Action. That was it! Action was the true healer, not time. This would be his medicine.

He noticed his father dithering at the table.

'Dad, aren't you supposed to be at work?'

'It's all right, I can go in later if you want to talk.'

'Not now, I'm exhausted, I'm going to bed,' Leo said, and walked out of the kitchen.

Frank watched him go, then he scraped his heart from his sleeve, carefully folded it up and hid it away. That evening he went up into the attic and rooted out an old leather suitcase. He dusted it down and took it to his study. He hadn't looked inside that case for fifty years. Inside was the inheritance, but there was a lot of work to do before he could give it to Leo.

Entry no. 6

Yesterday I read about a fifteen-year-old boy from Brisbane, Australia, who in 1989, as part of a school project, threw a bottle into the sea. In the bottle was a letter containing his name, address, a few details about his life and a plea that the finder write to him. Three years later, in April 1992, at the same time that I was flying back to Kithos with Eleni's coffin, the bottle was washed up on the coast of Wales. It was found by a girl who immediately wrote to say she had received the message. At the time that she wrote, the boy was travelling around Europe and his parents phoned him to tell him she had written. The boy decided to pay her a surprise visit. He went to Wales and knocked on her door. It was not long before they were going out with each other and she followed him back to Brisbane. She could not stop herself from telling the world how one day she found her love in the sand of a windswept beach on the Gower peninsula.

14

'AT LONG LAST. I CAN'T BELIEVE IT. I'VE ONLY CALLED YOU A thousand times. And it only took you a month to call back. I should be pissed off but for some reason I feel honoured because I know for a fact you haven't called anyone else.'

Hannah was one of the first people Leo had met at university. He was in the hall of residence queuing at the canteen on his first day and she happened to be behind him in the queue. A slim mousy-haired girl with impossibly high cheekbones and a natural toothy smile. In those early days all of the students were a little clingy and desperate, they would spend the first term making friends with anyone and everyone and the second term trying to lose them. But Hannah became an enduring friend. When Leo and Eleni moved out of their two-bedroom maisonette in Camden and left for South America it was Hannah who moved in.

'So what happened, suddenly find your address book?'
'I had a dream about you last night.'

'You lucky boy. Was it erotic?'

Leo laughed. 'No, the dream was about you but you weren't actually in it.'

'How intriguing, were people gossiping about me again? I am the subject of a lot of gossip, you know. The other day I was in the toilet at work when Janet and Lilly came in. Anyway there I was wiping my bum when Janet said to Lilly that I was sleeping with Mark, he's the chunky sandwich boy. Oh no, that doesn't sound right. He doesn't sell chunky sandwiches – they're actually quite meagre, no, what I meant was, he's chunky – works out and stuff. Sort of bloke that waxes unwanted hairy patches – you know, those scrappy little tufts you blokes get on your backs and upper arms. They all fancy Mark, that lot, always going on about peeling his wraps and getting their hands on his Cumberland and other perverse activities of which I am innocent. But he's not my sort. I swear to God, Leo, I haven't touched him.'

What relief to engage in a conversation about nothing. Hannah was the only person Leo knew who could turn trivia into a weapon against misery. 'It's all right, Hannah, you don't have to convince me. Even at college people always thought you were at it when you weren't.'

'Did they? Who? I want names. Who did they think I was shagging?'

'Well there was that anthropology lecturer, Jack Dunphy. Someone said they'd seen you under the table in his office, while he was sat on his chair with a big smile on his face.'

'I dropped my pen, for Christ's sake. He was laughing

because I was making such a fool of myself. God, did people really think I went down on Dunphy? That's desperate. What do they think I am? Why do they believe these scurrilous lies, Leo?'

'Because you smile at strangers? Because a lot of men fancy you? I don't know.'

Hannah snorted, 'The truth is I'm hopeless with men. I've not exactly had many and the longest relationship I've ever had was five months. That's crap, isn't it? You know we used to look at you and Eleni and say you were the perfect couple. I'm so used to saying your two names in one breath. Whenever a conversation came up about love we would quote you two as proof that it existed. I'm so sorry, Leo.'

There was a silence before she continued. 'Anyway, what about that dream you had? What were they saying about me?'

Leo took a deep breath, 'I've been having a lot of dreams about Eleni recently where she appears next to me and starts doing Eleni things like that crazy bouncy dance she used to do or singing away on her bike. She drifts into the dream and I think she's alive and then she waves goodbye and I know she's dead. Last night she came to me again, but she just sat staring at me and she said, 'Hannah', and then she disappeared.'

Hannah giggled, 'Is that it? She just said, "Hannah"? She didn't say, "Hannah had sex with the Archbishop of Canterbury"? Just "Hannah". That's weird. What do you think it meant?'

'At first I thought it had to be something deeply

significant from the way she said it, but now you're on the phone I think she was just saying, "Hannah will cheer you up". And she was right. You have.'

'Oh good, I'm not completely useless, then. So tell me when are you coming back to London, Leo?'

'Tomorrow,' he replied impulsively.

The following day he climbed the steps to his old flat, weighed down by the same rucksack that he had carried in a previous life, when he and Eleni had skipped down those stairs full of excitement and embarked on the adventure that was to separate them for ever. His heart filled with trepidation. How abject he felt coming home without her! There was a small, unwelcome, welcome committee waiting for him at the door. He would rather have entered the flat alone and spent a quiet moment with the memories that were beginning to flood his senses. As it was, Charlie greeted him first, throwing himself into Leo's arms and hugging him so tightly that it was difficult for Leo to breathe. Then came Stacey and Karen, Eleni's closest friends, and finally Hannah, who declined to kiss him, preferring instead to punch him hard on his upper arm. 'That's for not calling sooner,' she said.

As he followed them down the hallway towards the kitchen, Leo noticed two stacks of boxes. Still here, he mused, untouched. The thought of their contents made him shiver. His entire life with Eleni was packed up in those innocuous-looking brown boxes. Love tokens, letters, clothes, photos and books. Three years of a love now reduced to little things in boxes. He felt a certain ambivalence towards them. He did not relish the thought of sifting through them, a task he knew he would have to undertake soon. There were decisions to be made about what to do with it all and it had been so hard in Ecuador to even look at the clothes Eleni had once worn, or feel the objects she had once held. And yet he was desperate to reread her letters, rummage through forgotten photos and rediscover the accumulated paraphernalia that would allow him to travel back through their life together, leaping from memory to memory rather as a child might leap from stone to stone when crossing a stream.

Passing his old bedroom he couldn't help but look inside. Hannah had pushed the bed, which used to be in the middle of the room, up against the far wall under the window. She had offered to let him move back in, but he couldn't imagine sleeping in that bed without Eleni. There was a new rug on the threadbare carpet and a collection of Asian Buddha heads and statuettes above the unused fireplace. The doors on the large white fitted cupboard hung open. Leo saw Eleni standing there naked, wondering what clothes to put on. It was the gentle concave arch of her lower back, her rounded shoulders and the spread of her buttocks that were etched in his mind. She had the shape of a Botticelli goddess, neither fat nor thin but pleasingly fleshy. An unusual snapshot, he thought. Of all the things that had happened in that bedroom, why should this quiet and seemingly insignificant moment come to the fore? The image was frozen. He tried to make her turn round and smile at him but she wouldn't.

*   *   *

In the kitchen Leo was surprised to see a man standing by the table. He looked about twenty-five years old, with jet black hair and a handsome face.

'Leo, this is Roberto. Roberto Panconesi, love saying that. Pan – co – nesi. Sounds like an exotic Italian dessert. He's my new flatmate,' Hannah said.

Leo offered his hand. Roberto shook it warmly. 'Pleased to meet you,' Roberto intoned, with the slightest trace of an accent.

'Leo is doing a PhD on ants,' Hannah explained, playing the hostess.

'Really?' Roberto raised an eyebrow.

'Yes,' Hannah continued, 'he spends most of his time watching them fuck through a microscope like some sort of pervert. Isn't that right, Leo?'

'I watch them do all sorts of things, not just copulate,' Leo said in his defence.

'That's just a big word for the same thing . . . As for Roberto, he is a lecturer in the philosophy of physics, which basically means he talks incomprehensible bollocks all day. So you two should get on very well.'

'She's always teasing me,' Roberto protested.

'Am I? Oh I'm so sorry, I'll say something nice about you, then. Roberto is a genius. He's the youngest in the department. Students are all over him, they fight to get into his lectures – even people who aren't studying physics want to get in, and it's not just because of his general gorgeousness – although that helps – but also because he's got some mad theories and he is dangerously unconventional. How was that? Better?'

'Marginally, but thank you for trying,' Roberto laughed.

'Well it all sounds . . . I mean you sound . . . fascinating,' Leo said unconvincingly, and he felt the muscles in his face force a smile. He didn't want to have to make small talk with a stranger.

He sat down and looked about him. Nothing had changed in the kitchen; it was dominated by a large dresser filled with an assortment of plates and pots, none of which matched. The landlady and a parade of tenants had left them behind. There was the small balcony overlooking an inner courtyard, the unusual purple ceiling and the round pine table, now filled with salads and dips.

Hannah tried her best to be cheerful, flapping about the kitchen filling Leo in on gossip and politics, the momentous and the meaningless given equal weight; but the others were more sombre, and the conversation inevitably turned to what had happened in Ecuador. Leo patiently explained what little he remembered, omitting only the reason why they were sitting at the front of the bus. He couldn't bring himself to divulge that particular detail.

By the time Hannah served up dessert the atmosphere had lightened. She had started whipping a chocolate mousse in the afternoon, but after a while her hand had ached and she had become bored so she had abandoned it in the fridge, hoping that it would sort itself out. But when she took it out it had condensed to a lumpy sludge. 'Oh dear,' she said, 'I've made poo for dessert. Who's for poo?'

*　*　*

Later they retired to the living room and sank into the sofas. The conversation had died; the blood had been sucked out of their brains into their bellies. Their digestive juices wallowed in chocolate, occasionally gurgled, then abandoned their purpose. They were melting into the soft fabric of the furniture. Leo felt sick.

'Call an ambulance,' groaned Karen, 'I swear I'm going to die.'

'Well, you didn't have to eat it. This will teach you to be so bloody polite,' Hannah snorted.

'I can't move,' Stacey moaned.

'Actually, Stacey, you may not realize it but you are moving very fast.' It was the first time Roberto had spoken since he had greeted Leo. Everyone stared at him, slightly baffled by his strange interjection.

'Am I?' Stacey said.

'Yes, you are travelling at eighteen miles per second which is six thousand five hundred miles per hour around the sun. But the sun is also moving at a terrific speed and so is the galaxy. When you take all this into account we are actually travelling at two hundred and thirty miles per second which is . . .' he paused, 'eight hundred and twenty-eight thousand miles an hour.' He looked at his watch. 'I calculate that we've travelled almost a million miles since we ate that mousse.'

The others reflected on this fact in bemused silence. Roberto's outburst seemed to change everything, for now they felt like six bloated splodges slouched on couches in a lounge hurtling through space at terrifying speed.

'I think I need a seat belt,' Charlie said, eventually.

But out of all of them, Roberto's verbal foray into the cosmos had the most impact on Stacey, who had been looking for an excuse to fall in love with the mysterious Italian since she first clapped eyes on him.

It was not long before Stacey and Roberto had made a discreet exit so that he could explain, in the privacy of his bedroom, the philosophy of physics and of course, like all the best scientists, do a little probing experimental work. With their departure the party descended into a medley of smutty comments until eventually it fizzled out altogether. Leo had survived his first evening back in London, not only survived it but even enjoyed it.

That night Leo went back to Charlie's flat, which was above an all-night shop on Upper Street in Islington. It was supposed to be a temporary measure until Leo found his feet, but Charlie had made it clear that Leo could stay as long as he wanted. They hastily converted the lounge into a second bedroom by unfolding the sofa bed. They lugged the armchair and television into the hallway and put them in the only places they would fit: the chair next to the front door and the TV half-blocking the entrance to the kitchen. Leo's new room had a floor-to-ceiling window overlooking a bus stop on the main road. As he was unpacking his clothes a bus pulled up noisily and Leo was surprised to see, only a few metres away, the long, taut faces of the overtired passengers on the top deck staring absently at him. He hurriedly drew the blinds.

The bed was wretchedly uncomfortable. The mattress was old and thin, and when he lay down he found that his head was lower than his feet. But when he lay the other way he could feel the springs in his ribs. He closed his eyes but his ears remained stubbornly open to the symphony of unfamiliar sounds that filled the room. There was the indistinct music and chat from the shop radio, the drunken conversation of a couple of beggars who were camped outside the door, and the screeching brakes of the night buses.

All night he chased sleep, but each time he caught hold of its soft wings and felt himself drifting into its feathery embrace he was awoken by a subtle change of sound. With each pursuit his desire for sleep grew stronger and more desperate. By morning he felt like a stalker whose love had been cruelly unrequited. Crashing on friends' sofas was a throwback to a life before Eleni. It had been fun then, but now he felt as if he had fallen from a warm nest and was lying lonely in the mud.

Entry no. 2

Before Eleni's death I feared
nothing and I did as I pleased,
now I am frightened of:

* 1) travelling overseas
* 2) sitting at the front of buses
* 3) lorries
* 4) starting new relationships
* 5) being miserable for the rest
     of my life
* 6) talking to people who don't know
     what's happened to me
* 7) finding no meaning.

15

WHAT IS THERE TO DO, OTHER THAN WHAT I DID? LEO thought to himself as he boarded the 73 outside Charlie's flat, taking care to sit in the middle of the bus, which would take him to University College. He had no deep desire to resume his studies – or any not to. He merely sought a framework, like a coat hanger, on which he could hang his life. At least then it might look like a life which was ready to be inhabited, rather than a crumpled garment on the floor.

He unzipped his shoulder bag and pulled out the small red album which he had bought that morning after collecting his photos of Latin America. As he was leafing through them deciding which ones to put in, an image caught his eye. It was the photo that Eleni had taken of them on the beach in Colombia on New Year's Eve. Their heads were glued together at the ear and their beaming faces filled the photo entirely; how serenely beautiful they had been then. He melted into the picture for a moment, and emerged with the feel of Eleni at his side and a smile on his lips. He slid the picture into the first page of the album and carried on skipping through the photos, selecting only pictures of Eleni to put in after it. When he got to the final image his heart nearly stopped. There was Eleni on the bus with the ice pick in her hand, pulling a comic face like the grim reaper. Leo studied the detail. She was sitting in the first seat to the right of the aisle. In front of her legs was a hardboard panel above which was a horizontal steel bar that connected to a vertical used by passengers to board the bus. Behind Eleni he could make out the high Andean plateau. The picture must have been taken only half an hour before she died. Something was coming back to him: it was the conversation that preceded the taking of the photo. They had been joking about a hundred and one things to do with an ice pick. He had laughed at the time, but now it seemed like a sick joke and Leo couldn't help feeling that death really had visited them that day and briefly revealed himself in their game in readiness for the deed ahead.

At the university Leo made his way down the familiar corridors to the zoology department where he checked his pigeonhole for mail. There was an out-of-date invitation to a convention in Boston, three department circulars and a letter from a professor at the University of Zurich whom he had written to in order to gain clarification on an aspect of ant behaviour for his doctorate. He was dithering between going to the café to read the letter and dropping in on his tutor, when he was swept up in a tide of excited students heading into a lecture theatre. He overheard the name of Roberto Panconesi and remembering Hannah's effusive description of his lectures he decided to follow them.

He sat on the back row near the door so that he could make a discreet exit after a few minutes. The lecture theatre, which held a couple of hundred students and raked steeply down to a small stage, was full by the time Roberto arrived. He was dressed casually in a pair of jeans and a sky-blue shirt with a button-down collar. He put his briefcase on the table, switched on the microphone at the lectern and, impressively, proceeded to talk without any notes at all.

'Firstly I'd like to thank you all for coming to this opening lecture in my summer-term series, I doubt there will be so many of you by the end,' he laughed. 'Physics is merely a description of reality, but the more deeply we look into things the more extraordinary reality appears. At the quantum level there is stuff happening that is so strange, it challenges the way we see the world. By the end of this course not only will you be rethinking the world, but also how you act as individuals within it. For me the ramifications of quantum physics stretch not only into philosophy but into religion and politics. It is a kind of poetry. It is also an addiction. It is my purpose to convert those of you who are not already converted, to its beauty.'

It was as brash and arrogant an opening statement as Leo had ever heard. Roberto was laying down the gauntlet and simultaneously raising the stakes. He had certainly captured everyone's interest, but Leo wondered how on earth he was going to live up to such hefty claims.

'Ever since Newton played with his balls,' there was a roar of laughter from the young audience, 'scientists have seen themselves as objective outsiders. When Newton observed balls colliding he could calculate every force that acted upon them and predict exactly what would happen. For him there were no surprises, he claimed that the universe ran like a machine, consisting of millions of separate entities which interacted with each other in predictable ways. Newtonian mechanics made for a very safe and deterministic world in which nothing was connected.

'How wrong he was. The latest scientific discoveries have proved beyond doubt that at the quantum level everything is subtly connected. Even the scientist is part of his own experiment because every choice he or she makes changes the results. We can now prove scientifically what the founders of some of the world's greatest religions knew instinctively: that we live in a holistic universe.

'But we have been in thrall to the likes of Newton and Descartes for so long that it has infected our reason and our politics. We still run the world as if we are separate from it and not part of it. Holism has not yet taken root but it will. For you to get anywhere in the philosophy of physics you have to engage with the notion of holism in a personal way. I want you to feel it in your bones and not just as a conceptual theory . . .' Roberto suddenly broke off. He had noticed Leo sitting at the back of the theatre.

'Ah, hello, Leo,' he said casually. Leo flushed with embarrassment. 'Ladies and gentlemen, let me introduce you to Leo Deakin.' Two hundred heads turned and pinned Leo to his chair; there was no escaping now. 'Leo is doing a PhD on ant behaviour. I think we may be able to learn something from his experiences.' Leo squirmed in horror; he would rather drown in acid than talk about Eleni in this arena. And now Roberto was walking up the aisle towards him like a chat-show host. 'Tell me, Leo, you spend a lot of time observing ants. I want to ask you a very simple question. Are you an ant?'

Leo laughed, relieved that the question was about ants. 'No.'

'So you are a separate entity from the ants you observe?'

'Yes.'

'How do you know? What is the difference between you and an ant?'

'Size, for starters,' Leo said, wondering where all this was leading.

'Interesting. So how big do you feel next to an ant?'

'Enormous.'

'So next to an ant Leo Deakin is enormous. But now tell me: how big do you feel in relation to that oak tree we can see through the window there?'

'Pretty small.'

Roberto returned to the stage. 'So I have a question for you, ladies and gentlemen. Is Leo Deakin enormous or pretty small?'

'It depends who he's with,' a voice from the front called out.

'Exactly. So we can conclude from this that in a universe where we see ourselves as separate from the ant, a Newtonian universe if you like, we tend to define who we are by comparing ourselves to the things around us. So for example, I know I am not an ant because I look at an ant and I say I am not one of those. I know I am male because I look at a woman and I say I am not one of those. I know I am a tall man because in relation to others I am taller than most. I know I am no good at football because I see others who play better than me. On every level I define myself in relation to the things around me. And when I look at the world I do the same. I get a sense of what things are by comparing and contrasting them with everything else. Our very separateness is at the core of our identity. Do we agree?'

There were nods in the audience.

'But what if all those things against which you measure yourself weren't there. How tall would you feel then?'

There was a silence.

'OK, let's do a thought experiment. I want you all to close your eyes.' Leo allowed his eyes to shut as Roberto continued softly, 'Imagine that you are floating in an absolute void and any memory of your life on earth has gone. Here there are no concepts of space or time. You are just a naked human being suspended in nothingness.'

Leo pictured himself dangling in darkness.

'Now take all the "I am's" with which you define yourself and see how they fare in this void. I am English, I am tall, I am young and so on. Be ruthless, be honest in exposing the image of yourself. One by one let these notions parade before you like contestants in a beauty contest and examine them with a fresh eye.'

Leo swam off into his void armed with a long list of

adjectives that he would use to describe himself. As Roberto had asked, Leo tried to imagine that he had no memory of earth. But with nothing to compare himself to, with no tree to stand under, he found it impossible to say who he was or what he was like. To be English in a void was meaningless. How could he be sure that he was young when there was no one older to whom he could compare himself? He didn't even know that he was a man.

All his self-perceptions were delusions. They had nothing to do with the essence of being alive. The only thing that survived the void were his senses, for when he touched his face he could still feel it, and he heard the panic in his own breath. Leo opened his eyes to see Roberto smiling Buddha-like at his students.

'When I do the void experiment I perceive man as limitless,' the Italian said, 'free from that which shackles him to ideas, places, things and time. Free from triviality. Man becomes an ageless, sizeless, possessionless organism without racial, national or religious identity, a receptacle for higher emotion and thought, a master of the senses. He becomes a giant of possibility. How does it feel?'

'Terrifying,' a boy shouted out.

'Of course, that's the problem we physicists have in explaining this stuff,' Roberto mused, like an evangelist warning his converts of the travails ahead. 'People are very uncomfortable with the infinite and the eternal, especially when applied to themselves. We are a clannish and small-minded race. We feel more comfortable defining ourselves by our jobs, our social class, and our religions than by our boundless potential. The average person is happier saying he is a member of a badminton club than a member of the human race, let alone a part of the universe. But where does that small-mindedness lead? If you are a member of a club you will want to beat the neighbouring club. If you consider yourself a member of the human race there are no humans to beat but you can still subjugate the planet instead. But if you see yourself as a vital part of a holistic universe then any battle is ultimately against yourself.'

Leo looked at Roberto, bewildered.

'Don't you get it, my friends? If you are part of unity what is there to fight against? Leo is only different from the ant in the same way as his arm is different from his leg. We do not question that his arm and his leg are part of the same entity. Is it so difficult to imagine then that Leo, the ant and indeed all of us are small parts of a bigger whole? We are like characters in a painting who do not know the painting exists, and that everything we see is part of the same picture and painted with the same brush. We are each a small piece of infinity and in some form or other we will live for eternity. Quantum theory proves that the world is neither fragmented nor divided.'

As Roberto expanded on his theme of the holistic universe built on hidden connections, chaos and un-certainty, Leo began to feel comforted. There were particles that never died. There was the magic of light in which photons travel so fast that time slows to a virtual standstill and a beautiful moment might last for ever. (If only time had stopped on New Year's Eve 1991 in Colombia, when Eleni had taken that picture of their happiness!) There was the notion that there was an infinite number of universes that ran parallel but invisible to our own, and that in each of those universes an alternative outcome to every conceivable situation was played out. So Leo floated off into parallel universes where he and Eleni had missed the bus, where accidents didn't happen, where they were still together. They would now be in Peru, as they had planned, overlooking the Inca ruins of Machu Picchu. At least somewhere there was a world where he was happy, even if he could not access it.

'To end this lecture,' Roberto concluded wryly, 'I would like to start at the beginning. In the beginning there was a . . .' he paused. 'No. I am misleading you. The beginning does not exist; it is indefinable, indefinite. We can only talk of where our knowledge begins. It is *a* beginning, not *the* beginning. In *a* beginning our great scientists tell us there was an enormous fireball, and in this fireball trillions of electrons and other particles jostled together in a sublime cosmic dance. Then there was a big bang and these electrons were scattered forming the universe. Some of these electrons came together to form stars. In time some of these stars exploded and deposited a shroud of carbon dust into the atmosphere. Layers of carbon dust settled on earth. As you know, carbon is life. Every living cell, be it in plants, animals or humans, contains carbon. So my friends, as you leave today console yourselves with this thought: you are literally made of stardust, and whatever becomes of you the particles from which you are made have been around since the dawn of time and will continue to live for ever. You are inseparable from your forever teaching, holding court at parties, provoking and cajoling his students. As for Leo, he was as vulnerable as a beetle on its back: he was seeking answers to big questions and in Roberto he recognized a man who was ready to provide them.

'I thought a lot about Eleni during your lecture, and about the nature of death,' Leo said, sipping at his coffee.

'I wonder if the dead really die,' Roberto reflected, 'or do they just evolve into something else? On the quantum level everything is made up of tiny sub-atomic particles. Imagine then the universe as a sea of timeless electrons extending to infinity. What is a human being in that sea? A human being is merely a beautiful bag of particles. There is not much that distinguishes us from our surroundings other than shape and colour. But when we die our little electrons live on and blend into trees, flowers, sky and animals. Those we have lost are with us for ever, only a whisper away, in new shape and colour. It's a kind of life after death. Eleni is nowhere and everywhere.'

This was a paradox of clarifying insight for Leo, for though Eleni was gone she was ever-present. From that moment forth he was hooked to the gospel according to Roberto. Over the course of the following weeks Leo immersed himself in introductory books on physics and attended more of Roberto's lectures, from which he would often leave on a high, carrying an imaginary Eleni laughing and screaming on his back.

Roberto encouraged his students to carry a notebook with them at all times, in which they were to write down any illuminating thoughts. It was part of his crusade to get students to think more about the world in which they lived. He told them not to limit themselves to physics, but to take note of anything which inspired them, be it self-generated ideas, quotes from books, even photos from magazines. Leo obediently purchased a notebook, but struggled at first to find anything to write in it.

Entry no. 37

The female crab has an impenetrable shell, she is so hard on the outside and yet so soft within. There is no possible point of access. The male crab must wait a whole year until the female decides to shed her shell to grow a new one. And it is only at that moment of vulnerability that the patient crab can triumph in his love.

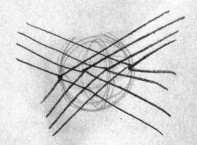

16

'BE CAREFUL WITH ROBERTO,' HANNAH WARNED ONE evening as they were sitting in Charlie's ex-living room, 'he likes to think he has all the answers. He is the vicar of physics and you can't turn him off. He spends his entire life proving himself correct. He may be a great thinker but he's not great with feelings.'

'And what about you?' Leo asked.

'I'm a crap thinker and a crap feeler, in fact I'm crap all round – which has its advantages because whoever spends time with me is bound to feel good about themselves,' she said.

'And what about me?'

'You think too much and you feel too much. You're intense about everything.'

'So I have no virtues?' Leo laughed.

'I didn't say that. Intensity has its virtues when applied to some things.'

'Such as?'

'Love. Passion. Romance. We girls were all jealous of the

commitment you showed to Eleni. That virtue alone would probably make up for all of your dreadful weaknesses,' she said.

'You think you're very clever, don't you?' Leo said, prodding her in the ribs.

'Yes – I am the oracle.' She giggled. 'Ask any question and you shall be answered.'

'All right, your problem is that you don't think about anything.'

'Correct,' she said in a deep monotone voice, 'but that is not a question. The oracle can only respond to questions.'

'Oh wise and all-knowing oracle, please tell me what's wrong with thinking?'

'It's a waste of time and it's boring,' Hannah boomed.

'Oh great one, what should one do with one's time?'

'Do.'

'Do?'

'The washing-up will never get done if you think about it. And when the washing-up is done do something else to take your mind off thinking.'

'So action is better than thought?'

'Don't think about it!'

'Thank you oracle, for illuminating me with the blinding power of your ignorance.'

'It's a pleasure, Leo. Now are you ready to go?' Hannah asked impatiently.

'Can the oracle ask questions?'

'The oracle can do what the fuck it likes, smart-arse. Get your shoes on or we'll miss the show.'

Hannah had bought two tickets to see *The Winter's Tale* at the Barbican. It was an unremarkable production until the final act when Leontes stands before a statue of his wife Hermione, who died sixteen years previously. He stares in amazement at the likeness. He draws closer.

> *There is an air comes from her. What fine chisel*
> *Could ever yet cut breath? Let no man mock me,*
> *For I will kiss her.*

Leo, who had never seen or read the play before, felt a bolt in his heart. Immediately he was transported back to Eleni's bedside at the hospital in Ecuador as he tried desperately to resuscitate her. How her raspy breath had simulated life for an instant and brought him joy! Paulina pulls Leontes back: 'You'll mar it if you kiss it'. She offers to cover the statue but Leontes will not let her, he cannot leave its side. Paulina claps her hands: 'be stone no more; approach'. Slowly Hermione comes to life; her dead eyes awaken and look down on Leontes. For a long while he cannot move, but stands in awe. Eventually he raises his arm in disbelief and touches her face.

> *O, she's warm!*
> *If this be magic, let it be an art*
> *Lawful as eating.*

He gasps with such longing, such tenderness that Leo instantly burst into tears. He had played out this scene every night since Eleni's death. Instinctively he grabbed

Hannah's arm and hung on like a rock climber who had lost his footing. The play was over.

'I'm so sorry, what an idiot I am. I wasn't thinking . . .' Hannah apologized.

Leo took a deep breath in an effort to master himself.

'It's all right. It's good for me.'

A young usher interrupted them and asked them to leave the auditorium.

They walked back to Charlie's silently. Hannah remembered how as a girl she had found a baby bird with a broken wing under a tree in the garden. It was tweeting forlornly. She had scooped it up carefully; how utterly helpless it was. Its tiny heart was racing and for the first time she had felt the fragility of life in her own hands, just as now she could feel it in Leo. She had taken the bird to her mother, who had bound its wing to a splint, and over a couple of weeks they had nursed it back to health. When later her mother was diagnosed with cancer Hannah had done everything a ten-year-old could do to help. She had tidied up after herself, looked after her little brother, Ed, brought her mum breakfast in bed, held her hand in hospital, but there was nothing she could do to make her fly again. Her mother had deteriorated rapidly, until one day her father had come out of the bedroom and told Hannah that she was dead. At the end of the play, when Hermione embraced her long-lost daughter Perdita, Hannah had melted into her seat as if into the arms of her own mother.

Back at Charlie's Leo found some ginger cake in the fridge and made a pot of tea. Hannah sat with him on his bed while he showed her all his photos from South America and related his adventures with Eleni. Hannah could be a good listener when she had to be. Patiently she let him paddle woefully back through his story, even though it was the second time she had heard it, and when finally he finished there was a long silence. They stared at each other for a moment.

The evening had triggered an unexpected swell of nostalgia. Hannah looked at her untouched ginger cake. A fortnight after they had released the bird Hannah had returned from school to find a huge cake in the shape of a butterfly on the table. She had wondered what the occasion was. Her mum had sat her down and cut her a slice. 'I need to talk to you, sweetie,' she had said in a quiet voice as she handed it to her. Hannah had skipped lunch and was ravenous. Greedily she had devoured the cake whilst her mother revealed that she had cancer. Hannah's only response had been: 'Can I have another piece, Mum?' Cake had since lost its sweetness, for now she could not disassociate it from death.

Hannah's face flushed, she had to be alone, she grabbed her coat, got up and left abruptly. A few seconds of silence, a blush and a hasty departure. It should have been the most insignificant of events in a friendship, but Leo put a microscope to those few seconds and imagined an entire culture of hidden meaning.

Why had she not broken that silence with words, what was on her lips that she hadn't been able to say out loud? Whatever it was it must have been embarrassing, for why would she blush? And then, of course, she had looked down. No, wait, it had been the other way round, she had looked down and then blushed; so staring at him must have been the source of her embarrassment, and she had had to look away. And what of her leaving without so much as a kiss? She always kissed him goodbye. Perhaps the kiss had suddenly taken on a new importance? Was she harbouring a secret affection for him? If she were would she dare admit it? Eleni had only died three months previously. Hannah and Eleni had been friends. Would Hannah dare step over the grave and declare her love? Leo thought that she wouldn't, which would explain the silence. So that was it. She had fallen in love with him.

For the first time since Eleni's death he allowed himself to consider what it might be like to be with someone else. Hannah was gorgeous, she was witty and compassionate, but he could not imagine having a relationship with her. They were very different people, she had said as much herself; he was intense and she was flippant, besides there was no room in his heart for anyone else. Although he desperately craved warmth and love, he was careful not to mistake his cravings for affection. If he were to start a relationship now it would be for all the wrong reasons.

He persuaded himself that he could not possibly love her, but he would not dismiss from his restless mind the notion that Hannah was in love with him. Every time they met he coloured her words with his suspicion. She gave herself away with her frequent hugs, inappropriate jokes and an apparent willingness to spend long hours listening to the outpourings of his tortured soul. She never once spoke about her feelings, but this, too, Leo interpreted as a sure sign. He even began to pity her; a love that cannot declare itself is a heavy burden to carry.

These thoughts began to infect his reasoning. Confusion seized him. He began to compare her unrequited love with his own. Leo was as unattainable for Hannah as Eleni was for him. I know what she's going through, he thought to himself, maybe I can help her deal with it.

He invited her round for dinner and asked Charlie to go out. He tidied the flat, turned his bed back into a sofa and moved the kitchen table into his room, where there was more space. He bought flowers and candles to make the place look less grim. The previous day he had marinated some chicken breasts, and now he removed the marinade from the fridge, added vegetables for a tagine and slow-cooked it in a clay pot. When Hannah arrived he had already drunk a couple of glasses of wine.

'Wow, Leo!' she said as she came in. 'I was expecting fish fingers in the kitchen as usual. Is it your birthday? Did I forget?'

'No, Hannah, I wanted to thank you for being such a good friend.' Leo could see she was touched. He offered her wine, but she refused, so he poured himself another glass. The meal lurched from one awkward conversation to another. Hannah was less humorous than usual; she was uncomfortable and refused to drink even when Leo opened the second bottle and proclaimed it a particularly good wine. Hannah's edginess did not concern Leo, this was part of the challenge. She was struggling with her feelings for him, looking for the right moment to open up. He asked her several times if there was anything she wanted to talk about; he even asked her if she had met anyone she liked recently. She would not be drawn. She was proving a difficult nut to crack. She had resolved not to confess at any price. Leo would have to adopt a more overt strategy.

Coffee was on the table when Leo broke the unbearable impasse. 'Hannah, do you fancy me?'

'What?'

'I want you to know that it's fine if you do. I mean I know there are a lot of reasons why you wouldn't want to say anything, what with it being so close to Eleni's death and her being a friend of yours . . . but that's just convention. I mean, emotions aren't convenient, you can't control them just because you're supposed to . . . they . . . they pop up at the strangest times and demand to be heard . . . so I thought that you should know that I can handle it and I'm ready for it . . . we can erm, you know, discuss anything you want, Hannah.'

'But I don't.'

'Don't what, Hannah?'

'Fancy you, Leo.'

'Look, I don't mind if you do. Really, it's OK, Hannah. It won't upset me. You know maybe . . . look, I love Eleni but I might like you too.'

Hannah laughed. 'You'll never pull with lines like that.'

'I'm not trying to pull, I just wanted you to know that we can get things into the open . . . that there's no point hiding things from each other. We'll be the stronger for it.'

'Why on earth do you think I fancy you, Leo?'

'Oh come on, Hannah, don't put me through this, you know why. You've made it so obvious.'

'I don't know what you're talking about.'

'All that blushing the other night and running off in a hurry. Come on, Hannah. I told you I don't mind. You see, you're doing it again.'

'What?'

'Blushing, you're blushing right now.'

'Am I? It's because I'm embarrassed, Leo.'

'Oh, thank God, at last you're prepared to admit it.'

'No, you don't understand. I'm embarrassed because you've got it completely wrong. If I was blushing it was because I was thinking about my mum . . . about when she died. The last thing I wanted to do was cry on your shoulder when I was supposed to be helping you deal with your own grief. So I kept it bottled up inside and it got too much. I had to leave before it all came out.'

Leo was crushed. 'Well, why didn't you say so at the time?' he complained.

'I told you I didn't think it was appropriate,' she said.

'But I've poured my heart out to you and the very least you could do is reciprocate . . . you've been patronizing me. It should be equal. I've given so much time, so much of myself to you, and you're giving me nothing in return.'

Hannah shuddered. 'How can you say that? I've spent hours listening to you . . . supporting you . . . I don't know what you want from me . . . you're pissed . . . we'll talk about it tomorrow.'

'I want you to be fucking honest with me like I am with you,' Leo shouted.

'I'm really sorry. I'm going home now. Thank you for a lovely meal,' she said, standing up and reaching for her jacket.

Leo would not let it go. 'There you go again . . . patronizing me . . . It wasn't lovely, it was bloody awful every sodding minute of it. You hated it from the start. Why can't you admit it? Why can't you just be honest for once in your life?'

'Leo . . .'

'No, I won't stop. The problem with you, Hannah, is that you're all bluster and smiles. You're a fake. You never let anyone know what you're thinking. Everyone likes you but no one knows you. That's why you can't hold down a boyfriend . . . it's because you're shit scared that they might get to know you . . . and we can't have that, can we, Hannah? That's why you always go out with jerks who you know you're going to chuck in a month's time. You'd never go out with someone who could actually love you and make you open up, because you're too scared. Admit it . . . go on, admit it.' Leo was off his chair haranguing her all the way to the door. She was crying but he didn't notice.

'I'll speak to you tomorrow,' was all she said as she left the flat. She walked down the stairs with Leo shouting after her. 'If you'd only be honest with me I could help you, Hannah. I could love you. I could show you . . . if

you'd let me. But you wouldn't dare, would you.' Leo
kicked the wall.

Hannah was gone. It was some time before he saw her
again.

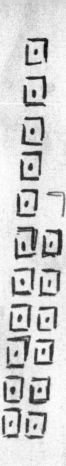

Entry no. 70

Look at every path closely
and deliberately. Try it as
many times as you think
necessary. Then ask yourself
one question... does this path
have a heart? If it does
the path is good; if it
doesn't it is of no use.

Carlos Castaneda

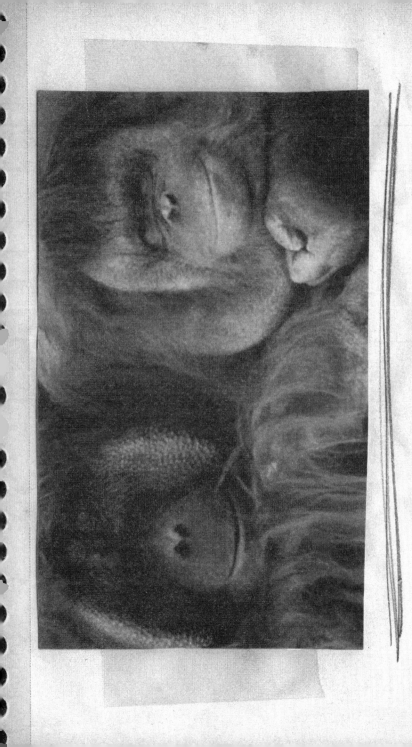

17

I WAS STRANGELY EXCITED TO HAVE BEEN CAPTURED; MY LETTERS to Lotte at the time were full of hope. It may seem odd, Fischel, but capture actually improved my chances of survival no end. For the first time since the war had begun I felt confident that I might come home alive. There were rules governing prisoners of war. We had to be fed, housed and treated humanely. I wanted Lotte to know that I would be safer behind enemy lines than at the front, so all we had to do now was wait until the war ended and we would be wed.

Thank goodness I spoke Russian so well, because it bought me respect and I was often used as a translator. A Russian officer told me to keep hold of my letters until I arrived at my final destination. From there normal POW mailing procedures would apply.

Those early feelings of jubilation were soon dashed. The Russians were overwhelmed by our numbers. They simply couldn't provide for us in the combat zone nor could they transport us quickly to the rear. We were clogging up their supply roads and using up precious resources, so they hastily frog-marched us back through Galicia and gave us a miserly twenty-five kopeks a day to buy our own food from the villagers we passed on the way. It was barely enough to survive on.

It took twelve days to get to Lemberg and I was followed every step of the way by Király. We were no longer obliged by company rules to march together and yet he shadowed me like a stray dog. At first I found his presence irritating, but the daily tedium wore down my resistance to him and we began to talk. Király was a man who needed a wall to kick against, he needed to hear himself shout and complain to know that he was alive. Put Király on a beach with a beer and a cigarette and he would still moan. This was his way; he was happiest when most provocative. He would push and push until he got you riled, and then he would laugh in pleasure at his victory. I learnt to humour him and even enjoy his offensive outbursts. If I reasoned with him he would weary of me, but if I insulted him he would rub his hands together and show me his crooked teeth in a twisted smile. I disliked everything he stood for, and he despised me for what he called my 'pathetic romantic inclinations'. So a friendship grew, borne of mutual hatred.

In Lemberg there was a rail connection to Kiev and we were shifted by the trainload to a huge POW holding station on the outskirts of the city where the Czechs, Slovaks and Southern Slavs were separated and transported to nearby camps. The rest of us were herded into freight wagons and sent further east. These *teplushka*, as they were known, had been fitted with a few wooden bunks, a stove and a solitary latrine bucket. There were forty of us to a car, wounded and non-wounded alike. We were on this train for weeks, cooped up like chickens, stewing in the stench of our own waste. Every foul, biting, crawling and flying insect in Russia seemed to sniff its way into our *teplushka*. The walls were a parade of cockroaches and fleas. There were lice, mites, and great flies that would swoop in and out of the latrine bucket and spread invisible particles of excrement all over us, causing sickness and disease. My body covered over in sores and mysterious rashes and as usual I was the first to come down with diarrhoea and vomiting, which of course made our intimate hell more intolerable. I thought of Lotte's letter in which she had written of the need to keep one's dignity. In the *teplushka* the most dignified thing a man could do was maintain his humour and morale for the sake of the others. So we sang, told jokes and swapped anecdotes of our disasters in the field. These last were often recounted with a light-heartedness that masked the horror of the events.

Sometimes we spent days stuck on sidings with nothing to eat, wondering whether we had been left to die. Then without any warning the doors would open, a guard would throw in some black bread, we would roll out a corpse or two in exchange, empty our festering bucket, and the train would lurch forward again. The journey east was broken up by various stopovers where we would be put up in some converted brewery or theatre, while petty

Russian bureaucrats agonized over what to do with us. Inevitably after a month or so we found ourselves back on the trans-Siberian railway. One day in November the train came to a definitive screeching halt, I could hear voices yelling down the platform. The doors rolled open, a blast of cold air rushed in and we stumbled out once more into the unfamiliar daylight.

'Where are we? Have we arrived?' we asked each other. I looked about me and saw the name Sretensk written in Cyrillic on a station signpost. I had never heard of it but I was sure we were somewhere in Siberia. It was several days before we realized we were in the triangle where North-Eastern Mongolia, China and Russia meet in the Chita province some seven thousand kilometres east of Moscow. I was a world away from Lotte.

Sretensk POW camp was an out-of-use summer camp designed for a few hundred soldiers but soon to be the home of ten thousand Austro-Hungarians. There were two parts to the camp: a military barracks in the town itself and a collection of decrepit wooden and brick buildings on the opposite bank of the Shilka River. I was taken to the latter, and what was so startling about our arrival there was that the place was empty. We were the first arrivals, and by the look of the dusty, unswept floor no one had stayed there for quite some time. Nor was there much by way of facilities: the kitchens were under-equipped and there was not nearly enough bed space for all of us. The only water supply was from the frozen river to which one had to descend a slippery steep bank with a hammer and bucket. The toilet situation was no better than the train. It appeared no preparations had been made for us whatsoever; even our guards did not know their way around the place.

The sleeping quarters consisted of two long wooden platforms one above the other running along the walls. These platforms were our beds, the occasional ladder giving access to the top bunks. Our dormitory was also our dining room and parlour. I bedded down with Király on the bottom bunk, and the space was so cramped that we all had to sleep on our sides like spoons in a drawer, with our knees tucked up under the next man's bottom. We were terribly thirsty that first evening after our long trek, but with no water some bright spark had the idea of breaking off ice from the windows, so we sat there licking water lollies like overgrown children and there was much merriment and song. But reality soon hit and the grit of daily survival robbed us of humour.

Occasionally we were ordered to carry water up from the river or to cut logs, both of which were gruelling in sub-zero conditions. Otherwise we hung around with little to do other than smoke or crush the lice that crept into our clothes and flick them on the floor. The vile stench of buckwheat porridge, stale tobacco, damp laundry and filthy men was all-pervading. But when I opened the window to clear the air, a blast of icy Siberian wind rushed through the barracks and immediately condensed into a misty vapour which settled over our bedclothes and made them wet. The men were furious with me and the window was never opened again, and so we mulched in our own rancid juices throughout the winter.

I expected at the very least to be able to keep clean but the bathhouse was run by a little Russian guard called Spansky who would not let anyone bathe unless they tipped him on entry. Some soldiers, especially the NCOs, could afford to pay each day, but most of us went very sparingly and some never went at all. When I was desperate I would pour tea on to a flannel and wipe myself down with it.

Corruption and bribery was a way of life in Russia and the camp was no different. If you had the money you could even buy butter or sugar from one of the guards. It cost me half my weekly stipend to bribe the postman to do his job and post a letter for me. I wrote more letters than I could afford to post. At least when I was writing those wasted letters I felt connected to my loved ones, even if this was in reality a fiction. Each month I selected one letter to post and kept the others in case the opportunity came to send them later. Even the bribe could not guarantee delivery; the mail service was notoriously bad and all letters were censored. Incoming packages always arrived open with half their contents missing. In all my time in Sretensk I received only one letter, and it came from my parents. They said that life under the Russians had been very difficult, and that the old Jews who stayed were treated as spies and often lynched. That Polish peasants from the countryside had moved into vacated Jewish properties and that even when the Austrians retook Galicia and the Jews returned, these peasants had refused to move out. That there were legal actions pending but now an atmosphere of intimidation and hostility was tearing the community apart. Accusations of treachery and theft were flying in all directions. The worst part of all was that during the occupation the Steinberg mansion had become a billet for Russian officers, and in May they had set fire to it before retreating. The Steinbergs had returned to find their house in ruins and all their possessions gone. They were now living in their factory while Mr Steinberg tried to build his business again. My parents said they no longer felt safe, but they did have some good news to report, and that was that all my brothers and sisters were safe in Berlin. They said they had sent me some warm clothes and some Sarotti bonbons but they must have been stolen en route because the package was empty.

Time slowed to a crawl and I sank deeper and deeper into depression. Day and night merged into one endless cycle of tedium. There was nothing to distinguish one day from the next. I began to doubt that I would ever see Lotte again. Ulanow might well have been back in Austrian hands but there were no signs of surrender. My mind latched on to Lotte as a drowning man clings to a raft. I relived every moment that I had spent with her, retraced every step of every walk along the San, replayed every conversation again and again until my head ached and the memories streamed into each other. I clung on to her letters and read and reread them, digging deeper and deeper into every word to see what lay beneath them. I tried to imagine where she was sitting when she wrote those words, the position of her legs, the curve of her body, the angle of her hands to the paper, the fall of her hair. I lived her letters to the final full stop. I packed her bags with her and loaded the cart when she left Ulanow, and I trudged through the mud at her side worrying about her when she lost her footing. I laughed with her when her father was selling furs from his cart. I lay with her under the bear hide and sank into her sweet-smelling skin. She permeated my dreams.

Then I began to suffer strange physical side effects. I found it increasingly difficult to swallow. My stomach distended and I couldn't defecate. Soon I began to splutter and over-heat. I stopped getting out of bed in the morning. When finally I woke up with my torso covered in red spots I knew I had typhus. It was my great fortune that, as usual, I was one of the first to be struck by the epidemic, for at least I was given a proper bed. Those who caught it later were not so lucky. I found myself in the hospital building. I don't know how I got there, because by then I was delirious and obsessive. Lotte was flying and spinning before me. Sometimes she was inside me, sometimes she was dead; now she was eating my innards like a rabid dog, now she was caressing me. I had the odd flow of lucidity in which I saw other patients lying on the floor or leaning against the wall next to my bed waiting for me to die, for indeed I was slowly ebbing away. One night a fire raged inside me and I saw Lotte in flames, a tremendous heat burned through me, and my lungs clogged up with smoke. I could hardly breathe; I had to escape. My every pore craved water and cold. I must have rolled out of bed and crawled to the door gasping for an icy Siberian wind to cool me, for in a flash I realized that I was at the entrance of the building and the hospital was on fire. An orderly found me and carried me to safety. There was great clamour and shouting and the camp woke from its slumber. The water supply was all used up fighting the fire but it was not sufficient to extinguish it. The men ran down to the river and smashed through the ice layer that had formed overnight. They hauled out water by the bucket-load and passed it along human chains up towards the hospital. But by the time they had got it there our hospital had been razed to the ground. It was never rebuilt.

The following day I was put in a makeshift infirmary that had been set up in a few rooms. My new bed was by a window overlooking the hill behind the camp. I saw a man pulling a sledge towards a small wooden outhouse halfway up. It was difficult at first to make out exactly what was on the sledge because the ice lay so thick on the window that it made everything blurry, but when the man arrived at the door he leant down and with great effort dragged his charge across the snow and rolled it into the outhouse. By its weight and shape I realized that it was a body. Further up the hill, a fire burnt day and night. The next day more sledges arrived at the little house and more bodies were piled up inside. The traffic steadily increased, and then after a week or so a work party of men carrying spades marched up the hill to where the fire still burnt. The frozen ground had thawed enough for them to turn their spades in the soil. So they put out the fire, dug a mass grave and, without ceremony, emptied in the now-rigid corpses from the house.

I was so close to death that the orderlies had already been through my pockets to see what was worth stealing and Király came to pay his last respects. This was a fool-hardy thing to do – no one in their right mind would visit the typhus ward for fear of catching it themselves – so Király's appearance was particularly touching. For the first time ever he addressed me by my first name.

'Moritz, you stupid arse,' he said, 'I curse the miserable day I had the misfortune of meeting you. You were always a useless piece of shit and now you're going to be a dead piece of shit. They're going to chuck you in that cesspit on the hill with the rest of your gut-rotting compatriots and I won't be sorry to see you go. No, Moritz, I won't miss you for a minute. Anyway I've come to say goodbye and fuck off . . . Well haven't you got anything to say for yourself, you bastard, or are you just going to slide off without a word?'

I was shivering uncontrollably and something that felt like a knife pressed into my kidneys. I could not speak but I was able to raise my hand and give him the finger. Király was delighted. 'That's the spirit, Moritz!' he roared, and he left the ward laughing . . . Oh dear . . . talking about it is bringing back the symptoms . . . Fischel, please hold out the spittoon for me . . . thank you, my boy . . . urgh . . . look away . . . I'm sorry. Perhaps you could fetch me a bucket and a cloth. I'm in a sweat, I need to cool down . . . thank you . . . Oh, and Fischel, could you bring Dovid and Isaac in? I would like to see them.

Entry no. 25

The eel is carried away, despite
itself, by a great current from
its birthplace in the Sargasso Sea
near Bermuda. Eventually it finds
itself thousands of miles away in
Europe, where it matures in freshwater
streams, sometimes climbing high
into the Alps or reaching the
Black Sea. But after several years
the urge to go home and spawn
becomes insuperable. Using some
unknown navigation system eels
will climb out of ponds and wriggle
across fields, if they have to, until
they find a stream that will lead
them to the sea. There they stop
feeding and swim as fast as they
can. Within six months they are
back in the Sargasso. At last they
spawn and then, perhaps because
their life's work is done or because
of exhaustion, they die.

18

AH, MY THREE BOYS, I'M GLAD YOU ARE ALL HERE. COME, Fisch, pass Izzy to me. There you go, little one. Lie there. Always asleep, so quickly asleep. Lucky boy . . . Dovid, you can play with your train in the corner if you like. You two little ones will understand nothing of all this other than that you are loved, but you, Fischel, must take note and explain it to your brothers when they are older and, in time, to your own children. So where was I? I can't remember. Ah yes, Sretensk. As I lay on that bed in Sretensk I had never been further from Lotte and I had never been so close to death. The corpses were piling up outside my window, there were dying men on the floor next to my bed, even under my bed, waiting for me to be thrown on the heap so they could have one last feel of a mattress before joining me. The war still raged with no end in sight. There were many who thought it would not end in their lifetime and that they would spend the rest of their lives in Siberia. I was staring into the tunnel of death and it did not look unattractive. The pain I felt was so

227

acute that I was ready to give my life to make it stop. I slipped into a strange state of unconsciousness that was neither coma nor sleep. I felt myself rising upwards through space, the pain was gone and I could see myself lying on the bed as if from above. Ahead of me was a bright light, indeed so bright it was impossible to look at. I felt as if I was accelerating up towards it, leaving my body far behind.

Now, I have heard from people who came close to death that they saw their whole life pass before them, but for me it was different. I saw children, dozens of them. They were naked, their eyes were as clear as mountain water and their beauty was indescribable. At first I thought they were the angels and cherubs of heaven, but then they started calling me 'Daddy, Grandpa, Great-grandpa', and I understood that these children were my children and my grandchildren and my grandchildren's children. They did not look as I now know you to be, but there was a Fischel, a Dovid and an Isaac amongst them. These children – you – were my future and I knew that you needed me. I tried to reach out to you and hug you, but though I was moving towards you and you were standing still I could not touch you. I realized that I would never reach you this way. I had to go back. I had to live.

Sometimes the future visits us and tells us what we should be. We think that we are in control of our destiny, that we are walking towards it. We think we are following our ambition, but perhaps it is the other way round and our future is hauling us in like fish on the end of a rod. Certainly that is how it felt to me, and I thank you for it.

When I came to my senses there was no doubt in my mind that I would survive. I had turned the corner and there was fire in my belly. I would not wait for the war to end; I would escape and find my way home. I would go as soon as I had my strength.

With the arrival of spring a new lease of life came to the camp. The men had resigned themselves to a lengthy stay. The news from the front spoke of stalemate. In the west, trenches had been dug and the French and British were fighting huge battles with the Germans over a few metres of territory. In the east, the Russians had been pushed out of Poland but the Germans did not have the resources to advance.

We had so much time on our hands that a kind of university sprang up in Sretensk. Virtually everything was taught there, from history to engineering. I taught Russian to the Germans, the Germans taught German to the Hungarians, but nobody wanted to learn Hungarian. I learnt how to carve wood and make cabinets from a Viennese craftsman. I made that chair you're sitting on, Fischel, and that cupboard over there; in fact everything I make in the workshop I learnt in Sretensk. Books flooded into the camps from the various Red Cross agencies and we were able to organize a little library. In the evenings we could listen to the camp choir or watch theatre shows, a thing I had never seen before. We had political debates and played every board and card game known to man.

I was still weak and could not do any hard labour, but

when the thaw came in May Király and many others were sent out to build roads or work on farms. These men kept the Siberian economy alive in the absence of the Russian workers who were still at the front. They also kept the womenfolk happy. Király would come back from his farm stays with lurid stories of peasant girls he had deflowered in haystacks . . . Oh, you find that funny, do you, Fischel? You too will understand such pleasures before long; although you will have to go a few kilometres from Berlin to find a haystack. Király said that someone had to do it while the Russian boys were at war. Apparently Siberian women were much less prudish than European women, a claim substantiated by many others, in particular a certain breed of Hungarian male who prided himself on his voracious womanizing. Király insisted that no man was a man unless he exercised his sexual function. I found his tales both amusing and educational, for I had never seduced a woman and Király took great pleasure in divulging detail.

Király's German greatly improved in Sretensk; it was unusual for Hungarian peasants to speak any German at all and even rarer for them to be fluent. I wondered where he had picked it up from in the first place. I discovered that his mother had been an Austrian, hence the name Frantz. His father was a cruel man who had beaten him senseless as a child, before leaving his mother for another woman when Frantz was twelve. His mother had become an alcoholic, they had been saddled with debt and their house had fallen into neglect. He had joined the army as soon as he could.

*　　*　　*

I was biding my time, getting stronger every day. I worked in the kitchens making kasha which was our staple diet. It is a buckwheat soup laced with pig fat. Don't look so shocked, Fischel, all the Jews ate it; a hungry man must eat. I even ate the scraps because all I wanted was to be strong. I did it for Lotte. I did everything for Lotte. It was not healthy but it kept me alive. I was still writing scores of letters, which were never posted. I was saving my money for the escape, besides, the Russian postal service had virtually collapsed and I did not have an address for her after her house burnt down. These letters were ever more nostalgic and passionate since I knew she would never read them.

Dear Lotte,
For a whole week I have thought only of the curve of your cheek and the lushness of your lips . . .

Dear Lotte,
Do you remember that time when the snow was so deep that the Kaminskys couldn't open their front door and we spent hours playing roly-poly down the hill?

Dearest Lotte,
Please wait for me, oh God please wait for me. I am sick without you. Don't go with another man, please, I'll die if you do.

Dear Lotte,
Last night I buried my nose in the soft fur of your waistcoat
where your body once lay, and breathed you in . . .

I was teaching Király to play chess and we spent many hours playing and arguing. I always won the games but I often lost the arguments. I could never quite work out what made Király tick, so I would challenge him over chess.

Once I asked him, 'What do you think about at the quietest moment in the middle of the night? The last moment before you sleep?'

'What? What are you talking about?' He was pondering his next move.

'You know, the one thought that holds up all the others, the one you can't ever escape from. The one which is you,' I probed.

Király lifted his eyes for a moment from the board and reflected. 'I think about death. I see death in the faces of the men, I see it in the snow and I see it in the blood-red battlefields of Europe. Even I am death. I live but I am dead, my life is useless, a waste. Knight takes pawn.'

'So why live – what for?' I asked.

'Oh, it's just a bad habit I got into,' he said. 'Play, you're losing.' His position was far weaker than he thought and I put him in check. 'Hmm,' he mused, 'I missed that.' And then he turned on me, as I knew he would. 'And as for you, you don't even have to tell me, the whole camp knows, it's your damn Lotte. Writing letters to the snow. Waste of time. And if you ever get home, what makes you think she won't have married someone else? She's probably fucking someone else right now, just like these little Russian girls.'

Excuse my language, Fischel, it was as shocking to me then as it is to you now. I could not hide my fury. 'My God, Frantz, you really are a pig,' I shouted. 'It's true I live on hope. Why shouldn't I? Every day I see her beauty while you rot in hell. You will tell me that I'm deluded but we are all deluded in some way. The question is which is the best delusion.'

'Oh ho,' Király mocked, 'Moritz the dreamer. One day the wind will leave your sails and you will see the world the way it is.'

'Maybe, but I will not be in here when it happens. I have to get to Lotte before my heart breaks.'

I should never have said such a thing in front of Király, it was fuel to his fire. He burst out laughing.

'And what are you going to do? Escape? From Siberia? You are mad. You will perish in the snow blizzard like all the other dreamers before you. Don't you see? The guards won't even chase you; you will just be one less to deal with. Moritz, you can't do it because it's impossible.'

He looked down at the board and realized his position was lost but the argument had been won. He was right: it was impossible.

There were two ways to escape, south into China or west through Russia. We had been warned by our own government not to attempt to go into China because we would be captured and treated much worse than under the

Russians. Rumour had it that the Buryats of Mongolia were so ruthless they would murder you for a silver button. We could not know whether this was true or not, but for sure a white man in China was easy to find. Most attempted escapes thus far had been to the west and by the summer of 1916 no one had succeeded. Those who had left in winter had been found frozen to death a couple of days' walk from the camp. Those who had escaped after the thaw had either been robbed by Cossacks and turned in, or captured by policemen tipped off by Russian villagers hostile to the Central Powers. I had only one advantage over all those who had failed and that was that I could speak Russian. I would bide my time and wait for the right moment.

As winter drew in there was a feeling of unrest amongst the prison guards. Inflation was so high that their salaries were becoming worthless. The Siberian grain producers began hoarding their grain because it was no longer profitable to market it and consequently European Russia, which was dependent on it, began to starve. When things started getting bad in Moscow and Petrograd the tsar got blamed for it. Even the army were losing faith in him. The front-line soldiers were demoralized and under-equipped. Imagine, Fisch, some of them were fighting bare-footed.

We were now receiving Bolshevik propaganda written in German and Hungarian and specifically targeting prisoners of war. They saw us as their natural allies in the struggle against the nobility of Europe. Our political debates during the long winter months became particularly heated. Many of the prisoners and guards were sympathetic to the cause of Bolshevism. They began to organize themselves and talked of revolution. This was froth, it would never happen as far as I was concerned. The tedium of camp life often brought debate to extremes. I shared the Bolshevik belief that the working man had become the plaything of the landed aristocracy, but I felt the people of Europe were sick to death of war, and did not have the stomach to wage a civil one as well.

How wrong I was. In March 1917 we were in our dormitories eating kasha when an Austrian activist prisoner burst in. He had just been in town and was breathless with excitement.

'Comrades,' he announced, 'revolution is in the air. I just heard the tsar has abdicated.' The room erupted in shouts of jubilation; more men came crashing in from other dormitories until ours was packed to the rafters. Everyone wanted to know if this meant the war was over. The Austrian brought the room to order with a wave of his hands. 'No,' he said. 'A provisional government has been declared, but look who the new ministers are: Prince Lvov, Milyukov, Guchkov and Kerensky. All members of the tsar's duma greedy for power. But who are they really, if not puppets of the ruling classes? This is no revolution but a bourgeois palace coup, there will be no land reform. Kerensky may call himself leader of the socialist revolutionary party, but really he is no better than the tsar because he too vows to continue this futile war, he too promises to use the workers as cannon fodder. The war still rages. Millions are dead. Our only hope is the Bolsheviks. It is now only a question of time before they take control. Every day the Bolsheviks are gaining support. They are calling for all Russian soldiers to stop fighting, and to join the workers in the great struggle. Landowners and officers are class enemies, their orders should not be obeyed. When the Bolsheviks take power they have promised to free all prisoners of war so that we too may join the revolution. Only the Bolsheviks will put an end to this futile war. The time has come to eliminate the ruling classes of Europe who have made our lives such a misery for so long.'

A prisoner at the back of the room shouted, 'Long live the Bolsheviks, long live the revolution!' And a throng of voices repeated the call. By now the guards had been alerted and were standing unnoticed in the doorway.

Frantz Király was on his feet. 'Propaganda. Rubbish,' he shouted. 'The Bolsheviks will be lucky to take Moscow but it will be years before they reach Siberia. And we will be here for ever.'

'Don't listen to this idiot. Let's go to Moscow. Who is with me?' the Austrian retorted. There was uproar as the men argued with each other.

A German took the floor. 'Why should we join the Russian working man, when he is our enemy? No, what we must do now is take the camp by storm. The Russian regime is weakening, imagine if every camp in Siberia was overthrown: we would be doing a service to the fatherland. We could be an army a million strong. It would hasten the end of the war.' There was a clamour of approval. The guards did not understand us but the atmosphere was becoming too heated for them, they barged their way in and one of them fired his rifle in the air. The room fell silent. The guard spoke in a quiet, assertive voice. No one understood him but the sense of threat was clear.

The Austrian asked if anyone could translate and Király pushed me forward. 'He says, try and escape if you want, and if you don't get shot by us you'll perish in the snow. No one has ever survived out there.'

As the day wore on we witnessed arguments among the guards. Some had not been paid for weeks and simply went home. Rumour was rife and the old colonel who was a tsarist through and through called his men together and ordered them to remain loyal to the old regime. There was such confusion that none of the guards went about their normal duty. This was the chance I'd been waiting for. That night as the other prisoners slept I packed my haversack. I had procured civilian clothing from the Red Cross and stolen two large salamis and some kasha from the kitchen.

Király saw me and whispered, 'What are you doing?'

'I'm leaving. I am going to walk straight out of the front gate. There's no one there,' I said excitedly.

'Don't be a fool, Moritz, where the hell are you going to go? This is March. It is still freezing – we are miles from anywhere. Only a madman would dream of escape. You heard what the guard said. You'll die out there. Here at least you have a roof over your head.'

'I'd rather die out there trying to get home than fester in here waiting for the Bolsheviks to free us, because it might never happen. Now is the time to go, the place is in turmoil, no one knows what's going on, or who to be loyal to. They are not going to worry about an escapee for the next few days,' I reasoned.

'Don't let hope blind you,' Király pleaded. But I would hear no more of it. I picked up my bag and walked out. Frantz came hurtling after me and grabbed me by the arm. 'Wait, Moritz . . . you can't leave without me,' he begged.

I was amazed. 'What do you mean?'

'I'm coming with you,' he said.

'I'm not asking you to come, Frantz. Besides, you think it's a stupid idea.'

'Please, Moritz, please let me come.' He was tugging at my coat.

It was extraordinary to see this big oafish man reduced to grovelling like a child. He had not done this since his father walked out on him when he was a boy. His eyes softened, the edge had left his voice. 'I'll go mad here without you,' he said forlornly. 'I have no friends, Moritz, you're the only one. I am dead without you. I'll bring the chessboard, I have to beat you at least once in my lifetime.'

I thought of all the reasons why Király would be a terrible liability. He didn't speak Russian, he was aggressive, and he whinged incessantly. But I was frightened and did not want to go alone so I relented. 'All right,' I said, 'get your things.'

He was so delighted he put his arms around me and hugged me. Just like a little boy. Then he scampered back into the dormitory, pilfered what he could from the sleeping men, stuffed his backpack and came back to me with a cheeky grin on his face. I had never seen him look so happy.

We made our way to the unguarded entrance of the camp and slipped out into the white night of Siberia. From now on each step would bring me closer to Lotte. My heart was dancing.

Entry no. 19

Emperor Penguins walk inland
together through miles of frozen
Antarctic wasteland. Then in some
desolate spot they mate and the
males are left carrying the precious
eggs between their legs whilst the
females go in search of food. As
the temperatures plummet the
males huddle together to share
their body heat, taking it in turns
to face the ice-cold winds and
endless night of winter.

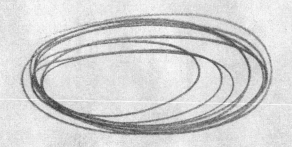

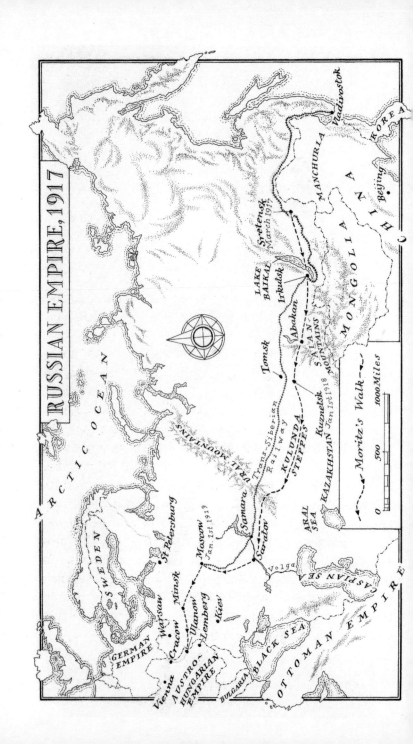

19

NOW SON, FETCH THE MAP OF RUSSIA. GOOD BOY. SO find Lake Baikal, you can't miss it . . . a little blue crescent above Mongolia. Now my plan was to get to the town of Irkutsk to the west and the quickest way was to cross Baikal while it was still frozen. Otherwise we would have had to walk an extra three hundred kilometres round the edge. Believe it or not it doesn't thaw out until May so we still had a couple of months to get there. In March when we set off it can still drop to minus 20 degrees centigrade, though a Siberian would tell you that it was warming up because in January you get minus 40. The worst was past, but the cold was still a big threat. Looking back I would say the timing of our escape was fortuitous because within days of our escape the provisional government ordered a vicious crackdown on POW camp security and began a virulent anti-German campaign. Rumour had it that captured escapees would be killed or at least tortured. If we had been heard talking German it would have been the end of us.

We had not been gone ten minutes when Király suggested we spend the night in Sretensk. He had some unfinished business with the young wife of a kulak whose wheat field he had harvested in the absence of her husband. I was regretting his presence already. We were barely out of earshot of the camp and we were at each other's throats arguing.

'Is that the real reason why you wanted to come? So that you could have your way with a Russian peasant? We'll be back in there by morning if we go into town. The place is crawling with soldiers,' I yelled.

'Don't you get it, you stupid Polish, Jewish, son of a lousy cobbler? She'll give us food. How far are we going to get on two bloody sausages and a flask of kasha?'

'It's not the food you want, you lying sod, it's her womanly charms, and you're prepared to risk my life to get them, because you don't care about anyone other than yourself. I should have known that when you watched me kill Jerzy Ingwer. What was I thinking letting you escape with me? You'd kill me for my waistcoat. You're worse to me than the enemy,' I cursed.

'I admit it, Moritz, I want to give it to her. Just like you want to give it to Lotte. Of course I do. What's wrong with that? The only difference is that you're going to have to walk ten thousand kilometres to get your oats and I can get mine right here. And by God I'm going to stuff her good and proper and the memory of it will keep me going to Hungary,' he scoffed.

'Hungary? Don't make me laugh, you're not even going to cross the Amur. You're nothing but a liability, and I wash my hands of you. Go to Sretensk if you must but go alone. We part ways here. Goodbye, Frantz.' And I stormed off.

Király came running after me.

'Oh no, not so fast, Moritz. Think about it for a minute. We don't have to cross town to get to her place; she has a good-sized plot right on the edge. She's wealthy by local standards and she has a larder full of food. If we can take a sledge from her and stock up for a month we might make it to Irkutsk. How the hell else are we going to get there without stopping in every village? It's worth taking the chance. Come on, Moritz.'

I hesitated. Now he was talking sense. But he mis-understood my silence. 'Oh, you're jealous! All right we'll share her, if that's what you want. She won't mind. Now tell me that isn't a good offer. Food, sex and a roof over your head.'

'You are an animal, Király, remember that. You are an animal and I am a human being. Don't ever confuse the two. I don't want your whore, but I agree that if we can get our hands on food we have a better chance of surviving. So let's go.'

Király had won again.

The woman heard the stones at her window, saw Király and came to the door in her bedclothes all excited. She was a handsome woman with broad shoulders and long wispy blond hair. She welcomed us in and blathered on at Király in Russian. She had been thinking about him and wanted to thank him again for saving her harvest.

He was better than ten Russians, he was so big and strong and more and more, none of which I bothered to translate. It was probably a good thing that they didn't understand each other. All she knew was that he had worked hard for her and saved her from destitution. Each day she had seen the soil on his hands and smelt the sweat on his back and she knew that no man would work harder for her. Király was a genuine farm labourer and not some soft-bellied POW teacher or peddler who pootled about the field like a pregnant pig. Of course, if she had been an old spinster he would not have gone to half the trouble.

Király duly got his reward and insisted that we stay another day. I must admit that I was happy to suffer their grunting and wailing a second night for the luxury of being in a room of my own in a proper bed. There was fresh linen and a fire in the room. I bathed in hot water from the stove and slept better than I had for three years. Heaven comes in simple pleasures.

Király would have stayed a third night if I had let him. As it was he finally agreed that we had to leave. The kulak woman, like most of the peasants, had been stockpiling her harvest, hoping for the prices to pick up. She had sheds full of food, and we loaded up a sledge with grain, potatoes, carrots, apples and many loaves of fresh bread which she had specially baked for us over the two days. She gave Király her husband's coat, a few bottles of vodka and an axe.

We trudged fifteen kilometres a day following the route of the trans-Siberian railway towards Lake Baikal. We never got too close for fear of being seen but made sure that we could hear the trains when they passed. The terrain was never-ending taiga: hilly, thickly forested with coniferous trees and nothing else. Wherever we looked it was the same to the horizon. The only interruption to the monotony was the occasional village that looked like an oasis in the desert. What we would have given to walk through those villages! Our eyes throbbed in the dazzling whiteness of snow and sky. It would have been restful merely to gaze on faces and buildings, to hear children's voices and to walk on cobbles. But we had to steer well clear of all that. I had learnt from the travelling merchants in my family how to build a lean-to from the branches and leaves of coniferous trees. Uncle Josef had taught me how to build a fire that would last the night and where to place it to keep the lean-to warm, and he had shown me how to navigate by the Pole Star after dark and in daylight by looking for where the moss grew thickest on trees.

For forty days we ploughed through this whitewashed wilderness and I swear we bickered every step of the way. We quarrelled about every conceivable detail of our tawdry existence: whose turn it was to pull the sledge in the morning, where to stop, when to stop, how much wood to gather for the fire, whose mess tin to use for cooking, how much snow to melt in the soup, when to eat one of our precious apples. Sometimes we would argue about the futility of the last argument we had just had, and on one occasion we were so mad at each other that we did not speak for three days. But no matter how much we professed to hate each other we always went to sleep in each other's arms because our survival depended on it.

The full ferocity of the Siberian winter had passed but there was a sting in its tail. When the northerlies blew they still blasted through our clothes and chilled our bones; they could still knock us off our feet and blind us in a blizzard. We never felt warm, and the cold began to nibble at my kidneys, which had never fully recovered from the typhus. Király began to moan about his feet; he had been ranting about the cold since we left, which was irritating enough given how futile it was to complain about the weather, but now his whinging took on dramatic new proportions even by his standards.

'Damn these useless, threadbare socks and the whore that knitted them, damn these pox-ridden bits of cow's arse and every flea-bitten labourer that laid his filthy fingers on them and dared to call them boots. Damn that drunken rotten mutton of a woman that called herself my mother and that fat-fisted mastiff of a man that stuck his dog-eared cock inside her. Damn them both for ejaculating me on to this windy septic bog of a planet full of loathing and death. Damn everything because my feet are frozen, do you hear me Daniecki? My feet are falling off, my feet have no feeling, why don't you care, you foreskin-hating fool? My feet are on fire. Oh Mary, mother of Christ, heal your humble God-fearing friend Király – that's Frantz Király, born in Sarospatak, Hungary 1897 – yes, me, heal me, don't make a mistake, don't go healing some dim-witted Romanian, do you hear me? Me.

Just me. And you can forget Daniecki, too, he doesn't even believe in you.'

And he would repeat and refine this tirade for hours on end as if it were some kind of mantra. I never took him seriously – not for a minute. On the contrary the more florid his insults the more they made me laugh, which enraged him, and led to more outrageous damnation. It was only when I noticed him limping and heard him sobbing in his sleep that I promised to carry out a proper inspection. It was a still night, the fire was roaring, the soup was cooking, Király was sitting on the sledge with his left leg stretched out in front of him, his foot resting on a rock. The sole of his boots had worn right down and there was a hole where the stitch-work on his uppers had come away. I untied the bindings and carefully loosened the boot; he winced and again cursed the Austrian cow for giving its hide to such a lousy piece of footwear. I tried to pull it off but it seemed to be stuck to his foot and he howled in agony. Snow had got into his boot. Foot and boot were frozen together. Together we rolled the rock nearer to the fire and he propped his foot up again as near to the heat as he could bear. Soon there was steam rising up from the toe and water dripping down the heel. I pulled again and this time the boot came off in my hands. His toes were sticking up rigid inside his socks as if he were stretching them. When I touched them they were cold and solid. I peeled off the first of his three socks; it was damp. With the second one the smell of rotting skin hit my nostrils. The third sock was impossible to remove: it had partly disintegrated and partly encrusted to his foot.

Bits of sodden wool hung off his scaly, blistered heel. Király was whimpering at the sight of it. He feared the worst. I took out my knife and cut carefully down the length of the sock to his big toe where the material was still frozen and clung tenaciously to his skin. Then I tugged at it until it came away in my hands. I winced at the sight that greeted me. The lower part of his foot was black. A white furry fungus covered all his toenails bar the big one, such that it was impossible to distinguish one toe from another. We had both seen this before in the Carpathians. It was a severe frostbite that had gone septic, and gangrene was setting in.

'My God, Frantz, why didn't you say something?' I asked.

'Very funny,' he said bitterly.

There was not much we could do until we got to Irkutsk. Király insisted that there was no point trying to thaw out his foot because it was known that a man with frostbite could still walk some distance, whereas once the foot was reheated it was much more painful and impossible to walk on for a while. Besides it would only freeze again over the next few days. I gave Király my spare socks and carved him a pair of crutches. From then on our progress was very slow, as he hobbled from hill to hill requiring frequent rests.

One day we trekked up a hill that looked like every other snow-covered hill but when we got to the top the land gave way before us and there was the vast and magnificent Lake Baikal. It was the end of April 1917 and the snow was melting but the lake was still frozen. I bounded down the hill in excitement with the sledge in tow. At the edge of the lake there were huge craggy edifices of ice that jutted upwards and outwards at strange angles pointing accusingly at the sky. These icy fingers must have been formed as the winter freeze sank deeper and deeper in the lake and the new ice pushed against the old ice, making it splinter and crack at the banks. But the centre of the lake was as smooth as a Viennese rink. I flicked one of the icicles with my finger and it responded by playing a beautiful clear note. Each icicle had a different song to sing. As I waited for Király to join me I amused myself by playing out a little tune. A surge of confidence swept through me. We had escaped and survived the winter, spring was a breath away and the most desolate and hostile terrain was behind us. It would not be my last winter in Siberia but the worst was past. At that moment under the blue skies of Baikal, I was happy merely to be alive and to know where I was going.

Király, on the other hand, was now so miserable he had even stopped cursing. His silence was tragic. He toiled down the hill like a great tortoise, his back arched like a shell over his crutches and his head rolling back and forth. There was a pained grimace etched on his face. He was so exhausted now that his breath was heaving and his bad leg dragged limply in the snow behind him.

I shouted up to him, 'We've made it, Frantz.'

When Király eventually joined me he slumped down on the sledge and waited until he had stopped wheezing. 'Made what exactly? We've made it to a frozen lake in the middle of nowhere. We've walked forty days and we're still six thousand kilometres from home.'

'Yes, but we're alive.'

'Barely.'

And then he looked hard at me and spoke from his heart: 'Moritz, I don't know where you get your energy from. Look at you, you're playing like a kid while I'm freezing to death. You move too fast for me. I'm holding you back. I can't go much further. I have to stop. There is a child in you that refuses to die. When I first met you I thought your naivety bordered on stupidity, you were a boy in a man's world. I hated you and yet I was drawn to you. I think it is because you have what I never had. So listen to me, Moritz, I want you to go and find your Lotte. Leave me in Irkutsk.'

'Don't be ridiculous, Frantz, we'll wait in Irkutsk until your leg has healed and then we'll set off again. I can't do this alone. I need someone to shout at.'

'My foot will never heal,' he said, 'it's gone. Besides I don't want to go back to Hungary. I have no love there. I'll only end up in the army again, at least here I can start afresh, be a new person. But will you promise to do one thing for me?' I nodded my head. At that moment I would have done anything for my best friend Frantz Király. 'Take an axe to my toes. Chop them off. If you don't do it now I'll lose my leg.' He picked up the axe that the kulak woman had given us and handed it to me.

'But we're only three days from Irkutsk. We'll find a doctor there,' I protested.

'It can't wait. Believe me, you have to do it now.'

I reluctantly built a fire while Király polished off the remaining vodka. It was the only anaesthetic we had.

When the fire was roaring I carefully placed the axe blade in the flame. Then I pulled off his boot and socks. His foot was barely recognizable; the gangrene had spread to his toes. The rest was a black icy stump and it reeked of putrid flesh. I placed it carefully on a boulder.

'You can save me the big one, it's not so bad,' he said in a tiny voice.

I looked down at his foot and doubted whether I could be that accurate with an axe. I picked up a pebble and forced it in the gap between his big toe and second toe. It bought me a couple of centimetres. I tore a strip of material from one of my shirts in readiness, then I took the axe from the fire and lined it up with the top end of the blade to the edge of the pebble. I hesitated a moment as I fought back a wave of revulsion.

'Do it, Moritz,' Király urged.

I quickly lifted the blade high above my head and smashed it down on to his foot. I felt the blade strike the pebble but not the boulder beneath. Király let out an animal-like scream the likes of which I had never heard from a human. It pierced my eardrums and echoed around the lakeside, making the crystalline icicles reverberate in sympathy. When I checked to see what I had done I saw that I had spared his big toe but that the pebble had prevented the blade from passing cleanly through the rest. His toes were half severed and still hanging by threads of bone and flesh. I grabbed a rock and, using the axe as a carpenter would a chisel, carefully lined it up once more and brought the rock down on top of it. The axe went clean through and his frozen toes rolled on to the ground all stuck together. I grabbed the strip of material I had torn from my shirt and bound it as best I could around his foot to stem the bleeding. Király was howling all the while. I felt sick but soon recovered my senses when a band of Buryat horsemen suddenly appeared over the brow of the hill and came thundering down towards us. Király was delirious with pain and hardly noticed them, but a chill went down my spine. Had we come this far for nothing? I told Király to shut his mouth and not say a word in German but I'm not sure he heard me. There were a dozen or so Buryats, mostly wearing dirty long brown robes held by orange sashes at the waist, but one of them wore a distinctive purple gown. Their black boots climbed high to their knees and they carried long scimitars. With their inscrutable Mongol features and large thickset shoulders they were as terrible a sight as anything I had ever seen. I had nowhere to run and nothing with which to defend myself other than an axe. They were shouting to each other in a language I did not recognize. It had no traces of Russian, nor did it sound Chinese. These strange guttural sounds added to my general feeling of apprehension, because I could not tell if their intentions were friendly or hostile. They came charging down and skilfully brought their horses to a standstill a couple of metres from us. I smiled at them weakly and offered a greeting in Russian. One of them responded courteously and asked what we were doing. I explained that my friend had frostbite and indicated his foot. They chatted in their language for a moment and then the one in the purple gown dismounted and walked up to Király to examine his foot. He pulled a yak-skin container from his neck, took out the stopper and poured some liquid on to a cloth. He then loosened my clumsy bindings, placed the cloth over Király's wound and rebound it with far greater expertise than I had done. When this was done he began to chant some kind of prayer in a deep resonant voice, the words of which he repeated over and over. His eyes were closed and he was locked in concentration; the man's belief in his own powers was total, Király was transfixed. The Buryat seemed to be weaving a blanket of sound over Király, lulling him and calming him. The other horsemen told me the purple-robed man was a Buddhist lama and that Király would heal quickly now. When the ritual was done they asked us which direction we were headed. They said they too were going to Irkutsk to trade and offered to take us there.

It is a mystery to me why they did not kill us. Perhaps it was because we had nothing worth stealing, or because on seeing Király they had taken pity on us. More likely, though, the Russian guards had exaggerated the threat posed by the Buryats to prevent us from escaping. These men seemed honest and simple. They knew little of the war and did not care to know. All of that was far away. They were not hostile to the Central Powers – they had never even heard of them.

They hoisted us up on the back of two horses and we galloped off towards Irkutsk. After plodding through the snow for so long it was delightful to move so fast. The

Entry no. 53

Species belonging
to different animal
kingdoms are in their
structure and shapes
related to the
movements of
the universe.

Louis Pasteur

20

IT WAS JULY, AND THE ANT-MATING SEASON WAS ABOUT TO begin. Most of the observational research took place in the hot months because of the short lifespan of male ants. Leo was now camped at the laboratory next to London Zoo hoping to break the back of his PhD. The pupae were about to hatch. The males had already developed their wings and he carefully separated them from the female workers. He transferred them out of Queen Bess's tank and into an isolated tight mesh cage where he planned to mate them with a new queen. At twenty-five Bess was the oldest ant they had. She was the same age as Leo. The researchers were very proud of Bess, they were hoping she might break the longevity record for a queen in captivity, which stood at twenty-seven years old. The thrust of Leo's research was to investigate how mating frequency was related to sociality. Queen Bess was a red ant, the Latin name *Formica rufa* made her sound like a type of kitchen worktop from Ikea. Red ant queens tend to mate only once whereas the giant leafcutter queens mate more often. This has a huge impact on their colonies. All the female workers in Queen Bess's colony were sisters and had a very high genetic relationship. A worker ant carries 100 per cent of the male genes and 50 per cent of the female, which means that the sisters have a 75 per cent similarity in their genetic structure, the highest in ant society. Higher than between mother and daughter ant and much higher than the 25 per cent of genes that human beings share with their siblings. The sisterhood are organized, structured and highly social, whereas the males just fly about looking for sex. The challenge for Leo was to recreate natural conditions in the laboratory so he could observe the mating. Humidity and light were key but no matter how perfectly regulated the laboratory the researchers were not always successful. The ants were very sensitive to captivity; some years they would not mate at all and come September an atmosphere of gloom would hang over the researchers. Red ants could mate on the ground or in the air, but they nearly always mated on the ground when they were kept in mesh cages. Indeed none of the young researchers had ever seen *Formica rufa* mate by air.

Leo took a new queen and placed her with the males. He had to give the queen a name so he called her Eleni. She would have been delighted to have an ant named after her; she had often come to see Leo at his laboratory and had spent hours watching them build nests.

'Oh look, Leo, they're chatting again,' she would say when ants going in opposite directions met along the trail and appeared to stop and talk. Eleni's main contribution to the science had been her vivid translations of these ant conversations.

'Hello, Sister, how are you?'

'I'm very well, thank you, Sister. What's that you've found?'

'Well you'll never believe it but a rotten apricot just appeared from nowhere and I thought Her Majesty the Queen might like some.'

'For goodness' sake, why don't you just call her Mum? I wonder where all this fruit comes from?'

'I don't know, Sister, but there's something new every day and it's always yummy.'

'There must be a God, Sister.'

'Yes, there must be. What shall we call him?'

'How about Leo?'

'Good idea, Sister. Well, really must dash. I've left a pongy path so you can find the apricot. Good luck.'

"Bye, Sister.'

Leo reckoned the males would hatch in two days and then Queen Eleni could take her pick. He spent those days mooching about the lab wondering why on earth he had chosen to do a PhD on ant-mating frequency. Four years spent producing a piece of research that no one cared about and that had no conceivable application. And when it was done it would be sent to the British Library where it would slowly rot. His passion for his subject had died with Eleni. It was quantum physics that excited him now, and instead of writing up his notes on the computer he sat there ploughing through Roberto's reading list. Leo had been meeting him on a regular basis in the student canteen and had persuaded Roberto to let him sit in on one of his tutorials. Leo wanted to be well-prepared for it.

There were ten students waiting for Roberto when he arrived, dressed as always in jeans and a light-blue shirt.

'I hate these classrooms,' he said, 'they remind me of school. We need to challenge the way we learn. Let's change the configuration. Can we get rid of these desks?'

Before long all the desks were piled up around the edge of the room.

'Put your books away. You won't need to write anything down. I'm hoping that by the end of the tutorial you will know everything you need to know. Great! Now there's nowhere to hide, no barriers between us. How can we open ourselves up to learning with all this crap in the way? Let us be demanding of ourselves: if I can't stimulate you enough for you to remember what I'm saying then I've failed. Today I want to look at the double-slit experiment. Before I open the subject up to discussion let's make sure we all understand what exactly is happening here.'

Roberto asked the students to line up their chairs in one long row across the middle of the room. He then removed one chair from the centre to create a small gap in the row and made the chair's incumbent stand against a wall like a naughty boy. The students giggled. Leo wondered what on earth was going on.

'Don't worry, Brian,' Roberto smiled at the student, 'you have a very important role to play. I want you to imagine you are an electron, and here before you is a barrier with a tiny slit where your chair used to be. You are about to be fired through the slit on to the back wall, which we shall imagine is a screen on which you can leave a mark.' Roberto gave Brian a piece of chalk and Brian charged through the gap, and when he reached the far wall he turned and looked hesitantly at Roberto. 'You want me to draw on the wall?'

'Yes, please, leave a mark,' Roberto insisted.

Brian put a cross on the wall.

'Good. When an electron is passed through a single slit it behaves like a particle and leaves a mark on the screen. Now, let's try to confuse Brian. Let's make a second slit in our barrier. Camilla, could you please take your chair away and stand aside.'

A girl stood up from further down the line leaving two gaps a couple of metres apart in the row of chairs. Roberto brought Brian back to the start.

'Now, Brian, what are you going to do this time?'

'I'm going to choose which gap to go through,' Brian said, and walked through the other gap. Some of the students were shaking their heads.

'Is that what happens?' Roberto asked.

'No,' Leo heard himself say, 'when there are two slits the electron goes through both of them at the same time because . . .'

'Stop there,' Roberto interrupted. 'Brian, can you do that?'

'No,' he said.

'Can a particle do that?'

'No,' Brian said.

'What can go through two holes at once?'

'A wave,' Camilla offered.

'Exactly, just like at sea, the same wave can pass through two gaps in a sandbank. So let's see what that looks like. If you could all come and stand with Brian. Now you are a wave. Please walk through the gaps.'

All eleven of them approached the chair barrier in a line like a wave, and one by one passed through the two gaps and fanned out again to reach the other wall.

'So, my friends, when there are two slits, the electron seems to behave like a wave, and what we see on the screen on the other side is a classic wave interference pattern. Please bring your chairs into a circle ... let's sit down.' When they were all gathered, Roberto grinned. 'So what is the question on every physicist's lips?'

'Is an electron a particle or a wave?' a lanky girl with plaits chimed in.

'Exactly, and the answer is it depends how you look at it. The observer's choice of whether to use one or two slits affects the result. What we learn is that the scientist is as important a part of this experiment as the electron, and that the scientist and the electron are in fact connected. This experiment is the cornerstone of the holistic universe theory.'

'But how can something be a wave one day and a particle the next? Just because you make a dog walk through a catflap it doesn't turn it into a cat,' Leo protested.

'It does with electrons. They are strange little things, terribly irrational, and we're full to the brim with them.'

Roberto pondered. 'Maybe that's why we're so emotional.'

'Yes, but a rock is full of them too, and a rock isn't emotional,' Brian said.

'How do you know?' Roberto retorted.

There was a silence whilst the students stretched their brains around the concept of emotional rocks. Roberto never took anything for granted.

Something was troubling Leo. 'What happens to the electron when no one is watching; is it a wave or a particle?'

'No one really knows, we can only say that the electron lives in the realm of possibility.'

So was every experiment subjective? Leo wondered what was the point of his own research. Did the behaviour of animals in captivity have any bearing on reality? What were those ants doing when no one was looking? What was Hannah doing when no one was looking? She always performed for her public, but what dark emotions bubbled up from her soul when she lay alone in her bed?

'Dr Panconesi,' Camilla asked, 'does this mean we could change the world simply by looking at it differently?'

Or by walking differently, Leo thought, remembering how uplifted he had felt when he copied Eleni's gait the very first evening he met her.

'It's a sweet idea,' Roberto responded. 'Normally these things apply only at the quantum level, but why not use the notion to change the world? Yes, yes, I like it, Camilla. Let's try it, let's all do a little thought experiment. Tomorrow we will change our world simply by looking at it differently. Let us imagine that this earth is actually heaven; that there is nothing more beautiful than the rolling hills, the rushing streams and the drifting clouds; that this planet, where water drops on to our heads and food grows beneath our feet is the ultimate paradise; that those who leave their bodies merely pass on to a higher level and enter into the fabric of this heaven to provide an infinity of pleasures, textures and vistas; that the dead literally turn into soil, flowers, air and animals.' Roberto was now pacing the room, visibly excited by where his thoughts were leading.

'What if we changed the story that has been peddled to us over thousands of years by those religions who want to control us, that this life is merely a stepping stone to something better or something worse, and that we can only achieve the better by passing through the doors of their institutions and following their rules? What if we trash this arcane story which has caused so much suffering and hostility, and accept that we have already arrived in heaven and that there is nothing more gorgeous than here and now? Oh yes, I like it, Camilla, let's change the world together.' Camilla blushed.

Leo walked home Eleni-style. He bounced along the pavement and imagined himself in heaven. And for the briefest of moments the world changed for Leo.

It had been an uneventful fortnight since the *Formica rufa* males had hatched; Leo was observing them despondently as they flitted around their cage. Queen Eleni was nibbling at some cereal when all of a sudden a male landed beside her. She stopped eating, turned to the male and sniffed him out. She took off and the male followed. Leo turned the video camera on in slow-motion mode. Queen Eleni had sniffed out a lot of ants, and he had already filmed a dozen rejections, so he was surprised when the two ants engaged in an aerial flirtation. The male latched on to Eleni's back and they began to mate.

'Quick, quick, everyone. Look at this,' Leo called out, jumping up from his chair. The other researchers and lab assistants gathered round. A ripple of excitement circled the group. Queen Eleni soared upwards with her charge hanging on determinedly. They alighted for a moment on the roof of the cage in a blatant display of exhibitionism. Five smiling faces stared at them. Then off they went again, wheeling around in a magnificent dance. A few seconds later it was all over. There was a great cheer and a lot of handshaking and hugging. The research group were all delighted that a new colony was likely the following year. No one noticed that in the commotion Queen Bess had died, eighteen months short of the world record.

The researchers left their stations and piled into the pub to celebrate. Among them was a young lab assistant called Amelia who secretly harboured a crush on Leo. Amelia was everything that Eleni wasn't: tall, blonde, slim and of English aristocratic stock. He had not been especially polite to her, if anything the contrary was true. But she perceived in the emptiness of his exchanges an emotional volatility that she found sexy. His aloofness was darkly attractive, for it gave the illusion of an unattainable yet tantalizingly complex soul. A soul that would have to be excavated with painstaking care, like ancient treasure lost in a sea wreck. For weeks she had fantasized how this man would ravage her silently and distantly, and as she closed in on him at the bar she knew that her time was now or never. She casually ordered herself a drink.

'Will you join me? You're almost empty.'

'Thank you,' Leo replied, 'a glass of red wine.'

They chatted long after the others had left. Leo exhibited his new-found weakness for alcohol and drank more than he should, and Amelia matched him glass for glass. And with the flow of alcohol Amelia's courage grew as Leo's resistance ebbed. She was attractive for God's sake, easy to be with. Eleni was dead. Dead. How long could she hold him in this emotional limbo? Suddenly he was desperate to break free of her, desperate for affection, desperate for Amelia. He urgently wanted to feel a woman's skin against his own, lose himself in passion, break away from the sterility of grief. She leant forward tentatively to kiss him and was shocked when he responded like a starving man to sustenance. One kiss unleashed a whirlwind of desire and pent-up frustration. He took her in his arms and embraced her deeply. He soared upwards, light and free. The dark walls of the pub fell away and he was gliding through sweet-scented pastures. He slipped his hand around her waist, under her camisole, and explored the gentle undulation across the small of her back. Her skin was as warm and smooth as a sun-drenched boulder rounded by the caress of wind and sea for a thousand years. She could feel the hunger in his fingers and managed to hold him off until she could drag him out of the door on to the street where she managed to hail a taxi. Before long they tumbled into her flat and made reckless love.

They lay breathless on the bed, Leo mistakenly building a love from a night's passion, Amelia delighted that for once a fantasy had lived up to expectations. If a relationship could be mapped in the warm post-coital glow of first love-making their future would have looked rosy. As their racing pulses began to settle, Leo felt compelled to speak. He wanted to spread his heart like strawberry jam at her feet so she might accept him, battered soul and all, for who he really was. So he related the entire story of Eleni: from their first meeting, to the moment they knew they were in love, from their adventures in Latin America, to the tumult of her death and the dreadful scenes at her funeral.

Amelia was appalled – not at the events he described – but rather by the way Leo was unravelling before her very eyes, denuding himself of mystery. When at last he finished she sighed heavily; a sigh that contained all the sadness and regret of a disillusioned woman. A sigh that told Leo immediately that their fleeting relationship was over.

His dalliance with Amelia left him drained of hope. He berated himself for falling for her so quickly and he was angry with her for judging his honesty so harshly. But when he replayed the events of that evening he realized that he had, in effect, conjured up a corpse and slapped it down in front of her. What was she supposed to think? The stench of Eleni was all over him. He was soiled goods. Hannah was right: he was intense – unbearably so. But worse than that, he had proved himself a fool. Why couldn't he take things for what they were? The daily sight of Amelia wandering around the laboratory pretending nothing had happened only compounded his feelings of self-pity and regret. One day he caught her shaking her head to herself and fancied she was thinking about him. That day Leo retreated into himself like a butterfly that takes one look at the miserable world into which it has emerged and decides to crawl back inside its chrysalis.

He brought home the video of Queen Eleni's spectacular aerial mating so that he could make his notes at home and escape Amelia's disappointed gaze. He watched it over and over again to the music of Puccini, which, coupled with slow motion, had the effect of transforming the act into ballet. The unselfconscious purity with which these two little creatures engaged with each other resonated inside him. It was as if for that brief instant they were immortal, hovering in the void that Roberto described, touching on infinity, masters of their senses, home at last in Eden. These ants were in paradise and Leo recognized it, for he had been there himself with Eleni in rare moments when love had freed them from self-consciousness and they had transcended their own sense of mortality.

As he was filing his video at the Institute of Zoology he wondered if he might find more images that captured that moment of freedom – which somehow encapsulated his relationship with Eleni – and happened across a tape entitled *Wild Love*. He took it to the viewing section and put it on. There before him were two small sea horses copulating. The video must have been part of a series on the mating habits of animals. Sea horses were followed by hyenas, salamanders, elephants and more. As he watched this great and beautiful parade of animals fornicating the universe into existence he was overcome by a feeling of humility. He began to recognize his friends in those coupling reptiles and mammals. The males who have six partners, the females who bite their partner's head off after sex, the ones who travel thousands of miles to mate, the ones who develop elaborate courtship practices, the ones who show off like peacocks, and the ones who stay with the same partner for ever.

It was the beginning of a new obsession. At last he had found something to fill the pages of his notebook. He jotted down descriptions of unusual mating practices and interspersed them with photographs that he bought or ripped out of books. Soon these animal stories were joined by quotations, poems and real-life love stories that he came across in magazines. Anything was worthy of entry if it triggered the intangible aroma of Eleni. The notebook became his best friend and confidant.

By December Hannah was back in his life. She had received a distressed phone call from Charlie about Leo. He was disturbed by Leo's behaviour; he was becoming increasingly reclusive. He spent all his time watching wildlife videos and reading romantic magazines. In

Entry no. 13

Today I awoke full of fear and uncertainty. When I met Roberto for lunch he said uncertainty was a good thing. Scientists were so certain about uncertainty that there was a universally accepted theory called the Uncertainty Principle. I liked that, it made me feel a little bit better. Roberto said he didn't think I was really interested in physics at all, that it was just an excuse to explore my feelings for Eleni. I guess he's right. He told me that I should consider the universe like a picture. Move one thing and the whole picture changes. Some people call it the great cosmic dance. Love is also part of the picture, every act of love affects the whole picture. It is like a small stone thrown in the middle of a lake, the ripples will reach the shore. He told me that I was indulging myself in introspection, and that I should cast my eyes outwards and chase the ripples of my love and maybe I will find love again and again mirroring itself throughout the universe. 'Look into the heart of the universe and you will discover the universe of the heart. Look for the Eleni in everything,' he said.

21

ANNAH'S RETURN WAS DRAMATIC. SHE STORMED INTO Charlie's flat uninvited, took hold of Leo's arm and dragged him to the door.

'We're going out, you miserable git. There's a Christmas party on. Oh, and by the way when are you going to move out and get your own place? Charlie has had enough of your self-indulgent moping. It's about time you stopped feeling sorry for yourself and got a life.'

'He hasn't said anything to me.'

'No, but he has to me. He thought you'd have made some effort to find somewhere by now. Take a jacket, it's raining outside.'

Leo grabbed his green raincoat and was pushed out of the door. 'Why are you being so horrible to me?'

'You can't have it both ways, Leo, you wanted me to be more honest, so I am. Don't tell me you don't like it. And while I'm at it, you know that girl Amelia you slept with? I met her and I thought she was a posh tart.'

'She is. You sound jealous?' he teased, but immediately regretted saying it.

'Oh my God, jealous! I am beside myself. I so wanted to be in her knickers listening to you pontificate about your favourite subject.'

'Oh God, she didn't tell you about that, did she?'

'Nice girl, huh! And before we go any further let's get one thing straight, Leo. I do not, have not and will never fancy you.'

Leo was stunned. They were at the bus stop outside Charlie's door; the rain was torrential. He dropped his head and turned back to the flat. Hannah pulled him back, spun him round and stared coldly at him.

'Aren't you going to ask how I am?'

'No.'

'Thank you for asking. I'm not great, Leo, in fact I would say I am positively miserable.' She clenched her fists around his wet collar. 'My dad is ill. They don't know what it is, but he can't eat.' Her eyes welled up. 'When Mum died I had a recurring nightmare that something would happen to my dad. Did you know that the partners of people who die of cancer are more likely to get it? Now they haven't said it's cancer but I can smell it, Leo. He's dying.' She burst into tears.

Leo gently took her hands from his jacket and hugged her. A speeding lorry drove through a little pool that had swelled up by the side of the road and sprayed them with water. Leo cursed. The world was full of stupid lorry drivers.

'Let's go back in and talk, shall we?' he suggested.

'No,' she insisted. 'If we stay here we'll just get depressed. I need to let my hair down. "Dance and forget," I remember my dad saying that after Mum died. He'd put some music on really loud and we'd dance around the house to cheer ourselves up.'

'Did it work?'

'Only while we were dancing.'

They arrived soaked at a small semi-detached house in Kilburn, notable only for the bedspreads hanging in the windows as makeshift curtains. A deep repetitious thud rocked the house. Hannah rang the doorbell but no one replied. She lifted the letter box to look and a whiff of smoke wafted into the damp air.

'Don't you just love student parties?' she said.

They made their way down a path that led past the side of the house to the back door. It was open and they stepped into a kitchen with a muddy floor. They passed a group of students necking beer and yelling above the music. Hannah dragged Leo deeper into the throbbing heat of the party, through knots of drunken girls and lairy lads. She headed for the living room where a mass of drug-sodden revellers swayed trance-like to the beat. Hannah furrowed her way to the centre of the dance floor and joined the horde, injecting an energy that enlivened those around her. Leo backed up to the wall and watched. He was still smarting from her comments. After a while he wandered into the kitchen and poured himself a glass of wine. But as he brought the cup to his lips he was knocked from behind and spilt the wine all over his jeans. He swore and turned sharply to see who was responsible. It was Stacey.

'Stacey,' Leo exclaimed, 'look where you're . . . Stacey, what's wrong?'

There were tears rolling down her cheeks. She pushed past him and out of the back door without so much as a word. Leo followed her out.

'Stacey, Stacey, are you all right?' He grabbed her arm and pulled her back. 'Talk to me, Stace, what's wrong?'

'It's Roberto,' she sobbed, 'he's in there with some bimbo. He was getting off with her right in front of me.'

'Oh God, that's awful. What's he playing at? That's not like him.'

'Oh yes, it bloody is. He refuses to be faithful for philosophical reasons. He's testing me, he wants me to be like him. It's not the first time. Well I've had enough of it. I've tried to put up with it but I'm sick of it, he's making a bloody fool of me. I'm going home, I never want to see him again.' She pulled a tissue from her pocket and blew her nose.

'Shall I walk you home?' Leo offered.

'No, it's all right, I need to be alone for a bit,' she said, and scurried off down the alleyway.

Leo wandered back into the house to see if he could find Roberto. In the corridor he bumped into Chris, a skinny rodent of a man who he knew vaguely from university. After initial pleasantries the conversation turned to Eleni. He was having to shout over the music but he was glad of someone to talk to. They sat down on the stairs and Leo explained that he had been trying to keep her memory alive through his research into love.

'I've kept this notebook, you see, and at first I just made random entries, but now I'm beginning to see a pattern. I'm beginning to realize that everything from the smallest particle, through the migrations of animals to the very movement of the stars is governed by one fundamental emotion . . .'

It was the sort of monologue to which his friends had become drearily accustomed. Chris stood up abruptly and said: 'You know what, mate? You're really screwed up. We're at a party, for Christ's sake. I really think you need help, all your friends are saying it but no one dares tell you because they feel sorry for you, Leo. You need therapy. Honestly, it will do you good. I'm the wrong guy to talk to about Eleni. I really am. I can't help you. So if you would excuse me . . .' and he walked off. Leo felt annoyed with himself, he kept forgetting that there was no point talking about Eleni. He heard Roberto's voice behind him, and turned to see the elegant Italian walking down the stairs.

'Hello, Leo,' Roberto said cheerfully.

'Roberto, what's going on? I've just seen Stacey . . .' Leo began, then halted as he noticed Camilla coming down behind Roberto.

'Camilla, this is Leo.'

'I remember you from the class,' she smiled.

Leo looked at Roberto fiercely.

'It's all right,' Roberto said. 'Camilla knows. Don't worry about Stacey, Leo, she's just jealous. She'll get over it, it's a petty emotion. So tell me, Leo, how are you?' He offered his hand. Leo shook it half-heartedly but made no reply.

'Oh come on, Leo, the world is here to be enjoyed. Don't be angry with me.'

'What about hurting other people's feelings?' Leo protested.

Roberto looked at him intently. 'I'm not hurting anyone's feelings, it's her choice if she wants to be upset. Look, if you've understood anything of what I've tried to teach you then you would know that everything is equal, nothing on this planet is more important than anything else. We should love everything equally. I think Camilla agrees with me.'

Camilla nodded.

'But is no one special to you?' Leo asked.

'Everyone is special. We are all part of the same unity.' Roberto smiled, and then he did something utterly extraordinary. He took Leo's head in his hands and kissed him forcibly on the lips. Leo was so shocked it took him a moment to realize what was happening. Camilla giggled nervously. Eventually Leo managed to push Roberto off.

'What the hell are you doing, Roberto?' he stammered.

'I'm proving a point.'

'What point?' Leo said angrily.

'There is no such thing as fidelity, there is not even such a thing as homosexuality or heterosexuality. These are just concepts, man-made constructs. They limit our infinite potential. Like I said, the universe is here for us to enjoy. If this is heaven, there is no judgement day. We should feast on our senses and feast on each other. Bodily pleasure should be derived from any and every source. I

love you, Leo, like I love Stacey, like I love Camilla.'
Roberto turned and kissed Camilla.

'Yeah, and you love me like you love the fucking wall-
paper. Is this where you've been leading me?' Leo
remonstrated bitterly.

'Absolutely,' Roberto said triumphantly.

Leo found himself alone in a small box room at the top
of the house. He had escaped up the stairs overcome by a
sudden wave of revulsion and panic. He switched the light
off and slumped on a pile of coats, clutching his stomach.
He felt betrayed. He heard a moth battering itself against
the paper lampshade, disturbed by the darkness, unable
to settle. He tried to breathe but his chest felt constricted.
His head was fire, flames licked the inside of his scalp,
turning his thoughts to ash. Now for the first time he saw
that he had been completely deluding himself. These past
few months he had been sliding into madness without
even realizing it. Eleni was gone and everyone knew it but
him. The dead only lived in the minds of lunatics. The
kiln in his head was unbearable, a fireball rampaged
through him incinerating every image of Eleni, and snuff-
ing out his fledgling theories. And when the furnace had
burnt itself out there was nothing. He was hovering in a
void, but instead of feeling immense as Roberto had
suggested, he felt alone and powerless. Ahead of him was
an eternity of emptiness. The moth had found the
windowpane and pounded its fragile body against
the glass until, exhausted, it found a resting place in the
shadows. They sat in the little room together, both
crushed.

They were disturbed by a sudden blast of light as the door swung open and two entwined bodies burst through. The couple were so involved with each other that they did not notice Leo and the moth sitting in the dark. The man kicked the door shut behind him and pushed his woman up against it. His face pressed against hers in lust. His hand reached down between her legs and hitched up her skirt. It was then that the woman felt another presence in the room. She screamed, 'There's someone in here.'

It was Hannah. She opened the door, and as the light burst in she saw Leo staring at her. She did not hear the small explosion in his heart, nor the quiet escape of hope that leaked from his veins, but the moth took off and headed for the light.

'Sorry, I was just getting my coat,' he said as he got to his feet and left, without a second look or a coat.

When he returned home he picked up his notebook in a rage, took it downstairs and threw it out on to a pile of rubbish by the bus stop.

The following day Leo called his GP and got the number of a bereavement counsellor, but immediately the woman's voice put him off. If marzipan could speak it would sound like Mrs Charlotte Philips. Her vowels were annoyingly long. Her comments were dripping with syrupy professional sympathy. She spoke too softly and was over-reassuring as though she was dealing with a very sick child.

'How aaaaawful,' she said repeatedly. 'You must feel tehhhhrrible.'

Charlotte Philips was one of those women who had been through 'the trauma of bereeeeavement' herself and had dedicated her life to helping others. Was this really what Leo needed? He resisted it. Nevertheless she lured him into her sticky trap and cudgelled an appointment out of him, the prospect of which hung over his head like a curse. He had nightmares of lying naked on her sugary couch with his breastbone peeled open and all his internal organs on display while Mrs Marzipan Philips spread treacle over them with a butcher's knife trying to make him 'feeeel' better. He couldn't go through with it. He waited until after six one day before calling back in the hope that he could cancel on an answering machine. The phone rang for a while before it was answered.

'Hello,' a tiny voice said.

'Ah, hello.' Leo could barely mask his disappointment. 'Can I speak to Mrs Philips?'

'I'm three and a half,' the voice said with great pride.

'Are you?'

'Yes, three and a half. How old are you?'

'Older than I was yesterday . . . Can you pass on a message to Mummy?' Leo continued rather hopefully. 'Could you tell her . . .'

'My name's Jenny, what's yours?'

'Mr Deakin.'

'Daddy says Mummy works with loonies. Are you a loony?'

Leo hesitated, 'Look, Jenny, can I speak to your mummy?'

'Mummy, Mummy, Mr Deak's on the phone. I think he's a loony.'

Leo could hear Mrs Philips in the background. 'Daaarling, please don't use that word.'

'Are you going to make him better with questions, Mummy?' was the last thing Jenny said before the telephone was snatched from her tiny hands and stuffed with fondant, long-vowelled apologies.

When he told Mrs Philips he wanted to cancel she was convinced that it must be because he was 'sooo tehh-hhrribly upset'. She said it was very common for people to cancel sessions because they were frightened, but really they had nothing to fear. Bereavement counselling was not like analysis, the source of the depression was known, there was no need to investigate the client's childhood or intimate relations. It was merely an opportunity for Leo to discuss what he was feeling right now with someone who had experience of those feelings. He would be reassured, she said, to learn that nearly all those who grieved follow a similar cycle of panic attacks, anger, pining and searching.

'Searching?' Leo heard himself ask.

'It is a restless drive to find the deceased.'

She explained how it was normal for bereaved people to lose all interest in humdrum daily activities while they directed all their attention to locating the lost person. Adopted children seek out their real parents, widows sit by the chair that their partner used to sit in or obsessively tend their grave. Some people catch sight of their loved ones in the street or think they hear them every time the stairs creak. Many feel that the deceased continues to be present in their lives, they may even talk to them. They will interpret unusual natural phenomena as signs from beyond the grave.

'All this is part of the process and I am here to affirm your experiences. These symptoms pass. You have to go through the darkness to find the light,' she said with zeal.

Leo dreaded the passing of the 'symptoms' of bereavement. At least the darkness held Eleni in its shadows; the light with its piercing clarity might reveal that she had gone for good, chased even from his dreams. Yes, it was reassuring to know that millions of others wandered the streets with angels at their shoulders, that the background hum of the city was actually the sound of people chatting to the dead, and that all day codified messages of love were being transmitted through rustling leaves and creaking stairs to the waiting ears of the lonely, but Mrs Philips's cure was worse than the illness. This was Leo's constituency and he had no desire to escape it. It would be treachery.

'Let yourself be helped, Leo,' she said.

He assured her that he was fine but he could hear the hollowness in his own voice.

'If you ever change your mind I'm only a phone call away.'

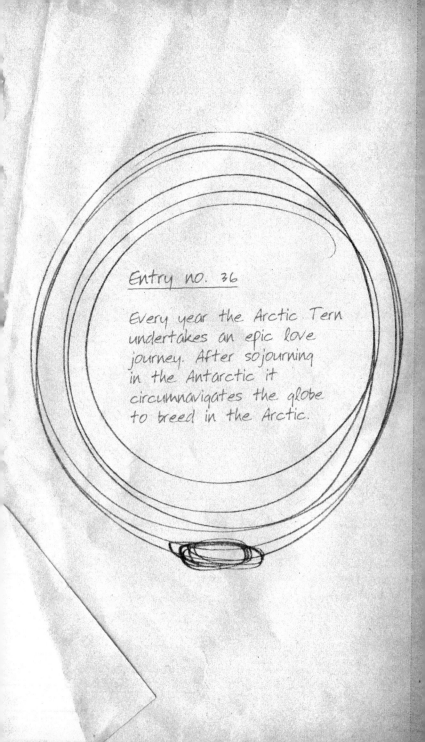

Entry no. 36

Every year the Arctic Tern
undertakes an epic love
journey. After sojourning
in the Antarctic it
circumnavigates the globe
to breed in the Arctic.

22

LEO HAD CAUGHT HUNDREDS OF FALLING LEAVES IN autumn, saved hundreds of souls. He had placed each leaf between the pages of the books on Charlie's shelf and forgotten about them. Every so often, when Charlie was reading, he would turn a page and a leaf would drift to the floor. He always picked it up and put it back out of respect for the lunacy of his friend.

Charlie returned home from work to find Leo's bags packed and their distraught owner picking painstakingly through the books. He had placed the leaves in pairs on the carpet.

'What are you doing, Leo?'

'I thought the leaves might be lonely in the books.' Leo was trembling, blinking nervously, 'Have you read Plato?'

'No,' Charlie replied. He took off his coat and sat down on the carpet, alarmed by Leo's strange behaviour.

'He wrote this story about how Zeus made these strange creatures with two heads and four arms and legs. They were always happy and had no inhibitions. And the world was full of laughter. But Zeus was having a bad time because his wife Hera was pissed off with him. They argued all day, and at night he couldn't sleep because his creatures were laughing so much. It got so bad that one day Zeus lost it and threw a load of thunderbolts at them. His creatures were split in two and scattered to the four corners of the world. Plato says that since that day the earth has been covered with restless one-headed creatures searching for their other half.' Leo's voice trembled as he spoke.

Charlie was unnerved, 'And the leaves?'

'Don't you understand, Charlie? Each leaf was a soul in freefall. I caught them before they hit the ground and now around the world hundreds of lonely people are in suspension awaiting their fate. I'm making matches for them, putting Zeus's creatures back together.'

Charlie looked in bewilderment at the leaves that Leo had lovingly put together. Beech, sycamore, oak and chestnut were arrayed in autumn tapestry across the floor. None of it made sense to him. Leo picked up another book from the shelf above Charlie's bed and rifled through the pages. Two maple leaves fell out and he put them together on the carpet. Then he went back to the shelf for the next book, but his hands were shaking and he dropped it on the bed. He blinked a couple of times in quick succession, as if he were not accustomed to the light, and reached down to the book. He took it in both hands and flicked through it carefully. Nothing. Another book revealed five leaves. Charlie found this sad and compulsive ritual difficult to bear. He got up and wrapped his arms around his friend. 'I'm worried about you, Leo.'

'Nobody caught my leaf. I am lost,' Leo muttered desolately.

'What's happened, why are you saying these things? Don't give up. You're going through a bad patch, but it's just a phase. It will pass,' Charlie reassured him.

Leo shook his head emphatically. 'You don't know how dreadful this is . . . I thought it would get easier to bear but the pain grinds on . . . it's relentless. It feels like it's going to last for ever. I've tried, Charlie, honestly I have. I've tried to live normally but I can't escape this weight. I haven't got the strength to keep looking for Eleni. I'm broken. I hate myself like this, but I can't find my way back and the worst thing is that no one understands . . . who am I meant to talk to?'

Charlie was stung, he knew he was at fault; he had never really sat down and talked to Leo about what was going on in his troubled head. The subject was too difficult to broach. A gulf had opened up between them and now his best friend was drowning. He looked at Leo's bags by the door. There was still a small spot of blood on the top of his rucksack from the crash in Ecuador.

'Why are you packed?' Charlie asked.

'I don't want to be a burden to you any more. I'll be off when I've sorted this out,' Leo said bleakly, opening another book.

'You're not a burden to me.'

'That's not what Hannah said.' Leo stared at him accusingly.

Charlie flushed with guilt. 'Look, I was frustrated. The

place is too small for two and I was feeling like an old housewife, cleaning up around you and doing all the shopping. Why don't we look for a bigger place?'

'No, I've made up my mind, I think I'm better off alone.'

'Have you found somewhere else?'

'I've got a bedsit.'

Charlie felt rebuked for the conditional nature of his hospitality. 'Oh for God's sake, don't go to a lousy bedsit. Please stay. I'm sorry, I've changed my mind. Stay here and I promise we'll do nice things together . . .' Charlie pleaded desperately. But his protestations were in vain, for that night the forlorn figure of Leo shuffled out of the door and on to a bus. As he took his seat on the top deck he could see Charlie standing in the big living-room window staring dolefully at him like a fish in a tank.

As the bus pulled away a creeping coldness percolated Leo's flesh, brought on by a growing feeling of scorn and resentment towards his friends. Not one of them understood him. They lived in the foothills of emotion and knew nothing of the extremes. They had no idea what love was, no idea how grief gnawed on the soul, no idea what it was like when the very air you breathed tortured you by keeping you alive. Had life ever mocked them as it did him? Each one had betrayed him in their own way. Let them rot. He had not given any of them his new address; an omission that would spare them from having to pretend to like him. Sure, he was envious of their easy lives but he knew that he would never be able to return to those carefree days. He was a young man robbed of youth, and time does not flow backwards. He was ready to start afresh, where no one knew him, where no one felt sorry for him, where he owed no explanations. Convinced that he would never love again he resolved to live without it. Perhaps he would be happier. Perhaps he would have been happier still had he never met Eleni in the first place.

Guests and shoes were banned from setting foot inside the house. No music after 10 p.m., no use of the bathroom between 8 and 9 a.m., no takeaways, no smoking, no drunkenness, no posters. Rent to be paid monthly in advance, any late payment would result in a warning; a second late payment would lead to eviction. The landlady had the right to evict any tenant for any reason whatsoever; the tenant had to give a month's notice. The tenant had his own cupboard in the kitchen and shelf in the fridge and was not to use the family's food. The kitchen should be avoided during family dinner times except in an emergency. Apart from these minor regulations Leo was free to do as he wished – as free as a bird in a cage.

He had never lived with a young family. Somewhere between five and six the baby woke up screaming. At seven the cat would jump on his head. If he was not up by eight a five-year-old would wander into his room with some toy or other which either spoke or had a siren and push it into his face. The house smelt of baby poo, which was collected throughout the day in a small nappy bin in the bathroom next to his room. And he often found bits of rotten food in the sofa or squashed between the floorboards. He received the occasional call from his parents, but apart from this he was never disturbed. He had no inclination to go out much, so he endeared himself to his uptight landlady by babysitting twice a week. At least on those evenings he had the living room to himself, which was infinitely preferable to the polite chatter he was subjected to in the family's presence.

His bedroom was large enough for a desk and a small sofa, but the single bed was disappointing. It had probably been chosen specially to discourage visits from the opposite sex – or any sex for that matter. It sagged in the middle from over-use by the exuberant onanists who inevitably found themselves in such establishments. A red Moroccan kilim covered the beechwood floor, and there were two landscape paintings, one above the bed, the other above the sofa, to transport the daydreaming bedsitter to rural paradise. He had the luxury of an old kettle, which left limescale in every cup of tea. It was a ruse to keep the tenant out of the kitchen. The window looked down two storeys on to a small back garden edged with a well-tended flower bed. Over the fence was a row of converted terraced houses, and directly opposite his window he could see into the kitchen and living room of one of the flats.

An old couple lived in the flat and Leo guessed that they were retired because they were always there in the daytime. Leo observed them as if they were ants in the laboratory. They would follow each other around from kitchen to living room, engaged in what seemed from afar to be a ritual mating dance. They often kissed or sat hand in hand watching the television; if one left the room the other would seem momentarily bereft. This would manifest itself through restless behaviour like switching channels on the television or fidgeting. He noticed that on average if left alone it would be five minutes before one would get up to find the other, whereas together they could sit for half an hour. Three times a week they unintentionally wore the same-coloured jumpers and trousers. They practised highly sophisticated and efficient task-sharing routines. At mealtimes he would chop and she would cook, then he washed-up while she made tea. On the whole Leo would have said that their lives were so intertwined as to be inseparable. Two people fulfilling the same objectives could be said to be functioning as one. This was the outward manifestation of love. Leo wondered if an empirical study of a hundred couples would reveal uniform behaviour.

He needed to broaden his study, so he began to take notes on his landlord and landlady. Excluding the husband's work, which Leo considered to be a social necessity, he charted the amount of time they spent together in the house sharing the same activity. He noticed that each would take responsibility for whole areas, which the other had nothing to do with. He bathed the children; she got them out of bed. She went to bed early; he stayed up late. They watched different television programmes at different times. They tended to play with the children separately. In general, they spent little time together. Leo concluded that although they were interdependent they were not unified. There was no love, only habit.

In the laboratory the next step would be to see whether one could create love by replicating the outward manifestation of love. If he could force his subjects to spend time together and work together to serve the same end would they be more likely to fall in love? How long would you have to sit on a sofa holding hands with someone before you fell in love with them? Ants only mated if the conditions were suitable; the same must surely be true of humans. In theory, if enough research were done it ought to be possible to structure our lives around the pursuit of love rather than the pursuit of money.

The new year passed quietly; Leo rarely left his room. On his desk was a stopwatch, a set of binoculars and two pads filled with data on the old couple and his landlady. He knew what papers they read, which friends came to tea, the extent of their wardrobes; he had even worked out which television programmes they were watching by cross-referencing viewing times with the television schedule. In his more lucid moments he was aware that a chronicle of the past year would reveal a man drifting dangerously from obsession to obsession.

The landlady began to take advantage of his constant presence in the house by asking him to help out from time to time with little chores. It began with popping out for the occasional pint of milk, but soon he was taking out the rubbish and moving furniture; before long he was tending to the garden and clearing out the garage. The chores were becoming more regular and time-consuming but he didn't mind because it kept him busy and took his mind off his problems. She seemed to enjoy finding things for him to do. One day she invited him down for a cup of tea, and soon he became a regular visitor to the kitchen. Little by little she went from Mrs Hardman to Katherine to Kath.

Kath was bored. She had sacrificed her career as a high-flying lawyer to look after the children even though she'd earned considerably more than her husband. It had soon become impossible for them to maintain the lifestyle to which they had been accustomed and over the past couple of years they had reluctantly taken in lodgers to boost their income.

A strange friendship founded on mutual loneliness grew between Leo and Kath; they had nothing else in common. Leo noticed that she had started wearing make-up in the daytime. The tracksuits disappeared to be replaced by bright flowery tops and leather skirts.

'Do you find me attractive?' she asked. The question came from nowhere. They were slurping soup in the kitchen. Leo wiped his chin with his napkin and looked at her, surprised. She was at least fifteen years older than him and the signs of age were showing. She was on the cusp of middle age: her body was not fat but had lost definition, her streaked shoulder-length hair had become wispy and her eyes lacked spark. She had once been very pretty; he had seen the wedding photos in which she stood straight-backed and imperious in a daring low-cut green dress, which proudly revealed her broad shoulders, angular collar-bone and fulsome breasts. She looked tanned, athletic and content. Now she looked weary, like a cut flower that had begun to wilt without having lost all its beauty.

'I haven't really thought about it,' he said evasively.

'I used to get a lot of attention,' she said nostalgically. 'I've let myself go recently, I've decided to make more of an effort. I wondered what you thought.' The desperation dripped off her and Leo sensed she was in need of a compliment.

'I like what you're wearing, Kath, it suits you.'

'Thank you, you're very sweet, you know. You've been ever so helpful since you came. We get on all right, don't we, Leo?'

'Yes, fine.'

'But neither of us are happy, are we?'

'No,' Leo admitted.

'And what would make you happy?'

'I don't know, Kath, I've given up on it. What about you?'

'Can I be honest with you?' she asked.

Leo nodded.

'I think what would make me happy right now is if you made love to me.' She looked at him pleadingly.

Leo blushed and pulled away, 'No I don't think that's the answer for either of us . . . but . . . anyway, what about your husband?'

'It's not working between us. But I'm not going to leave him, if that's what you mean. Look, Leo, I like you, but let's not be unrealistic about this, it would just be a bit of fun, Christ we both need it . . . even if it was just sex and no strings. We could enjoy it for what it was. What do you think?' She had never been so blunt in her life. Before her marriage she had had many lovers; perhaps she had given herself too freely but it had been so easy for her in those days, there were always men to choose from. Nowadays she would lie awake at night next to her husband revisiting the affairs of her youth, feeling old and unwanted. When Leo arrived he had reminded her of those lovely young men she had known and her fantasies had turned to him. Like a vampire needs blood, she wanted him inside her so she could feel young again.

Leo was as appalled as he was tempted. 'I don't think I can do that . . . I mean it's not me.'

It was not as categorical a rejection as it might have been and they both knew it.

'That's all right, Leo,' she said, refusing to be downhearted, 'think about it, it's an open offer, you can change your mind whenever you like.'

Kath could smell a victory; it was just a question of time. She knew men and how to seduce them. First plant the seed and then water it well.

A thing offered freely plays on the mind; it is almost irresistible. Who can refuse a 'free gift'? Who is not tempted by the two-for-one deals in the supermarket? Leo would always end up with bargains in his trolley that he had never intended to buy. Her offer stuck to him like an oil slick on a seabird. He couldn't shake it off. That night he was unable to sleep until he had masturbated.

The following day there was a knock at his door. Leo quickly hid his papers and parked himself guiltily on the sofa.

'Yes, come in,' he called out.

'It's only me.'

The door slowly swung open, Mrs Hardman stood non-chalantly in the doorway. She was totally naked. Leo gasped with embarrassment and turned his gaze down-wards. 'Ellen's asleep, we could do it now.'

'No, please, Kath,' he stammered, 'I'm not interested.'

'Leo, look at me.' He did not move. 'Please look at me.'

Leo lifted his head and stared reluctantly at her. She put her hands on her hips and then turned full circle.

'It's just a body, Leo, you can look at it without feeling ashamed. Tell me what you think of it. I'm not in such bad shape, am I?' As a prosecution lawyer Kath had been skilled at making the innocent feel guilty. Her biggest thrill had been winning a difficult case. She sauntered into the room and brazenly sat on the bed.

'Say yes, Leo. You'll be surprised how quickly you get over your embarrassment.'

'No, please don't do this . . . you disgust me.' Leo shrank into the sofa.

'Don't be ridiculous,' she said confidently, 'I tempt you and that's what makes you feel uncomfortable. You are not a boy any more, come on; give yourself some pleasure, that's what most men would do. There's nothing wrong with it.' Leo could have left the room but didn't.

She walked over to the sofa. 'Please, Leo, don't be mean to me. Let me help you.' She took his hand and placed it on her breast. He felt her nipple harden between his fingers and a rush of blood to his loins. His resistance van-ished, she was right; take solace in sex, there were no reasons not to.

At first Mrs Hardman was delighted with her muse: he

was discreet, available, and did not want a relationship, which suited her for she had no higher goal than self-gratification. She wanted nothing more than her orgasm and the whiff of power gained from dominating a younger man. But the initial pleasure soon subsided, to be replaced by a sense of futility and guilt. She began to resent Leo and her reliance upon him. Their trysts merely highlighted the breakdown of her marriage and her own neediness.

It had begun as a business relationship, dispassionate but cordial. Kath had laid out clear rules of engagement. She worked to a strict timetable, favouring times when her eldest was at school and the youngest was asleep. But as the weeks passed Leo no longer visited the kitchen to chat and Kath no longer asked him to help out with the chores. Their relationship diminished to the efficient and mechanical achievement of sexual climax. To this end they became more aggressive with each other. Theirs was the chemistry of violence, and the violence infected Leo's sleep until his nightmares were filled with images of scratched skin, distorted limbs and goaded genitalia, spurred until they vomited up their hideous loads. He dreamt that she was the devil, scraping the last remnants of respect from his plummeting soul, gutting his insides, draining his blood, wrenching, ripping, splitting himself from himself and sending him spiralling hopelessly down into a cesspit of self-loathing. 'Make hate to me,' she cackled.

If love begets love then sex begets sex, but love is hard and sex is easy. Sex and hatred are bedfellows, and hatred has its joys. Think of war. In war there are those who rape for victory; the enemy is destroyed through sex, forced and violent. The oppressors return home triumphant, with their seed littered in the wombs of those they have crushed, so that their hatred may be reborn and live for ever. And this was a subtle form of war, waged in the bedroom by two bodies locked in mutual disdain as they shunted and slithered on top of each other, until love was dead and Leo had sundered his body from his soul. His self-esteem was in free fall and yet a dark calling shovelled him like filth into her venal arms, driving him again and again to seek sex with his nemesis.

How quickly the fallen spirit can be stripped of its veneer by a vulture. How quickly the mind loses its ability to regulate the desires of the body. They had fucked in every room, mauled and bruised each other. And if Leo felt like a zombie ground into the earth by a siren he could not complain, because he had consented to everything, even encouraged it.

The days blurred into one until 2 April reared up in front of him. A year had passed since Eleni's death. That morning he did not emerge from bed, he could hear Kath putting Ellen to sleep in her cot. He knew that any moment the door would open. He pulled the sheets over his head and groaned. He felt something stir in his gut, he did not recognize it at first, but it bubbled quietly until she walked in and pulled his covers off. It was the tiniest of rebellions, barely a croak when it came out. 'Stop,' he whispered, 'we have to stop this . . . I hate it . . . I've had enough.'

*   *   *

Deep down she knew he was right. It had to stop. Her addiction to Leo was like a cancer eating away at her family life, but she had been unable to kick the habit. Now the drug had rejected the addict. Yet still she craved him; their liaison had marked her sexual renaissance, she felt rejuvenated, attractive and powerful. She could neither explain nor contain the rage that was welling up inside her or understand why, when there was no love between them, she should feel so spurned.

'Then you'd better leave now,' she exploded. 'I don't want you in the house. Go on, get out.' She pulled him out of bed and frogmarched him down to the front door in his pyjamas. 'Piss off and don't come back,' she yelled. It was raining hard. Leo stood bewildered on the doorstep whilst Kath returned upstairs to throw his things from the window in a whirl of fury. Leo gathered his goods from the wet pavement and staggered down the road, chased all the way by Mrs Hardman's splenetic insults and the sorry screams of her abandoned baby.

Entry no. 7

The oceans echo with the calls
of whales sending messages
under the sea to their loved
ones hundreds of miles away.
Come home, I miss you.

23

IMAGINE IF YOU OPENED ALL THE PRISONS AND LET ALL THE murderers and thieves out – now imagine if all those lunatics were put in uniforms and given power . . . Actually it's not so difficult to imagine, is it, Fischel? Because that's pretty much what Hitler is doing here. And that's exactly what had just happened in Irkutsk when we got there. Except that Kerensky's plan to boost the Russian Army with criminals backfired somewhat because, while half the prisoners joined him, the other half mocked him by joining the Bolsheviks. The town was full of no-go areas, particularly at night on the roads towards the barracks, where it wasn't unusual to find an empty pocketed corpse in the gutter at dawn. Of course we had no idea about that, so we blundered straight into the most dangerous part of town without even realizing it. We found an empty guest house and couldn't understand why the landlord immediately offered us a discount and agreed to let us pay at the end of the week. We didn't have enough money to pay up front. He didn't even ask any questions when he heard

Király speaking German. I don't think he had seen a guest for months.

All we had to do now was find some money for the rent. I suggested carving figures from wood and selling them at the market, but Király had other ideas. He said he had a way of 'finding' money that would prove far more lucrative. I thought he was crazy – if we were caught stealing, the authorities would punish us severely and we would probably end up back in Sretensk. A huge argument ensued and Király set out alone, armed only with the crutches I had made for him.

That evening I was disturbed by shouting in the street. When I looked out of the window I could see two shadowy figures fighting in the dark; then I heard Király screaming at the top of his voice. I picked up the axe and rushed downstairs. The landlord tried to grab me in the hallway. 'Don't go out there, it is not safe,' he pleaded.

I pushed him aside and burst out of the door. Király was on the ground flailing around. A soldier stood over him, knife in hand. As the blade glinted in the moonlight I could see that it was already dripping with blood. I lifted the axe above my head and charged towards him, but he heard me coming and turned to face me. I brought the axe down towards his head, he managed to dodge it and it caught his arm. He howled, turned on his heels, picked something up from the road and ran off into the night. Király managed to pull himself up, and wielding his crutch he fired a salvo of Hungarian expletives after him. Then he checked his pockets, gathered up a few wallets that lay strewn on the ground and said, 'The bastard stole my handbag.'

Oh, you think that's funny, do you, Fischel? Well, yes I suppose it is funny . . . ha . . . Oh ow . . . you're making me laugh now . . . no, please no laughing, it's not good for me . . . I didn't find it funny at the time, I was furious with him for getting into trouble.

'Oh, he's the bastard, is he?' I yelled. 'And where did you get the handbag from?'

'I found it,' he smirked.

'Where?'

'You'll never believe it, but it was on a lady's shoulder, it had just been left there unattended. But don't worry, I found these wallets too, we're going to be all right. Now, get me inside. Can't you see I'm in pain?'

I helped him through the door, and in the light of the gas lamp I could see that he had been slashed across the stomach.

'Don't worry about that,' he grimaced, 'that's just a scratch. It's my foot that's killing me.'

It had started bleeding again. The landlord quickly ran for a towel; he didn't want blood on his rugs, it would never come off.

'We need to get a doctor. Do you know one?' I asked.

The landlord scratched his bald head and sighed, and that's when he told us that nobody in their right mind walked that road at night, and even during the day it was best avoided. There wasn't a doctor in town that would go near the place. I had seen and heard enough. I resolved there and then to leave the next day. 'You could have warned us,' I said angrily. 'I don't want to stay here any more.'

The landlord nodded sadly, then he looked at Király's foot, and a thought crossed his mind; there was no way the injured one would be leaving in the morning. 'If he agrees to stay here until he can walk, I'll take him to a doctor in the morning. A good man who will ask no questions,' he offered.

'What the hell are you two talking about?' Király asked in frustration.

God knows how he would survive without me.

That night we played our last game of chess. I still hadn't told him that I was leaving. I felt guilty and didn't know how to break it to him. After an hour or so I had played myself into a hopeless position. I studied Frantz closely to make sure that he knew he had won. A toothy grin had spread across his ruddy face, he was a lousy chess-player but even a fool could see that it was mate in two. I toppled my king and watched it roll on to the floor. Frantz let out a shriek of delight that must have disturbed the thieves outside, and for a moment victory numbed the pain in his foot: he jumped up and hopped around the bedroom gleefully. Then, suddenly, a thought crossed his mind and he came to an abrupt halt. 'Did you let me win on purpose, you son of a whore?' He was staring at me intently.

'No, of course not.'

'You did, didn't you?'

'I would never do that,' I protested. 'I'd rather see you bleed to death than lose and watch you dance around like a freshly branded pig.'

He hesitated. I could see his mind working as he paddled back from his desire to believe me. The next thing I knew he was on top of me swearing in Hungarian. The cynic in him had overcome the believer, and for once he was right: I had lost deliberately. 'Why did you do it, you bastard?' he yelled, and a gobbet of saliva involuntarily flew from his mouth and landed on my cheek. 'I don't need your charity.'

I pushed him off me and brushed myself down. 'I did it because I wanted to make you happy before I left in the morning.'

He considered my response and his eyes welled up. I'm not sure whether he was moved because I wanted him to be happy, or because I was leaving. He turned away in embarrassment and left the room. He returned some time later after I had gone to bed, and I listened as he hobbled over to his bed and settled down to sleep. In the morning he lay watching me silently as I gathered my things. When I left he refused to shake my hand. I never saw Frantz Király again.

After the war I often thought about him nostalgically and wondered what had become of him, so I wrote to the guest house in Irkutsk and was amazed to find that he was still there. We exchanged a couple of letters, but soon realized that we had very little in common, and the correspondence died. He spoke in lurid detail of the women he had serviced during the war. He was the reluctant father of 'two poor bastards' who he refused to see. After the war some of the women's husbands had unexpectedly returned and he

311

had been beaten up, but survived to tell the tale. His foot had healed but he still walked with a stick and I got the impression he was a thief, because when I asked him what he did to survive all he said was that Irkutsk was an opportunist's paradise, and besides he spoke Russian, was a Bolshevik and had no interest in material possessions. I knew him well enough to take this last with a large pinch of salt. I haven't heard from him now for over a decade.

After Irkutsk I traipsed from village to village carving little pine effigies and selling them as I went. Uncle Josef was right – there is always a market for the small wooden crucifix – but the whole business of carving them and hanging around on street corners was slowing me down. Eventually, in desperation, I stole a horse from a kulak's field one night and was chased into the woods by its screaming owner and his tenacious dog. I got away and rode hard across the Saian Mountains. Ninety days later the horse dropped dead. When I looked at it I realized that my magnificent steed had never been anything more than an old carthorse. And now there was only one thing left to do. Eat it. For months I had been living off fruits and berries from the forest. To eat a horse is to take on its strength. So with as much of the horse inside me as I could eat, and as much in my pack as I could carry, I set off on foot once more.

One August day in 1917 as I was nearing Abakan I came across a small hut in a clearing in the forest. An old man was sitting peacefully on the wooden porch.

'It's a beautiful day,' he said cheerily as I marched by.

'Yes it is,' I answered politely, continuing on my way.

'How would you know? You're in such a hurry. You need a rest, come sit down. Have some vodka.'

I stopped for a moment and looked about me. The hut stood on the brow of a hill in a grove of wild flowers in full bloom, and from his porch the old man could see way down into the wooded valleys and across to the mountains beyond.

'That's very kind. I will join you for a quick drink.'

'Quick? Why quick? Let it take as long as it takes,' the man chuckled. I sat down on a wooden stool next to him and he poured me a drink. 'Oleg,' he said, offering a hand. 'And you?'

I hesitated. It would be safer to give a Russian name. 'Sergei.'

'Where are you going, Sergei?'

By now I was comfortable that I could pass myself off as Russian, it was such a vast country with so many tribes that I could have been from almost anywhere, and yet I was cautious. 'Home,' I said evasively.

Oleg smiled. 'Home is where you are. Why do you want to be somewhere else?'

'Love.'

'Ah, love,' he mused, 'but my friend, if you knew something about love, you would not be in such a hurry. You would sit back and enjoy this beautiful day. Your love is not somewhere else; you carry love with you. She is right here. She is the rustling in the trees. She is the scent of summer.'

I took in the magnificent view down the valley and felt the breeze play on my skin. It was truly a magical place. 'Maybe, maybe,' I sighed, 'but I won't be happy until I have her in my arms.'

Oleg ran his fingers through his beard and smiled. 'And how do you know you will be happy even then, if you're not happy now? Can having something really make us happy?'

The man seemed so benevolent I felt inclined to answer, even though no stranger had ever quizzed me like this before. 'Yes, why not?' I offered.

'Well, I once lived in a town full of ambitious people, people who aspired to having, be it wealth or power. It was an unhappy town. Your cause may be more noble than theirs, but nevertheless it is important to know the difference between having and being. If desire burns too strong in a man it will consume him. A man who says he will not rest until he has made a certain amount of money will not rest even then, for his desire will drive him to greater wealth. A man who says he will not be happy until he has obtained a certain woman will seek another once he has had her. I know this to be true because I was such a man. If you are not happy now you may never be happy.'

I wondered who this man was. I had heard that Siberia was awash with religious sects and false prophets, but this man had no followers with him. 'Are you suggesting I abandon my journey?' I asked.

'No, not at all. The opposite. Hear my story: one day a man sees the sun setting and decides that his fortune lies where the sun touches the land. He sets off towards it. He walks and walks and walks, and after a long time he arrives back in the village where he started. He has travelled the globe but when his friends ask him to describe the wonders of the world he is unable to reply, for his eyes have been blinded by the sun. Now, what I am suggesting is that you remember your journey and forget the arrival. Otherwise you too will be blinded, and you will grow old like me and wonder where your life has gone, and you will realize that you spent all your life planning for a future that never happened. Find your happiness now, and if you happen to find your love you will double it. Come have another vodka with me and listen to the birdsong. Why not live now, young man?'

We sat and talked for several hours until the vodka was finished. The alcohol in my empty belly reinforced my conviction that Oleg was a man I could trust and soon I had confessed everything: my nationality, my religion, and my status as a POW.

'Well then, we are both escapees,' Oleg laughed.

'And what are you escaping from?' I asked, wondering if he was a criminal.

'My enemies, my family, my life . . . myself.'

He was such a benign old fellow. With his long white beard and shiny eyes he looked more like a cuddly grandfather than a man with enemies.

'You seem surprised, my friend. But I won't say another word unless you agree to stay with me a couple of days and then I will fill your ears with stories. I have some

315

borscht inside and a squirrel pie. I would be glad of the company – and so would you, I think.'

In the end I stayed four days. We collected wood, hunted for deer and read. For a man of few possessions, Oleg had a magnificent collection of books. There was nothing much else for him to do but read. He was devouring in his age all the books he had been too busy to read in his youth. In the evenings we sat and talked in the firelight and Oleg entertained me and the forest spirits with folk tales and songs. Eventually, on my final night, Oleg rewarded me with his own story.

'I spent three quarters of my life in misery, my friend,' he said, tugging at his beard. 'When I was your age I also had many dreams. I was going to change the world. All I needed to do was get myself into a position of power. I worked so very hard as a merchant and then later as a politician, but still I was nobody. I learned that in Russia the strong man always wins. The big bully beats the small bully, the ruthless beat the honest, the greedy earn the respect of the poor and only the corrupt achieve power. I saw what I needed to do and I promised myself that once I had climbed the greasy pole of power I would change things for the better. But for every step I took away from my true path it was two steps back. Soon I had lost touch with my ideals. By the time I controlled the local duma I had subjugated everyone around me and I was surrounded by enemies. I lived in fear and now my only goal was to protect what I had. So much for changing the world.

'I turned my attention to my three boys. At least I could

help them grow up to be good Russians, but the more I exerted my authority the more wayward they became. I soon learned that I could not control them any more than I could control the world. They still despise me. Then my wife fell ill and on her deathbed she said she hated what I had become and accused me of being a tyrant. I had reached my dream only to discover that I had lost my soul.

'I broke down. No one understood and no one cared. I ran away and wandered alone for many months until I settled here. And here I have listened to my heart and it has begun to open again. And now I realize that the only power I have is the one I exert over myself. The world will bend around the man who knows his own power, for he is like a star that cannot be dimmed or a rock that cannot be moved. But use that power over others and the world will eventually crush you, for this is weakness disguised as strength. It is too late for me, I am cleansing my spirit for death, but you have everything ahead of you.'

I stared for a long time into the dying embers of the fire. Would I ever see Lotte again? The world was conspiring against us; did I have the strength of will to keep going?

'I'm afraid, Oleg. Terrified of what might happen to me. Half of Russia would kill me. I'm tired of hiding, tired of pretending.'

The following day Oleg was up early and I awoke to the smell of fresh bread. A steaming samovar of tea was standing on the table. Oleg had put three loaves of bread in my pack and filled my canteen with water. After a hearty breakfast I was ready to leave.

Oleg held me back.

'All night I have been wondering what story to send you away with and this morning it finally came to me. It's about a hunter who is in the forest chasing a deer. Suddenly he realizes he is being followed by a tiger. The hunter is now the hunted. He begins to run in fear through the trees, the tiger closing in. In his panic the hunter falls into a trap of his own making, and before he knows it he is tumbling down into a deep pit. He manages to catch hold of a root that sticks out halfway down and there he dangles. He looks down and sees a dozen deadly serpents writhing at the bottom of the pit. He looks up and sees the tiger prowling around the edge of the hole. Then he feels the root slowly loosening and coming away from the side. He hears a buzzing and notices a bee flying over him. A drop of honey falls on to a leaf near his mouth. And there, surrounded by death above and below, he sticks out his tongue and tastes the sweetness of life. Life is hard, Moritz, but there is always a drop of honey somewhere. Good luck.'

From there I walked through Abakan to Kuznetsk. But something had changed, Oleg's words had had a profound effect on me; I slowed down a little, became more curious about the places I passed through, met more people. I transformed myself from a vagrant into a traveller, and strangely enough I actually began to enjoy myself. But my pleasure was cut short when I arrived in that foul stinking town of Kuznetsk. I had been on the move for six months and I still hadn't left Siberia.

Further west the political landscape was changing rapidly, but the Bolsheviks were struggling to get a foothold in Siberia. You see the kulaks of Siberia were different from the poor peasants in Western Russia in that they despised the Bolsheviks. Why? Because the east was underpopulated, the peasants had more land and were generally much better off. But the irony was that the kulaks were inadvertently helping the Bolsheviks win power. Their decision to hoard their grain had sent prices rocketing. The grain surplus in the east could have fed everyone in the west. Kerensky issued decree after decree but the Siberians refused to hand it over. As a consequence the villages were well-fed but the towns starved. The undernourished soldiers on the front deserted in their droves, and the great cities of Moscow and Petrograd fell easily into the hands of the Bolsheviks.

I desperately needed some regular money; living off the land was getting harder and I was far too proud to beg in the city. Besides, I couldn't face another winter of walking. It wasn't difficult to find work. As more and more men were drafted to the army, jobs became vacant. Kuznetsk was a mining town and that's what I ended up doing.

Every day we would risk our lives and break our backs for long hours, only to return to our rented rooms with a handful of kopeks. And then one morning towards the end of October 1917 the pit came to life with jubilant voices that echoed down the mineshaft.

'The Bolsheviks have stormed the summer palace.'

'The revolution has begun.'

'The war is over.'

'God is dead.'

'Long live Lenin.'

'The workers are free,' the miners shouted. There was huge excitement and great optimism that their lives would improve. But that hope was misplaced, the local dumas in Siberia reasserted themselves and rejected the transition of power to the Bolsheviks. The workers were not free. We were a long way from Petrograd. And so the work continued just as it had before.

Another day without daylight, another breath of dusty air, a few more kopeks, backaches, leg cramps, and a wretched cough. The days began to lose their character, and life slowly ground down to a black, sooty smudge.

November and December came and went. Lenin signed an armistice with the Central Powers but for me life was nothing more than a black pit. I was losing hope that I would ever see Lotte again. She had not heard from me for a very long time. I was no longer on any of the Red Cross lists and she could only assume that I was dead. The mail service had collapsed, posting letters was pointless, and yet I still wrote my 'letters to the snow' as Király had called them. Those letters not only contained every detail of my life but they were my meditation, my fantasy, they were the tenuous thread that held me to life.

I had got into a dreadful rut; I was a slave to the pit. It was too cold to walk and I was too poor to live without the mine. By February 1918, crushed by meaningless routine, my spirit was fading and I had developed a hacking cough from which I have never fully recovered. There was a constant ache in my kidneys, which worsened by the day. All I remember of March was spitting blood, increasing accidents, fainting fits and collapse. One year had passed since leaving Sretensk.

It was then, my child, that I contracted this killing consumption which has plagued me ever since. Nevertheless I was not as ill as I had been in Sretensk. My symptoms were exacerbated by exhaustion. At my lowest point I was visited once more by those angelic children and I heard their voices driving me forwards. 'Come on, you can't stop now. Rise up, keep going. Walk, walk, walk. Don't give up on us,' they urged.

And that is exactly what I did. I got to my feet and I walked. I put one foot in front of another and walked towards the setting sun. I remembered Oleg's parting words to me, 'happiness is a choice and not a function of ambition'. So I walked for the sake of walking. I put one foot in front of the other and I looked for the Lotte in everything. From April to October 1918 I walked two thousand kilometres. I walked through the endless lowlands of the Kulunda Steppe. I walked through fields of wheat. I walked through corn, I walked over beetroot and potato. I put one foot in front of the other and I walked. I walked on black earth, I walked on pebble pathways, I walked on roads, I walked on goat tracks. I walked past villages and towns. Walking became an art, a philosophy, a way of life. There was joy in it. I walked to my love as if through a painting: melting into flowers, inhaling them, living them, riding on birdsong, dancing with the wind. I was the earth I walked on, blending with the vibrant colour of land and field, enveloped in the mighty flat steppes of Russia where the earth curves into the horizon and the sun bakes the crops. I carried the universe in the palm of my hand as a gift for Lotte. This planet does not spin of its own accord; it is we who turn it with our gentle steps. A man must always move, for the earth requires it and a nomad knows that nature conspires in love.

I met Kazakh herdsmen and black-veiled Uzbek women working the fields. I met Tadjiks and Jews, Turkmenians and Russians. I walked through a kaleidoscope of opinion, for each one I met had a different take on the historical events unfolding around us. None shared the same view but, one way or another, all were caught in the political fever that gripped the country. There were socialist revolutionaries and nationalists, there were intellectuals affiliated to the Kadets, and returning front-line soldiers known as *frontoviki*, there were tsarists, communists and a myriad other political groupings. There was such diversity under their banners that it would have been more accurate to say that each person was a party unto themselves. The latest developments were on everyone's lips. The road became my teacher. I learnt from a miserable Ukrainian that Lenin had signed an onerous peace treaty at Brest-Litovsk that gave Belarus and Ukraine to the Germans. Soon after, someone told me that Lenin had been shot in the neck by a socialist. I passed a farmer's wife who was weeping because she heard that the tsar and his children had been murdered in Ekaterinburg. Then I was staggered to learn that there was a civil war raging, but when I tried to discover who the Bolsheviks were fighting I got different responses. Some said it was a provisional Siberian government that had recently been set up in Omsk, others said the ex-tsarists, the Cossacks and the Estonians, yet more said it was a socialist organization called Komuch based in Samara, and, strangest of all, there were those who said it was the Czech Legion. This last one I dismissed as a wild rumour; nevertheless it seemed the Bolsheviks were fighting everyone on every front but that their enemy was as disparate, diverse and uncoordinated as the people I met on the road.

The closer I got to the Urals the wilder the rumours became and the more endangered I felt. People said that Lenin and Trotsky were German spies sent to bring the country to its knees, they said that the Germans had already taken Odessa. They claimed that Bolshevism was part of a Jewish conspiracy. I even heard that Poland had been given independence, and if that was true then where was Ulanow? In Poland, Austria or even Germany?

The countryside swelled with drunken deserters heading east. One day I was on a quiet pathway north-west of Orsk heading towards Orenburg. The chill of late autumn hung in the air like a threat and a thin mist blew down in gusts from the Southern Urals. I heard a moaning coming from the bushes. I put down my heavy pack and went over to see. There was a middle-aged man lying prostrate in the mud in a pool of blood. I asked him if I could help and he groaned incomprehensibly, so I pulled him up and sat him on his haunches. He was wearing a soldier's greatcoat but carried no weapons; he was no doubt a deserter. His forehead was lacerated, the wound fresh for it leaked blood, but the sheer quantity of it made the injury look worse than it was. I mopped his head with my handkerchief; he was disorientated and confused and it took him a few minutes to recover his senses.

'Who did this to you?' I asked.

'Cossacks,' he gasped. 'They robbed me. Why rob me? What do I have? I'm no kike.' I held my tongue. 'The bastards terrorize everyone in these hills. Be careful, friend, they must still be close by.'

I peered through the mist; there was no sign of anybody. 'Where are you going?' I asked.

'Away – away from the Germans, away from the Poles, away from the Yids.'

'What do you mean?' I couldn't help myself.

'Yids, Poles, Bolsheviks – call them what you like, they are one and the same. Didn't you know – Trotsky's real name is Bronstein? He's not even a Russian, and Lenin too.'

'Lenin's a Jew?'

'Well, he must be, they stick together don't they, like maggots in a nest.' He laughed and a trickle of blood rolled down his face and dropped on my trousers. I smiled and nodded. How easy it was to deny my faith. It was a game I played many times in my youth but refuse to play now I'm older.

'I didn't care much for the tsar,' he said, 'I was happy to see him go, but things have got so bad that I miss him now. Don't you agree?'

'Yes,' I sighed as ruefully as I could, 'he wasn't so bad after all.'

'There's less food now than there was before. West of the Volga the peasants are eating each other, they're so hungry. Can you imagine? People have been arrested for cannibalism. Those Bolshevik rats surrendered the best farmland to the Germans and now they're stealing the rest for themselves. Lining their pockets, as if the Jews aren't rich enough. And they say they are doing all this for the people. What a joke.'

'So why did you desert? Shouldn't we be fighting them?' I asked.

'I was forced into the army in the first place. They call it a volunteer force but the generals and their lackey Cossacks are rounding up men of all ages and enlisting them at gunpoint. Look at me: I'm forty-five years old, I've had no training. What use am I against the Red Army? If you go beyond Orenburg you'll get drafted whether you like it or not, and if you refuse to fight they'll assume you are a Bolshevik and throw you in the Volga or worse. I passed through one village where the body of a young girl hung from a telegraph post. Her head was shaved and her breasts had been ripped off. Her skin was burnt black. A piece of paper was nailed to her with the warning: "Anyone else who has any business with the Bolsheviks can expect similar treatment." I saw it with my own eyes.'

I was horrified. Just as I was congratulating myself for surviving the harshness of Siberia my hopes were dashed again. The only thing separating me from Lotte was the entire Red Army and a civil war of terrifying ferocity. I was entering the heart of madness.

'Where are you heading?' he asked.

'To the front.' It was a half-truth.

'Good man,' he said, slapping his bloody hand on my shoulder. 'Are you a *frontovik*?'

'Yes, I fought in the war, in Ruthenia.' That much was true.

'Ah, I thought you were Ukrainian from your accent, so you were with Brusilov, we need men like you. Who will you join now?'

I was confused by his question. 'The Whites,' I replied hesitantly.

'Yes, of course, but that could be anyone. Are you going to join Denikin in the Caucasus or Kappel in Samara?'

'Kappel,' I said off the top of my head. 'And what about the Czechs?' I ventured. 'Where are they?'

'The bloody Czechs, they've taken control of the whole trans-Siberian railway from Ufa to Vladivostok. They are a bunch of arrogant shits; nothing gets through without their permission. God knows what they're doing here. They're still fighting for their own independence. I've heard there's sixty thousand of them; all of them deserters from the Austrian Army. They switched sides because they wanted the Austrians to lose the war. Now they're stuck here and they hate the Reds for signing the peace treaty. They say they want to go home, but how can they unless Austria falls? So they're fighting with Kappel because they want the Great War to start again. I hate the bastards but thank God they're on our side because we'd be lost without them. They're organized and highly motivated, which is more than you can say for our rabble. You'll see our lot for yourself when you get to Samara. You'd better hurry up though, because I just heard the Reds have taken Syzran, it won't be long before they cross the Volga. It's going to be all hands on deck in Samara pretty soon. It's not for the likes of me but you . . . Oh Christ . . .' he tailed off as the thunder of galloping horses reached our ears. My heart skipped, a rush of blood surged into my head; quick as a fox the deserter scuttled into the bushes. I grabbed my pack and pelted into the scrub after him. The horses were nearing but I still couldn't see them through the mist. A thought struck me: they knew he was there, maybe they were coming back for him, he was spilling blood over the bushes, an easy target. I turned away and charged down the slope, trying to put as much distance between us as I could in the few seconds I had before the thudding gallop of horses sent me diving to the ground into a stand of nettles behind a bramble bush. I yelped but dared not move, for now I could see them: bearded, filthy and fearsome, astride their horses. I counted thirteen of them. They varied in age, two were grey-haired and perhaps in their late fifties – it was difficult to tell – but the youngest was no more than fifteen. They halted at the pool of blood on the track and looked around for their victim.

'The weasel's still alive,' one of them said. 'He's crawled away.'

'Won't be far. Let's have some sport, friends,' called another, and the men cheered.

A third called out to the bushes, 'I smell the blood of a coward, where can he be?' I held my breath. I could see the deserter's legs sticking out from a bush fifteen metres away. He was trembling like a lamb torn from its mother.

'Are we playing hide and seek, Yid?'

They could have been talking to me. My mind raced. I still had my Austrian papers; they would flay me alive if they knew who I was. I carefully reached inside my jacket pocket, stinging my hand on the nettles, and felt for my papers.

'Do we have to smoke you out, weasel? Or are you going to be clever and give yourself up?'

The deserter didn't budge. I pressed my papers into the soil and covered them over. One of the Cossacks steered his horse off the track. There was a sneering arrogance about him and a savage glare in his eye. I guessed he was their Ataman, or leader. 'Oh, what a careless little Bolshevik,' he gloated, 'you left your blood all over the place. Oh, look, here's a bit more. It's Red through and through.' The others roared with laughter. A couple of them jumped down from their horses and waded into the bushes straight towards their catch. I lost sight of them behind the bramble but I heard them taunting as they got closer.

'Why did you quit the battlefield, deserter?'

'There is no home for cowards in Russia!'

'Show yourself, chicken.'

Suddenly the deserter broke cover like a partridge at a shoot and hurtled off as fast as he could run. The Cossacks charged him down and dragged him back to the track, passing within feet of me but miraculously not seeing me. I began to shake with fear and prayed the deserter would not give me away. He was pleading with them now. 'I told you I'm not a Bolshevik and I'm not a Jew.'

'Why won't you fight them, then? You're with us or you're against us,' the Ataman said fiercely. 'We left you for dead; we'll not make another mistake.'

'No, no, don't kill me. I hate the Bolsheviks, with all my heart I hate them,' the deserter bleated. 'Please, I just want to see my wife and my three girls. You have families, don't you? You must understand. How will they live without me?'

The Ataman reflected a moment, then his face softened. 'Yes, I understand, little man, where are you from?'

'Kuvandyk.'

'I know it, a fine village, you're nearly home,' the Ataman smiled. 'And what do you do there?'

'I make hats. If you ever pass through ask for Lev Borisovich, everyone knows me. I will furnish each and every one of you with a fine hat,' the man simpered.

'You must be missing your daughters, Lev Borisovich, I have two myself. How old are they?' the Ataman asked politely.

'Yes, I haven't seen them for three months. The eldest is twenty-one, and the others are nineteen and fifteen. Each prettier than the last,' Lev said proudly.

'I'm so glad to hear that, Lev Borisovich, because we will be visiting them when you're dead.' The Cossacks sniggered with excitement.

Lev stared at the Ataman incredulously, then he let out

a high-pitched whine, his shoulders dropped and he began to sob: 'Not my girls, please don't touch my girls.'

His pleas were met with nods and smiles. He fell to his knees and beat the ground, cursing his stupidity. Then he raised his head and looked straight at the bush where I was hiding. My heart froze. It was a look of sheer desperation; he did not say a word but I knew that he was pleading with me to help him. What could I do? I kept still and waited to see what he would do. After a moment he looked away and I thanked God for blessing this man, anti-Semite though he was, with strength of spirit.

'What shall we do with him, boys?' the Ataman asked his henchmen.

'Cossack-charge him,' the youth replied.

The others hurrahed and turned their horses up the slope. The two men on the ground pushed Lev to the middle of the track and forced him to face the horses, which had retreated some way up the hill. They drew their swords and stood one on either side of the track a metre away from the kneeling deserter.

'If you move you'll lose your head,' one said.

The youth went first. Calling on his horse to run like the wind, he charged down the hill at full gallop straight towards Lev Borisovich. The others were cheering the boy on. His eyes were savage with excitement and as he got to Lev he readied himself for a jump. The horse sailed over Lev's head but a trailing hoof caught him full in the face, sending him reeling over backwards. The Cossacks laughed. Lev scraped himself off the ground and stared at me again. His nose was smashed and his face splattered in blood. I held my breath. His mouth opened as if to speak, but he swallowed and held his peace. The dismounted Cossacks grabbed him under the arms and turned his battered body to face the next rider, who had begun his charge.

'I'm looking forward to fucking your babies,' the rider jeered as he bore down on his victim. Lev was quaking as the horse bundled into him, trampling him with its hooves and knocking him down the hill. His body lay motionless for a moment, a twisted wreck in the mud. The two Cossacks pulled him up to see if he was dead. Lev coughed and spluttered, he was winded but trying to speak.

'I'm not . . . a . . . Bolshevik,' he gasped.

'You are to us. Come on, we've only just begun,' the older one said, yanking him back into position.

'I'm not . . . a Bolshevik,' he moaned. Then he turned his head towards my bush and said, 'Ask . . . him.' The words were like a bullet in my head.

'What?' they spoke together.

'Over there, ask him,' Lev said, a little more forcefully.

They both looked towards me. I could feel my face burning.

'Who?' the younger one asked.

'Me,' I said, getting to my feet. My appearance brought the other horsemen racing back down the hill. I made my way towards the track.

'So there's two of you?' the Ataman asked. 'Why didn't you say so earlier, Lev?'

'This man knows I'm not a Bolshevik or a Jew,' Lev wheezed.

331

'But you're both deserters,' the Ataman sneered.

'No,' Lev said, answering on my behalf, 'he's a *frontovik*.'

'I'm on my way to join General Kappel,' I added, trying to sound confident.

'This is true,' Lev assured him.

'How do you know each other?'

'He's from my village, he knows me well.'

He looked me in the eye; he was willing me to back him up. But I thought my accent would give me away, so I contradicted him. 'That's not the case,' I said, 'I found him in the ditch. We talked and I am sure that he is not a communist.'

'And where are you from, *frontovik*?'

'I'm from the Ukraine.'

'Is that so? You don't look like a Slav.' The Ataman stroked his beard, 'And what's your name, *frontovik*?'

'Sergei,' I said quickly.

'Sergei what?'

The only Russian names that came to my head were Pushkin, Tolstoy and Lermontov, all of which I had read in prison. The Cossacks didn't look like literary types so I plumped for: 'Sergei Lermontov, Sergei Alexandrovich Lermontov.'

The Ataman did not bat an eye. 'So, Sergei, if you are from Ukraine what are you doing here in the Urals?'

I was beginning to unravel. 'It's a long story. My mother is Kazakh and my father is Ukrainian, for many years we lived in Ukraine, but when my mother's sister fell ill we decided to move out here to look after her.' It was a story I had heard on the road, but no sooner had the words left my lips than they seemed to lose all credibility. A man will say anything to save his life. I could not tell whether he believed me.

'So, Sergei the Kazakh from Ukraine, what do you think should be done with traitors?' the Ataman asked.

'They should be shot,' I asserted.

'Is Lev a traitor?'

'No, he's too old to fight.'

'Is he indeed, and what of these men?' he said, pointing at the two greybeards in his company.

'They are trained. They can fight.'

'Mmm. Tell me, Lev Borisovich, is Sergei a patriot?'

'He is,' Lev said.

'Then both of you lie. A deserter is always a traitor. And a patriot should kill a traitor, or be branded a traitor himself. Is not that the case?' the Ataman said, in that gentle voice which he had used earlier as a precursor to violence.

Neither of us knew what to say.

'Well, friends, I have reached a decision on this day of sport. You are both liars, but to kill you both would be no fun, so in my infinite mercy I will let one of you live.' The Ataman paused and eyed us each in turn. 'Well, aren't you going to thank me?' he roared.

'Thank you,' we mumbled obediently.

'The problem is I don't know which is the bigger liar, so I will let you decide. Our entertainment shall be to watch. Andrei, Nikolai . . . give them your swords. Let them fight to the death. The winner will go free . . . No, on second thoughts let them use their hands.' The Ataman gesticulated and the Cossacks dismounted, tied their horses off and formed a circle around us. They were jeering and spitting. I looked at Lev Borisovich, with his face in shreds and his left arm hanging limply by his side, and I felt a great burden pressing down on my shoulders, as if God and heaven had come tumbling down on top of me. We had been cast as animals in a theatre of cruelty, thrust into a moral vacuum from which there was no escape.

Lev turned to the Ataman and said feebly, 'What chance have I against this soldier? I am already wounded; I think my arm is broken. If I die will you give your word that you will leave my family in peace?'

'What, and rob you of your reason to fight? I will give no such guarantee. No, no, if you lose, your three lovely girls will be ours. Isn't that right, boys?' The Cossacks cheered and began to chant my new name – 'Sergei, Sergei, Sergei' – but the Ataman cut them short. 'However, I am a fair man, so to account for your age and injuries I will give you a sword after all. Andrei!' Andrei unsheathed his sabre and gave it to Lev. The Ataman grinned and ran his dirty fingers through his matted beard. 'No more horse trading, let the scrap begin.'

We stood there for a moment, staring at each other. Lev felt more like my friend than my enemy, for we were in this nightmare together. We had no desire to hurt each other. But Lev would fight for his family and I for my future. The Ataman had decided that the two could not coexist. There could be no winner.

'I'm sorry,' Lev whispered as he lifted the heavy sword in his right arm.

'If you win, I forgive you,' I said.

'Likewise,' he replied, and suddenly he thrust at me, but there was no vigour in him and I side-stepped the blade easily. It brought hoots of derision from the Cossacks and spit rained down on us. I trotted round the edge of the circle and picked up a couple of large stones. Lev turned to face me once more. He wiped the blood from his eyes, cleared his throat and limped towards me. I threw one of the stones as hard as I could, and he did not even attempt to dodge the missile, for there was nothing nimble about him. The rock hit him in the ribs and he howled in pain. I threw the second but it sailed past his ear towards the youth, who ducked and hissed at me. The others laughed and teased the boy.

Lev swung at me; I stepped back but the tip of the blade caught the top of my leg and drew blood. There was an intake of breath from the crowd, followed by calls of 'Come on, Sergei.'

Lev swung again but lost his balance and followed the sword to the ground. I dived on top of him and pinned his right arm to the ground. I squeezed his wrist and tried to force the sword out of his hand, but he would not let go, so I grabbed another rock and brought it down on his hand. The sword fell from his fingers. He flailed hopelessly beneath me, but I could feel that he was spent. I lifted the rock again and smashed it down on his disfigured head, and a splatter of blood hit my face. I rolled off him and picked up the sword. He was in a pathetic state as he staggered to his feet. I made one sharp thrust towards his stomach, which he could not block, and felt the blade enter him. He slumped to the earth clutching his belly and looked up at me, waiting for me to finish him off. One swift blow to the head would have done it. I took a deep breath, and lifted the sword above my head ready to swipe, but I couldn't do it. I turned to the Ataman and said, 'He's finished. I've won.' I threw the sword down into the dirt.

'Kill him,' the Ataman shouted. The words echoed round the circle. Then there was a piercing scream from Lev, and suddenly the Cossacks were yelling at me to watch my back. I half-turned and saw that Lev had picked up the sword, and with the last of his strength was charging towards me. It was too late; I couldn't get out of the way. Time slowed down and for a split second I thought I would die, but Lev brushed past me and planted the sword in the Ataman's neck, puncturing it deeply. All hell let loose. Some of the Cossacks tore into Lev with their swords, hacking him to pieces. Others drew their guns and peppered him with bullets. The two greybeards were frantically trying to save their leader. No one was paying any attention to me so I ran as hard as I could into the bushes. I expected them to come after me but they never did. After half an hour or so I stopped in the woods and waited for nightfall. I had left my rucksack by the brambles and in it was my axe, mess tin and everything I owned. I had no choice but to go back and find it. I scrambled back through the trees and shrubs until I found the track. There was no sign of the Cossacks but the remains of Lev Borisovich were scattered across the way. It was dark and I could only make out shadows of flesh and bone. I found my pack and stumbled back into the woods.

From then on, I walked only at night, I steered clear of all pathways and avoided contact with people. It was several days before I realized that I had left my papers in the dirt. I actually had no idea where I was going. I followed the stars and walked in a westerly direction over the Urals, but that was all I knew. I didn't even know who was winning the war or where the various armies were camped. Food was hard to come by and I often went hungry. Occasionally I caught a squirrel or a rabbit at dawn but generally I survived on nettle soup, boiled dandelion and mushrooms. I made tea from mugwort leaves and scraped fungus from the trunks of elder trees.

The temperature was dropping rapidly. I had left Sretensk twenty months previously, my shoes were worn right down and I was unable to rid myself of the cough I had got working in the mine. It was raining, always raining. It was hard to navigate by night. At one point I slipped in the red mud, and bruised myself on a rock, but when I looked again I realized it was not a rock but a man's head. Then I saw another and another; I clambered over them trying to get away but the sea of bodies seemed to extend for some way. The rain had churned up a mass grave or a battlefield, and to this day I don't know whether they were Reds or Whites.

One morning in mid-November I arrived at the banks of a great river. I had reached the Volga.

Entry no. 71

I love you my sweety,
From your head to your feety,
From here to Haiti.
From an amoeba's dance
To a unicorn's lance.
From the smallest small to
    the biggest big.
From the stars in the sky to
    the pips in a fig.

I love you
Until eternity ends.
Till straight bends;
Till impossible is,
Till his is hers and hers is his.
May our souls entwine
Till there is no mine.
Till there is no war,
Till now is no more,
Till our spirits sing,
And our dreams take wing.

Siberia . . . so I'll carry on. But please be patient with me if I have to stop to catch my breath, or if I have to whisper. Pass me the spittoon . . . thank you . . . now sit down and hear the rest.

As I stood at the banks of the Volga I could hear distant gunshots coming from the woods to the north. To the south I could see the outskirts of a town emerging in the dawn light. I presumed this was Samara. On the other side of the river was another town rising up the hill.

I thought about swimming across, but the water was nearly frozen and the river was wide. I would never have made it. What could I do but surrender myself, exhausted and ravenous, to the hazards of the town? As I shuffled down the streets with the heels of my worn-down shoes dragging on the cobbles I passed several attachments of Red soldiers. They were not very well-turned-out but they looked as disciplined and determined as any good army. The latest Bolshevik decrees were plastered on every telegraph post. It looked as if the Whites had lost Samara already. I headed down towards the port, past queues of people waiting to buy butter or kerosene. All I could think of was food and how to get some. I felt around in my pocket; I still had five roubles. There was a bakery near the jetty and a long line of people were waiting patiently outside. I joined the back hungrily. After a couple of hours I wondered whether I shouldn't cut my losses and go and catch the ferry, but I had got trapped in that strange logic that afflicts people in queues; a logic which dictates that once you're in a queue you have to stay in it. It may not have moved all day but you become convinced that the minute you leave, it will start moving. And having spent so long there already it would be stupid to have wasted all that time for nothing. Even worse, once you get to the front you will buy something even if you don't want it because the queuing has to be for something.

It was four hours before I reached the counter, and then imagine my horror when I realized that the price of a loaf had rocketed from two kopeks to four roubles since the last time I had bought one. So there I am at the front of the queue dithering as to whether I can possibly afford myself the luxury, and the baker is sneering at me, and the people behind me are losing their patience as I ask the price of every roll. And in the end, after some deliberation, I settle for a tiny roll of stale bread which still costs me a precious rouble, and I leave the shop feeling guilty for having bought it, but in five seconds I've devoured it in one greedy mouthful, every crumb. And you know what? I feel hungrier than before.

I made my way to the ferry calculating that I would survive two days in Samara before I ran out of money. On the harbour was a sign that read 'Saratov crossing'. This confused me. Saratov? Where was Saratov?

Look on the map, Fischel, you see it? Go down the Volga . . . there, that's it . . . Saratov is about four hundred kilometres south-west of Samara. I really didn't have a clue where I was. I must have been in this town, here, on the eastern banks of the river – Pokrovsk it's called – and as you can see I was still a long way from home.

* * *

Another thing that baffled me was the date on the ferry ticket. It read 2 December. By my calculation it should have been 17 November. Where had the other two weeks gone? I tracked back in my mind to the last time I had seen the date, which was on a newspaper in a shop in Orsk in October. I had bought some paper there so that I could carry on writing to Lotte. It was a futile habit I had never broken. Letters were the engine of my journey and I wrote a few words every day describing my progress, a bit like a diary. The missing fortnight was a mystery to me, I wondered if I hadn't been walking in my sleep. I didn't realize that the Reds were already using a different calendar.

I sat next to a plump elderly lady whose hair was wrapped in a bright woollen headscarf. At first she eyed me suspiciously: I must have looked a dreadful mess. I was scrawny, dirty and malnourished, my beard was long and scraggly. But once I had spoken politely to her she softened and then nothing could keep her quiet. She had two large baskets at her side; one was filled with onions, the other held a rabbit, its stiff legs awkwardly hanging over the edge. She was delighted with her acquisitions. Finding food had apparently become a national sport. She said she knew of a peasant woman out in the country who had a good supply of onions. She had got up at four in the morning, crossed the Volga, and walked for three hours to her village, and once she had got there she was doubly rewarded when she came across a man selling rabbits. She was going to cook up a rare old feast for her family. She was a keen gossip and as we crossed the Volga she warmed my ear with news and rumour. Most significant was the news that General Kolchak had proclaimed himself the Supreme Ruler of Russia or at least White Russia and that the Central Powers had lost the war. The monarchies of central Europe had crumbled. What turmoil my country must have been in! And yet, despite my concern, the news filled me with hope that I would soon be home.

There was a man begging on the quayside in Saratov. He was perhaps ten years older than me and noteworthy for his old Austrian greatcoat and flap-eared hat. Despite the shabby state of his clothes there was a certain straight-backed elegance about him that seemed incongruous. He sported a distinctive handlebar moustache – a table for his large Roman nose to rest on – and his fingers were unusually long and thin. As the passengers disembarked he spoke politely to each one in turn: '*Tovarich*, please, one two kopek. Some food. Please, *tovarich*.' No one paid much attention to him. It was clearly a sight to which they had all grown accustomed. He earned a single rotten potato for his efforts. I waited for everyone to go before approaching him.

'Tell me, friend,' I said to him in German, 'what are you doing here?'

He eyed me mistrustfully, 'The same as all the others.'

'You've been released?'

'Weren't you?'

'No, I escaped from Sretensk.'

'Where's that? Siberia?'

I nodded. He grinned broadly, grabbed my hand and shook it warmly. 'Well done, old boy, I'm Oskar Schmidt.'

'Moritz Daniecki.'

'Been here long?'

'First day in Soviet territory.'

'Crikey, you're in for a shock. Come follow me, there's no point hanging around here, next boat's in two hours.'

He led me away from the docks towards the town. I felt deeply uncomfortable walking down a busy Russian street talking in German, but Oskar seemed unconcerned.

'So the Bolsheviks kept their promises,' I said.

'They certainly did, soldier, they lined up every German and Austrian officer they could lay their hands on and shot them . . . class enemies or some such nonsense . . . then they opened the doors to the camps and let the rest of us out to wander the countryside like vagabonds. Frankly I'd rather be inside; at least we were fed there. I never thought I'd miss kasha.' We both laughed.

'And the people won't kill you here for being Austrian?'

He lowered his voice, 'The people are terrified; they do whatever the Bolsheviks say.'

'Terrified of what?'

He tugged his moustache nervously, looked over his shoulder and quickly pulled me into a quiet alley. 'Ever heard of the Cheka?' he asked.

'No.'

'They are the secret police, they tolerate no opposition. If you cross them they'll butcher you without trial. They've been requisitioning apartments in the centre of town and moving anyone who looks like they've got a bit of money into the suburbs. They stick them in cellars and worse. We've had a few demonstrations here but they don't last long, the Red Guard fire straight into the crowd. Beggars are top of the heap. If I wasn't a foreigner I'd probably be given a dacha next week,' he joked.

'Are all the POWs begging?' I asked.

'No, some of them are fighting the Whites. I saw a platoon of Magyars heading for the front the other day. I don't know what's wrong with those bloody Hungarians, they are suckers for Bolshevism. There'll be trouble when they get home,' Oskar scoffed.

'Can't we just go home? After all, the war is over . . . isn't it?'

Oskar sneered, 'If only life were that simple. We are pawns in a political dogfight, soldier. Lenin's getting all excited, he reckons the whole of Europe will be Soviet by next year. Can't see it myself. The latest is they'll send you back if you agree to join the international revolution and spread the word back home.'

I was ready to agree to anything if it meant a ticket home.

'They won't just let you go, you know,' he said, seeing my eyes light up. 'You have to be brainwashed first. Only when you walk, talk and shit like Lenin will you be let out. It's dreadful.'

'Still, it's got to be worth the risk, hasn't it? What's the worst they can do? Fill us with ideas? Have you thought of volunteering?'

'I don't think someone like me . . . you know . . . but

yes, I have thought about it, if only because I'm bloody starving and I'm begging off people who are starving themselves. I can't live off rotten potatoes all my life,' he frowned and stuffed the potato in his pocket. 'And to think I used to have a cook!' If I hadn't already guessed from his aristocratic accent and the way he called me soldier, I knew it for certain now. Everything about his demeanour told me this man was an officer. Oskar stared at me guiltily, 'Christ, have I given myself away? Don't say a bloody word.'

'No, of course not. I don't care.'

'Thank you, I'd be hung and boiled like a beef *tafelspitz* if they found out.'

I was curious to know how he had escaped execution. He was wearing the coat and boots of a private, and perhaps he'd stolen them, but he would not be drawn on the subject.

'The less you know the better, and what you think you know already can harm us both. Remember I have told you nothing, soldier. Be happy in your ignorance and ask no more.'

We spent the night in the ransacked former residence of an escaped bourgeois. Oskar said he was never short of a good place to sleep: he'd keep half an eye open during the day to see where the Cheka had been, then steal a night in their wake, every night a different house, the grander the better. We shared his sad potato along with a loaf of dry bread that I bought with my last roubles, and discussed all the options open to us. By morning I had persuaded him, against his better judgement, to accompany me to Bolshevik headquarters in Saratov.

'They'll smell me out, Moritz, they're not stupid,' he said nervously as we made our way through town.

'How are they going to know?'

'The same way you did, you fool. It took you all of five minutes. Pedigree has no hiding place, soldier.'

'Keep your head down and stop calling me soldier, it gives you away. You'll be fine, Oskar, your inner peasant is just waiting to come out.'

Oskar roared with laughter, 'Good one, old boy. Think peasant! Think peasant! The bloody world has turned on its head.'

Our conversation was halted by a commotion coming from a grey stone apartment block ahead of us. A woman was screaming from somewhere inside. Suddenly we heard a window smash and a spray of glass rained on to the pavement in front of us; Oskar pulled me over to the other side of the road and quickened his pace. As we drew level with the building I could hear the dissonant barking of male voices. I looked up to the broken window and saw a flurry of movement; a man in a dark tailored suit was backed up against the frame clutching the curtains whilst several others appeared to be striking him. He took a blow to the head and fell backwards, the curtain rail gave way under the weight, and he plunged through the window hitting the paving stones with a dull thud and a bounce. The drapes drifted down to cover him like a ready-made shroud. I stopped in my tracks; I was ready to run over to him but Oskar shoved me in the back. 'Keep going.'

A boy ran out of the front door and threw himself on

top of the corpse, crying for his father. Not one person came to his aid, no one even stopped. We hurried on in silence, but as we neared the end of the street I turned back to see a woman being dragged by her hair on to the street by three plain-clothed men. Before I could see what was happening Oskar had dragged me round a corner.

'Don't get involved with the Cheka.'

Eventually we came to a magnificent tsarist square; on one side was a large brightly painted municipal building.

'There it is!' Oskar said, but he needn't have told me for the place was draped with red flags and four armed soldiers stood proudly at the door.

We queued for an hour before being granted an audience with a cheerless functionary. 'We wish to return to Austria to fan the flames of revolution, comrade,' I declared. For this noble purpose we were to receive special education, and the next thing we knew we were on a train bound for Moscow with hundreds of other POWs. This was the end of honesty with Oskar. From now on we had to lie, even to each other. From now on we would be Bolsheviks, committed communists, our very own thought police. There could be no cracks in the façade.

We were housed in a crumbling utilitarian school on the outskirts of town and taught in our own languages. It began with a strident address from a skinny, clean-shaven youth called Pototsky who had been given the grand title of Commissar of Education.

'Comrades,' he yelled in a throaty cry, 'the Bolsheviks

have been true to their word. We have fought on your behalf and freed you from the tyranny of the tsarists. Now it is your turn to fight for the Bolsheviks. You are the future of the revolution in Europe. Your importance cannot be overemphasized. We will teach you how to emulate the success of Comrade Lenin in your own countries. You will educate the workers, organize the unions, and spread the communist manifesto so that the working people of Europe may unite against their bourgeois oppressors. You are the spark that will light the fire . . .'

I glanced over at Oskar but he was too busy thinking peasant to honour me with a smile. When the speech was over he was quick on his feet to applaud.

Our teachers, many of whom had been POWs themselves, were passionate, highly articulate men. Some, such as Bela Kun, went on to become famous revolutionaries in their own right. They started from first principles, taking nothing for granted. It began with a Marxist analysis of poverty and social injustice. Little by little they revealed how capitalism necessitated the perpetuation of a downtrodden underclass and how the mechanisms of state allowed wealth to be concentrated in the hands of the few. Their arguments seemed irrefutable and I was, by my own admission, a rather brilliant student. But although I could recite great tracts of Marx and Lenin by heart, my heart was never in it. I could not reconcile the rhetoric with what I saw on the street. Nationalization and forced appropriations merely created a new underclass who were not only poorer than their predecessors but persecuted, too. This blunt tyranny smacked of greed and revenge. A few powerful Bolsheviks policed everything, even our language and our thoughts. And party bosses never went hungry. No, I didn't care much for the communists back then. Not like now. Now I know that only the communists have the courage to fight Hitler. The liberals and the democrats have let him in and only the communists can get him out.

Oskar and I hardly spoke during this period, in fact Oskar hardly spoke to anyone; he kept his head down and his hands in his pockets. We were never alone, the school was full to overflowing; there were no moments for quiet reflection, no opportunities for private conversation. We were carefully scrutinized for our enthusiasm and dedication to the cause. Every speaker, no matter how tedious, was given a tumultuous ovation and as the Bolsheviks pushed eastward we cheered their every victory. Oskar was working so hard at hiding that his shoulders began to bow under the strain, as if he alone was bearing the entire burden of what he considered to be an unjust system. Whilst Oskar was slowly diminishing in stature, the once downtrodden POWs, the cannon fodder of the Central Powers, were gaining in confidence.

When I did catch Oskar's eye, he would stare at me quizzically as if he was wondering whether I had been converted to the cause yet; he was at once terrified that I would give his status away and grateful that I had not yet done so. Each time I stood up in class to answer a question he would grimace, sure that the day of his betrayal was closer.

* * *

On New Year's Eve, we were granted leave to celebrate. It was the only chance Oskar and I would have to talk in private. Moscow was heaving with drunken peasants and Red Army soldiers toasting the revolution. We wandered aimlessly through the snow-covered streets until we found a busy tavern. There we used our meagre ration money to buy a bottle of vodka. Oskar told me that despite his initial cynicism he was now a committed Bolshevik. I wasn't sure whether this was what he wanted me to believe or whether it was the truth. If it was the truth I had to be careful; I didn't want to be considered a traitor either and blow my chance of being sent home, so I pretended to be as committed as him. For an hour we both extolled the virtues of the revolution until Oskar, who had downed the lion's share, was drunk and could lie no more. Something in him snapped and, like a dam bursting, three weeks of frustration poured out of him.

'So what do you think of that bloody commy tsar of education Pototsky, then, huh? Weasel-faced, trumped-up buffoon, who does he think he is? Not fit to clean a latrine, let alone give us bloody history lessons. These twits are so full of themselves . . . give them a bit of power and they behave like asses.' This from an Austrian officer! Oskar was shouting and I begged him to lower his voice but he was too far gone. 'If only we hadn't signed that damned treaty . . . we had them on the ropes . . . Christ, they're fighting each other now . . . the Germans could have walked in here . . . would have knocked this town into shape . . . got rid of this rabble for starters . . . you know what we're going to do, soldier . . . when we get

Oskar didn't say a word but downed his vodka in one gulp; his eyes were glazing over. The three of us sat in silence for several minutes watching the revellers.

As midnight approached the jig grew more frenzied; outside jubilant soldiers fired their rifles in the street. I felt a hand on my shoulder and turned to see a red-faced factory girl beckoning me on to the dance floor. She looked like a typical Slav, with a simple square face framed by long blond hair. 'You look miserable,' she slurred in my ear, 'no one should be sad tonight. Come and dance.' She took both my hands in hers and smiled. I shook my head and told her I was not a good dancer, but she wouldn't take no for an answer and yanked me off my stool.

'Don't worry about your friend, *tovarich*,' the burly man said, 'I'll look after him. Go and dance.'

The girl dragged me into the midst of the whirling Russian dancers. She knew all the words to the songs and belted them out as we danced. We charged about the floor careering into other couples as we went. Through the mêlée I saw the man talking to Oskar and plying him with vodka. My head was light and I heard myself laughing. The tunes were getting faster, and she began to spin me around and around, quicker and quicker until we were too dizzy to stand and we fell in a heap on top of each other. We lay there for a moment in a clumsy caress. She was howling with laughter. I grabbed her in my arms and held her tight to my chest. So tight I almost squeezed the air from her lungs.

'What's wrong?' she asked breathlessly as my eyes welled with tears. I could find no words to describe what

I was feeling; I had not touched a woman for four and a half years. Her breast heaved against mine, her damp hair clung to my sweaty forehead. I could feel her hot breath in my ear. I wanted it to last for ever. I wanted to love her. There awoke in me a carnal desire so deep that I could not fathom it. I forgot where I was and pressed my face against her cheeks like a kitten rubs up against its mother. She giggled and I took her head in my hands and kissed her passionately, not wanting ever to stop.

The next thing I knew I was being kicked in the back. Before I could turn round a bearded hog of a man took hold of my hair and dragged me off the girl. He was calling her a cheating bitch. I scrambled to my feet and ploughed through the revellers. The man charged after me. I looked for Oskar but he was unconscious on the floor by the bar; his burly drinking companion had gone. I hurtled out of the door. My assailant caught up with me halfway down the empty street and we tussled in the snow. I don't know which of us was more drunk, but we staggered about hurling ineffective punches, and slipping and sliding on the ice until the bells struck twelve and a volley of gunfire brought us both to a momentary standstill. A gang of off-duty Red Army guards came singing round the corner. 'Long live the revolution and a happy New Year, comrades,' they cheered.

My attacker backed off. 'Don't come back or I'll kill you,' he hissed and sloped away.

This transient embrace with a stranger, this meaningless moment of tenderness, was a catalyst to dread. My whole reason for living hung on one kiss in a forest in Poland. I had tramped the earth to be with my childhood sweet-heart. But who was this Lotte, other than a fading memory? I had nailed my sense of self to a romantic illusion, and if this edifice in my mind was toppled what would be left of me? So much had happened in four years that there was nothing left of the boy who once walked the banks of the San. I would never be that boy again. I had just got drunk, kissed a Russian girl and fought with her boyfriend, and what shocked me now was that had I not been disturbed I would have let it go further. I might have woken up in some shabby apartment with the name-less girl at my side. More alarming still was that such incidents were now normal to me. My life was a cycle of violence, illness and fear. I lurched from moment to moment in a stupefying moral void. The one beacon of hope on which my survival rested, namely the resumption of a far-off teenage relationship, which, at its best, was no more than soft words and light promises, now seemed as absurd to me as the existence of God. I did not even know what had become of my saviour princess. What horrors might she have seen? What torments might have ravaged her? A horrible thought exploded inside me. What if Lotte were dead? What if I arrived in Ulanow after five years and discovered that she had been torn to pieces by the Cossacks or the Poles? What then? Could I bear the truth after so long? For years I had been drawn inexorably towards my home, and that night I felt repulsed by it. I wandered the streets in a blind panic, sobering with each step. I was terrified of going home.

When I got back Oskar was nowhere to be found. He

showed up in the morning pale and shivering, with little memory of the previous night. We were all still a little groggy when we were called to an impromptu meeting in the lecture theatre. There were two armed Red guards waiting for us. The diminutive Commissar Pototsky stormed in, scowling. 'Comrades, we have a traitor in our midst.'

The students looked around at each other aghast. I felt my stomach tighten. Oskar sat with his shoulders hunched, staring at the floor. Pototsky walked over to him. 'Here sits a Lieutenant-General of the Austrian Army, Baron Oskar von Helsingen. Let me tell you about this man, comrades. He owns an estate in the Tirol and a mansion in Vienna. Is that right, Oskar?'

'Yes,' he whispered.

'You were captured at Przemyśl, were you not?'

Oskar nodded.

'We know all about you, Oskar. No one can hide from the state. Stand up.'

Oskar slowly stood up.

'What do you have to say for yourself?'

'Never trust a peasant,' he said, staring at me full of rancour. I bit my tongue. I dared not protest.

Pototsky gave a nod and one of the guards stepped forward and coolly shot Oskar in the head.

And I am ashamed to admit, Fischel, that your father was the first on his feet to cheer and applaud.

With our indoctrination complete, we were sent to the borders of our own countries and to our dismay we were not allowed entry. New countries had sprung up. What was once part of the Austro-Hungarian Empire was now Czechoslovakia or Poland or Hungary and these new states refused to accept responsibility for any POWs. We brave soldiers were suddenly treated like immigrants. They were paranoid about being infiltrated by agents of communism. Many prisoners were left stranded on the borders for over a year, especially those of us without papers. I was lucky because in June 1919, more than two years after escaping Siberia, I received a visa to my own country. I had been waiting in Minsk for only a month.

But despite our humiliation at the border, the Poles still wouldn't let us go home. They took us all for communists and sent us to a special camp for re-education. It really was just a question of time. I felt so close to Lotte now that I could almost feel her soft skin, but I admit that as much as I longed for her with every bone in my body, I was also terrified. I was having nightmares, terrible nightmares of arriving at her door and finding her with a child in her arms and a man at her shoulder. She stares blankly at me, no sign of recognition in her eyes. She turns to her husband and asks for some money to give to the beggar. I had survived all this time solely on the strength of a dream and now I feared that the dream would soon be shattered and a much harsher reality would emerge. Did I still love her? I thought so but, in a way, the logic of love is a bit like the logic of the queue. When you have waited so long there is no way you are going to walk away unless the shop closes and the door is slammed in your face. Did Lotte still love me? Sometimes it is easier not to know and live with hope than it is to know and live with truth.

Entry no. 29

Salmon are born in freshwater streams and rivers, sometimes high in the mountains. They then drift downstream until they find the sea. Here they feed, but salmon will not spawn in the open sea, they grow nostalgic for home. They never forget the smell and look of the place they were born. When they are ready to mate they swim back inland against the current. It is a journey fraught with danger. There are many obstacles on the way. All of these they navigate with Herculean strength, defying gravity with extraordinary leaps up rapids and waterfalls. When the male has climbed its mountain and found its home it bathes in the fragrant scent of female hormones, which have been secreted in the water to excite him. After such a remarkable journey can anything be sweeter?

25

IN AUGUST OF 1919 I WAS RELEASED FROM A MILITARY re-education camp having been no less brilliant than I had been in Moscow. I was suddenly able to refute every dogmatic Marxist assertion with convincing ease. I could even prove, citing biblical sources, that God loved capitalists. It is so easy to flatter one's teachers. No longer considered a communist threat, I was allowed to go home to Ulanow.

The streets and the houses were exactly the same as I remembered them, but in the five years I had been gone the population had grown tired and old. There were no children in the streets, no young lovers in the squares, and where once there was a spark in the eye now there was grief. I passed an old man carrying a loaf of bread in the street. He stopped and turned. 'Moritz?' he said shakily.

'Mr Kaminsky,' I spluttered.

'My God you're still alive . . . welcome home. What is this terrible cough? Are you ill?' I had grown so accustomed to it that I hardly noticed it. Kaminsky stared at me. He seemed shocked. 'Here, have some bread . . . You look . . .' He stopped short of saying 'old'. 'So tell me your adventures . . . where have you been all this time?'

'Siberia,' I said, eating his bread greedily.

'Siberia? Oh my poor boy, we heard about those camps . . . terrible. So you came back with the rest of our soldiers on the special trains, there's been a few boys returning to Ulanow, you know.'

'No, I wasn't with them. I walked back.'

'From Minsk? Good God.'

'No, from near Mongolia.'

Kaminsky was incredulous. His jaw dropped open and for a moment he was speechless. Eventually he said, 'Here, have some more bread . . . take it all. Your parents are in Berlin, Moritz. They left a couple of months ago. We thought you were dead.'

'What about Lotte Steinberg?' I felt my stomach churn in trepidation of the answer.

'Oh, she left last year. She went to Vienna.'

'Really . . . so she's still alive, then.' I was overjoyed.

'Oh yes, alive and well. She's engaged to a lawyer,' Kaminsky said cheerfully.

My legs almost gave way underneath me. I stumbled and began to cough more violently.

'Are you all right, child?' Kaminsky asked, placing his hand on my shoulder.

'Yes, yes, don't worry, I'm fine . . . just a little weak that's all,' I assured him.

'Come, I'll take you to the doctor.'

'No, no, really it's just a stupid cough. You must send

her my regards and wish her well . . . so when is the wedding?' I asked feebly.

'February.'

I don't really remember what happened next. I must have fainted, for the next thing I knew I was lying prostrate in the street, and my pack had come loose and spilled its contents on to the cobbles. Hundreds of letters were scattered around me. Kaminsky was at my side. 'We need to get you to the doctor. Let me help you with this,' he said, picking up a handful of letters and stuffing them back in my bag. After a minute he stopped and stared at the letters in his hand. He shook his head in disbelief, then, as if needing more confirmation, fanned out the heap of letters that were still on the ground. 'Lotte, they're all addressed to Lotte,' he murmured, aghast.

There was no point posting them in Russia so I had kept them, every single one of them. And each day my bag had grown a little heavier. See that case over there, Fischel, they are in there, go and lift it . . . you see how heavy they are? I want you to take this case, Fischel . . . so when you're older you won't forget my story. The closer I got to Lotte the more burdensome my love, until that day in Ulanow when I could bear the weight no longer. The doctor said I had tuberculosis but the truth was I was dying of a broken heart.

Entry no. 10

Imagine a nightingale that cannot sing
Imagine a butterfly without a wing
Imagine a baby that cannot cry
Imagine a landscape without the sky
Imagine a morning without the dew
I cannot imagine me without you.

26

LEO CLIMBED THE STEPS TO HIS BEDROOM IN LEEDS FEELING thoroughly defeated. He had barely uttered a word since Eve and Frank had collected him from the station. Frank was racked with guilt because he knew that Leo had learnt silence from him. He was determined to come clean with his son once and for all. In the few months since Leo had been gone he had worked every evening in his study with the old suitcase open at his side preparing everything that he wanted to give his son, and at long last he was ready.

When Leo opened his door he was surprised to see the floor covered in little neat piles of paper. His desk had been cleared but for the brown leather suitcase, which lay shut in the middle. He'd never seen the case before – it looked very old, the corners were battered and the leather was peeling off in places – and he wondered what could be inside. He dropped his bags by the bed and navigated his way through the paper to the desk. As he sat down he noticed an ant crawling out of the case. 'Eleni,' he whispered, 'have you already had a look?'

He clicked open the metal catch and slowly lifted the lid. A musty smell filled his nostrils. He was brimming with anticipation, this must be the inheritance his father had spoken about. He half-expected to find it filled with money or treasures and trinkets from the past. But instead all he found was hundreds of old yellowing envelopes. As he rifled through them he realized that nearly all of them were addressed to a Lotte Steinberg. A couple of them bore the name Moritz Daniecki. Leo was intrigued. He took an envelope at random, opened it and slipped out the letter inside. It appeared to be written in an Eastern European language, perhaps Polish. Leo looked down at the papers on the floor and picked up one of the piles. It contained a handful of pages. These appeared to be translations of the letters in the suitcase because each began with a date and the words 'Dear Lotte'.

'Dad?'

The door opened immediately. Frank had been hovering nervously outside.

'What's all this?' Leo asked.

Frank sat down on the bed. 'These are love letters written by your grandfather Moritz Daniecki. Deakin comes from Daniecki.'

'Where was he from?'

'He was born in Ulanow in 1896. It's now in Southern Poland. But he died in Berlin in 1938.'

'But you always told me you were too young to remember your real parents?'

'I was lying, Leo. I remember them very well. I was at my father's side when he died.'

'I didn't even know you were from Poland.'

'I'm not, I was born in Berlin in 1927 but we spoke Polish at home, I even know a little Yiddish.'

'Yiddish?'

'I am Jewish, Leo.'

Leo could feel the tectonic plates shifting beneath his feet.

'So how did you get here?'

'On a boat from Hamburg.'

'With your mum?'

'No. I was on my own. It was the twenty-ninth of August, 1939, to be precise . . . just a few days before the war started. The boat I was on was full of Jewish kids like me. My mum and my brothers were . . .'

Leo raised his eyes in disbelief.

'Yes, I had two little brothers, Dovid was five and Isaac . . . Isaac was only three . . . they were supposed to come on the next boat but there never was a next boat because the war broke out . . .'

Frank's voice trailed off and he brought his hands to his face. Suddenly he was standing at the docks in Hamburg. His mother was hugging him hard. He couldn't remember her face but he could remember that hug. Little Isaac looked on mystified, he didn't understand what was happening, and Dovid was crying because he wanted to go on the big boat with his brother but their mother said he was too young. Frank remembered telling her that he was scared. 'There's nothing to worry about,' she had said, but her furrowed brow and wet eyes betrayed a thousand worries. 'I promise that we'll come and join you in a week.'

Leo put a reassuring hand on Frank's shoulder. 'Go on, Dad,' he said softly.

'When I got to England I was placed with a family in Leeds . . . I say family but actually it was three middle-aged Jewish sisters, all spinsters . . . You never met them because they all died in the sixties. They were from that generation that lost its men in the First World War. They were delighted to have a little boy to look after but I proved to be hard work; you see, every day I expected my mum to come for me just as she'd promised, and I kept seeing her on street corners.'

'You must have felt so sad,' Leo reflected.

Frank sighed and moved over to the window. 'Sad, yes, but after a few weeks I began to feel angry with her. Why hadn't she come? I thought maybe I had done something wrong, that my mum was trying to get rid of me. The old spinsters told me that it was because of the war and that it would be over soon, but I didn't receive a single letter or any sign from her. You have to remember, Leo, that at that time we had no idea what the Nazis were doing to the Jews. I just felt terribly abandoned. And things only got worse because then I was sent to school, but I couldn't speak a word of English. The other kids bullied me because I was German – as far as they were concerned I was the enemy.'

'So what did you do?'

'I spent all my time studying English and perfecting my accent so that no one would ever know I was a German.

This went on all through the war, then in 1946 I got a letter from the Red Cross saying that my mum and brothers had died in Auschwitz.'

Leo was staggered. 'Why didn't you tell me, Dad? And why did you change your name to Deakin?'

Frank dropped his head in shame. 'Not just my surname, Leo, once upon a time I was called Fischel Daniecki. When I got the letter about my mum I went crazy for a while, and then I reinvented myself as an Englishman. I suppose it was cowardly but all I had known of being Jewish was that it brought misery on my family. I thought it might happen again and I didn't trust anyone. I'm so sorry, Leo, I know I should have told you all this ages ago, but for as long as I can remember I've been in the habit of hiding my past. At first it was to escape the bullying, but then it was to avoid the pain. As time has gone on I've found it harder and harder to break that habit. If it wasn't for your mum I probably wouldn't be telling you this now.'

Leo stared at his father. It was too much to absorb in one go. It was as if he had fallen headlong into a parallel universe where everything looked the same but was in reality completely different. And his father, who he had always thought of as dull and mildly irritating, had transformed into a man with an extraordinary history. Frank's idiosyncrasies, his fragility and anxieties, his evasiveness and silences suddenly began to make sense. Instinctively Leo got to his feet and threw his arms around his father. It took only one hug from his son to bring half a century of grief, anger, frustration and denial tumbling out of Frank. He burst into tears and wept uncontrollably, just as he had done as a child when he turned his back on his mother for the last time and boarded the boat. At long last man and boy had reached over the years to each other. Frank and Fischel were united.

Frank took out a handkerchief and wiped his eyes. 'I'm sorry, Leo, I shouldn't be crying.'

'Why not?'

Frank couldn't think of a good reason any more. 'I wanted to tell you about your grandfather. In fact he asked me to tell you his story. Would you like me to carry on, or do you want to unpack and have something to eat first?'

'No, no, please keep going. You've started this now, I want you to finish before you change your mind and decide to hold your peace for another twenty-five years.'

Frank laughed. 'All right, here goes . . . I don't know where to begin.'

'You said you were there when he died.'

'Yes, he died in his bed at our home in East Berlin, it was the thirtieth of November. Three weeks after Kristallnacht. His furniture workshop had been burnt down and he had been arrested along with all the other Jewish men. Some time round about then I stopped talking . . . I must have been in shock. He returned twelve days later battered and beaten with his head shaved. He had been taken to a labour camp – this was before the death camps, but it was a warning of what was to come. His health had deteriorated terribly but even so I remember him coming home with his spirit unbroken. It was not

370

his way to complain. Perhaps I idealize him, but no matter what happened he always managed a smile for his children. When he walked in the door it was as if he was coming back from a normal day at work; he lifted his cap to show us his 'new hairstyle' and if he hadn't laughed we would have been shocked. His wavy waxed hair had been shorn down to a patchy stubble. These were frightening times, but he tried to reassure us with, "Don't worry, remember, above the clouds the sun is still shining." He often said that but I didn't believe him, and by then I'm not sure he believed it himself. He must have been in a lot of pain that day even though he didn't show it, because the next day he couldn't get out of bed for coughing and spitting blood. In fact he never got out of bed again. I didn't understand what was happening. I was full of questions but still refusing to speak, so these questions flew around my head like bats trapped in a barn. Why did the world hate us? Why did my father have to go away? Why was he ill? Why did he have to lie in bed all day? Why did Mum stop me from seeing him when I wanted to? I was furious with them and could only think of myself. Silence was my revenge. I was so frustrated with the world.

'Then, on the day he died, he summoned me to his bedroom. I was secretly excited that he wanted to talk to me, but I made out that I didn't care. He was propped up against the pillows, his forehead dripping with sweat. Next to his bed was a large bowl of cold water and a flannel. They were on a table that he'd made himself; he made all the furniture in our house. It was a talent he had, he could make beautiful things from bits of rubbish, a skill he had acquired on his travels. We'd heard him coughing all night, it was worse than usual. Mum said that his back had given way and that his bones were too weak to carry him.

'He grinned at me and beckoned me over. He took hold of my hand and squeezed it. His palms felt clammy. Then he pointed to the large wooden chair in the middle of the room – another of his creations. I jumped on to it and dangled my feet off the edge. He said that time was running out and he wanted to tell me his story. I suppose I knew that he was dying but the last thing I wanted was for him to admit it.

'He was wheezing and coughing all the time he spoke. Every so often he would splutter uncontrollably and bring a hanky to his mouth to wipe away the phlegm, or ask me to hold the spittoon while he gobbed up bile from his rotten stomach. It was a foul reddish-green and when it hit the bucket there was an acrid smell that made me turn my head away in disgust. It's quite a shock for a boy to suddenly become aware of the ugliness of his own father. I was selfish; I felt no pity at first but as the afternoon went on his health deteriorated before my eyes and I began to worry about him.

'He was quite a storyteller, my father, but what struck me most was the way he addressed me as if I were an adult. He spared me no gory detail, and even though there were things I didn't understand he knew that what he said would one day make sense to me. I think he was telling the story as much to himself as to me. As if he needed to validate his life before saying goodbye to it.

'Before long I was caught up in his story and I had

forgotten why I was angry. I could see that he was getting tired, but the more he told me the more I wanted to hear. His voice was weakening, and he broke off ever more frequently to catch his breath. The cough was worsening and he was spitting up blood. Towards the end I think he wanted to stop and rest but I wouldn't leave his side, I wanted him to finish.

'I don't know how long he talked; it must have been most of the day. He kept me busy too, sending me on little errands here and there to fetch him water or empty his spittoon. In the afternoon he asked me to bring in Dovid and Isaac. Of course they were too little to understand his story, but I think he just wanted to see them one more time. Isaac fell asleep on the bed beside him. He lay there until Father died.

'Towards the end he was coughing and spitting a lot, I could hardly hear him, and sometimes he croaked as if death himself was speaking through him. Every now and then he took a sharp breath, I think he was getting shooting pains in his kidneys. His eyes would bulge and go red but he never spoke about the discomfort, he never complained. He would just wait for each episode to pass and then carry on with a kind of dogged determination. It was hard to bear; something in me knew that death had lost patience with him and wouldn't walk away empty-handed again. I was losing my daddy, my hero; I was still at an age when a boy worships his father. I began to fret, although I did my best not to show it. But even though I knew he was in severe pain, and even though he had told me several times that he wanted to finish off later, I pushed him and pushed him to the very end. All I wanted to know was what happened next.'

'And did he ever finish?' Leo asked.

'Very nearly,' Frank whispered.

'So what did he say, Dad?'

'I would never have remembered the details but thankfully he gave me these,' Frank said, indicating the letters. 'Why don't you read them, Leo? It's all there, I've laid them out in date order. Each pile represents a month. You don't have to read them all if you don't want to, but you should try, because you and him have a lot in common. I haven't looked at this for years, but when I started translating I got totally carried away with it. My dad was an amazing man. Go on, get started.' Frank squeezed Leo's arm and left the room.

Over the course of the next few days Leo read the letters obsessively. They were so vivid and heartfelt that it was as if he had been given privileged access to his grandfather's soul and he could step inside the man and consider him in every detail. He could swim down rivers of longing, sink into the immeasurable pain, and bask in the rays of hope that drove Moritz to walk across Russia. Leo had been feeling like a one-dimensional speck in time with no past and no future, but now he had context and history. He had roots that went deep into the earth. Roots that would hold him in place and help him stand firm against the misfortune that was threatening to blow him away.

Entry no. 46

The Royal Albatross can live more than sixty years but is very young and still sexually immature when it begins courting. The courtship is tender but polite, perhaps lasting four years. Once the birds have chosen each other they will never choose again. However, life dictates that they cannot always be together. Sometimes they have to separate for a whole year, but they always come back to the same craggy rock where they first met to mate again. Their bond is unbreakable throughout their long lives and no matter where they travel they will always find each other.

27

LEO WAS ALONE READING IN THE LIVING ROOM WHEN THE phone began to ring. He ignored it, he had nearly finished and he didn't want to interrupt his flow; but when the answering machine clicked on he could hear Hannah and the desolation in her voice made him listen.

'Hello, Mr and Mrs Deakin,' she said, 'I'm trying to get hold of Leo. I need to speak to him urgently . . . My . . . erm . . . no . . . well . . . anyway it's really important . . . I'm not sure where he is right now. Please could you ask him to call. Oh it's Hannah by the . . .'

'Hello, Hannah, I'm here,' Leo said, snatching up the phone. 'Are you all right? You sound upset.'

'My dad died . . . this morning . . . oh God . . . I love him so much . . . I don't know what to do,' she sobbed.

'Where are you, Hannah?'

'I'm at his house in Richmond.'

'Listen, I'm going to catch the next train, I'll be with you as soon as I can,' Leo reassured her.

'Leo?'

'Yes?'

'I hope you don't mind, I've been reading your note-book.'

'My notebook?' Leo was confused.

'You know, the red one.'

'But I threw it away.'

'I know. After that party when you saw me with that guy. I knew you were upset and I was worried about you so I followed you home. I saw you come down and chuck it in the rubbish, so I rescued it.'

'Thank you, but don't read it, it's embarrassing, it's full of rubbish.'

'No, it's not, Leo, it's the most beautiful thing I've ever read. I'm sorry; I should have asked you first. I was going to give it back to you when I saw you but I just came across it now. I haven't finished it yet, I've been flicking through, reading entries at random.'

'It's OK, Hannah, if you like it you can have it.'

Leo decided to take the last few letters with him to London. Moritz was nearly back in Ulanow; Leo was desperate to know what happened next, but he couldn't let Hannah down. He threw some clothes into his back-pack and ran out of the door.

As he left Frank smiled at Eve, Leo already had more purpose in his step. The inheritance was beginning to exert a strange kind of magic over all of them.

'How are you feeling?' Eve asked.

'I miss my mum and dad,' Frank said, 'I still think about them every day. Poor Hannah.'

'Poor you,' Eve whispered, snuggling up to him.

'Yes, poor me,' Frank sighed.

'I can't believe you've done it, darling. You've gone and told him. Well done.' She squeezed him proudly.

'Eve?'

'Yes.'

'I love you.'

'Why?'

'Why?'

'Yes why?' she repeated with a wry smile.

Frank thought for a moment. 'Well . . . erm . . . for all sorts of reasons.'

'But for what reasons? You've never told me before.'

'Haven't I?' he mumbled.

'No, Frank, you know you haven't.'

'No, no, well . . . I suppose . . . I suppose it's time I did, then.' He coughed and grimaced; Eve was pinning him to the sofa with her eyes. Frank took a deep breath. Think, he said to himself, desperately trying to lasso his errant thoughts. Why do I love Eve? What was it that made Eve Eve? If she died tomorrow what exactly would I miss, and what would I regret? 'I love you because . . . I love you because you won't use public toilets and . . . because you punch me when I snore, and make me eat all the left-overs . . . because you take strange pleasure in squeezing spots . . .'

Eve laughed.

'No . . . I'm not joking,' Frank said seriously. 'What I'm

379

trying to say is that I've sort of got used to these things. That's how I know I love you . . . I mean I don't really like people's strange habits, but I like yours. But also I love you because you look after me, and because you are terribly sweet to me; and I don't know why because I'm not an easy person to be with. And, of course, you gave me Leo and I watch you with him and I think you're the best mother in the world . . . and you've waited so patiently for me to tell him my story. Sometimes, Eve, I think your heart is made of chocolate and gold because I don't know how you manage to be so . . . so lovely.' He stopped and looked at her, surprised. These words, which were alien to him, were stirring his heart like a stick in a pot of old paint, and he was overwhelmed by the effect it was having on him.

'Thank you, Frank.' Eve would have liked him to continue, indeed she could have listened all day, because she wondered whether she would ever receive such praise again.

'I want to sleep with you,' Frank said suddenly.

'My goodness, Frank, that's not like you.'

'Well?'

'It sounds like a jolly good idea.'

Entry no. 91

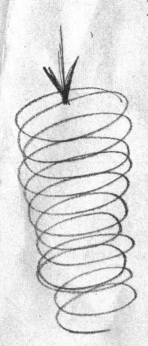

African Fish Eagles soar together, flying up to incredible altitudes. The male then flies up even higher and hovers momentarily above the female, perhaps appreciating her beauty. Then he tilts his beak and dives steeply down at terrific speed towards her. With perfect timing, the female rolls over on to her back, now gliding upside down. The male enters her. They clasp talons and cartwheel downwards, spiralling over and over. They hurtle to earth in a dizzying embrace, and just as it seems they might hit land they separate and spread their wings. Together they skim the ground and head up to take the sky once more.

28

I T WAS A TORRID FEW DAYS AS LEO HELPED HANNAH AND HER younger brother Ed deal with the mountain of official documents, insurance claims, bank notices and funeral arrangements that accompany death. They were visited by the vicar from the parish church in Surrey where Hannah's mother was buried. He had only ever met Hannah's father, Alan, once, and that was at the funeral of his wife. Unlike his wife, Alan was a fervent atheist and never set foot in a church unless invited for weddings and funerals, or unless the church was deemed to be a national treasure and he happened to be on holiday. The vicar's mission was to glean some useful information about Alan so he could make pertinent personal comments over the coffin in the church. Everyone knew that it was the last thing Alan would have wanted, and yet it was the last thing he was going to get before his interment because he had wished to be buried with his wife. The vicar probed gently to discover the names of Alan's family, his achievements and his passions. At one point

Hannah brought her hand to her mouth and looked down, and Leo could see she was trying to hide a smile. The vicar manfully continued with his questions, but Hannah burst into giggles. Eventually the vicar made some feeble excuse about parking meters and left.

'What was so funny?' Leo asked Hannah.

'I had a vision of Dad looking down on us having tea with the vicar, and he was laughing his head off. And then the more I tried to stop myself from thinking about it the funnier it got. And the odd thing is that if I wasn't laughing I'd be crying.'

In the event the vicar's eulogy seemed hollow and flat and the references to Christ inappropriate to those who knew Alan. Hannah read her father's favourite Ted Hughes poem and the amateur organist blundered through some obscure Elizabethan requiem. Leo sat at the back of the church and listened to the rain thunder on the roof. Did it always rain at funerals?

The door creaked open and Leo felt a shot of cold air and a damp presence at his side, it was Roberto. 'Oh Leo,' he whispered, 'I was hoping I'd see you here. Are you OK?'

'Yeah, fine. You?'

'I hate funerals. We've got to talk. I think I've found what you're looking for.' He grinned and flicked back his wet hair.

'I'm not looking for anything any more.'

'You're just on holiday from it. People like you will always look for answers.'

'Maybe.'

'Are you still mad at me?'

'Not really. We're just different.'

'Or the same but on different paths. Perhaps it is our destiny to diverge and converge and only meet at crossroads,' Roberto mused.

Leo had missed his conversations with Roberto, who was, despite all his foibles, relentlessly interesting.

The service died its own death, probably much to the corpse's relief. And it was only as the coffin was being lowered into the ground next to Hannah's mother that the enormity of the tragedy really hit home. The congregation stood huddled under umbrellas, remembering the last time they had stood at that spot fifteen years ago. Their eyes passed to the neighbouring gravestone: Sophie Johnson, née Lucas, born 1943, died 1978. 'Beloved mother and wife, an inspiration to all who knew you.' Hannah and Ed stood at the graveside holding hands like two small lost children as the tears rolled down their cheeks. The coffin was sunk, the ropes released, a prayer uttered, flowers thrown and a clod of earth dropped on the coffin.

Mother and father, husband and wife were together again.

Leo sought out Roberto and pulled him away. 'Come on, let's go for a coffee.' They found a quiet place on the high street where they could dry off and talk. 'So what have you got for me?' Leo asked.

Roberto chuckled and licked the froth from his cappuccino. 'It's a beautiful experiment by a Frenchman called Alain Aspect.' Roberto picked up the salt with his left hand and the pepper with his right and ritualistically banged them together. 'When two particles collide or kiss, like this, and then bounce off in their separate directions, something very strange happens. One would suspect that, having collided, these particles would go off and live their separate lives.' He placed the salt and pepper at opposite ends of the table. 'But no, Aspect proved that even though these particles are separated in space they behave as if they are still magically connected. He did this by "spinning" one of the two particles and noting that the other particle would "spin" instantly in the other direction. And when I say instantly I mean literally at the same instant – there's not a millionth of a second's delay. They are in total harmony.'

'And what if the particles hadn't kissed? What then?' Leo asked.

'Then they behave totally independently. Kissing is everything in this experiment.' Roberto laughed. 'Let's say the table is the universe and the salt is at one edge and the pepper is at the other. Even at this great distance the rule holds true. Spin the salt and the pepper cannot help but respond.'

'What does this mean?'

'Well, ever since the big bang, particles have been colliding with each other and forming secret liaisons. There are particles in me that are twinned with particles in the sun. There are particles in you that once danced together with particles in Eleni. And what Aspect proved was that even though these particles may be millions of light years apart they are still dancing together. They are like lovers, like you and Eleni. You are separated by death and yet somehow you remain invisibly connected.'

'What's this experiment called?'

'Passion at a distance. It is the best explanation of love physics can offer.'

Leo stayed with Hannah and Ed in Richmond for a few days as they went through their father's belongings and packed them in boxes. They had decided to put the house up for sale and split the proceeds. Neither of them felt they could live there. They spent the long evenings talking about life and death and what it all meant. They plundered religion, myth, poetry, anything that might shed some light on the subject. They discussed the concept of fate, reincarnation, and heaven. They even got on to quantum physics, in which Hannah had shown no previous interest.

'What were you thinking with that notebook?' Hannah asked.

'I don't know . . . when I started I didn't know what I was looking for, but by the end I realized that I was trying to prove that love exists.'

'But you know it exists, Christ, you should know better than most.'

'Yeah, but when Eleni died it wasn't enough. I needed to believe that love could conquer death, because if it couldn't then Eleni was lost for good, and what was the point of living? Everything rested on it.'

'Why did you throw it away, then?'

'Because I saw the stupidity in what I was trying to do. In the end what had I proved other than that I was desperate, deluded and in love with a corpse?'

'Well, it worked for me, and I loved all those photos of mating animals that you ripped out of library books. So naughty, but very sweet.'

Leo was finding strength. He was finding it for Hannah. All the awkwardness of their previous contact had dissolved and a new friendship grew from the ashes of the old. Sometimes they stayed up all night sipping wine because Hannah couldn't face going to bed and being alone with her thoughts. And Leo would wait for her to drift off on the couch in the early morning before gently laying a blanket over her.

After ten days Leo was itching to get back to Leeds to talk to his father. He had read the final letters and was confused. Lotte was going to get married in Vienna and Moritz had tuberculosis. His final letter was the sad diatribe of a man who had given up all hope. It was the most wretched of all Moritz's letters to the snow.

Why had Moritz stopped writing then? Had Moritz's desire run out of fuel and the great love of his life been unrequited? Maybe he never saw Lotte Steinberg ever again. So what could Leo take from this story, if that's how it ended? Moritz had crossed a continent for love, that in itself was beautiful. Whether Lotte knew it or not she had helped him survive the Great War and kept him warm in

Siberia. But there had to be more to it than that. His father must have had another reason for giving it to him. Leo imagined what it would be like for his grandchildren to read his own story. What would his story look like if seen from above, so to speak? What would they be feeling if they were looking at him now? They would also see a beautiful love story which ended tragically; they would also see a man who tried his best to get his life back but who failed and was now broken and on the verge of giving up. And they would be screaming at him to find the strength from somewhere to keep his heart open and keep going.

Leo raised his eyes to the heavens. 'This can't be it, Granddad,' he said over and over again. He was leaning forward, his hands clasped tightly to his knees, his foot tapping unconsciously. He pictured himself as one of the little angels that Moritz had seen when he was close to death, one of the cherubs of the future that had raised his grandfather's spirits. 'Come on, don't give up on her, Granddad,' he urged silently. 'Keep going, think of the future, think of Dad and me. You're not alone, we're all here with you, making the same journey. See how the moose journeys way up north to find a mating ground, and the whale calls out "I love you" to its partner two hundred miles away across the ocean, and the eel crosses the Atlantic to give birth, and the incredible Arctic Tern circumnavigates the world every year to mate? Please hear me, you are not alone on this planet hurtling through space, solitude is an illusion, come let me help you, rise up, walk forward, walk tall, walk straight, let nothing stop you.'

Ed was going back to work, but Leo didn't feel that Hannah was ready to be alone. He persuaded her to take another week off work and come back home with him. He knew that his parents would welcome her warmly, as they did all his friends. On the train Leo filled her in on his grandfather's story all the way up to that last letter in Ulanow, and surprised himself with just how many details he could remember. He had never been one for story-telling, but watching the effect of the story on Hannah made him wonder whether there wasn't still magic in this most ancient art form. He also noticed the effect of the telling on himself. He had never had a story to tell, never felt the power of a narrative bubbling up from his soul. For though the story was not yet finished, he already felt as if he owned it. This was his story, his father, his grand-father, and it filled him with pride. He felt like an artist who has been given a completely new palette with which to paint. And he was staggered by the depth of colour at his disposal. He found a rhythm and grace in the telling, he discovered nuance and intrigue, and the very sound of the words falling from his lips conjured an emotion that he did not know he could portray. And as he left the story with Moritz in a wretched state apparently dying from tuberculosis in 1919 he sighed and said wistfully: 'He lived such a remarkable life. I wish I could go back in time and meet him.'

'Maybe you can, Leo,' Hannah said, 'in your dreams. You always tell me that Eleni is alive in your dreams, and now that my dad has died I know exactly what you mean.

Maybe you can enter his dreams on a beam of light and pull him back from the brink.'

Leo smiled because he'd had the same thought. 'You know what, Hannah Johnson?' He chuckled.

'What?'

'You're beginning to think too much.'

'It's an affliction of the bereaved.'

Frank and Eve had a rosy glow.

'You guys look well,' Leo remarked as they came in the door. 'What have you been up to?'

Frank glanced at Eve. 'Nothing much, we've been . . . erm . . .'

'Gardening,' Eve suggested.

'Yes, gardening,' Frank repeated.

'Oh! That's great,' Leo said.

Eve had got the camp bed out for Hannah but said that she was not sure where to put it. It could either go in Leo's room or in the living room; it was up to them. Hannah said that so long as Leo didn't mind she would rather be in his room, because she still didn't want to be alone. Eve busied herself with the bed and Frank put the kettle on. Leo noticed that a snail had crept up the bottom of the windowpane. Back again, Eleni?

When at length they were all four sitting with their tea in the living room Leo asked the questions that he'd been desperate to ask for days, 'How did Moritz survive, and what became of Lotte?'

'What do you mean?' Frank asked.

'The letters stopped in Ulanow. I don't know what happened after that.'

'Oh I see . . . yes, of course, how silly of me . . . let me explain . . . you see in 1917 Lotte must have assumed my dad was dead. The Red Cross had made lists of the POWs in Sretensk and probably his name wasn't on them. She must have grieved for him terribly. After two years her father made a *shidduch*, an arranged marriage, with a wealthy Viennese lawyer and she agreed to it . . .'

Entry no. 42

The tortoise is a funny creature. Its protection is so disproportionately heavy that it has lost all sense of speed. It is a wonder that anything with such an impenetrable shell can ever open itself up to love. And yet somehow there is always a way into the heart of even the toughest customer. The tortoise will, eventually, lift up its shell and let its partner in...

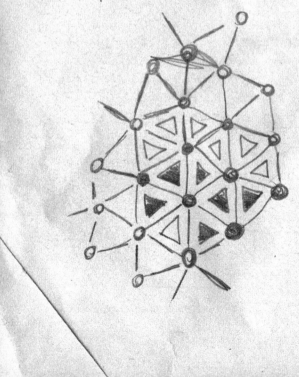

29

I WENT TO STAY WITH COUSIN MONYEK AND FOR THREE MONTHS I lay in bed wasting away . . . Fischel, my throat is dry . . . please pass me the water . . . Oh dear . . . I'm sorry . . . has it smashed? Fetch a broom and a cloth . . . careful, don't step in the glass . . . I said go and fetch the broom . . . Fischel, please . . . I haven't got the strength to . . . Fisch, please. Your silence is so demanding . . . don't just stare at me . . . Fine, have it your way but now you're beginning to upset me.

I still had those letters and the only thing I could think of doing with them was to post them. I sent her a few a day in the order I had written them. Goodness knows how she felt, suddenly receiving hundreds of letters from a man she didn't know was still alive. One day she wrote back.

Dear Moritz,
I have been moved by your letters. I do not know if I can love you as you love me. I need to see your face. It has been so

long. Please come to me.
Lotte

The letter sent me into a rage. Three non-committal lines. Was that it? I sat in front of the mirror and stared at the pock-marked face that she 'needed to see' and I cursed her: 'You want to see my face, what is that supposed to mean?' I yelled. 'And when you see me racked with consumption, wasting away, coughing blood, will you love me then? Haven't I proved myself enough to you? Have I not dedicated my life to you? No, I won't go to you, I've gone far enough. Now you make an effort. You come to me.'

And I tore up her letter like a petulant child and threw it in the fire. 'I don't care any more,' I screamed. 'I am too weak, I won't leave my bed. Go marry a Viennese snob, I don't care. You'll be better off without me, at least he might live to see his grandchildren. You broke your promise, I hate you, Lotte Steinberg, I hate you. Oh, what am I to do?' I flung myself on to the bed and beat the mattress until I felt ridiculous. My body went limp and I stared numbly into the fire. At length I fell asleep weeping with self-pity.

It was a week of fury and downward tilts, reassessment and panic. Ulanow had lost its charm, my family home was squatted in by peasants, the few relations that were left, like Cousin Monyek, were planning to leave, and Poland was at war with Russia. With a heavy heart I took to the road again, unsure of where to go, knowing only that given time the road provides all the answers. There were trains I could have taken but it's not the same, I needed time to think. The road led me through Czechoslovakia to Vienna. A voice told me I had to see Lotte one last time before coming to Berlin to find my family . . . ach . . . sorry . . . just a moment . . . it's getting a little difficult to talk . . . She lived on a quiet cobbled street in the west of the city. There it was, not as grand as I expected, a small Viennese house. It was 5 February 1920, a week before her wedding. It was early evening, dark, a cold bite in the air, the shutters were closed for the night but I could see light through the crack . . . excuse me a moment . . . ach . . . spittoon! Thank you . . . I stood for a long while just staring at the door from across the street. All I had to do was knock on it and my journey would be over, there would at last be some kind of resolution. I was petrified. I had prepared a little speech on the journey from Ulanow, with choice phrases that I thought best expressed my feelings. Each day I had honed and improved it. I had imagined various scenarios and planned different responses to each one. Now I was repeating these words over and over like a student standing outside the exam room. My hands were trembling, my legs were wobbly and the words, which had seemed so apt only an hour ago, sounded limp and hollow. Between the door and me was a bottomless pit. I had grown roots and could not move. I gazed at the door and wondered about the lives behind it; what if she were to refuse me? For more than five years I had dreamt of this moment, and now I felt the blood leave my heart like an army in retreat.

Out of the corner of my eye, I saw a man scurrying

down the street carrying a large bag. He wore a goatee beard and had an air of self-importance about him. He walked straight to Lotte's door and rapped loudly on it twice. I retreated into the shadows and watched the door slowly swing open . . . Please wait, wait . . . ach . . . yes, wipe it off . . . good boy . . . It was Lotte's mother who stood on the other side. Her hair, greyer than I remembered, was tied up in a tight bun and she wore a long, elegant, green dress. She seemed excited to see the gentleman.

'I've made all the alterations that you requested,' the man said, handing over the bag gingerly.

'Thank you, thank you so much, Herr Klein. Lotte will be delighted.'

The man bowed. 'Happy to be of service, Frau Steinberg,' he said ingratiatingly. They said their goodbyes and the man hurried away.

I guessed what was in that bag and it was more than I could bear. I turned on my heels and walked away. At the end of the road I had a change of heart and turned back. I paced the street in this way for some time. I was in a pathetic quandary. All reason demanded that I should not subject myself to the humiliation of rejection; compassion demanded that I shouldn't muddy Lotte's feelings a week before her wedding. In the end it was only the weight of a ten-thousand-kilometre walk that pushed me over the road. They were the most difficult few steps of my long journey. The air was thick like water, my heart was pounding, it was intolerable. A brass knocker on a blue door. I was transfixed by it. I raised my shaking hand and grasped the knocker and brought it down hard against the door. Mrs Steinberg opened the door and in the hallway mirror I could see Lotte standing behind her, wearing her wedding dress. I think my heart stopped.

Mrs Steinberg hadn't recognized me, she was asking me what I wanted. I just stared and stared at Lotte . . . couldn't speak . . . she was not the girl from my dreams. I had changed her, distorted her over the years. I had lightened her hair, heightened her cheekbone, wrapped her in melancholy. In the flesh she was darker, softer, more smiling. It took a moment for me to recognize her as my girl from the San. Now she was someone else's, so lovely, so perfect in that white dress. Strange that I should see her in that dress before he did. I wanted to say her name, but my tongue died in my mouth. Then she turned from the mirror to look, and when her eyes fell on me I wanted to stand tall and smile but I broke down, fell against the doorpost and wept. I felt weary, tired to my core, but worse than that, utterly forlorn. What was I doing there torturing myself? At last Mrs Steinberg realized who I was, she mumbled something and went away.

But Lotte knew me immediately. For a long time there were no words between us, no movement, not even a breath. I found her pitying gaze intolerable; through her eyes I saw how ugly I had become, how wretched, and I was ashamed. I felt humbled, unworthy. I was like a man waiting for his execution, and suddenly the moment had come; everything was to be settled once and for all, here and now. In my heart I knew that it was over, that the walking had saved my life but not my love. There was nothing more I could do, it was up to her now, my fate was in Lotte's hands. And all I wanted was for her to dispatch me quickly, send me away with a gesture; it would have been unbearable to be patronized by politeness. Now I could see her mouth open. She was about to speak . . . 'Moritz,' she whispered, 'you're home' . . . such tenderness in her voice . . . Oh, her voice. I felt a bolt of electricity rip through me and I knew from that sweet sound that she was mine, had always been, would always be. She flung herself into my arms. From a standing start my heart was galloping with hers . . . two wild horses . . . then we kissed like the children we once were on the banks of the San.

I still love her. I always have . . . Shh Isaac . . . awake at last . . . sweet boy. Now listen carefully, you two, life is a journey, you don't need power or wealth to survive it but with love in your heart you can face down a snowstorm. Your mother and I can only give you one thing and it is the only thing you need to make your journey beautiful. We love you more than life itself. Let this story be your inheritance . . . . . .

'Daddy?'

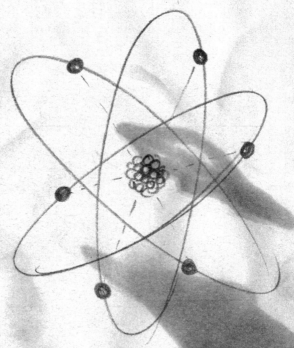

Entry no. 103

Any time not spent on
love is time wasted.
Tasso

30

'THE WEDDING PLANS HAD ALL BEEN MADE WHEN ONE DAY a bundle of letters arrived. You can imagine the shock, Leo, Moritz was back from the dead. Lotte couldn't believe he was still alive, she had completely given up on him. And the letters kept arriving; great piles of them every day for weeks on end. They had an extraordinary effect on her; his love for her was pouring from every page. Her life turned upside down. What was she to do? The invitations had been sent. One day she went to her father and begged him to call off the wedding. At first he was furious but she reminded him of his promise that she could marry Moritz if he came back alive. Eventually he agreed, but on one condition; that she wait until she saw him before deciding to marry him.

'Many soldiers had lost their minds after the war and couldn't adapt to normal life. He didn't want to lose his daughter to a lunatic. The wedding dress, however, had already been paid for, and everyone including the old man secretly hoped that it would still be put to good use.

'It felt like an age before Moritz showed up in Vienna and when she saw him at the door she was shocked by his appearance. He was emaciated and filthy. He looked much older than before, but frail though he was, he still had something about him. After all he'd just walked half the globe to be with her. She was in awe of him. When she hugged him he was shaking like a newborn lamb and later she noticed dirty hand-prints on her dress, but she didn't care, for she knew that no one could ever love her like Moritz. He had proved himself a thousand times over. Within a month they were married.

'After my dad died I had trouble sleeping and I would get my mum to tell me stories about him. I think she enjoyed remembering him through stories, and he took on this mythical status. She would always begin with, "One day, your dad, the great Moritz Daniecki . . ." She told me that Dad was the most extraordinarily intense and passionate man that she had ever known. He made the mundane seem miraculous. It was hard not to love him.' Frank sighed and shook his head. 'So there it is, Leo. It's your story now. Let it work for you.'

Leo got to his feet and wandered towards the window. 'I can't believe he did it . . . Moritz did it, he married Lotte . . . she's my grandmother.'

'Yes,' Frank said, 'but you already knew that. I told you about her putting me on the boat.'

'Yes, you talked about your mum, but you didn't tell me her name. I wasn't sure.'

All his life Leo had shuffled around the gaping hole of

Frank's past. He had never been told explicitly not to ask questions about it, and yet he had grown up knowing not to probe. Frank had been living on a high wire not daring to look down, and something in his sensitive demeanour told those around him not to push. All that was behind them now, and Leo realized that he had never really known his father at all.

'Mr Deakin, there's one thing I don't understand,' Hannah asked after a while. 'Why did you run away from the story for so long?'

'Because I couldn't separate the story from the grief and guilt I felt.'

'Guilt?' Leo queried.

'I thought that my father had died that night because I had made him finish the story. Not only that, but I watched him die in silence. I berated myself for not talking, not telling him I loved him, not even saying goodbye. Then, when my mother put me on the boat and didn't come to England as she had promised I thought that it was because she was angry with me for killing my dad. I know it sounds ridiculous but . . .'

'No it doesn't, Dad,' Leo interrupted, 'it's the same for me. I can't forgive myself for making Eleni sit at the front of the bus. She was on her way down to the middle and I called her back. She only came because she would have done anything I asked.'

'Well, you're already a better man than me for saying so,' Frank said. 'I didn't want anyone to know what a bad person I was. When I met Eve and we had you I thought

I was the luckiest man in the world. But my grief lay twisted like a knot in my heart, it felt so heavy that the last thing I wanted was to pass it on to you.'

Leo nodded, 'I know, Dad. Maybe you were right to wait. I'm glad I've heard it now.' He went over to Frank and gave him a hug, 'I love you, Dad, I'm so lucky that I've got you.'

Hannah bit her lip and looked away. She felt over-whelmed as if she were suffocating, and suddenly she jumped up and ran out of the room into the garden. Leo made to follow her, but Frank held him back.

'Let me talk to her, Leo,' he said firmly, and followed her into the garden. Leo raised an eyebrow at his mother and they both started to laugh.

'Wow,' Leo exclaimed, 'all of a sudden he's John Wayne.'

'Or just plain Fischel Daniecki,' Eve suggested.

The air in the house felt lighter. Eve had become so accustomed to the great silent weight that hung over her home that it was only now it was gone that she wondered how on earth she had been able to bear it.

Frank sat down on the garden bench next to Hannah and put his arm round her shoulder. 'It's no fun being an orphan, is it?' he said softly.

'No.'

'Wherever they are right now, they'll be looking down on you,' he assured her.

'Does the pain ever go away, Mr Deakin?' Hannah asked.

'Not really, but at some point life starts up again, the present slips into memory, and it becomes easier to bear.

What do you think they'll do up there now they're together again?'

Hannah thought for a moment. 'They'll probably go on some long walks, they used to love that.'

'Yes, and I'm sure your dad will tell your mum what you've been up to and how proud he is of you.'

'Mmm, and then they'll do some gardening. I never saw the attraction when I was growing up. It was this boring thing my mum and dad did every weekend.'

Frank nodded. 'When you've had kids you become more interested in watching things grow,' he said. Hannah looked around the garden, at the herbaceous borders and well-mown lawn; Frank and Eve had obviously spent a lot of time nurturing their own garden. 'Don't fall into the same trap I fell into, Hannah,' Frank warned. 'My mum put me on that boat so that I could be free. But I realize now that I've been oppressed all my life. I got to the point where I was so remote from my feelings that I didn't even know I had any. I honestly believed I had conquered them. It was only when I saw Leo go inside himself that I saw what was inside me. Does that make any sense?'

Hannah nodded. She took her mind back to the time when Leo had mistaken her blushes for affection and that dreadful dinner when he had accused her of hiding behind her smile. She had been badly stung by that attack, she had gone home and asked herself whether there was any truth in it, and had had to admit that he was right: after the death of her mother she hadn't let anyone get close to her. 'Yes, Mr Deakin, it makes a lot of sense,' she said.

'I can't have you calling me Mr Deakin any longer. Please call me Frank, and I want you to know, Hannah, that if there's anything I can do for you I will. If you want to talk about anything then call me any time, or even if you want to come and stay our door is always open.'

'Thank you. I really appreciate it, Mr Deak— I mean Frank.' Hannah smiled.

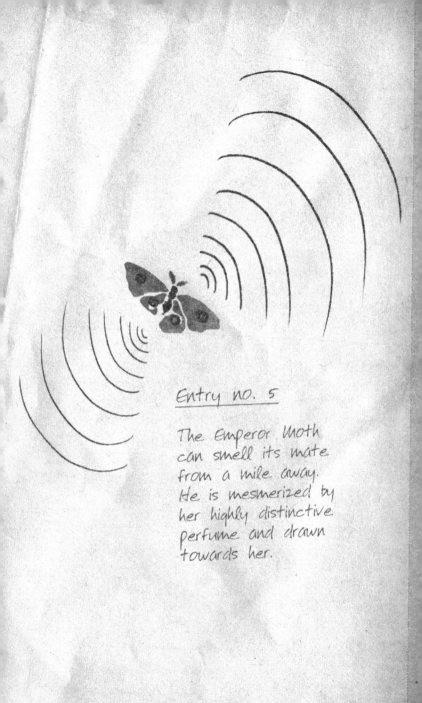

Entry no. 5

The Emperor Moth
can smell its mate
from a mile away.
He is mesmerized by
her highly distinctive
perfume and drawn
towards her.

31

'THIS THING IS REALLY BLOODY UNCOMFORTABLE,' HANNAH grumbled. 'It's more like a hammock than a bed. It's like sleeping in a bag. I'd get more rest on a bed of nails.'

'All right, all right, let's swap,' Leo offered, throwing back his duvet.

'No, I couldn't rob you of your bed, Leo. Can't we both sleep in it?' It was an innocent question and Leo read it as such.

'Well, I suppose so, it's not very big.'

'We'll snuggle up, it'll be OK. How old is that camp bed?' she asked as she jumped into Leo's.

'Put it this way: I remember my mum's brother sleeping on it when I was four or five and it wasn't new then.'

'Christ, it's an antique. It should be in a museum.'

'In a camp-bed museum?'

'Yeah, something like that.'

There was a long silence.

'Leo, what are you thinking?'

'I was thinking about Eleni. I was wondering why she is still following me around everywhere. It's as if she wants something from me.'

'Really?'

'Yes, I have this idea that wherever she is right now she can't rest until I've done what she wants. Or maybe it's me that's hanging on to her, holding her back. We're both in a kind of no-man's-land, unable to really live fully.'

'And what would you want for her if she were still alive and you were dead?'

'I'd want her to be happy.'

'And how would she achieve that?'

Leo reflected a moment. 'I think she would have to love and be loved in the same way we loved each other. I can't see any other way. Once you've been in love like that, how can you be happy until you've tasted it again?'

'But wouldn't you be jealous?'

'Yes, terribly. But what is my jealousy to her happiness?'

'Maybe she wants the same for you. Maybe she won't go away until she sees you happy.'

'I don't think I could ever love anyone like I loved Eleni.'

'How do you know? Maybe you could love someone more than Eleni, if you let yourself.'

'I don't know. It would have to be someone extraordinary.'

'Someone like your grandfather, who would go to the ends of the earth for you.'

'That's only half of it. I'd have to be prepared to do the same for her.'

'Leo, what do you think will happen to you if you don't find someone?'

'I see myself as a very sad old man. In fact I'm already a very sad young man so not a lot will change.'

'Mmm, me too – I'm sad too. You'd better find someone then, and let Eleni rest in peace.'

'Where, though?'

'I don't know,' Hannah sighed, 'I just don't know. I'll think about it.'

Leo rolled on to his side and hugged her. 'Sleep well.'

They lay spooned together in the single bed. Neither slept.

'Leo?'

'Yes.'

'Can you hear that noise?'

'Yes.'

'What is it? It sounds like two cats fighting.'

'It's Mum and Dad having sex.'

'My God, do they always do that?'

'They haven't done it within living memory.'

'Wow. G'night then.'

''Night.'

'Leo?'

'Yes.'

'Do you know what I'd like to do?'

'What?'

'I'd like to phone my job in the morning and quit.'

'Oh.'

'And then I'd like to go on a long walk like your granddad.'

'Good idea. You might get to Bradford.'

'Leo?'

'Yes.'

'You're right, there's no point walking. Where's your atlas?'

'On the shelf.'

'Can I turn the light on?'

'If you must.'

Hannah got out of bed, found the atlas and brought it back to bed.

'What are you doing, Hannah?'

She opened it on the general map of the world and picked up a hairclip from the bedside table.

'I'm going to shut my eyes, and you have to turn it round so I don't know which way up it is.'

'Hannah, what are you doing?'

'Are you turning it?'

'Yes.'

'Right, here I go.' She stabbed her hairclip into the map and opened her eyes. 'Where did it land?' she asked.

'In the Philippines.'

'Where, exactly?'

'On an island called Mindoro.'

Hannah opened her eyes and inspected the map. 'Mmm . . . Never in a million years would I have thought of going to the Philippines. I wonder what it's like there?'

'I've no idea,' Leo said.

'Right, tomorrow I'm going to book a flight.'

'You're nuts.'

'Thank you.'

'Can we turn the light off now?' asked Leo.

'Yes, sorry.'

'Goodnight, Hannah.'

Something was changing, Leo's heart was racing. He had no idea why. It could have been anything: the contact of his knee on her thigh, or the residue of the story working through his system. Or maybe it came from Hannah? Had he sensed a shift in her affections? Whatever it was there was something in the air. Perhaps it was a little electron creating random havoc with his emotions as it made invisible connections with its friends on the other side of the universe. So if an electron suddenly begins to spin does it always know why? Does it know what event on the other side of the universe has triggered it? When the pepper began to spin did it know the salt was spinning, or did it just experience a new and bizarre impulse, such as Leo felt now, and wonder where it came from? What was the universe trying to tell him at that moment? As he lay there wondering in the dark, he felt a vision of piercing clarity burn through him as if the world itself had unveiled its secrets. He saw that for every act of love or hatred a whole universe is sent spinning; for every loss, for every pain, for every hope, for every joy, the cosmos shifts. At every level through space and time, from past to future, from amoebas to humans, from particles to galaxies, from what is seen to what is unseen, all things vibrate as one, creating invisible harmonies and never-dreamed-of connections. A calmness and warmth enveloped him. He basked in it for a while, before a dark cloud drifted through his mind.

If this really was a holistic universe, as Roberto insisted, and all things were, by dint of billions of collisions, spinning together, then why was it still possible to feel so alone? There it was again: loneliness. It hadn't taken long to blot out his moment of bliss. Was holism a delusion? He remembered one of Moritz's letters where he said all souls are deluded and the only pertinent question to ask is: what is the best delusion? What belief system will bring most joy to you and those around you? Even if nothing was connected to anything else, wasn't it more romantic to believe that it was?

He had put all his efforts into keeping Eleni alive inside him, but what was Eleni, what did she represent? Eleni was the vehicle of love. Eleni herself was not important, she was merely the face of love; somehow he had confused the two. She had gone but love remained. She had set Leo spinning and he would never stop; now it was his duty to make others spin with him. It wasn't Eleni that he needed, it was love. And to find it he would have to take risks, go into the lion's den and confront the demons that were stopping him moving forward. There was only one thing troubling him. He got out of bed and wandered towards the door.

'Where are you going?' Hannah asked.

'I need to make a call.'

'Leo, it's three in the morning.'

But he had disappeared.

'Roberto, are you awake?'

'I am now. Christ, Leo!'

'I wanted to ask you something.'

'It had better be important.'

'It is to me.'

'OK, what is it?'

'What if an electron that's already spinning collides with a new electron – what happens then?'

Roberto sighed. 'If it was significant then . . .'

'Significant?' Leo interrupted.

'Not every collision will make an electron change its spin – an electron can have many affairs, if you like, but not all will be significant. If, however, the electron is profoundly affected by another electron it will become entangled with the new partner.'

'Entangled?'

'Yes, that's the technical term for the relationship: quantum entanglement.'

'I like that. But what happens to the old relationship? Is the electron now entangled with two electrons?'

'That's a moot point but most of us believe not. Each electron can only be in one relationship at a time.'

'So the original partner is released,' Leo said triumphantly.

'If you like . . . but, Leo?'

'Yes.'

'You're not an electron.'

'No, but I think I'm ready for a significant collision, I want entanglement.'

'I think we all do, Leo, but not at three in the morning.'

'Sorry. Thank you, Roberto, you can go back to sleep now,' Leo said, and hung up.

He returned to the bedroom excited. 'Hannah?'

'Yes, Leo.'

'Are you really going to the Philippines?'

'Yes.'

'Can I come?'

'Yes. I thought you'd never ask.'

Entry no. 1

Love can vanquish death

Tennyson

or six. Hannah leant out of the window and gave a dollar to a boy carrying a baby whose bald brown head was burning in the midday sun.

'I'm glad my hairclip didn't land in Manila,' she commented.

They got out at Baclaran flea market where Hannah bought a couple of sarongs while Leo stood nervously over their bags. Then they walked down a teeming boulevard towards the BLTB bus terminal. From here they were to take a coach down to the port of Batangas and from there a boat over to Puerto Galera on Mindoro.

When at last they came across the dilapidated terminal with its brightly coloured buses and street vendors, Leo stopped in his tracks. It was Ecuador all over again. He was in Quito with Eleni, lumbering under their huge rucksacks as they tried to find the bus to Latacunga. Eleni is singing a Spanish ditty she had picked up in Guatemala. '*Porque no me dijiste, cuando me . . .*' the words drowned out by the spluttering roar of an old bus engine. Leo is looking for their bus stop among the rows of buses. Now he sees Eleni wandering down to the middle of the bus, and he calls her back for the millionth time, and she turns round for the millionth time. Later he takes a photo of her with the ice pick in her hand and then puts it back in his rucksack. Cotopaxi looms into sight on their left. The lorry is veering across the road, straight for them, Eleni is screaming. Something new now . . . he is thrown against the driver's seat in front of him. He sees Eleni launch into the air and smash her right shoulder and chest against the vertical handrail but it does not break her momentum, her body

426

twists to the right and lurches over the barrier in front of her through a spray of shattering glass and crashes hard against the dashboard before falling back down the steps to land with her back against the door and her leg contorted upwards. The lights fade. There is no more.

'I have to get out of here.'

Hannah grasped his clammy hand in hers. 'No, Leo, you have to go through it.' She pulled him into the terminal and led him to their bus.

Leo was very tense as he sat in the middle of the bus waiting for the engine to start. The Hindu sages say that of all the miracles the greatest miracle of all is that even though we know we are mortal, we live as if we are immortal. Leo felt the paralysis of those who live with their mortality. He tasted the stultifying fear of the unlucky few who see death around every corner. He had lost the bravery of youth, he could no longer proclaim, as he had once done, when warned of the dangers of South America, 'well, it won't happen to me', for it had happened to him and every time he boarded a bus he thought it could happen again.

But fear was about to liberate Leo. Just like when a doctor tells a man he has a couple of months to live, the man will invariably put his house in order and say all those things he has been meaning to say for some time, so Leo was about to behave as if this day was his last. He turned to Hannah and kissed her. And at precisely the same moment she kissed him. In years to come they would argue about who initiated their first kiss. The only thing they did agree on was that it was the most un-romantic place on earth.

Hannah had taken one look at the terrified man beside her and had known that she had to help him. Was this what love felt like? It was nothing like she expected it to be: there was no wild fluttering of the heart, no aching lust, no bolt from Cupid's bow. She felt weirdly serene. All she wanted was to play a role in Leo's happiness. And although they were only one kiss old she couldn't think of a reason why it would ever end, and for the first time in her life that thought didn't scare her. It was as if she had been given a gentle nod from eternity.

When they arrived on Mindoro they took a Land Rover taxi along the rough coastal road until they left all the tourist beaches behind and arrived at a quiet stretch with only one small guest house made entirely from bamboo. It was situated, just as the guidebook had described it, at the far end of the beach, set back twenty metres from the seafront with a couple of palm trees leaning lazily over it.

They were shown to a room up a spiral bamboo stair-case with a magnificent view of the orange sun dropping into the sea.

'Come on,' Leo said, 'it's asking to be swum in.'

They put on their swimsuits, ran out with their towels to the water's edge and swam into the dipping sun. A golden fish brushed against Leo's leg and disappeared into the coral. Eleni was free.

'Oh, Leo, isn't this fantastic,' Hannah called out.

This is how it began and there was no end.

Epilogue

My grandfather Moshe Scheinmann was born in Ulanow in 1896. He fought in the Austro-Hungarian Army in the First World War. He was captured by the Russians and sent to a POW camp in Siberia. Determined to see his childhood sweetheart Lotte, he escaped the camp and walked home. It took him three years. No details are known of his journey. He eventually found Lotte and they married and moved to Berlin. In 1939 Lotte sent my father to England on the kindertransport. Lotte was due to follow but never made it. She was killed in Auschwitz.

Picture Acknowledgements

Acknowledgements

Six years, ten drafts and endless tweaking. I feel like I have been to Siberia and back. Sometimes I would dream of writing acknowledgements just so it would be over. I could never have got here without the support and advice of friends, the knowledge of experts and the guidance of people in the industry.

From Transworld I would like to thank Jane Lawson for her great editing, Neil Gower for his terrific map drawings, Julia Lloyd for her lovely notebook designs, Lucy Pinney, Deborah Adams, Claire Ward and Manpreet Grewal for all their hard work.

Thanks to Edina Imrik and Cristina Corbalan at Ed Victor Ltd, and to Philippa Harrison for knocking it into shape, but especially to my remarkable agent Sophie Hicks, who believed in me before I believed in myself and who has been my mentor and friend through some difficult times. Without her I would not be an author.

I am indebted to Yulia Mahr for her invaluable help, and to David Scheinmann, Rowena Mohr, Hannah

Kodicek, Jess Gavron, Amy Finegan, Jo Olsen, Olivier Lacheze-Beer and Julian Wells, who each suffered one of my early drafts and gave me useful feedback. You are the most generous, erudite, articulate and (of course) good-looking set of guinea pigs anywhere to be found.

I learnt everything I know about ants from Dr Rob Hammond, who was kind enough to show me around his laboratory and give me an insight into the sordid world of ant mating.

Thank you to Professor Mark Cornwall, who supplied me with a reading list for the Eastern Front and gave me clear answers to some knotty questions.

I was hugely inspired by my friend Dr Maurizio Suarez, with whom I had numerous conversations about quantum physics. I hope I will be forgiven for going so shamelessly off piste with both the physics and the physicist.

The story of my grandfather Moshe was told to me by my wonderful and charming uncle Adi. Mum and Dad added to it with memories of their own. I am grateful for their love, unconditional support and openness.

And a big thank you to the person I am bound to have forgotten: you know who you are – I just wish I did!

Deep love to my kids, Poppy, Sol and Saffron, who brought me back to earth when I returned home from the British Library with my head up my backside.

Last and most to my gorgeous Sarah, who, over the years, did more editing on this book than anyone and who for some inexplicable reason seems to love me whatever I do. Boy, did I get lucky!